Cavendon
Hall

Books by Barbara Taylor Bradford

Series
THE EMMA HARTE SAGA
A Woman of Substance
Hold the Dream
To Be the Best
Emma's Secret
Unexpected Blessings
Just Rewards
Breaking the Rules

Series
THE RAVENSCAR TRILOGY
The Ravenscar Dynasty
Heirs of Ravenscar
Being Elizabeth

Others
Voice of the Heart
Act of Will
The Women in His Life
Remember
Angel
Everything to Gain
Dangerous to Know
Love in Another Town
Her Own Rules
A Secret Affair
Power of a Woman
A Sudden Change of Heart
Where You Belong
The Triumph of Katie Byrne
Three Weeks in Paris
Playing the Game
Letter from a Stranger
Secrets from the Past

Barbara Taylor Bradford

Cavendon Hall

HarperCollins*Publishers*

HarperCollins*Publishers*
77–85 Fulham Palace Road,
Hammersmith, London W6 8JB

www.harpercollins.co.uk

Published by HarperCollins*Publishers* 2014

2

A catalogue record for this book
is available from the British Library

ISBN: 978-0-00-750316-2

Set in Sabon LT Std by Palimpsest Book Production Limited,
Falkirk, Stirlingshire

Printed and bound in Great Britain by
Clays Ltd, St Ives plc

For Bob, with all my love always

Author's Note

It often happens that a character springs quickly to life in my mind. A wholly formed person who I know intimately is hovering there.

That happened with Emma Harte, Blackie O'Neill, and later on Paul McGill, in *A Woman of Substance*. In *Voice of the Heart* I knew exactly who Victor Mason was when he was suddenly my mental companion. And in *The Women in His Life* Maximillian West came to me well-formed. The man was a crystal clear image in my head. I certainly knew Serena Stone when I started to write *Secrets from the Past*.

About six years ago the same thing happened, when suddenly a lovely young girl called Cecily Swann was dancing around in my head. I not only knew her intimately, but I also knew what her entire life was going to be. I also had images of DeLacy Ingham and Miles Ingham in my mind's eye. I knew that Cecily would be friends with the Ingham siblings all of her life. I worked on the outline of the book and saw that the story was covering many years. I understood suddenly, that it should be a series.

Unfortunately, other projects and books intervened and I put the Cecily Swann saga on hold. But finally, two years ago, it came to life once more. And I started to work on it after I finished *Secrets from the Past*.

Certain things changed in the storyline as I wrote the first chapter, but the house, *Cavendon Hall*, was born in all its wonderful glory and historical past. And of course the Swanns and the Inghams became truly real people to me. As I hope they will be to you. *Cavendon Hall* is the first book. You will be able to follow the ups and downs, joys and sorrows of all of these characters that you are about to read about now in the sequel. I can't wait to start *The Cavendon Women* and revisiting these fabulous characters. For me, when I begin a book, it's like going on a great adventure. I never know what to expect. Or what's going to happen as in *Cavendon Hall*. The Swanns and the Inghams will tell their own stories.

Contents

CHARACTERS

ABOVE THE STAIRS
THE INGHAMS IN 1913
Charles Ingham, 6th Earl of Mowbray, aged 44. Owner and
   custodian of Cavendon Hall. Referred to as Lord Mowbray.
Felicity Ingham, his wife, the Countess of Mowbray, aged 43.
   An heiress in her own right through her late father, an indus-
   trialist. Addressed as Lady Mowbray.

THEIR CHILDREN
Guy Ingham, the heir to the earldom, aged 22. Attending Oxford
   University. He has the title of the Honourable Guy Ingham.
Miles Ingham, the second son, aged 14, attending Eton College.
   He is known as the Honourable Miles Ingham.
Lady Diedre Ingham, eldest daughter, aged 20, living at home.
Lady Daphne Ingham, second daughter, aged 17, living at
   home.
Lady DeLacy Ingham, third daughter, aged 12, living at home.
Lady Dulcie Ingham, fourth daughter, aged 5, the baby of the
   family, in care of the nanny.

The four girls are referred to affectionately as the Four Dees by the staff.

OTHER INGHAMS

Lady Lavinia Ingham Lawson, married sister of the Earl, aged 40. She lives at Skelldale House, on the estate, when in Yorkshire. She is mostly in London. She is married to John Edward Lawson, known as Jack. He is a business tycoon.

Lady Vanessa Ingham, the spinster sister of the Earl, aged 34, who has her own private suite of rooms at Cavendon, which she uses when in Yorkshire. She spends most of her time in London.

Lady Gwendolyn Ingham Baildon, the widowed aunt of the Earl, aged 72, who resides at Little Skell Manor on the estate. She was married to the late Paul Baildon.

The Honourable Hugo Ingham Stanton, first cousin of the Earl, aged 32. He is the nephew of Lady Gwendolyn, the sister of his late mother, Lady Evelyne Ingham Stanton. He has been living abroad for years. His father was the late Ian Stanton, a racehorse breeder and owner.

BETWEEN STAIRS
THE SECOND FAMILY: THE SWANNS

The Swann family has been in service to the Ingham family for over one hundred and sixty years. Consequently, their lives have been intertwined in many different ways. Generations of Swanns have lived in Little Skell village, adjoining Cavendon Park, and still do. The present-day Swanns are as devoted and loyal to the Inghams as their forebears were, and would defend any member of the family with their lives. The Inghams trust them implicitly, and vice versa.

THE SWANNS IN 1913

Walter Swann, valet to the Earl, aged 35. Head of the Swann family.

Alice Swann, his wife, aged 32. A clever seamstress who takes care of the Countess's clothes and makes outfits and frocks for the daughters.

Harry, son, aged 15. An apprentice landscape gardener at Cavendon Hall.

Cecily, daughter, aged 12, who is allowed to attend lessons at Cavendon Hall with DeLacy.

OTHER SWANNS

Percy, younger brother of Walter, aged 32. Head gamekeeper at Cavendon.

Edna, wife of Percy, aged 33. Does occasional work at Cavendon.

Joe, their son, aged 12. Works at Cavendon as a junior woodsman.

Bill, first cousin of Walter, aged 27. Head landscape gardener at Cavendon. He is unmarried.

Ted, first cousin of Walter, aged 38. Head of interior maintenance and carpentry at Cavendon. Widowed.

Paul, son of Ted, aged 14, apprenticed to his father as a designer.

OTHER SWANNS

Eric, brother of Ted, first cousin of Walter, aged 33. Butler at the London house of Lord Mowbray. Single.

Laura, sister of Ted, first cousin of Walter, aged 26. Housekeeper at the London house of Lord Mowbray. Single.

Charlotte, aunt of Walter and Percy, aged 45. Retired from service at Cavendon. Charlotte is the matriarch of the Swann family. She is treated with great respect by everyone, and with a certain deference by the Inghams. Charlotte was the secretary and personal assistant to David Ingham, the 5th Earl, until his death. There was some speculation about the true nature of their relationship.

Dorothy Pinkerton, née Swann, cousin of Charlotte and the Swanns. She lives in London and is married to Howard Pinkerton, a Scotland Yard detective.

CHARACTERS BELOW STAIRS
Mr Henry Hanson, Butler
Mrs Agnes Thwaites, Housekeeper
Mrs Nell Jackson, Cook
Miss Olive Wilson, Lady's maid to the Countess
Mr Malcolm Smith, Head footman
Mr Gordon Lane, Second footman
Miss Elsie Roland, Head housemaid
Miss Mary Ince, Second housemaid
Miss Peggy Swift, Third housemaid
Miss Polly Wren, Kitchen maid
Mr Stanley Gregg, Chauffeur

OTHER EMPLOYEES
Miss Maureen Carlton, the nanny, usually addressed as Nanny or Nan.
Miss Audrey Payne, the governess, usually addressed as Miss Payne. The governess is not at Cavendon in the summer. The children are not in school.

THE OUTDOOR WORKERS
A great stately home such as Cavendon Hall, with thousands of acres of land, and a huge grouse moor, employs many local people. This is its purpose for being, as well as providing a private home for a great family. It offers employment to the local villagers, and also land for local tenant farmers. The villages surrounding Cavendon were built by various earls of Mowbray to provide housing for their workers; churches and schools were also built, as well as post offices and small shops

at later dates. The villages around Cavendon are Little Skell, Mowbray and High Clough.

There are a great number of outside workers: a head gamekeeper and five additional gamekeepers; beaters and flankers who work when the grouse season starts. Other outdoor workers include woodsmen, who take care of the surrounding woods for shooting in the lowlands at certain times of the year. The gardens are cared for by a head landscape gardener, and five other gardeners working under him.

The grouse season starts in August, on the Glorious Twelfth, as it is called. It finishes in December. The partridge season begins in September. Duck and wild fowl are shot at this time. Pheasant shooting starts on 1 November and goes on until December. The men who come to shoot at Cavendon are usually aristocrats, and always referred to as the Guns, i.e., the men using the gun.

PART ONE

The Beautiful Girls of Cavendon
May 1913

She is beautiful and therefore to be woo'd;
She is a woman, therefore to be won.

William Shakespeare

Honor women: They wreathe and weave
Heavenly roses into earthly life.

Johann von Schiller

Man is the hunter; woman is his game.

Alfred Tennyson

ONE

Cecily Swann was excited. She had been given a special task to do by her mother, and she couldn't wait to start. She hurried along the dirt path, walking towards Cavendon Hall, all sorts of ideas running through her active young mind. She was going to examine some beautiful dresses, looking for flaws; it was an important task, her mother had explained, and only she could do it.

She did not want to be late, and increased her pace. She had been told to be there at ten o'clock sharp, and ten o'clock it would be.

Her mother, Alice Swann, often pointed out that punctuality might easily be her middle name, and this was always said with a degree of admiration. Alice took great pride in her daughter, and was aware of certain unique talents she possessed.

Although Cecily was only twelve, she seemed much older in some ways, and capable, with an unusual sense of responsibility. Everyone considered her to be rather grown up, more so than most girls of her age, and reliable.

Lifting her eyes, Cecily looked up the slope ahead of her.

Towering on top of the hill was Cavendon, one of the greatest stately homes in England and something of a masterpiece.

After Humphrey Ingham, the 1st Earl of Mowbray, had purchased thousands of acres in the Yorkshire Dales, he had commissioned two extraordinary architects to design the house: John Carr of York, and the famous Robert Adam.

It was finished in 1761. Lancelot 'Capability' Brown then created the landscaped gardens, which were ornate and beautiful, and had remained intact to this day. Close to the house was a manmade ornamental lake, and there were water gardens at the back of the house.

Cecily had been going to the hall since she was a small child, and to her it was the most beautiful place in the world. She knew every inch of it, as did her father, Walter Swann. Her father was valet to the Earl, just as his father had been before him, and his great-uncle Henry before that.

The Swanns of Little Skell village had been working at the big house for over one hundred and sixty years, generations of them, ever since the days of the 1st Earl in the eighteenth century. The two families were closely intertwined and bound together; the Swanns had many privileges, and were exceedingly loyal to the Inghams. Walter always said he'd take a bullet for the Earl, and meant it sincerely.

Hurrying along, preoccupied with her thoughts, Cecily was suddenly startled and stopped abruptly. A figure had jumped out onto the path in front of her, giving her a shock. Then she saw at once that it was the young gypsy woman called Genevra, who often lurked around these parts.

The Romany stood in the middle of the path, grinning hugely, her hands on her hips, her dark eyes sparkling.

'You shouldn't have done that!' Cecily exclaimed, stepping sideways swiftly. 'You startled me. Where did you spring from, Genevra?'

'Yonder,' the gypsy answered, waving her arm towards the long meadow. 'I see yer coming, liddle Cecily. I wus behind t'wall.'

'I have to get on. I don't want to be late,' Cecily said in a cool, dismissive voice. She tried to step around the young woman without success.

The gypsy dodged about, blocked her way, muttering, 'Aye. Yer bound for that owld 'ouse up yonder. Gimme yer 'and and I'll tell yer fortune.'

'I can't cross your palm with silver, I don't even have a ha'penny,' Cecily said.

'I doan want yer money, and I've no need to see yer 'and, I knows all about yer.'

Cecily frowned. 'I don't understand . . .' She let her voice drift off, impatient to be on her way, not wanting to waste any more time with the gypsy.

Genevra was silent, but she threw Cecily a curious look, then turned, stared up at Cavendon. Its many windows were glittering and the pale stone walls shone like polished marble in the clear northern light on this bright May morning. In fact, the entire house appeared to have a sheen.

The Romany knew this was an illusion created by the sunlight. Still, Cavendon did have a special aura about it. She had always been aware of that. For a moment she remained standing perfectly still, lost in thought, gazing at Cavendon . . . she had the gift, the gift of sight. And she saw the future. Not wanting to be burdened with this sudden knowledge, she closed her eyes, shutting it all out.

Eventually the gypsy swung back to face Cecily, blinking in the light. She stared at the twelve-year-old for the longest moment, her eyes narrowing, her expression serious.

Cecily was acutely aware of the gypsy's fixed scrutiny, and said, 'Why are you looking at me like that? What's the matter?'

'Nowt,' the gypsy muttered. 'Nowt's wrong, liddle Cecily.' Genevra bent down, picked up a long twig, began to scratch in the dirt. She drew a square, and then above the square she made the shape of a bird, then glanced at Cecily pointedly.

'What do they mean?' the child asked.

'Nowt.' Genevra threw the twig down, her black eyes soulful. And in a flash, her strange, enigmatic mood vanished. She began to laugh, and danced across towards the dry-stone wall.

Placing both hands on the wall, she threw her legs up in the air, cartwheeled over it and landed on her feet in the field beyond.

After she had adjusted the red bandana tied around her dark curls, she skipped down the long meadow and disappeared behind a copse of trees. Her laughter echoed across the stillness of the fields, even though she was no longer in sight.

Cecily shook her head, baffled by the gypsy's odd behaviour, and bit her lip. Then she quickly scuffled her feet in the dirt, obliterating the gypsy's symbols, and continued up the slope.

She's always been strange, Cecily muttered under her breath, as she walked on. She knew that Genevra lived with her family in one of the two painted Romany wagons, which stood on the far side of the bluebell woods, way beyond the long meadow. She also knew that the Romany tribe was not trespassing.

It was the Earl of Mowbray's land where they were camped, and he had given them permission to stay there in the warm weather. They always vanished in the winter months; where they went, nobody knew.

The Romany family had been coming to Cavendon for a long time. It was Miles who had told her that. He was the Earl's second son, had confided that he didn't know why his father

was so nice to the gypsies. Miles was fourteen; he and his sister
DeLacy were her best friends.

The dirt path through the fields led directly from Little Skell
village to the back yard of Cavendon Hall. Cecily was running
across the cobblestones of the yard when the clock in the stable-
block tower began to strike the hour. It was exactly ten o'clock
and she was not late.

Cook's cheerful Yorkshire voice was echoing through the back
door as Cecily stood for a moment, catching her breath, and
listening.

'Don't stand there gawping like a sucking duck, Polly,' Cook
was exclaiming to the kitchen maid. 'And for goodness' sake,
push the metal spoon into the flour jar before you add the lid.
Otherwise we're bound to get weevils in the flour!'

'Yes, Cook,' Polly muttered.

Cecily smiled to herself. She knew the reprimand didn't mean
much. Her father said Cook's bark was worse than her bite, and
this was true. Cook was a good soul, motherly at heart.

Turning the door-knob, Cecily went into the kitchen, to be
greeted by great wafts of steam, warm air, and the most delicious
smells emanating from the bubbling pans. Cook was already
preparing lunch for the family.

Swinging around at the sound of the door opening, Cook
smiled broadly when she saw Cecily entering her domain. 'Hello,
luv,' she said in a welcoming way. Everyone knew that Cecily
was her favourite; she made no bones about that.

'Good morning, Mrs Jackson,' Cecily answered and glanced
at the kitchen maid. 'Hello, Polly.'

Polly nodded, and retreated into a corner, as usual shy and
awkward when addressed by Cecily.

'Mam sent me to help with the frocks for Lady Daphne,' Cecily explained.

'Aye, I knows that. So go on then, luv, get along with yer. Lady DeLacy is waiting upstairs for yer. I understand she's going to be yer assistant.' As she spoke, Cook chuckled and winked at Cecily conspiratorially.

Cecily laughed. 'Mam will be here about eleven.'

The cook nodded. 'Yer'll both be having lunch down here with us. And yer father. A special treat.'

'That'll be nice, Mrs Jackson.' Cecily continued across the kitchen, heading for the back stairs that led to the upper floors of the great house.

Nell Jackson watched her go, her eyes narrowing slightly. The twelve-year-old girl was lovely. Suddenly, she saw in that innocent young face the woman she would become. A real beauty. And a true Swann. No mistaking where she came from, with those high cheekbones, ivory complexion and the lavender eyes . . . Pale, smoky, bluish-grey eyes. The Swann trademark. And then there was that abundant hair. Thick, luxuriant, russet-brown, shot through with reddish lights. She'll be the spitting image of Charlotte when she grows up, Cook thought, and sighed to herself. What a wasted life *she'd* had, Charlotte Swann. She could have gone far, no two ways about that. I hope the girl doesn't stay here, like her aunt did, Nell now thought, turning around, stirring one of her pots. Run, Cecily, run. Run for your life. And don't look back. Save yourself.

Two

The library at Cavendon was a beautifully proportioned room. It had two walls of high-soaring mahogany book-shelves, reaching up to meet a gilded coffered ceiling painted with flora and fauna in brilliant colours. A series of tall windows faced the long terrace that stretched the length of the house. At each end of the window wall were French doors.

Even though it was May, and a sunny day, there was a fire burning in the grate, as there usually was all year round. Charles Ingham, the 6th Earl of Mowbray, was merely following the custom set by his grandfather and father before him. Both men had insisted on a fire in the room, whatever the weather. Charles fully understood why. The library was the coldest room at Cavendon, even in the summer months, and this was a peculiarity no one had ever been able to fathom.

This morning, as he came into the library and walked directly towards the fireplace, he noticed that a George Stubbs painting of a horse was slightly lopsided. He went over to straighten it. Then he picked up the poker and jabbed at the logs in the grate.

9

Sparks flew upwards, the logs crackled, and after jabbing hard at them once more, he returned the poker to the stand.

Charles stood for a moment in front of the fire, his hand resting on the mantelpiece, caught up in his thoughts. His wife Felicity had just left to visit her sister in Harrogate, and he wondered again why he had not insisted on accompanying her. Because she didn't want you to go, an internal voice reminded him. *Accept that.*

Felicity had taken their eldest daughter Diedre with her. 'Anne will be more at ease, Charles. If you come, she will feel obliged to entertain you properly, and that will be an effort for her,' Felicity had explained at breakfast.

He had given in to her, as he so often did these days. But then his wife always made sense. He sighed to himself, his thoughts focused on his sister-in-law. She had been ill for some time, and they had been worried about her; seemingly she had good news to impart today, and had invited her sister to lunch to share it.

Turning away from the fireplace, Charles walked across the Persian carpet, making for the antique Georgian partners' desk, and sat down in the chair behind it.

Thoughts of Anne's illness lingered, and then he reminded himself how practical and down-to-earth Diedre was. This was reassuring. It struck him that at twenty Diedre was probably the most sensible of his children. Guy, his heir, was twenty-two, and a relatively reliable young man, but unfortunately he had a wild streak that sometimes reared up. It worried Charles.

Miles, of course, was the brains in the family; he had something of an intellectual bent, even though he was only fourteen, and artistic. He never worried about Miles. He was utterly loyal: true blue.

And then there were his other three daughters. Daphne, at seventeen, the great beauty of the family. A pure English rose, with looks to break any man's heart. He had grand ambitions for his Daphne. He would arrange a great marriage for her. A duke's son, nothing less.

Her sister DeLacy was the most fun, if he was truthful; quite a mischievous twelve-year-old. Charles was aware she had to grow up a bit, and unexpectedly a warm smile touched his mouth. DeLacy always managed to make him laugh, and entertained him with her comical antics. His last child, five-year-old Dulcie, was adorable; much to his astonishment, she was already a person in her own right, with a mind of her own.

Lucky, I've been lucky, he thought, reaching for the morning's post. Six lovely children, all of them quite extraordinary in their own way. I have been blessed, he reminded himself. Truly blessed with my wife and this admirable family we've created. I am the most fortunate of men.

As he shuffled through the post, one envelope in particular caught his eye. It was postmarked Zurich, Switzerland. Puzzled, he slit the envelope with a silver opener, and took out the letter.

When he glanced at the signature, Charles was taken aback. The letter had been written by his first cousin, Hugo Ingham Stanton. He hadn't heard from Hugo since he had left Cavendon at sixteen, although Hugo's father had told Charles his son had fared well in the world. He had often wondered about what had become of Hugo. No doubt he was about to find out now.

April 26th, 1913
Zurich

My dear Charles,

I am sure that you will be surprised to receive this letter from me after all these years. However, because I left Cavendon in the most peculiar circumstances, and at such odds with my mother, I decided it would be better if I cut all contact with the family at that time. Hence my long silence.

I continued to see my father until the day he died. No one else wrote to me in New York, and I therefore did not have the heart to put pen to paper. And so years have passed without contact.

I will not bore you with a long résumé of my life for the past sixteen years. Suffice it to say that I did well, and I was particularly lucky that Father sent me to his friend, Benjamin Silver. I became an apprentice in Mr Silver's real-estate company in New York. He was a good man, and brilliant. He taught me everything there was to learn about the real-estate business, and, I might add, he taught me well.

I acquired invaluable knowledge, and, much to my own surprise, I was a success. When I was twenty-two I married Mr Silver's daughter, Loretta. We had a very happy union for nine years, but sadly there were no children. Always fragile in health, Loretta died here in Zurich a year ago, much to my sorrow and distress. For the past year, since her passing, I have continued to live in Zurich. However, loneliness has finally overtaken me, and I have a longing to come back to the country of my birth. And so I have now made the decision to return to England.

I wish to reside in Yorkshire on a permanent basis. For this reason I would like to pay you a visit, and sincerely hope that you will receive me cordially at Cavendon. There are many things I wish to discuss with you, and most especially the property I own in Yorkshire.

I am planning to travel to London in June, where I shall take up residence at Claridge's Hotel. Hopefully I can visit you in July, on a date that is convenient to you.

I look forward to hearing from you in the not-too-distant future. With all good wishes to you and Felicity.

Sincerely, your Cousin,

Hugo

Charles leaned back in the chair, still holding the letter in his hand. Finally, he placed it on the desk, and closed his eyes for a moment, thinking of Little Skell Manor, the house which had belonged to Hugo's mother, and which he now owned. No doubt Hugo wanted to take possession of it, which was his legal right.

A small groan escaped him, and Charles opened his eyes and sat up in the chair. No use turning away from the worries flooding through him. The house was Hugo's property. The problem was that their aunt, Lady Gwendolyn Ingham Baildon, resided there, and at seventy-two years old she would dig her feet in if Hugo endeavoured to turf her out.

The mere thought of his aunt and Hugo doing battle sent an icy chill running through Charles, and his mind began to race as he sought a solution to this difficult situation.

Finally he rose, walked over to the French doors opposite his desk, and stood looking out at the terrace, wishing Felicity were here. He needed somebody to talk to about this problem. *Right away.*

Then he saw her, hurrying down the steps, making for the wide gravel path that led to Skelldale House. *Charlotte Swann.* The very person who could help him. Of course she could.

Without giving it another thought, Charles stepped out onto the terrace. 'Charlotte!' he called. 'Charlotte! Come back!'

On hearing her name, Charlotte instantly turned around, her face filling with a smile when she saw him. 'Hello,' she responded, lifting her hand in a wave. As she did this she began to walk back up the terrace steps. 'Whatever is it?' she asked when she came to a stop in front of him. Staring up into his face, she said, 'You look very upset . . . is something wrong?'

'Probably,' he replied. 'Could you spare me a few minutes? I need to show you something, and to discuss a family matter. If you have time, if it's not inconvenient now. I could—'

'Oh Charlie, come on, don't be silly. Of course it's not

inconvenient. I was only going to Skelldale House to get a frock for Lavinia. She wants me to send it to London for her.'

'That's a relief. I'm afraid I have a bit of a dilemma.' Taking her arm, he led her into the library, continuing, 'What I mean is, something has happened that might become a dilemma. Or even a battle royal.'

THREE

When they were alone together, there was an easy familiarity between Charles Ingham and Charlotte Swann.

This unselfconscious acceptance of each other sprang from their childhood friendship, and a deeply ingrained loyalty that had remained intact over the years.

Charlotte had grown up with Charles and his two younger sisters, Lavinia and Vanessa, and had been educated with them by the governess who was in charge of the schoolroom at Cavendon Hall at that time.

This was one of the privileges bestowed on the Swanns over a hundred years earlier, by the 3rd Earl of Mowbray: A Swann girl was invited to join the Ingham children for daily lessons. The 3rd Earl, a kind and charitable man, respected the Swanns, appreciated their dedication and loyalty to the Inghams through the generations, and it was his way of rewarding them. The custom had continued up to this very day, and it was now Cecily Swann who went to the schoolroom with DeLacy Ingham for their lessons with Miss Audrey Payne, the governess.

When they were little, Charlotte and Charles had enjoyed irking his sisters by calling each other *Charlie*, chortling at the confusion this created. They had been inseparable until he had gone off to Eton. Nevertheless, their loyalty and concern for each other had lasted over the years, albeit in a slightly different way. They didn't mingle or socialize once Charles had gone to Oxford, and, in fact, they lived in entirely different worlds. When they were with his family, or other people, they addressed each other formally, and were respectful.

But it existed still, that childhood bond, and they were both aware of their closeness, although it was never referred to. He had never forgotten how she had mothered him, looked out for him when they were small. She was only one year older than he was, but it was Charlotte who took charge of them all.

She had comforted him and his sisters when their mother had suddenly and unexpectedly died of a heart attack; commiserated with them when, two years later, their father had remarried. The new Countess was the Honourable Harriette Storm, and they all detested her. The woman was snobbish, brash and bossy, and had a mean streak. She had trapped the grief-stricken Earl, who was lonely and lost, with her unique beauty, which Charlotte loved to point out was only skin deep, after all.

They had enjoyed playing tricks on her, the worse the better, and it was Charlotte who had come up with a variety of names for her: Bad Weather, Hurricane Harriette and Rainy Day, to name just three of them. The names made them laugh, had helped them to move on from the rather childish pranks they played. Eventually they simply poked fun at her behind her back.

The marriage had been abysmal for the Earl, who had retreated behind a carapace of his own making. And it had not lasted long. Hateful Harriette soon returned to London. It was there that she died, not long after her departure from Cavendon. Her liver failed because it had been totally destroyed by the huge quantities of alcohol she had consumed since her debutante days.

Charles suddenly thought of the recent past as he stood watching Charlotte straightening the horse painting by George Stubbs, remembering how often she had done this when she had worked for his father.

With a laugh, he said, 'I just did the same thing a short while ago. That painting's constantly slipping, but then I don't need to tell *you* that.'

Charlotte swung around. 'It's been re-hung numerous times, as you well know. I'll ask Mr Hanson for an old wine cork again, and fix it properly.'

'How can a wine cork do that?' he asked, puzzled.

Walking over to join him, she explained, 'I cut a slice of the cork off and wedge it between the wall and the bottom of the frame. A bit of cork always holds the painting steady. I've been doing it for years.'

Charles merely nodded, thinking of all the bits of cork he had been picking up and throwing away for years. Now he knew what they had been for.

Motioning to the chair on the other side of the desk, he said, 'Please sit down, Charlotte, I need your advice.'

She did as he asked, and glanced at him as he sat down himself, thinking that he was looking well. He was forty-four, but he didn't look it. Charles was athletic, as his father had been, and kept himself in shape. Like most of the Ingham men, he was tall, attractive, had their clear blue eyes, a fair complexion and light brown hair. Wherever he went in the world, she was certain nobody would mistake him for being anything but an Englishman. And an English gentleman at that. He was refined looking, had a classy air about him, and handled himself with a certain decorum.

Leaning across the desk, Charles handed Charlotte the letter from Hugo. 'I received this in the morning post and, I have to admit, it genuinely startled me.'

She took the letter from him, wondering who had sent it. Charlotte had a quick mind, was intelligent and astute. And having worked as the 5th Earl's personal assistant for years, there wasn't much she didn't know about Cavendon, and everybody associated with it. She was not at all surprised when she saw Hugo's signature; she had long harboured the thought that this particular young man would show up at Cavendon one day.

After reading the letter quickly, she said, 'You think he's coming back to claim Little Skell Manor, don't you?'

'Of course. What else?'

Charlotte nodded in agreement, and then frowned, and pursed her lips. 'But surely Cavendon is full of unhappy memories for him?'

'I would think that's so; on the other hand, as you've seen, Hugo says in his letter that he wishes to discuss the property he owns here, and also informs me that he plans to live in Yorkshire permanently.'

'At Little Skell Manor. And perhaps he doesn't care that he will have to turn an old lady out of the house she has lived in for donkey's years, long before his parents died, in fact.'

'Quite frankly, I don't know. I haven't laid eyes on him for sixteen years. Since *he* was sixteen, actually. However, he must be fully aware that our aunt still lives there.' Charles threw her a questioning look, raising a brow.

'It's quite easy to check on this well-known family, even long-distance,' Charlotte asserted. Sitting back in the chair, she was thoughtful for a moment. 'I remember Hugo. He was a nice boy. But he might well have changed, in view of what happened to him here. He was treated badly. You must recall how angry your father was when his sister sent Hugo off to America.'

'I do,' Charles replied. 'My father thought it was ridiculous.

He didn't believe Hugo caused Peter's death. Peter had always been a risk-taker, foolhardy. To go out on the lake here, in a little boat, late at night when he was drunk, was totally irresponsible. My father always said Hugo tried to rescue his brother, to save him, and then got blamed for his death.'

'We mustn't forget that Peter was Lady Evelyne's favourite. Your aunt never paid much attention to Hugo. It was sad. A tragic affair, really.'

Charles leaned forward, resting his elbows on the desk. 'You know how much I trust your judgement. So tell me this – what am I going to do? There will be an unholy row, a scandal, if Hugo does take back the manor. Which of course he can, legally. What happens to Aunt Gwendolyn? Where would she live? With us here in the East Wing? That's the only solution I can come up with.'

Charlotte shook her head vehemently. 'No, no, that's not a solution! It would be very crowded with you and Felicity, and six children, and your sister Vanessa. Then there's the nanny, the governess, and all the staff. It would be like . . . well . . . *a hotel*. At least to Lady Gwendolyn it would. She's an old lady, set in her ways, independent, used to running everything. By that I mean her own household, with her own staff. And she's fond of her privacy.'

'Possibly you're right,' Charles muttered. 'She'd be aghast.'

Charlotte went on, 'Your aunt would feel like . . . a guest here, an intrusion. And I believe she would resent being bundled in here with you, with all due respect, Charles. In fact, she'll put up a real fight, I fear, because she'll be most unhappy to leave her house.'

'It isn't hers,' Charles said softly. 'Pity her sister Evelyne never changed her will. My aunt *will* have to move. There's no way around that.' He sat back in the chair, a gloomy expression settling on his face. 'I do wish Cousin Hugo wasn't planning to come back and live here. What a blasted nuisance this is.'

'I don't want to make matters worse,' Charlotte began, 'but there's another thing. Don't—'

'What are you getting at?' he interrupted swiftly, alarm surfacing. He sat up straighter in the chair.

'We know Lady Gwendolyn will be put out, but don't you think Hugo's presence on the estate is going to upset some other people as well? There are still those who think Hugo was responsible for Peter's death, and—'

'That's because they don't know the facts,' he cut in sharply. 'Or they won't accept them.'

Charlotte remained silent, her mind racing.

Getting up from the chair, Charles walked over to the fireplace, stood with his back to it, imagining worrying scenarios. He still thought the only way to deal with this matter easily and in a kindly way was to invite his aunt to live with them. Perhaps Felicity could talk to her. His wife had a rather persuasive manner and much charm.

Charlotte stood up, and joined him near the fireplace. As she approached him she couldn't help thinking how much he resembled his father in certain ways. He had inherited some of his father's mannerisms, often sounded like him.

Instantly her mind turned to David Ingham, the 5th Earl of Mowbray. She had worked for him for twenty years, until he had died. Eight years ago now. As those happy days, still so vivid, came into her mind, she thought of the South Wing at Cavendon. It was there they had worked, alongside Mr Harris, the accountant, Mr Nelson, the estate manager, and Maude Greene, the secretary.

'The South Wing, that's where Lady Gwendolyn could live!' Charlotte blurted out as she came to a stop next to Charles.

'Those rooms Father used as offices? Where you worked?' he

asked, and then a wide smile spread across his face. 'Charlotte, you're a genius. Of course she could live there. And very comfortably.'

Charlotte nodded, and hurried on, her enthusiasm growing. 'Your father put in several bathrooms and a small kitchen, if you remember. When you built the office annexe in the stable block, all of the office furniture was moved over there. The sofas, chairs and drawing-room furniture came down from the attics and into the South Wing.'

'*Exactly.* And I know the South Wing is constantly well maintained by Hanson and Mrs Thwaites. Every wing of Cavendon is kept in perfect condition, as you're aware.'

'If Lady Gwendolyn agreed, she would have a self-contained flat, in a sense, and total privacy,' Charlotte pointed out.

'That's true, and I would be happy to make as many changes as she wished.' Taking hold of her arm, he continued, 'Let's go and look at those rooms in the South Wing, shall we? You do have time, don't you?'

'I do, and that's a good idea, Charles,' she responded. 'Because you have no alternative but to invite Hugo Stanton to visit Cavendon. And I think you must be prepared for the worst. He might well want to take possession of Little Skell Manor immediately.'

His chest tightened at her words, but he knew she was right.

As they moved through the various rooms in the South Wing, and especially those that his father had used as offices, Charles thought of the relationship between his father and Charlotte.

Had there been one?

She had come to work for him when she was a young girl, seventeen, and she had been at the 5th Earl's side at all times, had travelled with him, and been his close companion as well as his personal assistant. It was Charlotte who had been with his father when he died.

Charles was aware there had been speculation about their relationship, but never any real gossip. No one knew anything. Perhaps this was due to total discretion on his father's part and Charlotte's . . . that there was not a whiff of a scandal about them.

He glanced across at Charlotte. They were in the lavender room, and she was explaining to him that his aunt might like to have it as her bedroom. He was only half listening.

A raft of brilliant spring sunshine was slanting into the room, was turning her russet hair into a burnished helmet around her face. As always, she was pale, and her light greyish-blue eyes appeared enormous. For the first time in years, Charles saw her objectively. And he realized what a beautiful woman she was; she looked half her true age.

Thrown into her company every day for twenty years, how could his father have ever resisted her? Charles Ingham was now positive they had been involved with each other. And on every level.

It was an assumption on his part. There was no evidence. Yet at this moment it had suddenly become patently obvious to him. Charles had grown up with his father and Charlotte, and knew them better than anyone, even better than his wife Felicity, and he certainly knew *her* very well indeed. And he had had insight into them, had been aware of their flaws and their attributes, dreams and desires; and so he believed, deep in his soul, that it was more than likely they had been lovers.

Charles turned away, realizing he had been staring so hard she had become aware of his penetrating scrutiny. Moving quickly, saying something about the small kitchen, he hurried out of the lavender room into the corridor.

And why does all this matter now? he asked himself. His father was dead. And if Charlotte had made him happy, and eased his burdens, then he was glad. Charles hoped they had loved each other.

But what about Charlotte? How did she feel these days? Did she miss his father? Surely she must. All of a sudden he was filled with concern for her. He wanted to ask her how she felt. But he didn't dare. It would be an unforgivable intrusion on her privacy, and he had no desire to embarrass her.

Four

The evening gown lay on a white sheet, on the floor of Lady DeLacy Ingham's bedroom. DeLacy was the twelve-year-old daughter of the Earl and Countess, and Cecily's best friend. This morning she was excited, because she had been allowed to help Cecily with the dresses. These had been brought down from the large cedar storage closet in the attics. Some were hanging in the sewing room, awaiting Alice's inspection; two others were here.

The gown that held their attention was a shimmering column of green, blue and turquoise crystal beads, and to the two young girls kneeling next to it, the dress was the most beautiful thing they had ever seen.

'Daphne's going to look lovely in it,' DeLacy said, staring across at Cecily. 'Don't you think so?'

Cecily nodded. 'My mother wants me to seek out flaws in the dress, such as broken beads, broken threads, any little problems. She needs to know how many repairs it needs.'

'So that's what we'll do,' DeLacy asserted. 'Shall I start here? On the neckline and the sleeves?'

'Yes, that's a good idea,' Cecily answered. 'I'll examine the hem, which my mother says usually gets damaged by men. By their shoes, I mean. They all step on the hem when they're dancing.'

DeLacy nodded. '*Clumsy.* That's what they are,' she shot back, always quick to speak her mind. She was staring down at the dress, and exclaimed, 'Look, Ceci, how it shimmers when I touch it.' She shook the gown lightly. 'It's like the sea, like waves, the way it moves. It will match Daphne's eyes, won't it? Oh, I do hope she meets a duke's son when she's wearing it.'

'Yes,' Cecily muttered absently, her head bent as she concentrated on the hemline of the beaded gown. It had been designed and made in Paris by a famous designer, and the Countess had only worn it a few times. Then it had been carefully stored, wrapped in white cotton and placed in a large box. The gown was to be given to Daphne, to wear at one of the special summer parties, once it had been fitted to suit her figure.

'There's hardly any damage,' Cecily announced a few minutes later. 'How are the sleeves and the neckline?'

'Almost perfect,' DeLacy replied. 'There aren't many beads missing.'

'Mam will be pleased.' Cecily stood up. 'Let's put the gown back on the bed.'

She and DeLacy took the beaded evening dress, each of them holding one end, and lifted it carefully onto DeLacy's bed. 'Gosh, it's really heavy,' she said as they put it back in place.

'That's the reason beaded dresses are kept in boxes or drawers,' Cecily explained. 'If a beaded gown is put on a hanger, the beads will eventually weigh it down, and that makes the dress longer. It gets out of shape.'

DeLacy nodded, always interested in the things Cecily told her, especially about frocks. She knew a lot about clothes, and DeLacy learned from her all the time.

Cecily straightened the beaded dress and covered it with a long piece of cotton, then walked across the room to look out of the window. She was hoping to see her mother coming from the village. There was no sign of her yet.

DeLacy remained near the bed, now staring down at the other summer evening gown, a froth of white tulle, taffeta and handmade lace. 'I think I like this one the most,' she said to Cecily without turning around. 'This is a *real* ball gown.'

'I know. Mam told me your mother wore it only once, and it's been kept in a cotton bag in the cedar closet for ages. That's why the white is still white. It hasn't turned.'

'What do you mean?'

'White turns colour. It can become creamy, yellowed, or faded. But the ball gown has been well protected, and it's as good as new.'

On an impulse, DeLacy reached down, picked up the gown and moved away from the bed. Holding the gown close to her body, she began to dance around the room, whirling and twirling, humming to herself, imagining herself waltzing in a ballroom. The skirt of the gown flared out as she moved.

Cecily couldn't believe what she was seeing. She was totally speechless, gaping at DeLacy as she continued to swirl and jump with the delicate ball gown in her arms. Cecily was in shock, unable to do anything. She was afraid to grab DeLacy in case the gown was damaged in the process, and so she just stood there cringing, worried about the lace and the tulle. It truly was a ball gown, full-skirted like a crinoline, and it would easily rip if it caught on the furniture.

Finding her voice at last, Cecily exclaimed, 'Please stop, DeLacy! The fabric could get damaged. It's so delicate. Please, please put the dress back on the bed!'

Now Cecily took a step forward, moving closer to her friend, who immediately danced away, putting herself out of reach. She continued to clutch the dress to her body. 'I won't hurt it, Ceci,' DeLacy said, still whirling around the room. 'I promise I won't.'

'Stop! You must stop!' Cecily cried desperately, her voice rising. She was on the verge of tears.

DeLacy Ingham paid no attention to Cecily Swann.

She was enjoying herself too much, dancing around the bedroom, lost in a world of her own for a moment or two. And then it happened. The accident.

Cecily saw it start as if in slow motion, and there was nothing she could do to stop it.

DeLacy's foot got caught in the hemline of the gown. She wobbled. Then lost her balance. And reached out to steady herself. She grabbed the edge of the desk, still holding the gown. But as she did so, she knocked over the inkpot. It rolled across the desk towards her. She stepped back but she was not fast enough. The bright blue ink splashed onto the front of the skirt of the white lace ball gown.

Cecily gasped out loud, her eyes widening. Horrified at what had just happened, and frightened at the thought of the conse-quences, she was unable to move.

DeLacy looked down at the ink, her face stricken. When she glanced across at Cecily her eyes filled with tears.

'Look what you've done!' Cecily said, her voice trembling. 'Why didn't you listen to me? Why didn't you pay attention?'

DeLacy had no answer for her. She stood there holding the dress, tears rolling down her face.

FIVE

'Delacy! What on earth's happened?' Daphne exclaimed from the threshold of the room, and hurried forward, making straight for her sister.

DeLacy did not answer, quaking inside, knowing how upset Daphne would be when she saw the ruined ball gown. It had been chosen for her to wear at the summer ball their parents gave at Cavendon every year. Tears brimmed, and she swallowed hard, pushing back her fear. She knew she was in trouble. How stupid she had been to play around with this fragile gown.

'Why are you clutching the ball gown like that? My goodness, is that ink? How did *ink* get on the lace?' Daphne's normally soft voice had risen an octave or two, and she was startled, her face suddenly turning pale.

When DeLacy remained silent, looking more frightened than ever, Daphne turned, her gaze resting on Cecily. 'What on earth were you doing? How did this happen?'

Cecily, fiercely loyal to her best friend, cleared her throat nervously, not knowing how to answer Daphne without lying.

That she could not do; nor did she wish to explain the series of events that had taken place.

Her mind raced as she wondered what to say. Unexpectedly, she did not have to do that, since her mother was now entering the room.

Cecily began to shake inside. She was well aware how angry her mother would be, and *she* would be blamed. She had been in charge.

Alice walked over to join Daphne and DeLacy. When she spotted the ball gown in DeLacy's arms she came to an abrupt halt, a dismayed expression crossing her face. Nonetheless, Alice was self-contained, and she said in a steady voice, *'That's ruined!* It's of no use to anyone now.' Glancing at her daughter, she raised a brow. 'Well, what do you have to say? Can you please explain how this unique ball gown got so damaged?'

Unable to speak, her mouth dry, Cecily shook her head; she retreated, moving away, backing up against the window.

Alice was not to be deterred, and went on, 'I gave you a task, Cecily. You were instructed to inspect the frocks and the ball gown, which had been taken out of the cedar closet in the attic. I asked you to look after them. They were in your care. However, it is obvious you didn't look after this one, did you?'

Cecily blinked back the incipient tears. She shook her head, and in a whisper, she said, 'It was an accident, Mam.' She was still protecting DeLacy when she added, 'I'm sorry I let you down.'

Alice simply nodded, holding her annoyance in check. She was usually polite, particularly when she was in the presence of the Inghams. Then it struck her that it was DeLacy who was responsible for this disaster. Before she could direct a question at her, DeLacy stepped forward, drew closer to Alice.

Taking a deep breath, she said in a quavering voice, 'Don't blame Ceci, Mrs Alice! Please don't do that. She's innocent. It's my fault, I'm to blame. I picked up the dress, waltzed around the room with it. Then I tripped, lost my balance and knocked over the inkpot . . .' She paused, shook her head, and began to weep, adding through her tears, 'I was silly.'

Alice went over to her. 'Thank you for telling me, Lady DeLacy, and please, let me take the gown from you. You're crushing it. Please give it to me, m'lady.'

DeLacy did so, releasing it from her clutches at last. 'I'm sorry, Mrs Alice. Very sorry,' she said again.

Alice carried the ball gown over to the bed and laid it down, examining the stains, fully aware how difficult it was to remove ink – virtually impossible, in fact.

At seventeen, Daphne Ingham was a rather unusual girl. She was not only staggeringly beautiful but a kind, thoughtful and compassionate young woman with a tender heart. She stepped over to her sister and put an arm around her. Gently, she said, 'I understand what happened, Lacy darling, it was an accident, as Ceci said. Mama will understand. These things do happen sometimes, and we all know you didn't intend to do any harm.'

On hearing these words, and aware of Daphne's sweet nature, DeLacy clung to her and began to sob. Daphne held her closer, soothing her, not wishing her little sister to be so upset – and over a dress, of all things.

Surprisingly, Lady Daphne Ingham was not particularly vain. She only paid attention to clothes because it had been drilled into her to do so because of her station in life. Also, she knew that her father could easily afford to buy a new dress for her.

After a moment, Daphne drew away. 'Come on, stop crying, DeLacy. Tears won't do any good.' Looking over at Alice, she then said, 'Can the lace and the underskirts be cleaned, Mrs Swann?'

Alice shook her head vigorously. 'I don't believe so, m'lady. Well, not successfully. I suppose I could try using lemon juice, salt, white vinegar . . .' She broke off. 'No, no, they won't do any good. Ink is awful, you know, it's like a dye. And talking of ink, it's all over the desk, m'lady, and on the carpet. Shall I go and find Mrs Thwaites? Ask her to send up one of the maids?'

'That's all right. I'll ring for Peggy, Mrs Swann. She'll clean up the ink. None of us should go near it. We don't want it on our hands, not when there are other frocks around.'

'You're right, Lady Daphne. I was—'

'Mam,' Cecily interrupted. 'I can make the ball gown *right*. I can, Mam.' Cecily turned around, stared intently at her mother, suddenly feeling confident. Her face was flushed with excitement, her eyes sparkling. 'I'm sure I can save it. And Lady Daphne can wear it to the summer ball after all.'

'You'll never get that ink off, Ceci,' Alice answered, her tone softer, now that she knew her daughter had, in fact, not been responsible for the ruination of the gown.

'Mam, please, come here, and you too, DeLacy. And you as well, please, Lady Daphne. I want to explain what I can do.'

The three of them immediately joined her, stood looking down at the white lace ball gown stretched across the bottom of the bed.

Cecily said, 'I'm going to cut away the front part of the white lace skirt from the waist to the hemline. I'll shape it. Make it a panel that starts out narrow at the waist and widens as it goes down to the floor. I'll do the same with the white taffeta under-skirt, and the tulle. If the second layer of tulle has ink on it, I'll cut that off too.'

'And then what?' Alice asked, gazing at her in bafflement.

'I'll replace the panels of lace, taffeta and tulle. It'll be hard to find white lace to match the ball gown. You might have to go to London.'

In spite of her initial scepticism, Alice suddenly understood exactly what Cecily meant to do. She also realized that her daughter might have the solution. 'It sounds like a good plan, Cecily, very clever. Unfortunately, you're right about the lace, it will be difficult to match. I probably *will* have to go up to London. To Harrods.'

Alice now paused, shook her head. 'There are several other things we must consider. First, a panel of lace that's different from the rest of the overskirt would be extremely noticeable. Secondly, there would be seams down the front. They'd be obvious.'

'I've thought of that,' Cecily answered swiftly. 'I can hide the seams with narrow ribbon lace, and sew the ribbon lace around the waist as a finishing touch.' She bit her lip, before adding, 'Or we can make a *new* skirt out of new lace.'

'I understand,' Alice said. 'But the new lace wouldn't match the bodice. And don't even think of trying to remake the bodice, Cecily, that would be far too difficult for both of us.'

'We don't have to touch the bodice, Mam.'

'I think Cecily is right, Mrs Swann,' Daphne said. 'Her ideas are brilliant.' She gave Cecily a huge smile. 'I believe you will be a dress designer yourself one day, like Lucile of Hanover Square.'

'Perhaps,' Alice said quietly. 'I've always known Cecily had talent, a flair with clothes. And such a good eye.' Alice suddenly smiled for the first time since entering the room.

Pragmatic by nature, and wishing to continue talking about the ball gown, Cecily now said, 'The lace will cost a lot, won't it?'

She had addressed Alice, but before her mother could answer, Daphne said, 'Oh you mustn't worry about that, Ceci. I am quite certain you will be able to rescue the gown, and I know Papa will be happy to pay for the lace, and the other fabrics you require.'

Alice carried the ball gown over to Cecily, and gave it to her.

She said, 'We'll go up to the sewing room now and put this on the mannequin, so that we can examine the stains properly. I'll bring the beaded gown. It's heavy.' Glancing across at Daphne, she said, 'Will you join us, Your Ladyship? I think you should try on both of the dresses, so we can see how they fit.'

'I'll be happy to, I'll just go to my room and change into a dressing gown.' Turning to her sister, Daphne added, 'I shall ring for Peggy, and once she arrives to clean up the ink, you can join us in the sewing room. She can, can't she, Mrs Alice?'

'Of course she can, m'lady,' Alice replied with a friendly smile, and then she and her daughter left DeLacy's bedroom.

Cecily was relieved her mother was no longer angry with her. How foolish she had been, not trying harder to stop DeLacy, and DeLacy had been irresponsible, dancing around with the gown, the way she had. They should both have known better. After all, they were grown up.

'I think I'd better get the platform out,' Alice announced, walking over to the huge storage cupboard in the sewing room, opening the door. 'It'll make it easier for me to see the hemline when Lady Daphne stands on it.'

'I'll help, Mam.'

Alice shook her head. 'I have it, love, don't worry.' She now upended the square white box she had pulled out, and pushed it across the room to the cheval mirror. Several years ago, Walter Swann had attached two small wheels on one side of the platform so that it would be easy for his wife to move around.

At this moment, the door flew open and Lady Daphne came in wearing a blue silk dressing gown; DeLacy was immediately behind her older sister, creeping in, stealthily, almost as if she did not want to be noticed.

Cecily's eyes flew to her friend, and she nodded.

DeLacy offered a smile in return, but it was a wan smile at that. The girl looked shamefaced, subdued, and even a little cowed.

Cecily said encouragingly, 'Let's go and sit over there, Lacy, on the chairs near the wall.'

DeLacy inclined her head, followed her friend, but remained silent.

'Here I am, Mrs Swann,' Daphne said. 'I'm so sorry to have kept you waiting.'

'No problem, my lady. If you'll just slip behind the screen, I'll bring the beaded gown, help you get into it.'

Cecily felt sorry for DeLacy, and she reached out, took hold of her hand, squeezed it. 'Mam's not angry any more,' she whispered. 'Cheer up.'

DeLacy swivelled her head, looked at Cecily, and blinked back sudden tears. 'Are you sure?' she whispered. 'She was furious with me. I could tell.'

'It's fine, everything's settled down.'

Within seconds Daphne was standing on the wooden platform in front of the cheval mirror; even she, who so lacked an interest in clothes, was impressed with the way she looked.

The blue, green and turquoise crystal beads, covering the entire dress, shimmered if she made the slightest movement. It was eye-catching, and Daphne knew how well it suited her. Smiling at Alice, her bright blue eyes sparkling, she exclaimed, 'It undulates; it's unique.' She turned slowly on the platform, viewing herself from every angle, obviously taken with the long, slender column of beads and the magical effect they produced.

Alice was happy. The gown fitted this slender beauty as if it had been specially made for her, and also Daphne was finally showing an interest in clothes. Alice also realized how right the Countess had been to choose this particular dress from the collection of her evening gowns and other apparel stored in the cedar closets. It was . . . *wonderful* on Daphne. No other word to describe it, but then it *was* a piece of *haute couture* from Paris. It had been made for the Countess at Maison Callot, the famous fashion house run by the three talented Callot sisters, who designed stylish clothes for society women.

'The dress is most becoming on you, Lady Daphne,' Alice smiled, and went to stand in front of her. Very slowly, she walked around the platform, studying the dress, nodding to herself at times.

'The hemline dips in a few places; nothing to worry about, m'lady. That often happens with beaded gowns, it's the weight of the beads. I'll just put in a few pins where I need to adjust it. It's a perfect fit, Lady Daphne.'

'Thank you, Mrs Alice.'

Cecily said, 'There aren't many beads missing, Mam.'

Alice swung her head, smiled at her daughter and went on with her work.

Cecily sat back in the chair, watching her mother, always learning from her. Alice was now kneeling on the floor with a small pincushion attached to her left wrist. Every so often she put a pin or two in the hem, marking the exact spot for attention later.

Pins had a language of their own, Cecily was aware of that. It was a language her mother was going to teach her soon. She had made a promise, and her mam always kept her promises.

When Daphne finally got off the platform and walked towards the screen in a corner of the room, Alice beckoned to Cecily, and the two of them took the bouffant white ball gown off the mannequin. Alice followed Daphne, carrying the gown. She was certain this would fit her too. It had been made at the same time as the beaded column.

Daphne emerged a few seconds later, looking so beautiful, so ethereal, in the froth of white lace and tulle, that Cecily caught her breath in surprise. Then she exclaimed, 'You look like a fairy-tale princess!'

Daphne walked forward, smiling. She swirled around, the skirts billowing out, and then swirled again, and nobody even noticed the ink stains, so entrancing was she.

'The perfect bride for the son of a duke,' DeLacy blurted out, and then shrank back in the chair when they all stared at her.

The phantom duke not yet found, Alice thought, and therefore no son to marry. But there will be one soon enough, I've no doubt. After all, she's only seventeen and not quite ready for marriage yet. Still a child in so many ways. And such a beauty. But all of the four Dees are lovely, and so is my Cecily. Yes, they're the beautiful girls of Cavendon, none to match them anywhere.

Alice stood there smiling, admiring them, and thinking what a lovely summer it was going to be for everyone – the suppers, the dances, the big ball, and the weekend house parties . . . a happy, festive time.

Although she did not know it, Alice was wrong. The summer would be a season of the most devastating trouble, which would shake the House of Ingham to its core.

SIX

'It's extremely quiet in here, Mrs Jackson,' the butler remarked from the doorway of the kitchen, surveying Cook's domain. 'Did yer think we'd all died and gone ter heaven then?' Nell Jackson asked with a laugh. 'I just sat down ter catch me breath before I start on the main course. Can't cook it yet, though, not till the last minute. Dover sole is a delicate fish, doesn't need much time in the pan.'

Mr Hanson nodded and went on. 'I've no doubt the hustle and bustle will start up again very shortly.'

'It will. Right now everyone's off doing their duties upstairs, but they'll soon be scurrying back down here, bringing their bustle with them. As for Polly, I sent her ter bed, Mr Hanson. She's got a sore throat and a headache. It's better she's confined ter her room until she feels better. I don't want her spreading germs, if she does have a cold.'

'Good thinking on your part, Mrs Jackson. Lord Mowbray is a stickler about illness. He doesn't like the staff working if they're under the weather. For their sakes as well as ours. You'll be able to manage all right. It's only three for lunch, with the Countess and Lady Diedre in Harrogate today.'

'It's not a problem, Mr Hanson,' Mrs Jackson reassured him. 'Elsie and Mary will help me ter put the food on the serving plat-ters, and Malcolm and Gordon will handle lunch upstairs with ease.'

'And I shall be serving the wine, and supervising them as usual,' he reminded her with a kindly smile. Then he nodded and walked on down the corridor, heading for his office. The room was one of his favourites in this great house, which he loved for its beauty, heritage and spirit of the past; he looked after it as if it were his own. Nothing was ever too much trouble.

Hanson had occupied the office for some years now, and it had acquired a degree of comfort over time, resembling a gentle-man's study in its overall style. Henry had arrived at Cavendon Hall in 1888, twenty-five years ago now, when he had been twenty-six. From the first day, Geoffrey Swann, the butler at that time, had favoured him; he had spotted something special in him. Geoffrey Swann had called it 'a potential for excellence.'

The renowned butler had propelled Hanson up through the hierarchy with ease, teaching him the ropes all the way. Starting as a junior footman in the pecking order, he rose to footman, eventually became the senior footman, and was finally named assistant butler under the direction of Geoffrey Swann. He had been an essential part of the household for ten years when, to everyone's shock, Geoffrey Swann suddenly dropped dead of a heart attack in 1898.

The 5th Earl had immediately asked Hanson if he would take over as butler. He had agreed at once, and never looked back. He ran Cavendon Hall with enormous efficiency, care, skill and a huge sense of responsibility. Geoffrey Swann had been an extraordinary mentor, had turned Hanson into a well-trained major-domo who had become as renowned as Swann before him in aristocratic circles.

Sitting down at his desk, Hanson picked up the menus for lunch and dinner, which Mrs Jackson had given him earlier, and glanced at them. In a short while, he must go to the wine cellar and choose the wines. Perhaps a Pouilly Fuissé for the fish and a Pomerol for the spring lamb that had been selected for dinner.

Leaning back in the chair, Hanson let his thoughts meander to other matters for a moment or two, and then he made a decision and got up. Leaving his office, he walked in the direction of the housekeeper's sitting room.

Her door was ajar and, after knocking on it, he pushed it open and looked inside. 'It's Hanson, Mrs Thwaites. Do you have a moment?'

'Of course!' she exclaimed. 'Come in, come in.'

Closing the door behind him, Hanson said, 'I wanted a word with you . . . about Peggy Swift. I was wondering how she was working out? Is she satisfactory?' he asked, getting straight to the point as he usually did. 'Is she going to fit in here?'

Agnes Thwaites did not reply immediately, and he couldn't help wondering why. He was about to ask her if she was unhappy with the new maid, when she finally spoke.

'I can't fault her work, Mr Hanson. I really can't. She's quick and she's efficient. Still, there's something I can't quite put my finger on . . . something about her doesn't sit well with me.' Mrs Thwaites shook her head.

'So I've noticed,' Hanson replied pithily. 'She did work at Ellsford Manor, and you did get an excellent reference, but then the manor is hardly Cavendon. It's not a stately home.'

'Oh, yes, I understand that,' she answered, suppressing a smile. It was well known that Hanson believed Cavendon was better than any other house in the land, including Buckingham Palace, Windsor Castle and Sandringham, all royal residences. 'I have noticed there is a certain coolness between Peggy and the other maids. I'm not clear why,' Mrs Thwaites added.

'Has Mrs Jackson told you what she thinks of Peggy?' he asked, a brow lifting.

'Well, naturally Mrs Jackson is pleased with her efficiency, her quickness. It might be that Peggy is just not suitable for this house.'

'You'd better keep a sharp eye on her, since the maids are in your care, as the footmen are in mine. And I will as well, as I think two pairs of eyes see much more than one.'

Hanson left the sitting room and walked back to his office. He sat at the desk for a moment or two, thinking about the situation in general. They were still missing a third footman, and if they had to let Peggy Swift go, they would be short of a maid. This problem would have to be rectified by the summer, since His Lordship and the Countess had planned a number of events, and there would be weekend guests. Sighing under his breath, Hanson reached down, unlocked the bottom drawer, took out his keys and went to the wine cellar.

A short while later, he was returning to his office, carrying two bottles of wine, when he ran into Walter Swann, husband of Alice, father of Cecily, and valet to Lord Mowbray.

'There you are, Mr Hanson,' Walter exclaimed in his usual cheerful voice, smiling hugely. 'I was just coming along to tell you that His Lordship will make sure lunch finishes early today. He knows Alice and Cecily are joining us in the servants' hall, and he doesn't want us to be eating "in the middle of the afternoon", was the way he put it. He wanted you to know.'

'Very considerate, I must say,' Hanson replied, glad to have this bit of pleasant news.

'I'll go and tell Cook, and then I must get back upstairs. I've a lot of jobs to do for Lord Mowbray today,' Walter explained.

'I'll see you later, Walter. I'm looking forward to having lunch with Alice and your girl. Everyone loves Cecily.'

Walter grinned and hurried towards the kitchen, where he

hovered in the entrance, obviously explaining matters to Mrs Jackson.

Once he was back in his office, Hanson placed the two bottles on the small table near the window, and went again to his desk. He dropped the bunch of keys into the bottom drawer, glancing at the clock as he sat down in the chair. It was ten minutes to twelve, and he had a moment or two before he needed to go upstairs to check on things. He looked down at the list he had made earlier, noting that the most pressing item on it was the silver vault. He must check it, tomorrow at the latest. The footmen had their work cut out for them – a lot of important silver had to be cleaned for the parties coming up in the summer.

Leaning back in his chair, his thoughts settled on Walter. How smart he always looked in his tailored black jacket and pinstriped grey trousers. He smiled inwardly, thinking of the two footmen, Malcolm and Gordon, who had such high opinions of their looks. Vain they were.

But those two couldn't hold a candle to Walter Swann. At thirty-five he was in his prime – good looking, intelligent and hard working. And also the most trustworthy man Henry Hanson knew. Walter brought a smile to work, not his troubles, and he was well mannered and thoughtful, had a nice disposition. Few can beat him, Hanson decided, and fell down into his memories.

He had known Walter Swann since he was a boy . . . ten years old. And he had watched him grow into the man he was today. Hanson had only seen him upset when something truly sorrowful had happened: when his father, then his uncle Geoffrey, and then the 5th Earl had died. And on King Edward VII's passing. That had affected Walter very much: he was a true patriot; loved his King and Country.

The day of the King's funeral came rushing back to Henry Hanson. It might have been yesterday, so clear was it in his mind.

He and Walter had accompanied the family to London in May of 1910, to open up the Mayfair house for the summer season.

The sudden death of the King had shocked everyone; when Hanson had asked the Earl if he and Walter could have the morning off to go out into the streets to watch the funeral procession leaving Westminster Hall, the Earl had been kind, had accommodated them.

Three years ago now, 20 May: that had been the day of the King's funeral after his lying-in-state. Hanson and Walter had never seen so many people jammed together in the streets of London: hundreds of thousands of sorrowing, silent people, the everyday people of England, mourning their 'Bertie', the playboy Prince who had turned out to be a good King and father of the nation. There had been more mourners for him than for his mother, Queen Victoria.

Hanson knew *he* would never forget the sight of the cortège and he believed Walter felt the same – the gun carriage rumbling along, the King's charger, boots and stirrups reversed, and a Scottish Highlander in a swinging kilt, leading the King's wire-haired terrier behind his master's coffin. He and Walter had both choked up at the sight of that little dog in the procession, heading for Paddington Station and the train to Windsor, where the King would be buried. Later they had found out that the King's little white dog was called Caesar. They had wept for their King that day, and shared their grief and become even closer friends.

There was a knock on the door, and Hanson instantly roused himself. 'Come in,' he called and rose, moved across the room. He touched the bottle of white wine. It was still very cold from being in the wine cellar. He must take it upstairs to the pantry in readiness for lunch.

Mrs Thwaites was standing in the doorway, and he beckoned her to enter when she looked at him questioningly. As she closed the door and walked towards him he saw that her expression was serious.

She paused for a moment as she reached his desk and then said, 'Instinct told me there was something about Peggy that was *off*, and now I know what it is that bothers me. She's the type of young woman who's bold, encourages men . . . you know what I mean.'

Hanson was startled by this statement and frowned, staring at her. 'Whatever makes you say that?'

'I saw her just now. Or rather *them*. Peggy Swift and Gordon Lane. They were sort of . . . wedged together in your little pantry near the dining room. She was canoodling with him. I was coming through the back hall upstairs and I made a noise so they knew someone was approaching. Then I went the other way. They didn't see me. Instinctively, I feel that Peggy Swift spells trouble, Mr Hanson.'

Hanson didn't speak for a moment, and then he said, 'There's always a bit of *that* going on, Mrs Thwaites. Flirting. They're young.'

'I know, and you're right. But this seemed a little bit more than just flirting. Also, they were *upstairs*, where the Earl and Countess and the young ladies could easily have seen them.' Mrs Thwaites shook her head, continuing to look concerned. 'I just thought you ought to know.'

'You did the right thing. And we can't have any carrying-on of that sort in this house. It cannot be touched by gossip or scandal. Let us keep this to ourselves. Better in the long run, avoids needless talk that could be damaging to the family.'

'I won't say a word, Mr Hanson. You can trust me on that.'

SEVEN

Daphne sat at the dressing table, staring at her reflection in the antique Georgian mirror. And she saw herself quite differently. For the first time in her life she decided she *was* beautiful, as her father was always proclaiming.

Unexpectedly, she now had a different image of herself, and it was all due to the two evening gowns she had just tried on.

She had been taken aback by the way she looked in the blue-and-green beaded dress, that slender column glittering with sea colours, and also in the white ball gown. Even though this was stained with ink, it had, nonetheless, made her feel happy, buoyant, full of life, whilst the long, narrow dress of shimmering beads had given her a feeling of elegance and sophistication she had never known before.

Leaning forward, she studied her face with new interest, and saw a different girl. A girl a duke's son might find as lovely as her father did.

She thought he might have someone picked out for her, even though he had never actually said so. But he was determined to arrange a brilliant match for her, and she was certain he would do so. Her father was clever, and he knew everyone that mattered in society. After all, he was one of the premier earls of England.

A little spurt of excitement and anticipation brought a pink flush to her cheeks, and her blue eyes sparkled with joy. The idea of one day being a duchess thrilled her. She could hardly wait.

Next year, when she was eighteen, she would come out, be presented at court in the presence of King George and Queen Mary, along with other debutantes. Her parents would give a coming out ball for her, and there would be balls given for other debutantes by their parents, and she would go to them all. And after the season was over, there was no reason why she couldn't become engaged to whichever duke's son her father had selected.

A little sigh escaped, and she sat with her right elbow on the dressing table, her hand propping up her head. A faraway look spread itself across her soft, innocent face as she let herself float along with her romantic imaginings. Her mind was filled with marvellous dreams of falling in love, having a sweetheart, a true love of her own. A brilliant marriage. A home of her own. And children one day.

A sudden loud thumping on the door brought her out of her reverie, and she swung around on the stool as the door burst open.

A small but determined little girl with a flushed red face came storming in, heading straight for her. It was quite apparent the child was angry, and having a tantrum.

'Whatever's the matter?' Daphne asked, going to her five-year-old sister, Dulcie, who was usually all sweetness and smiles.

'I don't like this frock! Nanny says I have to wear it. I won't! I won't! It's not for *a special occasion!*' she shouted, and stood there glaring at Daphne, her hands on her hips, looking indignant.

Daphne swallowed the laughter bubbling in her throat, and

endeavoured to keep a straight face. In stark contrast to her own lack of interest in her clothes, her baby sister had been concerned with hers from the moment she could express an opinion. Diedre, their eldest sister, called Dulcie 'a little madam', and in the most disparaging tone, and avoided her as far as she could.

'And what is the special occasion?' Daphne asked in a loving voice, crouching down so that her face was level with her sister's.

'I'm having lunch with Papa,' Dulcie announced in an important tone. 'In the dining room.'

'Oh isn't that lovely, darling. I am too, and so is DeLacy.'

Dulcie gaped at her, a frown knotting her blonde brows. 'Nanny said *I* was having lunch with Papa. She didn't say you were, and DeLacy.'

'Well, we *will* be there. But I do have to agree with you about the dress,' Daphne now said quickly, wanting to placate the angry child. 'It simply isn't appropriate, not for lunch with Papa. You're absolutely right. Let's go and find something more suitable, shall we?'

Instantly the stormy expression fled, and a bright smile flooded Dulcie's face. 'I knew I was right,' she exclaimed, and took hold of Daphne's hand, her normal happy demeanour in place.

Together the two sisters went down the corridor to the stairs leading up to the nursery floor. At one moment, Daphne leaned down, and said softly, 'You must be grown up about this. Just tell Nanny you do like this dress, but that it's not quite nice enough for the special lunch. And you can say I agree with you.'

'I will.'

'You must say it sweetly; you mustn't be rude, or angry,' Daphne cautioned, as they mounted the stairs together.

'I'm not angry, not now,' Dulcie said, looking up at her adored Daphne, her favourite sister. She liked DeLacy, and they were good friends, but she was wary of Diedre. Her eldest sister constantly looked and sounded annoyed with her, and this puzzled and worried the child.

Nanny was waiting in the doorway of the nursery, and exclaimed, 'I was just coming to look for you, Dulcie!'

Dulcie was silent.

Daphne said swiftly, not wanting the nanny to scold: 'I think we've solved the problem.' She smiled warmly, then gave the nanny a knowing look, and added, 'It's not often Dulcie has lunch with Papa, and it's, well, rather a special occasion for her. And I do think she could wear a more appropriate dress. Something perhaps a little smarter. I'm sure you agree?'

'Of course, Lady Daphne, whatever you think is best.' The nanny opened the door wider, and they all went into the nursery sitting room.

Dulcie explained, in an earnest tone, her expression solemn, 'I do like this frock, Nanny, but I really want to wear the blue one with the white collar. Can I?'

'Of course, you can, Dulcie. Let's go and look at it, and won't you join us, Lady Daphne?'

'I certainly will.'

Dulcie was already halfway across the floor, making for her bedroom. 'Come on, Daphne, come and look at my best frock. Mrs Alice made it for me.'

As she followed the little girl, Daphne smiled to herself. She had long ago learned that the best way to handle her rather stubborn and independent youngest sister was to immediately agree with her, and then negotiate.

'Oh there you are, Hanson,' Lord Mowbray said, walking into the dining room. 'I was just about to ring for you. Dulcie is joining us for lunch today, a special treat for the child. So would you please add another place setting?'

Hanson inclined his head. 'Of course, my lord.' He excused himself and hurried into the adjoining pantry.

The Earl swung on his heels and returned to the library, where he sat down at his desk and perused the list of guests he and Felicity were planning to invite to the annual summer ball in July. He added a few more names, and then sat back, pondering, wondering who had been left out, who they might have forgotten.

It was at this moment that he saw a pair of bright blue eyes staring at him. They were just visible above the edge of the huge partners' desk. Then a moment later the whole face appeared, and he knew Dulcie was standing on her tiptoes.

She said, 'I am here, Papa.'

'So I see,' he responded, laughing. 'So come along, Dulcie, let me have a look at you.'

She did as he asked and he swung around in his chair and held out his hands to her. 'You look very lovely this morning.'

'Thank you, Papa. Mrs Alice made this frock for me. It's new. It's my favourite.'

'I can see why,' Charles answered, pulling her to him, bringing her closer. She truly was the most lovely child, with her almost violet eyes, and mass of blonde curls. Her pretty little face was still plump with baby fat, and she reminded him of a Botticelli angel. But one with a will of iron, he reminded himself. None of his other daughters was as stubborn.

Dulcie leaned against his knee, and looked up into his face. 'Can I have a horse?'

Her request startled him. 'Why a horse? Isn't a horse a bit large for you, darling?'

'No, I'm growing up fast, Nanny says.'

'I agree, but you're still not quite ready.'

'But I can ride, Papa.'

'I know, and you've enjoyed your little Shetland pony. I have an idea. I shall buy you a new pony. A better pony. Just until you can handle a horse better, when you're a bit older.'

Dulcie flushed with happiness at this suggestion and nodded. 'Thank you, Papa! What shall I call my new pony?'

'I'm sure you will think of the right name. In the meantime, we must join your sisters for lunch – and, by the way, let's keep the new pony a secret, shall we?'

'Oh yes. It's *our* secret, Papa.'

She clung to his hand as they went out of the library together. I do spoil her, Charles thought. But I just can't help it. She's the most adorable child. As they crossed the vast hall together, hand in hand, Daphne and DeLacy were hurrying down the grand staircase.

Both girls ran to greet him, and then DeLacy bent down, kissed her little sister on the cheek. 'I like your dress, Dulcie,' she murmured, smoothing a loving hand over the child's golden curls.

Dulcie smiled back and opened her mouth to speak, and then immediately closed it. The news about the new pony was a secret, her papa had said, and she must keep it.

EIGHT

After the special lunch, as Dulcie called it, the five year old was taken back to the nursery by DeLacy. Their father went off to the library to finish his correspondence, and Daphne, with nothing to do, decided to walk over to Havers Lodge.

The Tudor manor house was on the other side of the bluebell woods, and was the home of the Torbett family, old friends of the Inghams. Daphne and her sisters had grown up with the three Torbett sons, Richard, Alexander, and Julian. It was nineteen-year-old Julian who was Daphne's favourite; they had been childhood friends, and were still close.

Crossing the small stone bridge over the stream, she glanced up at the sky. It was a lovely cerulean blue, and cloudless, filled with glittering sunlight. This pleased her. The weather in Yorkshire was unpredictable, and it could so easily rain. Fortunately, the dark clouds that usually heralded heavy downpours were absent.

There was a breeze, a nip in the air, despite the brightness of the sunshine, and she was glad she had put on a hat, as well as a jacket over her grey wool skirt and matching silk blouse. She snuggled down into the jacket, slipped her hands in her pockets, walking at a steady pace.

Julian wasn't expecting her this afternoon, but he would be at the manor house. He always practised dressage on Saturdays. He was a fine equestrian, loved horses, and aimed to join a cavalry regiment in the British Army. In fact, his heart had been set on it since he was a young boy. He would be going to Sandhurst at the end of the summer, and he was thrilled he had been accepted by this famous military academy. He had once told her that he aimed to be a general, and she had no doubt he would be in years to come.

Daphne wanted to tell Julian that her father had given her permission, over lunch today, to invite Madge Courtney to the summer ball at Cavendon. The Torbetts always came, and were naturally invited again this year. Her father had now thought it only proper and correct to include Madge. She and Julian were unofficially engaged, and when he graduated from Sandhurst, several years from now, they would be married.

Off in the distance in the long meadow, Daphne saw the gypsy girl, Genevra. She was waving; Daphne waved back, then veered to the left, walking into the bluebell woods, which she loved.

They were filled with old oaks and sycamores and many other species, magnificent tall trees reaching to the sky. There were stretches of bright green grass and mossy mounds beneath them and bushes that were bright with berries in the winter, others which flowered only in the spring.

A stream trickled through one side of the woods. Rushes and weeds grew there, and when she was a child she had parted them, peered into the clear parts of the water, seen tadpoles and tiddlers swimming. And sometimes frogs had jumped out and surprised her and her sisters.

Occasionally Daphne had seen a heron standing in the stream, a tall and elegant bird that seemed oddly out of place. She looked for it now, but it was not there. Scatterings of flowers could be found around the stream, and in amongst the roots and foliage. And of course there were the bluebells, great swathes now starting to bloom under the trees; they made her catch her breath in delight.

All kinds of small animals made their homes in the woods – down holes, in tree trunks, under bushes. Little furry creatures such as voles and dormice, the common field mouse and squirrels . . . She had never been afraid of them, loved them all. But most precious to her were the birds, especially the goldfinch. She had learned a lot about nature from Great-Aunt Gwendolyn, who had grown up at Cavendon, and it was she who had told her that a flock of goldfinch was called a 'charm'. The little birds made tinkling calls that were bell-like and pretty. Her great-aunt told her they actually sang in harmony, and she believed her.

Once, her mother had called the tops of the tall trees a 'shady canopy' where their branches interlocked, and she had used that phrase ever since. Bits of blue sky were visible today, and long shafts of sunlight filtered through that lovely leafy canopy above her.

Their land was beautiful and she knew how lucky they were to live on it. Just to the left of these woods were the moors that stretched endlessly along the rim of the horizon. Implacable and daunting in winter, they were lovely in the late summer when the heather bloomed, a sea of purple stretching almost to the coast.

But as a family they had usually spent most of their time in the woods, where they had picnics in the summer. 'Because of the shade, you know,' Great-Aunt Gwendolyn would explain to their guests. She was a genuine stoic, the way she cheerfully trudged along with them, determined never to miss the woodland feasts or any of their other activities. And the ball was her favourite event – one she would not miss for the world, she would say, explaining she had never failed to attend since being a young woman. 'I was always the belle of the ball, you know,' she would add.

Daphne's thoughts settled on the summer ball. For a split second, she thought of the ink stains, and the image of herself in the gown was spoiled. Then, almost in an instant, it was gone, obliterated. She was absolutely confident Cecily would make the gown as good as new, and she *would* wear it after all.

Over lunch, DeLacy had told their father about the terrible accident with the ink, which had been her fault. He had been understanding, and he had not chastised DeLacy. Although he had said she should have known better than to play around with a valuable gown.

The one thing he had focused on was the way Cecily had behaved, how she had been willing to take the blame to protect DeLacy. 'She is a true Swann, instantly ready to stand in front of an Ingham. Remember our motto, DeLacy, *Loyalty binds me*. It is their motto as well. The Inghams and the Swanns are linked forever.'

It is true, Daphne thought. It always has been thus and it always will be. And then she stared ahead as the trees thinned, and she found herself crossing the road and walking onto Torbett land.

Daphne approached Havers Lodge from the back of the house, and she couldn't help thinking how glorious it looked today. Its pale, pinkish bricks were warm and welcoming in the sunlight. The Elizabethan architecture was splendid, and there were many windows and little turrets, as there always were in traditional Tudor houses. And some privet hedges were cut in topiary designs.

The long stretch of manicured lawn was intersected by a path of huge limestone paving stones, which led up to the terrace. Once she reached this, she turned the corner on the right, and walked towards the front door. It was made of heavy oak, banded in iron.

She had only dropped the iron knocker once when the door opened. Williams, the Torbett's butler, was standing there, and he smiled when he saw her.

'Lady Daphne! Good afternoon. Will you come in, please, m'lady.'

She inclined her head. 'Thank you. Good afternoon, Williams.'

After he had closed the door, he said, 'Shall I tell Mrs Torbett you are here? Forgive me, but is she expecting you, my lady?'

'No, she's not, Williams. I stopped by to see Mr Julian. If you would be so kind as to let him know I'm here.'

'Oh dear! He's gone out, Lady Daphne. He didn't say how long he'd be. But he didn't go riding. I saw him walking.'

Daphne gave the butler a warm smile. 'Just tell him I was here, Williams. And please ask him to come over to Cavendon in the next few days. It's nothing important, just an invitation I want to extend.'

'I will, m'lady.' The butler walked her to the door, and saw her out, and he couldn't help thinking she was the most beautiful woman he had ever seen. Going to marry a duke's son, she was. At least, that was what he had heard.

NINE

D aphne had been walking along the woodland path for only a few minutes when she heard a strange rustling sound. Looking around, she saw nothing unusual, so simply shrugged and went on at her usual pace. Squirrels playing, she thought, and then came to a sudden stop when she saw the heron at the edge of the stream, standing high on its tall legs in the shallow water. It was such an elegant bird.

A smile of delight flitted across her face. This was such an odd place for it to visit. She couldn't help wondering why it kept coming back, but then perhaps it liked the stream and the woodland setting. Maybe it feels at home—

This thought was cut off when something hard struck her back, just between her shoulder blades. She pitched forward, hitting her head against a log as she fell to the ground. She lay still for a moment, stunned and overcome by dizziness. Realizing she had been attacked by someone, she endeavoured to stand up; she managed to get onto her knees, was about to scramble to her feet, but instead she was pinned to the ground from behind, and with brute force.

She struggled to free herself but the weight on top of her was too much; suddenly she was turned over, roughly, and laid on her back.

Daphne stared up at her attacker, the man who was pinning her down with such strength. He had wrapped a dark-grey scarf around his head and face, and all she could see were his eyes. They were hard, cruel, and because of the scarf she had no idea who he was. And she was terrified.

Understanding that she had no chance of escaping him, she began to shake, apprehension overwhelming her. In one last valiant effort, she pushed at him hard, but it was impossible to throw him off.

When he brought his hand close to her neck, she cringed and held herself still. She thought he was going to strangle her. Instead he ripped the front of her blouse, bent over her; he found her breasts, began to fondle and then pinch one of them harder and harder. He hurt her, and she screamed. This he immediately stopped by putting his hand over her mouth. With the other he lifted her skirt.

Rigid with fear, knowing there was no escaping him, under-standing his intentions, Daphne snapped her eyes shut and prayed to God he would not kill her when he was finished with her.

He raped her.

The wild, rampaging man forced himself on her. He was hurting her; pain flowed through her, and she felt as though her insides were being ripped apart. She knew that to scream again would be useless, and gritted her teeth, turned her head to one side, straining away from him. There was nothing else she could do . . . except to shut it out.

All of a sudden the man began to move against her very quickly, shuddering and gasping. With a long groan he finally stopped moving, fell against her, all of his weight on her. And his body went limp.

In that instant Daphne seized the moment. She reached up, grabbed at the scarf around his face, tugged at it hard. When it came away, and she saw his face, she gaped at him in astonishment, horror and disbelief.

The man who had just raped her was Richard Torbett, Julian's older brother. Still stunned by the violent attack, aghast that someone she knew had done this to her, she was unable to speak.

As for Torbett, he was infuriated that his identity had been revealed. Bright colour flooded his face as anger took hold of him.

He leaned down, brought his head close to hers. Against her ear, he hissed, 'Speak of this to anyone and *they* will be killed. Your baby sister and your mother. I know men who'll do the job for a few pounds. Not one word. Understand?'

Shock and genuine fear rendered Daphne speechless. She could only nod.

He pushed himself to his feet, stood looking down at her. 'Remember, keep your mouth shut.'

Daphne closed her eyes. She heard him rustling through the bushes, obviously not wanting to be seen on the path. She felt as though her whole body had been bludgeoned. And so she lay very still, trying to breathe normally, hoping to get her strength back, wondering if she would be able to walk. She wasn't even sure she could get up. Tears seeped from underneath her eyelids and trickled down her cheeks, as she continued to lay there dazed, unable to focus, hurting all over. He would not return, of that she was certain. He had taken what he wanted.

Daphne felt a gentle finger on her face, smoothing away the tears, and then a voice was saying her name. 'Lady Daphne, Lady Daphne.'

She opened her eyes and saw the gypsy girl kneeling next to her, looking concerned.

'Genevra,' Daphne said, attempting to sit up.

The girl offered her hand, and helped Daphne into a sitting position. She said, 'Come on . . . let's go, m'lady. Dark clouds. Mebbe rain.'

With a bit of effort, Daphne managed to get to her feet, and immediately straightened her clothes, pulling her jacket around her torn blouse. Genevra handed Daphne her hat, which had fallen off in the struggle, and she put it on her head. Then she limped back to Cavendon, helped by Genevra all the way. When they came to the end of the woods, Genevra stopped, and gave Daphne a penetrating look. She said, 'Yer fell down, my lady.'

Daphne stared at her, puzzled. She frowned at the gypsy girl.

Genevra said again, 'Yer fell down, Lady Daphne. That's wot 'appened ter yer.'

Daphne nodded. 'I fell down,' she repeated, and realized immediately that Genevra had witnessed the attack on her. She shrivelled inside at the thought, a shocked look on her face.

The Romany nodded, swung around and pointed towards Cavendon on the hill. 'Go, Lady Daphne, go on! There yer'll be safe.' She smiled, raced off, heading for the long meadow.

Daphne watched her go, feeling grateful to her. I didn't even thank her for helping me home, she chastised herself, annoyed at her thoughtlessness. On the other hand, she was still reeling from what had occurred, her horrific violation, stunned that she had been attacked by one of her own kind, an aristocrat, no less, who had known her all her life.

TEN

Genevra had been right. It began to rain. Daphne felt the first drops on her forehead as she arrived at Cavendon. Avoiding both the kitchen and the front doors, having no desire to run into anyone, she slipped into the house through the conservatory. Only she and her mother used this room, and her mother was in Harrogate today.

Once she was inside the house, Daphne experienced an enormous sense of relief. She also wondered how she had managed to climb the hill. Walking the final stretch on her own had been difficult. It struck her that she would never even have made it through the woods, if not for the gypsy girl's help. Genevra had supported her, held her upright all the way.

Crossing the terracotta-tiled floor of the conservatory, Daphne went up the back staircase. Half way, she had to sit down on a step for a moment. Her back hurt, and she was sore and bruised. What she needed was a hot bath to ease her aching body. She must also calm herself, take control of her swimming and troubled senses, come to grips with what had happened. She was filled with fear, as well as horror-struck by what had been done to her with such force and cruelty.

Taking a few deep breaths, she finally rose and continued up the narrow staircase. When she finally stepped out into the bedroom corridor, she found herself standing in front of DeLacy and Cecily. Both girls had their arms full of summer frocks, and Alice was immediately behind them.

'Daphne!' DeLacy cried, when she saw her sister. 'Whatever's happened? You look as if you've been pulled through a hedge backwards!'

Cecily was also gaping at Daphne, looking startled, but she did not utter a word.

Filled with dismay, her heart sinking, Daphne remained silent. She had been taken by surprise, and was flustered, rooted to the spot. Cringing inside, she shrank closer to the wall.

It was Alice Swann who immediately took charge. She had noticed Daphne's dishevelled appearance at once, knew something was terribly amiss, and was alarmed by Daphne's stricken expression.

Turning to the girls, she said, 'Please take the frocks upstairs to the sewing room.' She smiled at DeLacy, 'And why don't you try on a few of them, m'lady? You and Cecily can decide which ones you like the best. I will join you shortly.'

They did as she suggested, knowing it was best not to say anything, and they did not linger a moment longer.

Daphne had begun to edge towards her bedroom; Alice hurried over to her. Putting her hand underneath Daphne's elbow, she gently guided her inside.

After closing the door behind them, Alice stood there, not only wondering what had happened to Daphne, but also seeking a diplomatic way to approach the matter.

Although Daphne was trying to disguise the fact, Alice noticed that her blouse was torn and the jacket sleeve ripped at the shoulder.

It was Daphne who spoke first. In a shaking voice, she whispered, 'Something happened . . .' She was unable to continue, turned around, and collapsed on a chair, her entire body shaking.

An exceedingly observant woman, Alice took in everything: Daphne's dazed and troubled state, the bleakness in her blue eyes, the trembling mouth, the aura of fear surrounding her. It was obvious she was in shock, and Alice could not help anticipating the worst.

Her eyes swept over the Earl's daughter. Her clothes were in a mess, not only torn, but there were grass stains and dirty marks on the skirt, mud on the jacket, and, as she peered closer, she thought she spotted blood on the skirt. Her chest tightened in apprehension.

Walking across the floor, she said softly, 'Something bad happened, didn't it, Lady Daphne?' When Daphne did not answer, Alice said, 'Am I correct, my lady?'

Daphne could not speak. She attempted to hold herself still, but the shaking would not stop. She wanted to confide in Mrs Alice, just for the relief of it, but she did not dare tell her the truth. Not after Richard Torbett's terrifying threat to have Dulcie and her mother killed. The mere thought of this brought tears to Daphne's eyes, and she started sobbing as if her heart would break.

Alice ran to her, knelt down at her feet and took hold of her hands. 'Lady Daphne, I am here to help you. Don't be afraid to cry. Let it all out. Tears help to release the tension.' She reached into her jacket pocket and gave Daphne a clean white handkerchief. Alice waited quietly, kneeling next to the young woman, wanting to give her support, and a measure of comfort if that were possible.

At one moment, Alice rose and went to the door, locking it to ensure their privacy. Then she returned to Daphne's side.

Slowly the sobbing abated. Daphne wiped her eyes again, and finally sat up straighter. She looked at Alice, explained, 'I fell down, Mrs Alice, and I—'

'Don't say anything else, my lady!' Alice interrupted. Drawing closer, she added, 'I don't need to know anything. Nothing at all.' In a lower tone, she whispered, 'Tell no one. No one at all. Understand?'

Daphne looked at her intently. 'Yes.'

Alice said, 'Do not trust anyone in this house. Not ever.'

On hearing these words, Daphne was puzzled, and also a little frightened.

Observing her reaction, and wanting to allay any fears, Alice reached out, took her hand. 'Only your parents. You can trust them. Naturally. And you can trust me. And Walter and Cecily. *We are Swanns.* We will always protect you.'

Daphne nodded her understanding, a look of relief entering her eyes.

'Our ancestors made a blood oath over one hundred and sixty years ago. It has never been broken. Please say the motto, Lady Daphne.' As she spoke Alice stretched out her right arm and made a fist.

Daphne placed her right hand on Alice's fist, and said in French, '*Loyauté me lie.*'

Repeating the motto in English, Alice said, 'Loyalty binds me,' and she put her left hand on top of Daphne's, and the young woman did the same. 'We are bound together into eternity,' they said in unison.

After a few moments of silence, Alice broke their grip, and stood up. She said quietly, 'I think you must get undressed, and then take a hot bath, m'lady. A good soak will bring ease to your body. Shall I help you?'

'No, no, thank you, Mrs Alice. I can manage,' Daphne said hurriedly.

Understanding that she wanted privacy, Alice nodded. 'Please give me your hat, Lady Daphne.'

Daphne did so, and rose, limping towards the bathroom, her mind racing, filled with all manner of thoughts, not the least being Alice's comments about not trusting anyone except her parents and the Swanns.

Alice explained, 'I'm going to take those clothes home with me later. I will clean and mend them, and no one will be any the wiser.'

Daphne paused, turned around and stared at her, 'But—'

'No buts, my lady. We can't have one of the maids finding them, now can we?'

Daphne simply nodded, realizing Mrs Alice was right.

Alice said, 'I shall go up to the sewing room and satisfy the curiosity of DeLacy and Cecily, put their busy little minds at rest. By the way, where did you fall, Lady Daphne? In the woods?'

'Yes,' Daphne replied, swallowing hard.

'I shall lock the door behind me, m'lady. You don't need anyone walking in on you unexpectedly. I'll only be a few minutes.'

'Is Daphne all right?' DeLacy asked as soon as Alice walked into the sewing room.

'Oh yes, she's perfectly fine,' Alice answered, smiling. She added, 'You look lovely in that rose-coloured chiffon, Lady DeLacy. I think this one will work beautifully for you, for the spring supper dance later this month. Don't you agree, Cecily?'

'I do, Mother, it is a wonderful colour for DeLacy, and a change from blue.' Cecily began to laugh. 'Everyone in this family wants to wear blue.' She glanced at DeLacy, and said, 'I'm sorry, Lacy, but it *is* the truth.'

'Oh, I know. Great-Aunt Gwendolyn says we're all stick-in-the-muds, and unimaginative. She thinks we should all wear purple – the *royal* colour. She even wonders aloud why we want clothes to match our eyes.'

Alice also had to laugh. 'She's been saying that for as long as I can remember.'

DeLacy swirled, the chiffon evening dress flaring out around her legs. She said, as she turned again, 'I suppose Daphne must have fallen in the woods. I know she was going to see Julian at Havers Lodge . . . to tell him he could invite his fiancée to the big ball. She must have been hurrying back because of the thunder clouds, and then tripped.'

'That's exactly what happened,' Alice agreed, her mind instantly focused on the Torbetts. She knew the Earl and the Countess had never been too happy about Lady Daphne's friendship with Julian, when they were younger. They were afraid the two of them might become too attached to each other. Fortunately, that hadn't happened, because of Julian's intentions to have a military career, and Daphne's lack of interest in him romantically.

They had only ever been platonic friends. This was also because Daphne's head was filled with dreams of a duke's son and a brilliant marriage, planted there at a very young age by her father.

To Alice's way of thinking, there was something odd about the Torbett family. They tended to put on airs and graces, but they weren't as wealthy as they liked the world to believe. Hanson had always told Walter that they were pretentious, jumped-up nothings.

On the other hand, Hanson was a bit of a snob and tended to dismiss anybody without a title. However, his damning statements had seemed to stick with her.

Going over to the rack of dresses, Alice looked at all of them with her beady eye; they were perfect for DeLacy, she decided, and also Daphne, as well. She took a honey-coloured taffeta ball gown over to DeLacy. 'I think this would be lovely . . .'

There was a knock on the door, and when Alice called, 'Come in,' it was Walter who poked his head into the room. 'Sorry to disturb you, ladies, but His Lordship would like DeLacy to go down for afternoon tea. Lady Gwendolyn has just walked over, and they are waiting in the drawing room.'

Alice nodded, and exclaimed, 'Tea, of course! You'd better hurry along, DeLacy.' And I'd better go and look in on Daphne, Alice thought, as she gave the honey-coloured gown to Cecily, then hurried out to join her husband.

In the corridor, Alice took hold of Walter's arm, 'Has the Countess returned from Harrogate yet?'

'No, she won't be back for another hour or so.'

'I'll see you at home tonight,' Alice said, and went down the stairs to the bedroom floor. Walter followed her, and squeezed her arm affectionately, before they went in different directions. DeLacy was already halfway down the main staircase, on her way to tea.

Alice unlocked the door to Daphne's bedroom, went inside, and quickly locked it behind her. Daphne was nowhere in sight. Alice noticed the small pile of clothes folded up on a chair. She went to examine them. The blouse was badly ripped; Alice thought she could mend it. As for the jacket, the back was smeared with green streaks from the grass, and splotches of mud. The skirt was in the worst condition, with dirty patches, grass and bloodstains. She could clean them successfully. She had good products and special methods.

Carefully, Alice folded them up again, and finally picked up the underskirt. There was blood on it, and some other damp patches. Alice bent her head and sniffed, and then turned away, grimacing. Her worst fears had been confirmed. A man had attacked Lady Daphne out in the woods, no two ways about it.

That male smell clung to the underskirt. Carefully, she folded it and put it under the pile, shaking her head.

Alice sat down heavily in the chair. She felt as if a lump of lead was lodged in her chest. Her mind floundered for a moment, and her heart went out to Daphne, so sweet, so lovely. Whoever had done such a thing to a seventeen-year-old innocent girl should suffer the severest punishment. She wondered then if any of the woodsmen or gardeners had seen anything; several Swanns worked on the outside at Cavendon. Walter would have to ask them if they had noticed anything untoward this afternoon.

A moment later the bathroom door opened and Lady Daphne came out in her robe. She smiled at Alice, but then the smile instantly faltered. 'I hoped I hadn't bruised my face, but there's a mark, here, on the cheekbone,' Daphne said anxiously, touching her face. 'How will I explain it to Mama and Papa, Mrs Alice?'

Alice hurried across the room, peered at her face. 'It's not so bad, Lady Daphne. I think it can be covered up with a few touches of powder and rouge. And you fell, remember, and if you fell forward then you would easily hit your face on a rock, a tree trunk or roots. You'll explain it that way. What about the rest of you, m'lady?'

'Just bruises, nothing broken. Did you see DeLacy and Cecily?'

'Yes, they were in the sewing room. I told them you'd tripped and fallen. DeLacy assumed it was in the woods, because she said you'd gone to Havers Lodge to see Julian Torbett this afternoon.'

'That's true. I went to tell him his fiancée could come to the big ball. Obviously DeLacy heard me telling father after lunch that I was going there.'

'By the way, DeLacy has gone down to tea to join your great-aunt and your father. Walter brought a message from His Lordship. What about you? Do you want to join them, m'lady?'

Daphne shook her head. 'I think I should rest. I'm hoping I'll be able to go down for dinner later, but for now . . .' Her voice trailed off.

Alice nodded, 'Yes, stay and have a rest. I'd get into bed if I were you, m'lady. If it's all right with you, I will tell Walter to inform your father that you're resting after trying on dresses most of the day. I'll say you're a bit tired.'

Daphne inclined her head. 'Thank you, Mrs Alice. I'd appreciate that. And thank you . . . for everything.'

ELEVEN

Lady Gwendolyn Ingham Baildon stood in the centre of the great entrance foyer at Cavendon Hall, glancing around, a beatific smile on her face. She had been in London for the past week, and this was her first visit since her return to Yorkshire two days ago.

To her, Cavendon was the most sublime place. There was nowhere else like it, and only here did she experience a feeling of euphoria, a sense of genuine happiness and contentment. So many memories, so many emotions were wrapped up in this house; her entire life had been spent here.

The smile lingered as her eyes rested on the oil paintings of her ancestors, which lined the wall above the grand curving staircase. Looking down at her were her parents. Her beautiful mother, Florence, wife of Marmaduke, the 4th Earl, her father. Next to her father was a striking portrait of her brother, David, the handsomest of men. He had been the 5th Earl, and next to him was a lovely oil painting of his wife, Constance, who had died far too young. She sighed to herself. Her own husband, Paul Baildon, had died young; she had been a widow for a very long time.

Turning away, Lady Gwendolyn walked across the hall in the direction of the small, yellow sitting room, where afternoon tea had been served for years.

Gwendolyn had been born in this house seventy-two years ago, and brought up here with David and their sister Evelyne. She knew every nook, cranny, corner and secret hiding place. In fact, there wasn't much she didn't know about Cavendon and the Ingham family. Well, that was not exactly true. She was ignorant about any number of things, as was her nephew Charles.

A small, amused smile struck her face fleetingly. Only the Swanns knew everything, and what they knew had been passed down from one generation to the next. There were notebooks filled with endless records, so she had been told once, and this information had come from the best source – a Swann, no less.

Ah well, Gwendolyn said under her breath, what would we have done without the Swanns? And they're on our side, thank God, stand sentinel beside us. She would trust a Swann with her life if she had to.

Her nephew was the only occupant of the yellow sitting room, and he jumped up, came towards her once he saw her appear in the doorway.

After kissing her cheek, he said, 'It's lovely to see you back at Cavendon, Aunt Gwendolyn.'

'Thank you, Charles, I feel the same.' She glanced around. 'Am I the first?'

'Yes, actually, you are. I'm afraid our ranks are a bit diminished today. Felicity is still in Harrogate, visiting Anne, and Diedre accompanied her. But DeLacy will be joining us.'

At that moment Hanson glided into the room and, after greeting Lady Gwendolyn, he addressed the Earl. 'Do you wish tea to be served immediately, m'lord?'

'Yes, Hanson, thank you. But perhaps you could send a message to Lady DeLacy to come down.'

'I took the liberty of doing that a short while ago, my lord.'

Charles nodded. 'Thank you, Hanson. Very astute of you. I'm afraid punctuality is not her strong suit.'

As Hanson left the room, Gwendolyn said, 'Isn't Daphne joining us as well, Charles?'

'I don't think so. Apparently she has been busy with dress fittings for most of the day, and feels tired. She has asked to be excused.'

'Sorry I'm late, Papa!' DeLacy cried as she came racing into the room, a bright smile on her face. She ran over to her great-aunt, kissed her on the cheek, and then went to kiss her father.

'You are coming to the supper dances and the big ball, aren't you, Great-Aunt Gwendolyn?' DeLacy asked, a moment later, sitting down next to her. 'It's never the same when you're not present.'

'How nice of you to say so, Lacy, and of course I plan to come, my dear. I've always thought the entertaining we do at Cavendon at that time of year, in the summer months, was the best, the most fun.' Leaning slightly closer, she said in a low voice, 'Please do try to avoid sky blue this season, darling. The obvious is rather boring, you know?'

DeLacy stared at her, saw the amusement flickering in the deep-blue eyes, and began to giggle. 'I will certainly do that,' she answered, still laughing, and then glanced at the door as the two footmen came in, both pushing laden tea trolleys, followed closely by Hanson, as always present to make sure nothing was amiss or went wrong.

As they went through the ritual of afternoon tea, Charles silently debated whether or not to tell his aunt that Hugo was about to make a visit. In the end, he decided he must do so. He preferred not to spring it on her at the last minute. But he would certainly avoid mentioning anything about property and Little Skell Manor.

After DeLacy insisted he try a piece of the Victoria sponge, Charles tasted it, and then put it down. Looking across at his aunt, he said, 'I had a letter from Switzerland today. And you'll never guess who it was from.'

Lady Gwendolyn threw him a puzzled look. 'No, I'm afraid I won't . . . I don't know anyone who lives in Switzerland.'

A smile touched his mouth, and was gone. 'It was from Hugo Stanton,' he said in a level voice, wondering how she would react to this news.

'Goodness gracious me!' Lady Gwendolyn exclaimed. 'Hugo Stanton, of all people, and after these many years of silence.' She frowned, and peered at Charles. 'I thought he was sent to live in America?' A brow lifted.

'He was—'

'Quite the wrong move in my considered opinion,' Lady Gwendolyn cut in. 'Very rash.'

'He was rather successful there, apparently, according to his letter, Aunt. He did well in business, and married well. However, sadly his wife died last year. From what I gather, they had been living in Zurich for several years.'

'I see,' Lady Gwendolyn observed noncommittally, and took a sip of her tea.

Charles continued, 'In any event, Hugo wrote to tell me he has to come to London on business, and he asked me if he could come here for a visit. I suppose he was wondering if he would be made to feel welcome.'

There was a short silence, then Lady Gwendolyn said, 'Of course he would be welcome as far as I'm concerned. I always liked Hugo, and I never believed for one moment that he had anything to do with his brother's death. Stuff and nonsense that was.'

'I couldn't agree more.'

'When is he coming?' she asked.

'Oh in the summer. I thought perhaps June or July. I'll suggest that when I reply.'

'And I shall look forward to seeing him again,' Lady Gwendolyn announced with a warm smile.

Charles nodded, and decided to say nothing further. Why bring up Little Skell Manor or property, and who owned what at this stage? 'And so shall I,' Charles agreed amiably, and took a bite of his cake. 'He will always be welcome at Cavendon.'

A few minutes later, DeLacy cried, 'Mama! Diedre! You're back early, and just in time for tea.'

The Earl glanced at the door, appearing to be as startled as DeLacy had sounded. He immediately rose, and walked across the floor to greet his wife and eldest daughter.

As he escorted them into the room, he asked Felicity, 'I hope you had a lovely visit with Anne, my dear.'

'Yes, we did,' Felicity answered softly, trying to keep her voice steady, her expression neutral, not wishing to display any of her flaring emotions.

Diedre said, 'Hello, Great-Aunt Gwendolyn,' and went to kiss her.

Felicity followed suit, and touched DeLacy lightly on her shoulder as she passed by. Then she took a seat in a chair opposite them.

Hanson, as usual ever ready, appeared with a footman in tow, who proceeded to pour tea for the Countess and Diedre. And the ritual of afternoon tea began all over again.

Moving slightly on the sofa, Lady Gwendolyn focused on her niece-in-law, thinking once again that she looked slightly on edge. Felicity's face was taut, and she was instantly aware of the sorrowful look in her light green eyes. Something's wrong, Gwendolyn thought. *Terribly wrong*. I'm looking at a troubled woman, beleaguered by worries. What's going on with her? She appears to be more nervous than ever.

TWELVE

D iedre Ingham, the eldest daughter of the Earl, had a great affinity for Lady Gwendolyn, and they had always been good friends since she was a little girl. They were cut from the same cloth, had similar characteristics, both being practical, down-to-earth and well organized. They also had a look of each other, and were of similar build.

Although Diedre did not have the alluring beauty of Daphne, nor the shining prettiness of DeLacy, she was still a good-looking young woman, with even features and those lovely blue eyes that were the Ingham trademark.

Tall, like her great-aunt, she had inherited Lady Gwendolyn's elegance and style, and had her taste for strictly tailored clothes and understated jewellery, costly but not flashy or vulgar.

It was their down-to-earth natures that had bound them together over the years. They saw eye-to-eye on most things, and whenever Diedre had a problem, or a decision to make, it was to Lady Gwendolyn that she went.

At this moment, Diedre wished she could talk to her

great-aunt, but that was not possible. She could hardly interrupt afternoon tea, and led her away to a quiet corner.

Perhaps later she could walk back with her to Little Skell Manor, and talk to her then. Earlier today a great difficulty had arisen unexpectedly. Their aunt, Anne Sedgewick, was dying; Diedre needed someone to confide in, and to ask for advice. Intelligent, and blessed with common sense, she was, nonetheless, only twenty, and sometimes wisdom from the older woman helped her to see things more clearly.

Suddenly, Diedre sat up straighter in the chair, and paid attention. From the sound of his voice, her father was speaking about something important; she pulled herself out of her reverie to listen to him.

'And so, Felicity, my dear, I can't tell you how surprised I was to receive this letter from Hugo, after his silence all these years. The crux of it is this. He will be visiting London shortly, and he asked if he could come to Cavendon to see us.'

Diedre, observing her mother, saw how her face instantly brightened, and there was a sudden flash of pleasure in her eyes. 'How wonderful that you've heard from him at last, Charles,' Felicity said, her voice warm. 'I've spent quite a few years worrying about little Hugo, on and off, and wondering how he had fared, hoping he was all right. Such a tragedy . . . being sent away.'

'Wasn't it in disgrace?' Diedre ventured, looking at her father.

Before he could answer, Lady Gwendolyn said in a stern voice, 'He was not at fault in any way, and my sister was wrong in her ridiculous attitude. And I told her so, and in no uncertain terms. It made no difference, but I've always regretted not being more forceful with her, or more persuasive.'

'It wouldn't have made any difference,' Felicity remarked. 'Aunt Evelyne had made up her mind that he had not helped his brother, and there was no changing her opinion. She was an extraordinarily stubborn woman, and needed a scapegoat, by the way.'

'Didn't his brother die in the lake . . . drown?' DeLacy began, and stopped abruptly when she saw the warning look on Diedre's face.

Charles said, 'Enough of the past. We are now in the present, looking towards the future, and the future is very bright for us. And for Hugo. He has done well in the world and, although his wife died a year ago, I think he will bravely march on. He is an Ingham, after all, and we do that. We don't crumble and give in. Also, he's only thirty-two. He has his life ahead of him.'

'Quite so,' Lady Gwendolyn agreed in a firm voice.

'When is he coming?' Felicity asked softly, staring at her husband.

'That's really up to me, or rather to us, darling. He plans to visit London within the next few weeks. So I am going to suggest he comes here in July.'

Felicity simply nodded.

Lady Gwendolyn announced, 'I believe a weekend visit would be most appropriate, Charles.' She glanced at Felicity. 'Don't you agree, my dear?'

'That would be nice,' Felicity nodded, leaning back in the chair, tired after the long and difficult day in Harrogate.

Charles beamed at them. 'That settles the matter. I shall write to him after I've had a chance to consider the engagements we have in the next few weeks, to ascertain which is the best weekend for him to come.'

'Oh Papa, please invite him here when there's a supper dance. You know there's always a shortage of men at these dances, and some of us have to partner each other.'

Always indulgent with her, Charles couldn't help laughing at her eagerness for male dancing partners. 'Now, now, DeLacy, you're only twelve, you know,' he answered. But he could not keep the amusement out of his voice, nor did he ever chastise her when she was cheeky or forward. He just didn't have the heart, and she was his favourite; he rather liked her cheekiness.

Lady Gwendolyn was also amused, and it showed on her face when she stood up. 'Thank you, Charles and Felicity, I must go back to the manor, to rest. London was rather hectic, you know.'

'May I walk back with you, Great-Aunt Gwendolyn?' Diedre asked, also standing.

'Of course, my dear. I would enjoy the company.'

'May I come, too?' DeLacy jumped to her feet, and looked at Diedre pleadingly.

On the verge of refusing this request, Diedre instantly changed her mind. 'You can come with us, if you wish.' DeLacy might as well know the truth, the way things are, Diedre thought, as they trooped out of the yellow sitting room together. She's old enough to know how hard life can be, and what we are facing: the imminent death of our mother's sister; a bereavement in the family, which will make Mama more upset than ever.

Once they were alone, Felicity went and sat on the sofa with Charles; leaning closer to him she said, 'I have bad news . . . Anne is dying.'

A look of astonishment crossed his face, and his brows drew together in a frown. 'How can that be? You told me she was better! That she had said she was all right. You went to have a celebratory lunch with her today.'

'That's what I thought it was. She told me on Friday that she had seen her doctors, that they had given her the results of the last tests. And then she added she was all right. The problem is, she didn't mean it the way I took it.'

'How did she mean it?'

'That she was all right, because at last she knew what the outcome of her illness was going to be, and how long she has to live.'

Charles cringed at these words. He took hold of his wife's hand, held it tightly. His expression was one of compassion. 'I'm so sorry, so very sorry, Felicity. For Anne and for you, darling.' He gazed at her intently, took in the beauty of her delicately wrought face, surrounded by a halo of red-gold hair, and looked deeply into her light green eyes, and he felt himself choke up with emotion. He knew how much this bad news would affect her.

Felicity edged even closer to him. He put his arms around her and held her against him, fighting back the tears. His sister-in-law, Anne Sedgewick, was a woman of intelligence, kindness and humour. And an extraordinary artist. Her glorious, still-life oil paintings had become collectors' items over the years, and she was now famous for her work. This aside, she was a lovely woman, and one of great depth, whom he cared about enormously. He wanted to ask how long she had, but he didn't dare. His nerve had left him.

Felicity drew away from him, and looked up into his face. She said, 'I'm so sorry I put it so bluntly, Charles. I just didn't know how to break the news to you, since you believed we were celebrating her recovery at lunch today . . . I felt I just had to say it, and without any frills.' Tears flooded her eyes, and she began to weep.

Bending over her, Charles held her close once more, and wept himself. And so wrapped up were they in their pain and grief, neither of them saw Hanson silently gliding away, shooing the two footmen ahead of him, using his discretion as he inevitably did.

Upstairs at Cavendon, in her darkened room, Daphne lay curled up in a ball in her bed. Sorrowing and bereft, she had cried until she had no tears left in her. And finally she had slept, exhausted from the assault on her body and on her senses.

Now that she was awake, her mind was racing with all kinds of worried thoughts, and raw anxiety had surfaced. She had no idea how to deal with the situation she found herself in. She could not confide in anyone, because of Richard Torbett's threat. Also, Mrs Alice had told her to tell no one, to trust no one, except her parents and the Swanns. She did not have the nerve to tell her parents, and she felt sure Mrs Alice already knew what had happened. She had guessed when she saw the stained clothes, and took them away.

Right from the start of the attack in the bluebell woods, Daphne believed the man was going to murder her, after he had raped her. He had not killed her. But he had taken her life. And left her with nothing of value. Her virginity had been destroyed and so had her chance of becoming the wife of the son of a duke. Or wife of anybody, for that matter.

Her future was meaningless now . . . there was nothing left for her. There was only bleakness in store. And loneliness.

THIRTEEN

arry Swann, Cecily's fifteen-year-old brother, had her full attention, and she was listening to him closely, impressed by his knowledge.

'And so,' he said, 'it was Richard Neville, the Earl of Warwick, who put Edward Plantagenet on the throne of England, and when he was very young. Only eighteen. Imagine that!' he ended in an excited voice.

'You certainly learned your history well, Harry,' Cecily responded, giving her much-adored brother a warm smile. 'No wonder you were top of your class when you were at school.'

Harry grinned at her. 'The Earl of Warwick lived at Middleham Castle. We once went there, if you remember, with Aunt Charlotte. Do you think we could go up there again sometime? Would she take us? It's such an historic place. And history is my hobby.'

'It's not very far away. We can ask her tomorrow when we go to tea. Perhaps she'll go with us in the summer.'

Harry nodded, bent his fair head, ate his baked apple in silence, savouring it. Ever since childhood, it had been his favourite dessert. The two of them were in the kitchen of their home, finishing supper.

Sitting back in her chair, watching him, Cecily couldn't help thinking that he looked older than his age, perhaps because of the intelligence in those light grey eyes, and his serious nature. And also his build. Like his father, he was tall; certainly there was no mistaking that Harry was a Swann. Not only because of his looks, but his bearing, his self-confidence, and his natural charm as well.

Cecily was aware that he had always been diligent, and he was quick, clever, and articulate. She knew he would go far in life, given the opportunity. Aunt Charlotte had told her the same thing: they were in agreement about his abilities and his talent as a landscape gardener, working with his cousin Bill at Cavendon.

Suddenly, he glanced up at her, asked, 'When is Miles coming home from Eton? For the summer, I mean.'

'I don't know, but it'll be soon. By the end of the month.'

'I hope we can all go fishing one weekend. What do you think, Ceci?'

'Yes, we'll go fishing, and bird watching, and we'll have picnics in the woods. DeLacy will come with us.'

'We always have fun together,' Harry said.

'Now then, how are you both doing?' Alice asked, sounding as cheerful as usual when she came hurrying into the kitchen. But her heart was heavy with worry about Daphne, and she felt unsettled, at odds with herself. She could not get the girl's predicament out of her mind.

'We've enjoyed our supper, Mam. Haven't we, Ceci? The cottage pie was nice, and thanks for my baked apple.'

Alice stood looking at them, filled with sudden joy. They were her adored children. She knew they were special, each in their own way, at least to her and Walter. They would have good lives. She smiled at them, picked up their empty plates and carried them to the sink. As she began to run the tap water she thought once more of Lady Daphne, and sadness flooded through her. She simply couldn't bear to think of her pain.

'We'll help you, Mam!' Cecily jumped up and so did Harry, and the three of them washed and dried the dishes together. They chatted to their mother about what they would do the next day with Walter. Their father had tomorrow off, as he did every other Sunday. This was a privilege given to any Swann who was the Earl's valet.

Much later that evening, when Walter had returned from Cavendon to Little Skell village, he and Alice went to see Charlotte. She lived across the street from them, and it was a late-night ritual they often enjoyed. They would have coffee and cognac as they chatted about the goings-on at Cavendon, and catching up with each other in general. They were close, and bonded to each other.

Although it was May, it was a cool evening. Charlotte had a fire blazing in the parlour; the coffee and brandy were ready for them on the sideboard, and she was waiting with a smile on her face.

Once they were settled in front of the fire in the cosy room, sipping their coffee, Charlotte said, 'I have a bit of news. Something unexpected, and it upset the Earl this morning. I happened to be going down the terrace steps, when he saw me, and came out of the library to speak to me about it.'

'What kind of upsetting news?' Walter asked, eyeing her keenly, as always concerned about anything affecting Cavendon.

'You're not going to believe this, but Hugo Stanton's coming back here to see the Earl.'

'That's a turn-up for the books!' Walter exclaimed. 'What's

prompted him to come home? He was packed off without so much as a goodbye.'

'I always liked Hugo, and he didn't kill his brother,' Alice interjected, sounding defensive.

Walter burst out laughing. 'No one ever said that he did, Alice.'

'But they thought it,' she shot back swiftly. 'It was never even a possibility. Just his mother talking nonsense.'

'Why was His Lordship so upset?' Walter asked, focusing on his aunt.

'Because he thinks Hugo wants Little Skell Manor, which is his by rights, and that he'll turf Lady Gwendolyn out.'

'Hugo wouldn't do that,' Alice protested. 'He's not that kind of person.'

Charlotte gave Alice an odd look, puzzlement surfacing.

Walter explained. 'Don't you remember, Aunt Charlotte? Alice's father worked for the Stantons.'

'How silly of me. I'd forgotten for a moment. Of course your father was a trainer, wasn't he? He looked after the Stanton yard near Ripon, helped Major Gaunt train their racehorses. That's right, isn't it?'

Alice nodded. 'Yes, and Hugo wouldn't turf her out. His aunt was always on his side.'

'If he does, Lady Gwendolyn can move into the South Wing. It's like a self-contained flat, and large. She would be comfortable there. I explained this to Charles,' Charlotte told them.

'Good thinking on your part.' Walter took a sip of coffee. 'Anyway, it might not come to that.'

Alice said, 'No, I'm sure it won't.'

'I have a bit of news too,' Walter now put in. 'But it's rather sad I'm afraid. Mrs Sedgewick has not recovered from cancer, after all. She's dying . . .' Walter paused, looking sorrowful. 'His Lordship told me tonight. The Countess is devastated, she thought her sister was better, and that they would be having a celebration luncheon today, believing her to have years ahead of her. Seemingly, that's not so.'

'How terrible for Her Ladyship. She must be suffering. She and her sister are very close.' Charlotte reached for her glass of cognac, took a swallow. She was filled with sympathy for Felicity Ingham.

Alice murmured, 'What an unfortunate mistake to make.'

The three of them sat in silence for a short while, sipping their cognac, lost in their own thoughts. There was no sound except for the crackling of the fire, the ticking of the clock, and the rustling of the trees outside. They were wise enough to understand that the unexpected frequently happened, and inevitably it was unfair. Life had a way of making its own rules, dealing its own cards, and the cards were rarely lucky.

It was Alice who finally roused herself, knowing that she would have to inform her husband and Charlotte about Daphne's terrible ordeal. After a moment, settling herself, she said in as steady a voice as she could muster, 'I'm afraid I have the worst news of all . . .' Alice glanced at her husband, and then Charlotte, who was the matriarch of the Swann family. Barely audible, she whispered, 'Lady Daphne was attacked this afternoon.'

'*What?*' Charlotte exclaimed, her voice rising. She sounded shocked, and gaped at Alice. '*Attacked?* What do you mean by *that?*'

'Someone attacked her. Physically.'

'I hope you don't mean what I think you do, Alice?' Walter gave his wife a penetrating look, frowning at her.

Alice glanced from one to the other. She saw that Charlotte was aghast, a stricken expression on her face, and Walter had disbelief in his eyes, and she knew he was filled with apprehension. It showed in the tautness of his face, the way he held his body so rigidly.

Swallowing, her mouth dry with anxiety, Alice said slowly, carefully, 'When Lady Daphne came back to the house this afternoon I ran into her. She was dishevelled. Once I got Cecily and DeLacy out of the way, I ushered her into her bedroom. She told me something had happened. I asked her if it was something bad, and she didn't answer me. Later she said she'd fallen.'

'But are you certain she was *assaulted?*' Walter probed, finding this hard to believe.

'I am positive.'

Charlotte asked quietly, 'Are you telling us she was *raped?*'

'Yes, I am.'

'Oh my God!' Charlotte was horrified, and a look of fear spread across her face. She sat there unable to speak, utterly shaken.

Walter was also shocked into silence for a moment, as the words sank in, and then he cried, 'Who would dare to go near Lady Daphne? Touch her? In God's name *who?* Where did this happen, Alice? Did she tell you?' His voice sounded harsh in the quiet room.

Alice shook her head. 'No. However, later, when I explained to DeLacy and Cecily that Daphne had had a bad fall – remember Daphne was dishevelled, so I had to tell them something, DeLacy said that it must have been in the woods. She added that Daphne had gone to see Julian Torbett after lunch, and that she always went to Havers Lodge through the bluebell woods.'

'Our land! She was raped on our land!' Walter cried angrily. 'By God, whoever did this I'll beat the living daylights out of him.'

Charlotte was as white as bleached bone, and she spoke in a low, worried voice. 'You are very *sure* of this, aren't you, Alice? She did tell you she was raped?'

'No, she didn't, Charlotte. When she confirmed that something bad had happened to her, I silenced her at once. I said I didn't need to know any more. And that she must not tell a living soul about it. I also warned her to trust only her parents, and us, the Swanns.'

'*She's ruined*,' Walter lamented in a sorrowing, almost mournful voice. 'Her life is over. Gone, just like that, in a flash.'

Alice said quietly, 'Although she didn't confide in me, I know it's true, because of her clothes. Her jacket and blouse were torn, and there were stains on the jacket and skirt.' Alice paused, gave Charlotte a meaningful look, then added, 'Her underskirt was stained as well.'

'Where are those clothes?' Charlotte asked, concerned.

'I brought them home, washed and cleaned them earlier this evening. I will repair them, they'll be as good as new.'

'Wise move,' Charlotte answered, and sat back in the chair, her mind racing. She was thinking of Felicity and Charles Ingham, and of all their plans for Daphne, and the anguish they would suffer if they ever got to know about this.

A sudden thought struck Charlotte and she took a deep breath. 'She's not necessarily ruined, not as long as nobody knows about the rape but us. Because there are ways of concealing the loss of virginity . . . we'll have to go to the old medical books, Alice.'

'You have them all, don't you?' Alice asked, sitting up alertly.

'Yes. They are locked up with the record books covering generations of our history . . . the history of the Inghams and the Swanns and their intertwined lives.'

Walter turned to his wife. 'Are you positive she won't tell anyone, Alice? Sometimes a young woman has a need to unburden herself.'

'Who can be sure of what anyone will do?' Alice replied. 'On the other hand, I've known Lady Daphne all of her life, and she's a loner, not one given to confessions about anything. And who would she confide in? Not Diedre, there's a certain distance between them. And, frankly, she would think DeLacy is too young. She won't talk, I just know this. Don't ask me how, but I do.'

'We Swanns must close ranks, and do all we can to keep her safe in every way,' Charlotte announced in a strong voice. 'Walter, talk to our other Swanns, those who work outside, and let's throw a ring of protection around her.'

'It's done,' Walter said at once. 'I'll see our lads tomorrow, and the woodsmen. I'll tell them to be on the lookout for trespassers. I'll talk about poachers, suggest we've spotted one, and I'll tell the Earl the same thing.'

Charlotte leaned forward. 'We can't have anyone wondering why Lady Daphne has to be protected, therefore rumours of poachers on our land *is* the best reason to give. Use it.'

Alice said, 'Lady Daphne was distraught, still in shock when I helped her this afternoon. She was . . . dazed and fearful, the poor girl. I tried to do everything I could to comfort her, Charlotte.'

'Keep on doing that, Alice. Stay close to her.' Charlotte stood up, went and brought the bottle of cognac to the fireside, poured the golden liquid into their glasses. 'We're going to make everything right. Expunge that rape . . . make her whole again. As best we can. And she *will* marry the son of a duke if we have anything to do with it.'

'That's the right way to think,' Walter asserted. 'And don't forget, the Swanns always win.'

Alice said a silent prayer, hoping that this would be the result, that they would save Daphne's future. The problem was, she wasn't sure they could.

Fourteen

Daphne sat at her dressing table, studying her face in the mirror. The bruise had finally faded away. It had only been a scrape really; powder and rouge had done the trick. No one had noticed it except Dulcie, who had prattled on about it but had fortunately been ignored. Everyone else was concentrating on other things.

Her aunt had been given only six months to live at the most, and so her mother and father had been preoccupied with this tragic news all week. They had also been concerned about the upcoming arrival of Hugo Stanton, her father's cousin, and making plans for his weekend visit in July.

And so they had not paid much attention to their four daughters these past few days, much to her relief. They had not noticed the bruise; she had not mentioned her fall in the woods. Neither had DeLacy. She had asked her younger sister not to bring it up, and DeLacy had agreed to keep silent.

So, all in all, she had managed to get through the week without any explanations. But it had not been easy for her. Her body had begun to heal, the bruises and scratches calming down, but her mind was extremely busy.

It was virtually impossible for her to expunge that violent physical attack from her mind. The angry face of Richard Torbett, when she had pulled off his disguise, and his deadly threat to have her mother and Dulcie killed, were engraved on her brain.

When Mrs Alice had returned her clothes in perfect condition, and put them away in her wardrobe, she had thanked her, but made no reference to them. And neither had Mrs Alice. Instead she had said in a low voice, 'I understand that there are poachers on our land, so don't be surprised if you see more woodsmen around than usual. They're keeping their eyes open for trespassers.'

Daphne had nodded, and later wondered about this comment. Yet she fully understood that no Swann would ever discuss an Ingham with someone else. Her secret was safe, there was no question about that. Still, it had occurred to her that the woodsmen were out and about because of her, without any of them knowing it. The Swanns were making sure she was protected. That was the way they worked. In clever ways. Secret ways.

Smoothing her hand across her hair, Daphne then dabbed a bit of powder on her cheeks, and adjusted the jabot of her white blouse.

Last week, when Madge Courtney and Julian Torbett had come to call, she had passed on her father's invitation to Madge to come to the summer ball. And she had agreed to go riding with them this morning. It was Saturday morning, and she was dreading it all of a sudden. Julian was nothing at all like his dangerous older brother, who was known to be a reprobate and a gambler. But, nonetheless, she couldn't help feeling uncomfortable, even though Julian was her childhood friend. Being near him made her think of the rapist.

Madge was joining them, and she had asked DeLacy to come

94

along as well. Her sister was delighted to be invited to go riding with this older group, and had accepted with alacrity and pleasure.

There was a knock on the bedroom door, and DeLacy, her face full of smiles, came in, asking, 'Are you ready, Daphne? Everyone's waiting for you.'

Daphne reached for her elegant lady's bowler hat; looking in the mirror, smoothing her hand over her bun, she perched the bowler on top of her head. 'Yes, I'm ready,' she answered, and stood. Picking up her gloves, she pulled them on, and continued, 'I don't feel like riding today, but I didn't want to disappoint Julian and Madge.'

'You don't want to disappoint Papa, either,' DeLacy exclaimed.

'Papa! Is he joining us?' The thought of her father being with them cheered her up enormously, brought a smile to her bright blue eyes.

'Yes, he is. He told me a good gallop would do him good, that he needed to clear his head. Mama is not going to Harrogate today, and she invited Julian and Madge to join us for lunch, after our ride.'

'That's nice,' Daphne nodded, attempting as they walked downstairs together to shut out the vivid image of Richard Torbett's angry, snarling face.

The Earl, Julian and Madge were waiting outside, standing next to their horses and chatting amiably. Daphne and DeLacy went over to join them; after greeting her father, Daphne stepped over to welcome Julian and his fiancée.

Madge Courtney was a striking redhead, good looking, forceful in her manner, and taller than Julian; she had a friendly personality, was outgoing, and good company.

Daphne had always thought they looked odd together. Julian, of medium height, fair of colouring and with soft features, appeared to be much younger than her. Yet they were the same age; Julian was introspective, less flamboyant.

Julian hugged her, as always gentle and loving with her, and told her she looked beautiful. 'So elegant, Daphne, in your dark blue riding habit. An unusual colour. And I love the bowler. That's a snappy touch.'

'Thank you, Julian,' she answered graciously, and said to Madge, 'I'm so glad you can come back for lunch with us.'

'I'm looking forward to it,' Madge answered, and then turned to DeLacy to speak to her.

A few minutes later, they were all mounted. DeLacy was riding Dreamer, a horse she had long favoured, whilst Daphne was on Greensleeves, a beautiful roan, which she had owned for several years, a gift from her father.

Within minutes they were trotting out of the stable block, heading for the long stretch of fields where they would be able to enjoy their gallop, racing each other, and giving their horses a good run.

As they swept across the open fields, Daphne began to feel better. Her father was right, fresh air cleared the head. Blowing the cobwebs away was a grand idea, she decided, and settled into her saddle, handling her horse with her usual skill and finesse.

Once they came to the end of the fields, exhilarated by the race, they slowed down, and wheeled their horses to the left. They headed along one of the wide bridle paths that ran along the right side of the bluebell woods, slowly progressing back to Cavendon.

It was a beautiful day, sunny and mild, with a blue sky, and no hint of rain for once. Daphne blocked out the image of her assault in the woods last week. These were *their* woods, and she would not avoid them, even if she had to grit her teeth to forget her ordeal. But she would put it behind her. It wouldn't happen again, she was certain of that. Their land would now be patrolled regularly by their own men, thanks to the Swanns.

As she trotted along the path behind DeLacy, enjoying the shade created by the overhanging branches of the trees, Daphne noticed that her lovely heron was back. It was standing in the pool of water in the middle of the woods, and it brought a brief smile to her face. It had found a home, she decided.

Unexpectedly, she caught sight of Walter's brother, Percy, who was head gamekeeper at Cavendon. She saw her father beckoning him over, and Percy started to run. Then he stood talking to the Earl for a few moments before he hurried off.

Suddenly, in the distance, there was the sound of gunfire. Shots rang out, startling them all, especially the horses. Greensleeves snorted and reared up on her hind legs, tossed her head, frightened by the sudden noise. Daphne tightened the reins, tried to calm her, to gain control of her. Somehow she managed it. And then she saw, much to her horror, that Julian's horse had not only panicked but bolted.

It was galloping down the bridle path, hell for leather, obviously totally spooked by the rifle fire. And then she filled with fear as she saw Julian thrown off his horse. He landed heavily, hit a large boulder, rolled over onto his back, and lay still.

Daphne noticed that the other horses were in the same state of great agitation, pawing, tossing their heads, and rearing up. DeLacy was still struggling with Dreamer, trying to calm her. But finally her father had his stallion Blackstar under control, much to Daphne's relief.

Julian's horse ran on, galloping down the bridle path, still a terrified animal.

DeLacy and Daphne galloped forward. As they drew closer

to Julian they reined in their horses, and jumped to the ground. Their father was running towards Julian, where he lay unmoving on the ground. He was obviously badly hurt.

Only Madge remained on her horse, frozen by shock and fear, and unable to move a muscle. She had lost all colour, her eyes wide with horror.

Glancing around, DeLacy asked no one in particular, 'Where did those shots come from?' And then she went to join her father, who was kneeling next to Julian.

The Earl shook his head. 'I've no idea, DeLacy. But we never have guns out at this time of year.' He felt Julian's pulse. It was faint but it was there. The young man was deathly white, and Charles noticed that the gash on his forehead was deep, bloody. His eyes were closed; blood was splattered on his fair hair. He was still, very still indeed, hardly breathing. Charles was filled with fear for the young man. The fall had been bad, awkward, and his legs were skewed, looked as if they were broken.

Percy Swann was suddenly back with them, panting from running hard. 'Our lads weren't shooting, m'lord. None of our men have guns out here. I'm not sure where those shots came from, m'lord.'

'Torbett land,' Daphne interjected, certainty ringing in her voice. Half turning, she pointed behind her. 'Definitely back there.' She couldn't help thinking it was Richard Torbett, up to his tricks. Then she looked down at Julian, and was struck by his total inertness, his extreme pallor. She was afraid for him. She knew he was in a bad way. Her chest tightened, and anxiety flared in her as she wondered if he would recover. She doubted it. He looked so . . . *damaged*. He lay there like a broken doll.

The Earl said, 'I don't think we should move Mr Julian, Swann. Or carry him away. It could be dangerous to do so. He's lying in a funny way. His neck could be broken, or his spine. If I remember correctly, don't we have some sort of makeshift stretcher at Cavendon?'

'We do, Lord Mowbray. It was made for Sir Redvers Andrews, when he had a heart attack on the grouse moor last August. And it's still there in the cellars, as far as I know. I can get it, m'lord, and be back in a few minutes with some of the woodsmen.'

'Thank you, Swann. Have Hanson make a phone call to Dr Shawcross. He should tell the doctor we need an ambulance. Mr Torbett will have to be taken to hospital. Harrogate's the nearest.'

'Right-o, m'lord,' Percy answered, and began to move away.

Daphne said, 'Papa, Swann should take my horse, it's faster riding than running, surely.'

'Good idea, Daphne. Take Her Ladyship's horse, Swann,' the Earl said.

DeLacy was kneeling on the ground next to her father, and she now asked in a concerned tone, 'Do you think Julian is going to die, Papa?' She thought he might actually be dead already, but didn't dare say that out loud.

'I've absolutely no idea. I pray to God not. He took a terrible, very hard fall. He must have damaged his spine, and he must have a bad head injury. Look at all the blood on the grass. He's certainly unconscious.'

'I know,' DeLacy said. As her sister spoke, Daphne walked back to Madge. She knew she must offer some sort of comfort to the young woman, who was still sitting on her horse, as if frozen in place. She was like a statue. Her face was the colour of chalk, and looked unnatural. It was stark against her vivid auburn hair.

Touching her on the arm, Daphne said gently, 'Can you dismount, Madge? Or do you need my father to help you?'

Madge gazed at Daphne and, observing her sympathetic expression, she began to weep. Tears rolled down her cheeks. 'I don't need help, I can manage now. But I'll need help later . . . of that I'm quite sure.' She threw Daphne a sorrowful look, shaking her head in disbelief.

After she had managed to dismount somewhat awkwardly, Madge and Daphne walked back to the Earl and DeLacy. They were still kneeling on the grass, their eyes riveted on Julian, who looked like a corpse to them.

Madge crouched down next to her fiancé. She touched his face, smoothed her hand over his brow. 'It's me, Julian,' she said, drawing closer. 'I'm here, my darling, I'm here.'

He did not answer her. She began to weep, and Daphne comforted her as best she could.

Even though Percy Swann and the woodsmen, as well as all the other staff at Cavendon, moved with great swiftness and efficiency, it was two hours before Julian Torbett arrived at the hospital in Harrogate. He had suffered a fractured skull and a broken back, but he was still alive. By six o'clock that same evening he was dead, never having regained consciousness.

The funeral of Julian Baxter Torbett was held at Ripon Cathedral by his family four days later. The great families of Yorkshire were in attendance, and other friends came in droves.

The Earl and Countess of Mowbray, their three oldest daughters and other Inghams were present, seated at the front of the cathedral.

The women were dressed in black from head to toe, and all wore hats, some with veils. It was Lady Daphne Ingham who had chosen a large-brimmed hat with a black tulle veil, one that totally obscured her face. She made sure she was seated between her father and mother in the pew, where she felt totally protected and safe.

Not once did she look at the Torbetts.

At the end of the service, accompanied by her sisters Diedre and DeLacy, she paid her condolences to Julian's mother, and to Madge. And then the three of them left the cathedral, crowded out by everyone else, Diedre later explained.

Daphne felt sad that her childhood friend had died the way he had, and so young, but she had no feelings at all for the Torbetts – except hatred, of course, for the rapist in that family.

PART TWO

The Last Summer
July–September 1913

There has fallen a splendid tear
From the passion-flower at the gate.
She is coming, my dove, my dear;
She is coming, my life, my fate.

Alfred Tennyson

O Lyric Love, half angel and half bird,
And all a wonder and a wild desire.

Robert Browning

But I, being poor, have only my dreams;
I have spread my dreams under your feet;
Tread softly because you tread on my dreams.

W. B. Yeats

FIFTEEN

'Is there something wrong with Daphne?' Miles Ingham asked, looking across at Cecily, giving her one of his very direct stares. 'Everyone I've asked in the family says that she's perfectly fine, but I don't think she is. In fact, I know she's not.'

Cecily moved her position slightly on the thick car rug spread out on the ground, silent for a moment, then she shrugged. 'She does seem sort of distant . . . far away. But I don't think there's anything *wrong* with her. *Honestly.*'

Miles sighed. 'I believe you, because you've always told me the truth, and vice versa. But you know I'm close to her, Ceci, and she's just not herself. Whatever anyone says.' He poured lemonade into two old silver mugs, forced on him by Cook, who didn't like the family using glasses outside, because of previous accidents.

He handed one of the mugs to Cecily, who thanked him. Miles took a long swallow of the lemonade, then reached for a cucumber sandwich. His mind was racing. He had been home from Eton for almost a week, and he had known the instant he'd arrived at Cavendon that his sister was troubled. He had even wondered if she was ill. There was a listlessness about her; she was paler than usual, and appeared preoccupied. When he'd questioned her, she had vehemently denied there was anything wrong. But *he* wasn't convinced.

Miles and Cecily were sitting under a large sycamore tree in a glade at the edge of the woods, having one of their special picnics. It was a beautiful morning, and all was well at Cavendon. At least on the surface. The family was coping with Anne Sedgewick's fatal illness, and the sudden unexpected death of Julian Torbett, which had been so upsetting to them.

Daphne's horrendous experience had remained a secret known only to the Swanns, and was, therefore, buried deep. Her parents didn't even know that Daphne had fallen in the woods. Daphne had kept quiet and so had DeLacy. Cecily, a Swann, knew not to utter one word about it.

With Miles home from Eton and Guy from Oxford, the entire family was in residence. Normally they would all have been at the London house for the Summer Season, but the Countess had asked the Earl if they could remain in Yorkshire for the summer. She was concerned about her sister, and wanted to be nearby in case she was needed.

The Earl, who adored his wife and wanted to please her, had agreed. They had not even gone up to London for Royal Ascot Week in June.

Suddenly, Miles said, 'Do you think that perhaps she's so quiet because of Julian's death? Surely not, Ceci. After all, they were only chums, and childhood chums at that.' He frowned, threw her a puzzled look. 'She can't be grieving, can she?' Miles, at fourteen, was unusually insightful for his age, and had always understood Daphne had no interest in Julian.

'No, of course not, don't be silly. She's sad, but no more than you or me . . .' Ceci stopped abruptly, looked off into the distance.

Miles probed, 'What is it? I know that look on your face only too well.'

'It's just that . . . well, she had a fall in the woods a little while ago. She was worried about a bad bruise on her face. It got better quickly, but she didn't want your father to know. Daphne kept quiet about her fall, so it must be our secret, Miles. Promise me.'

'I promise. Cross my heart and hope to die. I understand about her problem, you know. Father has his heart set on her marrying the son of a duke, and she's acutely aware of her great beauty. But then who isn't? Anyway, she wouldn't want Papa to know she'd fallen. He'd chastise her for being careless. He's drilled it into her for years that her beauty is her greatest asset.'

'That must be a big responsibility for her to carry,' Cecily muttered, making a face.

Miles nodded. 'It's made Daphne cautious, very careful. She knows she can't damage her face, or any part of her body.' He looked at Cecily with his warm, steady gaze, added in a lower voice, 'You're beautiful, too, Ceci.' Leaning across the food in the middle of the car rug, he kissed her on the cheek. 'And you're my special girl. You are, aren't you?'

Whenever he kissed her like this, or spoke in this affectionate manner, Cecily turned bright pink, and she did so now, really blushing. Looking at him from under her long, dark eyelashes, she whispered, 'Yes, and you're my special boy, aren't you?'

He offered her a loving smile, nodded, and finished his sandwich.

Cecily picked up the silver mug, which she knew Hanson had relegated to the kitchen because it was dented. She drank some of the lemonade, and then glanced at the crest engraved on the side. '*Loyalty binds me*,' she said. She knew that motto by heart; she had heard it all her life.

Miles smiled at her, his blue eyes full of admiration for Cecily, whom he had grown up with and couldn't imagine being away from for very long. He heard a faint noise and glanced behind him. Footsteps were coming down the path, and he wondered who it was. He sat up, fully alert.

It was Genevra who appeared; she came to a sudden stop the moment she saw them, obviously taken by surprise.

'Aw, liddle Miss Swann. And Master Ingham himself, come a courtin'.' She laughed, pirouetted, drew closer to them, peering at Miles. Suddenly she asked, 'The Lady Daphne? How be she?'

Miles stared at her, speechless, not knowing how to answer her.

Cecily jumped to her feet. 'What do you mean, Genevra?' she demanded.

'Be she better?' Genevra asked.

'She's not better, because she's not been ill!' Cecily exclaimed sharply, glaring at her.

'I know that, liddle Cecily.'

The gypsy girl looked from Cecily to Miles. She held his gaze for the longest moment, and she saw the light around him, saw his destiny in a flash. Immediately her eyes settled on Cecily, and her heart leapt when she caught a glimpse of her future, as she had only a couple of months ago.

Without saying anything, Genevra turned around and walked away. She stood for a moment, when she came to the edge of the woods, gazing up at Cavendon sitting there high on the hill. Her eyes swept over its glittering windows; the sheen on its walls was like a coating of silver. Blinking in the intense brightness, she closed her eyes.

When she opened them a moment later, the great house looked dark, ominous, and the future was so clearly visible to her she was startled. A shiver ran through her. Nothing had been so clear to her ever before.

Genevra, the Romany girl with the gift of sight, ran into the fields, tears blinding her as she went. She could not change anything. What was meant to be was meant to be. *Che sarà sarà.*

SIXTEEN

Alice Swann walked down the corridor to Lady Daphne's bedroom, carrying three lovely summer frocks for her. They had been altered to fit her, were freshly ironed, and Alice hoped they would bring a smile to her face, cheer her up.

Over the last week, Alice had become concerned about the seventeen-year-old, who seemed lost, helpless and lacking in enthusiasm for anything, even everyday, simple things.

Arriving at the room, Alice knocked, and when there was no answer she turned the knob, only to discover the door was firmly locked. Drawing closer to it, she said in a low, urgent voice, 'Lady Daphne, it's me, Mrs Alice. Please let me in. I have your dresses.'

When there was no sound, Alice knocked again, rapping a little harder. There were muffled sounds from behind the door and finally she heard the key being turned. The door was opened just a crack, and Alice slipped in swiftly. When she saw the state Daphne was in, she was alarmed and locked the door immediately.

The girl was standing there, looking forlorn and dishevelled. She had obviously been crying and her eyes were red rimmed, her hair rumpled, and her clothes seemed to have been thrown on without much care.

'Whatever is it, Lady Daphne?' Alice asked as she walked across to her.

Daphne said nothing, but stared blankly at Alice, her face a picture of dismay. She started to say something, and stopped abruptly.

Alice showed her the dresses. 'Look, Lady Daphne, the summer chiffons. They're ready for the parties coming up. You'll look lovely in them, I'm certain of that.'

'Thank you,' Daphne whispered, and immediately fell silent again.

Walking across to the wardrobe, Alice put them inside, sliding the hangers onto the rail, and closing the door. She returned to the middle of the room, firmly took hold of the young woman's elbow, and ushered her over to the sofa.

'Please sit down, Lady Daphne, and tell me what's the matter. You know I will help you if I can, and you know you can trust me.'

Daphne became distressed. Tears began to run down her pale cheeks, splashing onto her hands clasped in her lap. Alice noticed that she was trembling, and there was such a stricken look in her eyes that Alice was afraid. Something was terribly, terribly wrong. Her heart plummeted, and she hoped to God her worst fear wasn't about to come true. Pulling a side chair over, Alice sat down in it, and reached out. She took hold of Daphne's hand and held it tightly in hers.

Her voice was low, gentle, when she said, 'Take a deep breath, Lady Daphne, and tell me why you are so troubled.'

Lady Daphne Ingham, second daughter of the Earl of Mowbray, the family's great beauty, of whom so much was expected, could not speak. For days she had been in a stunned state of disbelief, hardly able to function, and now she was running out of excuses for spending so much time alone in her room. She did not know what to do, or where to turn, except to Mrs Alice, who had told her not to trust anyone except her parents and the Swanns. But she could not go to her parents. That was unthinkable.

Trying to control her swimming senses, Daphne groped for the handkerchief in her pocket and dried her eyes. She looked at Alice Swann, and nodded, but once again she discovered she could not speak. The words just wouldn't come out. She was unable to say them.

Leaning closer to the young woman, Alice said softly, 'Are you pregnant?'

Daphne drew back swiftly, staring at Alice, a terrified expression settling on her face. She began to shake uncontrollably. Tears swam in her bright blue eyes. Suddenly she began to sob. Then, unexpectedly, she reached out to Alice, who pulled her closer, held her tightly in her arms, attempting to calm her, while fully understanding the girl's fear.

Daphne whispered, 'I've missed two courses and I'm now sick every morning.'

Oh my God, Alice thought, this is a disaster. Whatever are we going to do? An Earl's daughter, pregnant out of wedlock. That was ruinous to any family, and the grander the family, the worse it was. The Inghams would be shattered when they found out. Charlotte, she thought, I've got to go to Charlotte. Only she can work this out, help the Earl and the Countess. They trust her implicitly, and she's very clever.

Releasing Daphne from her tight embrace, Alice said, 'This is a dreadful problem, you know that as well as I do. But I think we can prevent a huge disaster for the family if we handle it correctly.'

'What do you mean?' Daphne asked, patting her eyes with her hankie. 'Handle it how? My . . . condition is not going to go away.'

Barbara Taylor Bradford

'No, it isn't, but there are ways to *conceal* the condition, shall we say. Ways to make certain things . . . *invisible.*'

Daphne bit her lip, shaking her head, 'My parents are going to be furious, Papa in particular—'

'Let's not think about that right now, Lady Daphne,' Alice cut in. 'Just leave things to the Swanns for the moment. I have to speak to Charlotte. She will come up with a plan, I promise you. In the meantime, I want you to do something for me, and for yourself. And it's very important.'

'What do you wish me to do, Mrs Alice? I'll do anything if it helps.'

'I want you to take charge of yourself. And at once. *Now.* This afternoon. I want you to put up a front, and a good one at that.'

Frowning, Daphne said, 'I'm not sure I understand.'

'You've always been a good little actress when we've put on the family plays over the years. I want a performance. The performance of your life. You must behave as normally as possible, and look extremely beautiful. Radiant, in fact. You have to fool your family. They must not think that anything is wrong, or that you're ill or unhappy. You can't mope around, or remain in your room. Otherwise they'll become suspicious, wonder about your health.'

'Yes, yes, I see what you mean. And I will be my normal self, I promise. But what will we do about . . . the other thing?' she asked anxiously, frowning.

'As I told you, I shall speak to Charlotte, and she will deal with everything. That's all I can tell you just now. Listen to me carefully, m'lady. Everything depends on you and your behaviour. Nobody, and I do mean *no one at all*, can suspect anything. Secrecy is the key. You do understand, don't you, Lady Daphne? You can't confide in anyone.'

'I do know that, Mrs Alice.' She sat straighter in the chair. 'Tell no one. Trust no one.'

Alice nodded, stood up. She walked across the room, but paused just before reaching the door. Turning, she said softly, 'The Swanns will protect you, m'lady. You must remember that when you feel despondent or worried.'

The kettle was whistling when Alice opened the front door of their cottage in Little Skell village, and went inside. Cecily was in the kitchen preparing their tea, and Alice noticed how nicely the table had been set. Everything was ready for the two of them, and there were delicious smells permeating the air.

'You're a bit late, Mam,' Cecily said, smiling at her mother. 'I expected you ages ago.'

'I had to help Lady Daphne try on the summer chiffon frocks,' Alice improvised. 'And I must say she looked beautiful in them.'

'She is beautiful. But Miles is worried about her,' Cecily blurted out, and stopped, wishing she hadn't mentioned it.

Alice was startled by the comment, but she did not allow her expression to change. Instead she took off her light cotton jacket, and began to potter around in the kitchen, allowing Cecily to finish her preparations. But Alice's mind was in a whirl; Miles was very close to Daphne, and it was only natural that he would spot any differences in her. She could only hope no one else had. We must be quick, nip this in the bud, she thought, and sat down at the kitchen table.

She said casually, after a moment or two, 'Why is Miles worried about Lady Daphne?'

'He thinks she doesn't seem like herself. "Listless" was the word he used,' Cecily explained, not wishing to make things worse by repeating everything. She certainly didn't want her mother to know she had told Miles that Daphne had fallen in the woods. Alice would be angry if she knew.

'I think she *has* been under the weather a bit,' Alice finally remarked, trying to sound offhand. 'She told me she's been fighting a cold . . . I can only say that she was in blooming health when we tried on the dresses,' she lied, and immediately changed the subject.

Later, Alice couldn't help thinking that it was a good thing she had talked to Daphne today. In doing so she had probably averted a family crisis, an explosion of no mean proportions.

Cecily had made bacon-and-egg pie for their tea and, as they ate, Alice complimented her daughter, exclaiming how delicious it was. A bit later she got around to Miles Ingham; she wanted to find out more.

'So how was your picnic with Miles?' she asked with a warm smile.

'Nice, Mam. DeLacy wasn't allowed to come, though. She had to go with her mother and Diedre . . . to see the dentist in Harrogate.'

'Yes, so I heard. The Countess went to visit her sister while the girls were at Dr Potts's. Poor Mrs Sedgewick. I hear she hasn't been too well over the past few weeks. Quite ill, Cook told me.'

'Miles said his aunt's poor health is affecting his mother, and that she doesn't seem to be interested in anything else except her sister's condition.'

Alice sipped her tea thoughtfully. As heartbreaking and sad as it was, this illness in the family was a blessing in disguise, in a sense. It was distracting the Countess, and she had obviously not noticed her daughter's listlessness, as Miles had referred to it, or that anything was amiss with the family beauty. Daphne had been lucky to have avoided her mother's scrutiny.

'Miles told me that the Earl's cousin, Hugo Stanton, will be arriving soon. For a weekend visit,' Cecily confided to her mother, before finishing her slice of bacon-and-egg pie.

'Your father told me that the other day,' Alice answered, and continued, 'I have to go across to see Aunt Charlotte shortly, Ceci. But first I'll help you clear the dishes.'

'No, no, Mam, I can do it. You've been sewing all day. You must be worn out. You know your eyes get tired.'

Alice smiled at her lovingly. Cecily was such a good girl. And she would leave Cavendon one day, and make a name for herself in the big wide world out there. She would design extraordinary clothes and be somebody. Alice knew that in her bones; she knew how truly gifted her daughter was, and that she was bound for success.

SEVENTEEN

Hanson sat in his office, staring at the calendar on his desk. It was Friday 11 July, and next Friday, just one week from today, they would be holding the first supper dance of the summer season. This event was usually met with great anticipation and excitement. That was absent this year, and he was disappointed, and a little worried.

The butler sighed as he stared down at the date, wondering what sort of evening it was going to be. The Countess, very sadly, was focused more on her sister's cancer than the upcoming dance, whilst the Earl was worrying about his wife and her state of mind, and was preoccupied.

Lady Diedre was more aloof and distant than ever, and appeared distracted, whilst Lady Daphne had spent days moping around and looking tearful. He wondered now how much her demeanour had to do with Julian Torbett's death. He didn't have an answer for himself.

Thankfully, the family's favourite had somehow sprung back to life in the last couple of days, and was more like her old self. She'd been looking beautiful, sounding cheerful, giving everyone smiles, and generally being the charming Lady Daphne they were accustomed to, and loved.

Hanson was saddened that young Julian Torbett had died in such a tragic way. The woodsmen and gardeners were still talking about the rifle shots, which had been so unexpected, and hadn't come from any of their men. It was a mystery, and troubled them all.

But shots had been fired by somebody, and as a result a young man was dead . . . because his horse had been spooked by the shots, had bolted and thrown him.

The Torbett family had sent their regrets that they were now unable to attend the supper dance. The whole family was in mourning and had cancelled all engagements.

Everyone in the area was wary of the Torbetts, considering the family to be arrogant, snobbish, and far too big for their boots. And so, in one sense, Henry was not particularly displeased that they would be absent. He was just sorry the young man was dead before he had lived his life. He had been the nicest of the three Torbett sons. Alexander was a pathetic drunk and Richard, the eldest, was something of a martinet, thoroughly disliked by the entire staff.

Henry Hanson picked up a red pencil and put a line through their names, crossing them off the list. Good riddance to bad rubbish, he thought.

Next, the butler studied the champagne and wine lists, which he and the Earl had created last week. He nodded to himself. Their choices were good. He moved on, picking up the menu for the supper. It had been prepared by Cook, who knew the family's tastes and preferences, and those of their guests. The Earl had approved it, because the Countess had been in Harrogate.

A sudden rapping on the door made Hanson lift his head. 'Come in,' he called.

A second later, Lady Daphne was standing in the doorway. The moment he saw her, he jumped to his feet. 'Good morning, m'lady,' he exclaimed, surprised, and then he stared hard at the young woman with her, who was holding a tiny child in her arms.

Aware that he was taken aback, Daphne explained, 'I'm sorry to trouble you, Hanson, but I ran into this young lady in the back yard. She was looking for Peggy Swift. She's Peggy's sister, and she needs to speak to her about a family matter.'

'I see,' Hanson responded, walking around the desk, his eyes riveted on the young woman. She was simply but neatly dressed, and did indeed have a look of Peggy.

'Please come this way. I will take you to the servants' hall, and you can sit there whilst we find Peggy. And what is your name, may I ask?'

'It's June, Mr Hanson. Mrs June O'Sullivan. My husband brought me over to Cavendon from Ripon. In the horse and trap. He's waiting outside.'

Inclining his head, Hanson said, 'Follow me,' and led the way down the corridor. He was surprised to see that Lady Daphne was still with them, and turned to her. 'Thank you, my lady, for bringing Mrs O'Sullivan to me, but I can take over now.'

'Oh that's all right, Hanson. I don't mind staying with Mrs O'Sullivan until Peggy arrives.' She smiled at the young woman, who looked rather wan. 'Please sit down. Could I get you a glass of water, or something else to drink?'

'Oh no, thank you, my lady. I'm all right. But I will sit if I may, thank you very much. The baby's a bit heavy.' She half smiled. 'Boys are.'

Although Hanson was slightly put out, not liking the idea of Lady Daphne lingering here downstairs with a relative of one of the staff, he was clever enough not to display his feelings. He hurried away in search of Mrs Thwaites.

Daphne continued to stand in the doorway of the servants' hall, and as the silence lengthened she said, 'How old is your little one?'

'He's eighteen months, and doing well, Lady Daphne.'

'And what's his name?'

'It's Kevin, m'lady.' There was a pause, and then she said, again with the small smile, 'Patrick, that's my husband, is Irish. So obviously we picked an Irish name.'

Before she could respond, Daphne heard clicking heels running down the corridor, and suddenly Peggy Swift was rushing into the room, slightly flustered, her expression anxious. When she saw her sister she rushed over to her, flung her arms around her and the youngster. And then looked down at the child, touched his cheek with a finger.

And in that instant Daphne knew that Peggy was the mother of this child, not June. There was such adoration and motherly love reflected on her face, it was patently obvious. Daphne continued to watch her, wondering what her situation was.

As if Peggy had somehow become aware of Daphne's fixed scrutiny, she swung around and stared at Daphne, and then her face flushed bright red.

She knows what I'm thinking, Daphne realized, and instantly wanted to put the young maid at ease. 'Your nephew's a lovely little boy, Peggy,' she said brightly, and edged out of the doorway. 'I'll leave you both alone now. You've things to discuss.' With another smile and a gracious nod of her head, she hurried down the corridor to the back stairs and went upstairs.

A few seconds later, she found herself in the conservatory, her favourite room, where she sank down into a chair, still thinking of Peggy Swift and June. She couldn't help focusing on June, whom she had found wandering around at the back of the house. She had known that something was amiss from the moment June had spoken to her, asking about Peggy. And she was even more convinced of this now. Everyone knew better than to seek out a relative who was in service. It never happened. So there was a problem. A big problem. Her heart went out to Peggy. Perhaps the O'Sullivans could no longer look after the child . . .

Daphne's mind drifted as she leaned back against the cushions . . . and thought about her own predicament. She was pregnant, and single, as Peggy more than likely had been. The difference was that she came from a rich and powerful family who could help her through her trouble, and would do so lovingly. At least Charlotte Swann had assured her of that. But was Charlotte right? She was not sure. Throw a pebble in a pool and watch the ripples spread out, Daphne thought. I am a pebble, and the ripples are about to spread and spread. And my life will never be the same ever again. Rape she could have perhaps hidden. But pregnancy? That was hardly likely.

'She's nice,' June said, sipping the cup of tea Peggy had just brought to her from the kitchen.

'You mean Lady Daphne?'

'Yes, of course. But Cook's nice too. Can you take Kevin for a minute, Peg? So I can drink my tea.'

'Here, give him to me,' she answered, and took the child in her arms. But she did not sit down. Cook had already told her to get her business done quickly. Visitors were frowned on, she'd said. 'Mrs Thwaites came to the kitchen to ask why you're here,' she explained to her sister.

June nodded her understanding. 'What did you tell her?'

'I said you needed my signature on a piece of paper to do with Dad's farm. So I'll sign it when you've finished your tea.'

'Thanks, Peg, it's good of you to give up your share, and we appreciate it. Patrick'll make a go of the farm, and it's a home for you, too, when you need it.'

'I know,' Peggy nodded, having understood right from the beginning of their marriage that they'd want the farm one day. Anyway, what use was a farm to her? She wouldn't be able to run it. Still, they were using the baby as a tool, to get her to give them her half. A fool she wasn't. She'd only been a fool giving into Andy Newson, who'd got her in the family way and then run a mile. Three thousand miles, actually, since he'd gone to America.

Peggy looked down at her son and smiled at him, touched his cheek, kissed his nose. He was a gorgeous baby. She was suddenly glad June was taking care of him. She trusted her sister when it came to the child. June would love him, nurture him, keep him safe. She had no qualms about that.

'Is it Lady Daphne you look after, then? Are you her maid?' June asked, her curiosity getting the better of her.

'No, I'm more of a general parlour maid. All of the four Dees are nice, but—'

'Who are the four dees?'

Peggy grinned. 'Diedre, Daphne, DeLacy, and Dulcie. The four daughters of the Earl. All beautiful, in their own way, but the terror is Dulcie. Five going on fifteen, and very cheeky.'

This comment made June smile, and she shook her head. 'Some little girls are like that, grown up before their time. So you *do* like it here at Cavendon?'

'Sort of, the housekeeper's quite nice, and so is Cook.' She shrugged. 'The footmen are full of themselves, think they're the bees knees.'

'I thought there was one you liked.'

'Yes, Gordon Lane. He's pleasant, and has been kind to me, and he's not too conceited.'

'Be careful, Peg,' June warned, staring at her sister pointedly.

Peggy flushed. 'I won't be going that route again, I can tell you that.' She paused, listened, and then swiftly handed the baby back to June. 'Give me the document to sign. Come on, be quick. I can hear Hanson coming down the corridor. He runs this place with an iron hand. He won't like it that you're still here. He'll say I'm wasting time.'

'We have to have two witnesses when you sign,' June cried as she put the envelope on the table.

'Oh my God! No!' Peggy became flustered as Hanson hurried into the servants' hall looking somewhat put out.

'Now, now, what's all this?' he asked, eyeing Peggy suspiciously. 'Your sister's begun to outstay her welcome. You're in dereliction of your duties, Swift.'

'Yes, I know. I'm ever so sorry, Mr Hanson. I need to sign this paper, a legal document. But I need two witnesses,' she wailed, looking suddenly panic-stricken.

Anxious to remove the woman and the baby, and get Peggy Swift back to her work, Hanson exclaimed, 'Well, then let me get a pen, and I'll sign, and I'll bring Mrs Thwaites with me. Once the document is dealt with, your sister must be on her way. Immediately.'

'Yes, sir, thank you, Mr Hanson, I'm ever so grateful.'

EIGHTEEN

The Inghams were on the very edge of a precipice. One false step would prove fatal. If they fell they would be doomed forever.

The fall of the house of Ingham, Charlotte thought. No, no, I can't allow that to happen. I can't be the only Swann in over one hundred and sixty years to fail in my duty. Since 1749 the Swanns have protected the Inghams, starting with my ancestor James Swann, liegeman to Humphrey Ingham, the first Earl of Mowbray.

I must pull some tricks out of the hat, she told herself. I can't be shamed, can't be a failure.

But she knew she couldn't make the pregnancy go away, just like that, with the snap of her fingers. There was only one solution: she had to conceal it, camouflage it, and keep it a secret. And she needed a foolproof plan.

Charlotte sighed to herself as she walked on, her mind turning swiftly, endless possibilities occurring to her. She glanced around, thinking that the park was lovely on this sunny July morning. She usually took this route, avoiding the dirt road from the village. That happened to be the quickest way, but not as pretty to traverse.

When she came to the walled rose garden, she pushed open the heavy wooden door and went in, sat down on a garden seat, breathed in the fragrance of the roses. They were in full bloom, and their scent was very heady, almost overpowering, but then roses were her favourite flowers.

Leaning back against the wooden seat, Charlotte closed her eyes, relaxing a little, concentrating on an almost insurmountable problem: on a pregnant, unwed girl, the seventeen-year-old daughter of one of England's premier earls, from a pre-eminent and very powerful family; on the great beauty who was expected to achieve important things for them, through a brilliant marriage to a duke's son.

Her father's dream . . . a dream now destroyed, and in an instant of unthinkable violence.

An involuntary shiver ran through Charlotte, and she squeezed her eyes tighter, not wanting the welling tears to seep out. And she *was* on the verge of tears. This was a terrible tragedy, heart-breaking, and the girl wasn't to blame at all. She was the innocent victim. A raging maniac, a pervert, had raped an innocent young woman, had taken her life away. Daphne's future *would* be gone . . . if Charlotte didn't save her.

Daphne. Poor Daphne, Charlotte thought, seeing her in her mind's eye . . . the image of her yesterday had been memorable. She had looked truly beautiful, and so much so Charlotte had been stunned for a moment, had caught her breath in surprise when Daphne had come out onto the terrace to speak with her that morning.

She had been wearing a peach-coloured dress, with a cowl neckline, full skirt and long flowing sleeves. The soft colour had emphasized her peaches-and-cream complexion, the blueness of her eyes. Charlotte had realized, at that precise moment, that a young man, any man, would be completely bowled over by her, caught up in the sheer loveliness of her.

The floaty dress, its warm peach hue, her smiling face, her cheerful demeanour . . . all this was to do with Alice, who had told Charlotte everything immediately after she had found out about the pregnancy. 'I explained to Daphne that she had to give the performance of her life for the next few days, until you came up with a plan. I told her she could not fail.'

And I can't fail either, Charlotte reminded herself as she left the rose garden, hurried on up to Cavendon, sitting high on the hill above the Dales, its windows gleaming in the bright northern sunlight.

She knew that Charles and Felicity were expecting her. Yesterday she had asked if she could see them both the next day, to discuss something very important.

In his usual easy-going way, Charles had agreed, and had not even asked what she wanted to discuss. He had also said that Felicity would be at Cavendon because she was not going to Harrogate. Apparently, Anne Sedgewick's only child, Grace, and Grace's husband, Adrian, had arrived from Cairo at last, and were staying with her.

Later, Charlotte had met with Daphne on the terrace again, and had asked her to be available the following day. The girl was terrified of facing her parents, even though she was totally innocent of any wrongdoing. So much so, she was a nervous wreck, and when Charlotte had volunteered to talk to them first, Daphne had leapt at the idea. Anxiety-ridden though she was about the meeting, she was much calmer when Charlotte had finally gone home later that afternoon.

Charlotte glanced at her fob watch as she walked around to the back door of the house. It was just ten minutes past ten. She had time for a quick cup of tea, and a word with Hanson before her meeting.

When she walked into the kitchen, Cook's face brightened at the sight of her. 'Charlotte! It's grand ter see yer, luv! I knows yer always popping in and out, but yer never pop in here, not these days, yer don't.'

Charlotte went over to Cook, took hold of her hands affectionately, held them in hers for a moment. 'I hate to come bothering you when you've so much to do. But I've a few minutes to spare today, before a meeting with Lord Mowbray, so I knew I just had to come and say hello.'

'Well, then, let's have some tea. Or would yer prefer a cup of coffee? I've just made a pot.'

'Why not? That sounds nice, Mrs Jackson.'

'Do yer know, young Cecily gets ter look more like yer do every day, Charlotte, and she's going ter be as beautiful,' Cook said as she went over to the stove, poured the coffee, then brought the cups to the table. 'A lovely girl, that she is.'

'Yes, I know, she's a darling,' Charlotte agreed, and took a sip of the coffee. 'And she's so talented, I can't believe how clever she is with a needle and thread.'

'Lady Daphne thinks she's going ter be a designer one day, making frocks. In London, she said. What do yer think of that then?' Mrs Jackson gave Charlotte a knowing look. 'And she really did manage ter repair that there frock that got damaged with ink.'

'So I heard,' Charlotte smiled.

Stepping closer, Cook whispered, 'Mrs Sedgewick's been really poorly, that she has! And the Countess has been out of her mind with worry. But things seem ter be calming down. Oh, and the Countess's niece has come back from Egypt.'

'Yes, I know.' Charlotte picked up the coffee cup again, took another sip. 'There aren't many secrets around here.'

'Only too true. No doubt yer've heard that Master Hugo's coming back for a visit. I always liked that boy, I did that. Pity he got shipped off to heathen lands.'

Charlotte laughed. 'He went to New York, Mrs Jackson, not darkest Africa. From what I gather, everyone's rather looking forward to seeing him again.'

'That's so, yes.' Cook hurried over to her boiling pots, took the lids off, peered inside, and stirred one of the pots.

Charlotte said, 'I'm afraid I've got to be off, Mrs Jackson. Thank you for the coffee. It really hit the spot.'

Cook beamed at her and blew her a kiss as she slipped out of the kitchen.

Charlotte found the butler in his office, as usual poring over a collection of papers on his desk. He glanced up as she knocked and went in, saying, 'Good morning, Mr Hanson. I just wanted to let you know I am meeting the Earl and Countess in the South Wing in a few minutes. For a private meeting. I didn't want you to be alarmed if you saw a lot of lights on in there on a Saturday morning.'

'Thank you, Miss Charlotte. I appreciate your thoughtfulness. But I did know about that. His Lordship told me earlier.'

Charlotte smiled and retreated. She went down the back corridor, and upstairs to the front entrance hall. Then she headed in the direction of the South Wing, bracing herself for her encounter with the Earl and Countess.

NINETEEN

Charlotte heard steps behind her, and she recognized them. She paused and swung around. Just as she had thought, Hanson was hurrying after her, a determined look on his face.

'I do apologize, Miss Charlotte,' he said as he drew level with her. 'I didn't ask if you would like some refreshments served during your meeting. The Earl didn't give me any instructions, and it was remiss of me not to mention it a moment ago.'

'I don't think we do, Mr Hanson, but thank you for thinking of it.' She smiled at him warmly. He was special to her; she had a soft spot for him, and took comfort from his calm authority. His constant presence had been reassuring in times of trouble and problems; also, his devotion to Cavendon and the family was commendable. Although Hanson could be stern with the staff, he never raised his voice, nor was he unkind. It was a gift, the way he managed the staff. And the family, she added to herself, smiling inwardly.

Hanson said, 'If you don't mind, I will accompany you to the South Wing. I can help you put on the lights. There are a lot of switches you know. Still, I'm thankful the 5th Earl put in electricity. We couldn't do without it now.'

'Please come with me, Hanson, you'll be a great help.' Realizing that he was riddled with curiosity about the meeting, and wanting to allay any concerns he might have, Charlotte said, in a confiding tone, 'I suggested to His Lordship that we should consider using the South Wing again. To open it up would be useful, because there's so much wear and tear on the East Wing. However, I also brought the matter up because I thought the Earl should consider it for Lady Gwendolyn.'

Hanson stopped abruptly, stared at her, obviously surprised. 'I don't understand. Lady Gwendolyn is happy where she lives now, isn't she?' He sounded genuinely puzzled.

Charlotte nodded. 'She is, yes. But I will confide in you, Mr Hanson, and this has to be between us.'

'But of course. I would never break a confidence: you must know that after all these years.'

'I do. I'm afraid the Earl is rather troubled, in a sense, about Mr Hugo's return. You see, Little Skell Manor is actually *his*. It belonged to his mother, but Lady Gwendolyn continued to live there after her death. However, it is his legally.'

A look of comprehension crossed Hanson's face. 'Lady Evelyne never changed her will in favour of her sister. That's the problem, isn't it?'

'I'm afraid so. Mr Hugo would be within his legal rights to claim the house. I've been trying to find a solution, if that should happen. Where could we put Lady Gwendolyn? Obviously the South Wing came to mind. What is your opinion, Hanson?'

'It's the perfect solution, Miss Charlotte. Lady Gwendolyn does enjoy her privacy, and the South Wing is beautiful, and very comfortable. Ah, here we are. Let's go in and put on the lights.'

As he spoke, Hanson opened the double mahogany doors,

and ushered Charlotte inside. Together they went around the rooms, flipping light switches, and discussing the different spaces. Charlotte knew this wing inside out, because she had worked in these rooms for years with David Ingham, the 5th Earl.

'Thank you for helping me,' she said in an undertone, when she heard footsteps and voices. She and Hanson went out to meet the Earl and Countess as they came into the gallery of the South Wing.

Hanson immediately excused himself and hurried off.

Charlotte said, 'Hanson volunteered to help me turn on all the lights. Quite a task.'

Lady Felicity was glancing around the pale green living room, and she exclaimed, 'I'd forgotten what a lovely room this is, Charles, and the antiques are quite extraordinary. Aunt Gwendolyn would be happy here. Who wouldn't? You had a good idea, Charlotte.'

'You might have forgotten, but the other rooms are equally as lovely. Let's walk around, Your Ladyship, shall we?' she suggested.

The Countess agreed at once, and hurried ahead, leaving Charles and Charlotte to follow. 'The more I see this wing, the more I like it.' Charles turned to Charlotte. 'I'm seriously thinking of opening it up for the summer events, even if Hugo doesn't want the manor.'

Charlotte simply nodded.

He mentioned this to Felicity as they caught up with her, and she immediately agreed.

They returned to the pale green sitting room, and Felicity said, 'Thank you again, Charlotte, and now I must be off. I have so many—'

'You can't leave, darling,' the Earl interrupted swiftly. 'When I told you earlier I wanted you to see the South Wing, I also explained that Charlotte wished to speak to us. About something important.'

The Countess looked at Charlotte, frowning. 'Do you have some sort of problem?'

'No, I don't, my lady. You and the Earl do. And when the Inghams have problems, so do the Swanns.'

'What is it, Charlie?' the Earl asked, reverting to his childhood name for her, suddenly aware of her troubled expression, the worry flooding her eyes.

Taking a deep breath, she replied, 'I think it would be a good idea if you both sat down . . .' Her voice trailed off.

Felicity appeared to hesitate, obviously longing to go about her own business, but Charles knew instinctively that something was awfully wrong. 'Come along, Felicity, sit next to me here on the sofa,' he insisted.

Reluctantly, Felicity did so, her eyes now riveted on Charlotte. 'What is it you want to discuss? Surely it can't be that bad?'

Lowering herself into a chair next to them, Charlotte answered quietly, 'It is indeed very bad, Lady Mowbray. You are both facing a situation that is almost insurmountable. It could be ruinous. It could easily bring down the House of Ingham.'

Felicity was gaping at her, her eyes filled with bafflement, obviously unable to come to grips with such a preposterous suggestion.

Charles Ingham, the 6th Earl of Mowbray, trusted Charlotte Swann with his life. He knew she was not exaggerating. That was not her way. His face paled and apprehension filled his light blue eyes as he focused on her.

'Let's have it, Charlotte,' he said, bracing himself.

Twenty

Taking a deep breath, Charlotte said, 'Daphne's pregnant.' Her eyes did not leave their faces as she uttered these fateful words.

They fell into the room like an exploding bomb.

For a moment Charles and Felicity could not say a word, so stunned and shocked were they. They looked at each other in alarm, and then gaped at Charlotte, obviously filled with total disbelief from the expressions on their faces. It was as if they couldn't comprehend what she had announced so bluntly.

'No! No! That can't be!' Charles exclaimed in a loud, angry voice. 'Not Daphne! That's not possible! She doesn't know any men. So how can she be pregnant?' He shuddered as he said that word, shaking his head vehemently. Charlotte is mistaken, he thought; she has to be. It can't be true. Daphne cannot be pregnant. Not my Daphne.

Felicity found her voice at last. 'I agree with Charles,' she exclaimed, her voice shrill, harsh. She brought a trembling hand to her mouth in an effort to stifle the sobs bubbling up in her throat.

'She would never break her code of honour, or let us down. She is part of Charles's plan; she wants to marry the son of a duke. She has integrity, and it's true, she doesn't know any men, other than Julian Torbett, but—'

Felicity could not control her raging emotions, and she began to sob once more, tears coursing down her cheeks.

Charles moved closer to her on the sofa, and put his arm around her, endeavouring to calm her. But she was distraught, just as he was himself. He was still suffering from shock, and he felt as though his strength had drained away. For the first time in his life he was floored, so startled by this horrendous news that he felt undone.

Holding his weeping wife in his arms, he looked across at Charlotte helplessly, and cleared his throat. His voice shook when he finally asked, 'Who did this to her?'

Charlotte swallowed, and answered unsteadily, 'I don't know. We don't kn—'

'Do you mean she hasn't told you who her . . . lover is?' Felicity cried, the pitch of her voice higher than ever, her face white as bleached linen.

'There is no lover, Your Ladyship. Daphne did not have a liaison with a man. She is the innocent victim. She was attacked by a man – either a stranger, or someone she knew. She was raped.'

'Are you saying Julian Torbett raped her?' Charles exclaimed, his voice echoing with anger. He was astounded, and added, 'Surely not Julian . . . he was so meek.'

'I don't know that it *was* him. She hasn't been very forthcoming about what actually happened—'

'When did this take place?' Charles demanded.

'On the Saturday you had lunch with her and the girls. May the third. She went to Havers Lodge after lunch—'

'I remember that!' he interrupted, cutting her off. 'Daphne

told me she was going to Havers Lodge to see Julian, to tell him that he could invite Madge Courtney to come to the annual summer ball. Perhaps I'm wrong about him. Maybe he did force her; yes, that's what happened.'

'You're right, Charles,' Felicity said quietly, now attempting to control herself. 'It must have been at the lodge, when she was there.'

'No, No,' Charlotte interjected. 'It was in the bluebell woods . . .' She let her voice trail off when she saw the shock on their faces once again. This was hard for them to bear.

'On our land!' Charles shouted, his usual constraint evaporating. His anger was spiralling once more.

Felicity, looking thoughtful, confided in a low voice, 'I know Julian was engaged to Madge Courtney, but mostly that was because Daphne never showed any interest in him romantically. Her heart was set on following the plans Charles had made for her. However, I always believed Julian was enamoured of her. In my opinion, Madge was second choice. Anyway, Madge is rich, let's not forget. The Torbetts favour women with great fortunes, you know.'

There was a long silence.

Charlotte broke it when she said, 'I think I should tell you everything I know. After that you must talk to Daphne. She is terrified, and beside herself with grief and sorrow. She's trying to keep up a good front, encouraged by Alice to do so. But she really needs you, needs your comfort, your love and understanding.'

'Of course she does,' Charles agreed, trying to calm himself. The shock had not yet receded. 'Daphne is a wonderful young woman, and obviously she is totally innocent. We must reassure her that we are on her side, and that we will help her in every way we can.'

Felicity took a deep breath. 'We will make sure she gets through this, Charlotte, but what are we going to do about her condition? How will we keep it a secret? Hide her pregnancy? Lead a normal life? What if the secret leaks out? She'll be ruined. The family will be ruined, as you warned. And what about next year? She's supposed to come out as a debutante, be presented at Court? What can we do to sustain the family's reputation?'

'I've come up with a plan. First, I would like to fill you in about Daphne's ordeal.'

'Yes, do that, Charlie, tell us everything.' Charles sat back, waiting, an expectant expression on his face.

Charlotte, leaning forward, her hands clasped together, did exactly that . . . told them everything they had to know, however unpalatable this was.

Once she had concluded her story, Charles rose. After thanking her, he looked at his wife. 'We must now go and find Daphne to console her, and give her our support. She must be beside herself.'

'Yes, she must be.' Felicity also stood up, but at that precise moment there was a knock on the door of the South Wing. It was Charlotte who ran to open it.

Daphne was standing there, looking truly beautiful in a pale blue outfit, and it was obvious she was apprehensive.

'Come in, come in, Lady Daphne. Your parents were about to come looking for you,' Charlotte told her with a wide smile. 'They understand you are totally innocent,' she finished in a slightly lower tone.

Daphne stepped into the gallery. Her mother ran to her at once, embracing her. Charles followed swiftly, and put his arms around both women, holding them close to him protectively.

After a moment, Charlotte said quietly, 'I shall be in the

lavender bedroom, here in the South Wing. And when you are ready to hear them, I will tell you my plans for Daphne. For the moment you must be together to discuss this problem, and comfort each other.'

Charles simply inclined his head, half smiled at Charlotte. 'Thank you,' he murmured softly, and turned back to his daughter and his wife. His concern for them was apparent, as was his deep love.

Sitting at the small antique writing desk in the lavender bedroom, Charlotte used this time to refine the plans she had made in her head over the last few days. She thought they would work; she prayed they would. Once they were put into operation, she believed she and the Inghams could save Daphne, and their reputation as a family. That was her aim, and her duty. She was a Swann. And there were other Swanns to assist her.

A short while later, Daphne found Charlotte in the lavender bedroom and they went back to the sitting room together. She could tell that the Inghams were supportive of their daughter, very loving with her. Daphne was more relaxed, and relieved.

Once they were seated, Charles asked, 'Who else knows about this situation, Charlotte?'

'The four of us, and Alice and Walter.'

'So we're safe, it's a secret.' He glanced at Daphne. 'You haven't told any of your sisters, have you?'

'No, Papa, I haven't. Mrs Alice told me that I shouldn't . . . She said, "Tell no one. Trust no one in this house, except your parents and the Swanns." I listened to her, and I did as she said.'

'I'm glad to hear that, Daphne.' Turning to Charlotte, he asked, 'So, what plans have you developed?'

'Maintaining the secret is the first *vital* rule,' Charlotte replied. 'If you feel the need to talk, if you're troubled –' she looked pointedly at Daphne and Felicity, then continued – 'then you should talk to each other, or to Alice, or me. Try to speak in a private place where you can't be overheard. All right? Remember, there must be no gossip about you, Daphne.'

They both nodded, and Charlotte went on, 'The next thing is your demeanour. You must behave as normally as possible. All of you. Not one single person should think something is wrong or amiss. That is especially important as far as you're concerned, Daphne. As Alice told you, please keep up that happy front.' She sat back in the chair, pausing for a second before saying, to Charles, 'Your father once told me something I've never forgotten, and it's this: *Never show weakness, never lose face.*'

Charles nodded. 'He said the same thing to me, and it's good to remember his advice.'

'Now, let's get to the pregnancy. The attack on Daphne was on May the third; today is July the twelfth. By my calculation that's around two months into the pregnancy. So, for the next four months I feel certain we can conceal Daphne's condition.'

'How is that possible?' Charles asked, raising a brow questioningly.

'Daphne will be able to wear the clothes she has now and for quite a few weeks. During that time, Alice will make some very well-cut outfits for her; these will hide her condition. Also, Daphne is tall and slender like her mother, which helps. As I recall, Her Ladyship didn't show for a long time.' As she said this, Charlotte looked at Felicity for confirmation of her statement.

The Countess nodded and said to Charles, 'I didn't actually show until at least six months into my pregnancies. Let's hope Daphne is the same.'

He was silent, hoping his wife and Charlotte were right.

Charlotte leaned forward, and turned again to Felicity. 'I believe Daphne can safely stay here at Cavendon through the summer season, and attend all of the events without anyone knowing a thing, Your Ladyship. The clothes she wears, her bearing and the way she's built will all work in her favour. Don't you think?'

'I certainly do, and it's good that things continue in a normal way.'

For a moment Charlotte sat thinking, before finally saying, 'Daphne will have to disappear at one moment, and I came up with another idea. Why not have her take a European tour? Many young women do that before becoming debutantes, and being presented to the King and Queen at Court.'

'That's an excellent idea,' Felicity replied, and glanced at Charles. 'Don't you agree?'

'Yes, I do. But who will accompany her?'

'If you wish, Your Lordship, I could do that, act as a chaperone and companion. I do think there will come a time when Daphne *must* leave here, when she begins to show.'

'I would like her to do a European tour,' Charles answered, finding himself more at ease the more Charlotte talked this through with them. 'How do you feel about it, darling?' he asked Daphne, smiling at her, resisting the impulse to grab hold of her, keep her close, and safe always.

'I would like that, Papa – and anyway there aren't many other solutions. I couldn't live at the Mayfair house, because of the staff. So this tour sounds like the answer.' Turning to look at Charlotte, she added, 'I would enjoy being with you, Miss Charlotte, and certainly it would mean I could relax. Because I would be showing by October, don't you think?'

Charlotte nodded.

'And after the tour?' Felicity asked, eyeing Charlotte. 'What is the next step?'

'Perhaps Daphne could come home to Cavendon for a couple of weeks, and then she would tell you she would like to attend a finishing school in either Paris or Switzerland. Obviously, she won't be going to a finishing school, but she will have the proper tutors, and will learn a lot. We would be using assumed names.'

'And Daphne could come home in the New Year, well-polished, with French on the tip of her tongue, and a bit of real Parisian chic?' Charles threw Charlotte a questioning look.

'That's exactly what I had in mind, Lord Mowbray.'

'Where will Daphne give birth?' Charles enquired quietly.

'In a good hospital in the south of England, maybe in Kent – one of the southern counties, anyway. And again, under an assumed name.'

'And what happens to the baby?' Felicity asked in a low, troubled voice.

'That's up to the family, but I think you have plenty of time to make a decision about adoption. I'm not sure you have any other choice,' Charlotte answered gently.

'Well, I think you've helped to ease our worries,' Charles said, giving Charlotte a faint smile. 'We're very grateful to you. We'll be discussing things and making the right decisions when the time is appropriate. Now, Charlotte, won't you join us for lunch?'

'Thank you, Your Lordship, but I did make an arrangement with Alice that is a bit hard to break. However, if you like, I could come to tea this afternoon. Would that be all right? I would love to see Guy.'

'That would be perfect,' Felicity said swiftly. 'Aunt Gwendolyn is coming; in fact, the whole family will be present. And naturally you are welcome.'

Twenty-One

Later that afternoon, Charles Ingham, 6th Earl of Mowbray, climbed the moors to an outcropping of giant-sized rocks. They dated as far back as the glaciers that had covered Yorkshire in the time of the Ice Age, and they were known as High Skell.

The monolithic rocks were formed in a semicircle and created a secluded and protected area. It was a place Charles had always favoured since his childhood.

The weather had clouded over slightly, and as he strode towards the rocks he glanced up at the sky. Despite its leaden aspect, he knew it wouldn't rain. He went and sat down on one of the flat stones and leaned back against a wall of rocks, closing his eyes for a moment, relaxing his taut muscles. He thought of High Skell as his private place, where he could think more clearly and sort out all of the machinations rumbling around in his head.

In this vast and desolate stretch of moorland, he found a certain tranquillity, a deep sense of peace. There was nothing here but sky and moors, and the keening of the wind coming off the North Sea when the weather was inclement.

The vast emptiness was a blessing. Nothing intruded. He had only his thoughts to contend with. Here he could sort them out, find the focus to solve his problems. And so he had come up here to be alone. And to mourn.

He had been shaken to his very core by Charlotte's revelations a few hours ago. What had happened to his beloved daughter, his darling Daphne, had been a million-to-one chance. For a child of his to be raped on his own land was unimaginable, utterly appalling. It had broken his heart today; destroyed all of his plans and dreams for her. And her dreams as well.

She had led a quiet, sheltered life within her own family; she never been exposed to the outside world, and was inexperienced in every way . . . and then she had been assaulted in the most savage and cruel manner.

How shocked and frightened she must have been – and still was, if the truth be known. She had been courageous and strong, and that told him just how much of an Ingham she truly was. He was proud of her stoicism.

Charles sighed under his breath, thinking of the worst possible scenario. She could easily have been murdered after the rape; that man, whoever he was, could have ended up killing her to protect himself.

Every time he thought of this his mind froze at the mere idea of it, and now he pushed the thought away once more.

They were lucky that she was still alive, that the rapist had not taken that ultimate step and killed her. Fortunately, her facial beauty was unmarred. She had begun to recover physically, if not mentally; obviously that would take time, and she would need very special care. He and Felicity would give her all the help she needed, as would Charlotte and Alice.

Apparently Alice had been stalwart and wise in her handling of the dreadful situation she had stumbled into accidentally, on that fateful Saturday in May. And, as it turned out, it had been truly propitious that Alice had found out first and acted swiftly to keep the matter quiet. Now they would protect Daphne, nurture her, until the baby's birth.

And what to do about the baby? When all was said and done, the child was part Ingham, blood of his blood through Daphne. He closed his eyes, let his thoughts float.

Who had raped her? It seemed unlikely that it could have been a stranger, some man who had wandered onto the estate and randomly attacked her, and then fled.

When he had mentioned Julian Torbett to her, Daphne had dropped her head, looking down at her clasped hands in her lap, and she had wept. At that moment, as he now looked back, he had genuinely believed she had been acquiescing, silently naming Julian.

Julian Torbett. Charles focused his mind on the young man. He had always appeared meek, gentle, even a little wishy-washy, as Felicity put it. How would he have found the nerve to force Daphne into a sexual act?

The answer came to him quite suddenly. The meekest of men often found enormous inner strength and purpose in order to gain something they longed for. Frustration, desire, love and lust could be forged together to become a powerful force. Had this happened on that May day? He did not know. He would never know. But it occurred to him now that Julian was the most likely candidate, the man who had done this to Daphne. Well, he was dead and buried. And that was that. They had to cope with the reality.

If they followed the plans Charlotte had made, Daphne would be able to pick up her life in February of 1914, as if nothing had happened. It would be their secret.

Daphne would come back from her sojourn in Europe, where she would have acquired lots of new knowledge about history and art, a new language, French, and that special kind of chic that was totally Parisian. She would have a new wardrobe of clothes from the best *couture* houses in Paris, and she would be launched as a debutante, just as they had always planned. She would be presented at Court to the King and Queen, and he and Felicity would give her a coming out ball. And she *would* marry the son of a duke.

Charlotte had told them everything could be fixed, and he trusted Charlotte Swann. He always had. His father had relied on her judgement for years, and so had he. Whenever he looked back, he realized how much he had depended on her in his childhood.

He knew she would not accept his lunch invitation when he had asked her earlier. That was too formal. But she would come to tea, because it was more casual. She wasn't a servant, and she wasn't an aristocrat; she was a loyal retainer. In between, in a sense, and she was aware of her place.

Charles took out his watch, glanced at it. Then he stood up and walked away from the little enclave of rocks, taking the moorland path back to the house. As he did so he ran across two of the woodsmen walking together along a lower ridge, and he raised a hand, waved. They waved back.

Ever since the morning meeting with Charlotte, he had fully understood why there were so many of his woodsmen roaming the property these days. Percy Swann, the head gamekeeper, had told him recently that there were rumours of poachers on the estate. That was not true. Charlotte had thrown up protection for the entire family by making sure the outside workers were everywhere. That was now patently obvious to him. He approved of her actions; the presence of his employees gave him comfort.

Walter Swann was waiting for Charles when he hurried into the dressing room adjoining his bedroom a short while later.

'I'm afraid I'm running late, Swann. Has the Countess gone down for tea?'

'Yes, m'lord, about ten minutes ago. Lady Gwendolyn arrived a little earlier than expected.'

Charles nodded as Walter helped him off with his tweed jacket. 'As usual,' he muttered, shaking his head knowingly. 'My aunt is always afraid of missing something, hence her overdone punctuality. She's been doing it for years.'

'Hanson gave me a message for you, m'lord. Mr Hugo Stanton telephoned from London. Hanson gave me the number.' Walter handed Charles a piece of paper; Charles glanced at it and put it on the chest of drawers.

'I'd better get dressed first,' Charles said, walking over to the bathroom. Over his shoulder, he added, 'I'll wear a grey suit, Walter, and would you be good enough to select a suitable tie, please?'

'Right away, m'lord,' Walter replied, and went over to the wardrobe.

In the bathroom Charles washed his hands and face, and then stared at himself. He thought he looked strained, and immediately reminded himself to relax, and to behave in the most normal way. He couldn't help wondering why Hugo was telephoning him. Hopefully he might be cancelling his trip. Now that would be a bit of good news for a change. The thought of Hugo's impending visit was upsetting, especially under the present circumstances. Any house guest would be a nuisance at the moment. He wasn't going to cancel Hugo's planned visit; with luck, Hugo himself might do that.

DeLacy sat down on the small sofa next to Miles. She said, 'It's a lovely tea today, isn't it? And Mama seems so much better.'

'That's true,' Miles answered, glancing around the room. In

the Ingham family, he was the most observant of anyone, missing nothing. He had already made a note of his mother's mood. She had gone from being worried and concerned about his aunt all week, to a woman who was now laughing and smiling far too much. She, who was never frivolous, now appeared to be just that. Miles frowned and glanced over at Daphne. She, too, had improved. She seemed calm; she was no longer moping or looking weepy. As for his father, he was positively genial.

Extremely perceptive for his age, fourteen-year-old Miles decided they were not behaving normally. He couldn't help wondering why they were so different this afternoon. What was going on? Miles was positive he detected an undercurrent and that something strange was happening within the family. However, he couldn't even hazard a guess as to what it might be.

'Penny for your thoughts,' DeLacy said, nudging him. 'You're very preoccupied. What's the matter?'

'Nothing, Lacy, honestly. I was just thinking about the supper dance next Friday. I can't say I'm looking forward to it,' he improvised.

'Oh, please, don't be stuffy, Miles. It's fun. And I'll dance with you, and Diedre and Daphne will too. Then you'll escape all those giggling girls who swoon all over you.'

'No, they don't!' he shot back, and then blushed. 'Stop teasing me. I don't like it, and you know that. Anyway, I'm not interested in any of those silly females from the local families. I don't understand why they're even invited.'

'Because Mama and Papa understand that as the premier family in Yorkshire they have to host a few social events in the summer.'

'I saw Harry Swann this afternoon, and I promised him that we'd all go fishing in the Skell next Saturday,' Miles announced, moving on, changing the subject. 'We can have a picnic in the woods. I know you and Ceci will enjoy it. Isn't that a grand idea?' Miles smiled at her, wanting to be affable, and a good brother. DeLacy was his favourite sister; also, he didn't want to arouse her suspicions about the family. He knew how curious she was, always poking her nose into everybody's business.

DeLacy exclaimed, 'That will be nice!' Her attention had been caught by the parlour maid, Peggy Swift, who was standing in the hall just outside the yellow sitting room. She was edging closer to the footman Gordon. DeLacy had to stifle a giggle. They thought no one could see them.

To avoid the sight of the two of them flirting, DeLacy jumped up and went over to sit with Daphne. She was looking wonderful this afternoon, wearing a lime-green silk afternoon dress. DeLacy thought it must be the latest model from Mrs Alice, and the colour was perfect. 'Is that a new frock?' she asked, gazing at her sister admiringly. 'It really suits you, Daphne.'

'No, it's not new. Mrs Alice made it for me last year. I only wore it once.'

'Look at Peggy flirting with Gordon,' DeLacy whispered, catching sight of them again.

Daphne followed the direction of her gaze. 'I don't think she's flirting, is she?' Daphne said softly, feeling the need to defend Peggy. Seeing the young woman with her baby had touched her heart, and she had felt sorry for the girl's predicament. 'I think they're probably checking if they should serve more food.' Daphne smiled at DeLacy. 'The white evening gown looks beautiful, brand new, Lacy. Cecily did a fantastic job; created something quite extraordinary.'

DeLacy smiled back, thrilled to have this news, and thought of the ink blotches. She pushed the bad memory away, and began to talk to Daphne about the coming supper dance, and what they would wear on Saturday night.

Across the room, Charlotte was seated next to Guy Ingham, and she was enjoying being with him. She was glad she had come to tea. She usually had a good time, mainly because the teas were more relaxed than the family dinners, which were formal and far too long. And often a little pretentious.

Guy, who usually managed to make her laugh, did so now when he said in a conspiratorial whisper, 'Aunt Gwendolyn just informed me she has found the most suitable girl for me. She is going to introduce me to her at the supper dance next weekend. You can bet she will be as ugly as sin, but an heiress with a vast fortune at her disposal.'

Once her laughter had subsided, Charlotte remarked, 'Lady Gwendolyn does try hard to be the matchmaker and, let's face it, she does manage to dig up heiresses, that's absolutely true.' There was a pause, and then she asked, 'But what happened to Violet Lansing? I thought you were rather taken with her, Guy. At least, that's the impression you gave me at Easter.' She sat back in the chair, gazing at him. He was special to her; she had known him since he was born. Now she noticed that his face had suddenly changed. His expression was unexpectedly sorrowful, his light blue eyes stricken.

After a moment, taking a deep breath, Guy said sotto voce, 'It was brought to my attention that Violet wasn't quite suitable for the heir to an earldom.' He sighed heavily. 'I was on the verge of . . . well, becoming rather involved with her, and just caught myself in time. So I let the situation . . .' He shrugged, and went on softly, '. . . just drift until it drifted away. I felt the need to be kind to Violet. I didn't want to hurt her.'

Guy sat back, and then offered Charlotte a warm smile. 'No point in bashing my head against steel. That's not going to do any good. They didn't want her in my life.'

'I'm so sorry,' Charlotte sympathized, then touched his arm lightly. 'You'll meet someone who is exactly right in every way. One day. You'll see, it will happen.'

'I know. That's what Papa said to me. But there will never be anybody like Violet . . .' He allowed his sentence to trail off, knowing his life had been settled for him long ago. So why belabour the point about his lost love . . . probably the love of his life.

Charlotte was about to sympathize with him, when Diedre came and sat down next to Charlotte. Addressing Guy, she asked, 'Did Papa say anything about the London season? Or aren't we going up to town this year?'

'I don't know, and frankly, Didi, I don't care,' her brother answered. 'I personally love it here at Cavendon in the summer. The tennis, the cricket, the swimming, the fishing, the supper dances and summer entertaining. And the shooting when it starts on the Glorious Twelfth.'

'But we're always here for the Glorious Twelfth in August. That's a given. I'm talking about now, Guy – July,' Diedre protested.

Guy said, 'I don't think we'll be going to London this year. At least not as a family, for the season. Because Aunt Anne is too ill, and Mama doesn't want to be too far away. At least, that's what Daphne told me.'

'Oh what does old Daphers know, she's only interested in how she looks.'

Guy threw his sister an odd look, wondering why she was being mean, and changed the subject. He started to talk about Hugo Stanton, who was coming to visit them soon, asking Charlotte a lot of questions about him, as she had known him years ago.

There was a sudden explosion of noise as a small figure, intent on making her presence felt, came rushing into the room, exclaiming, 'I've come to tea, Papa! I can, can't I? I have to be at the party.'

At the sight of Dulcie flying across the floor as fast as her little feet would carry her, Charles jumped up from the sofa where he was sitting with his aunt. He immediately grabbed hold of his youngest child and swept her up into his arms. She had been about to entangle herself in the feet of the parlour maid, Mary, who was carrying a tray of fresh sandwiches over to Hanson, waiting near one of the tea trolleys.

'There we are, my darling,' Charles smiled, holding Dulcie against his chest. 'Yes, you're going to have tea. But first, how would you like to come with me to make an important telephone call?'

'Oh yes, Papa, I would. Can I speak on the teffolone?'

Everyone laughed, enjoying the antics of the pretty, if somewhat boisterous, child. Charles laughed too as he hurried off to the library, relieved he had managed to avert an accident with the maid.

He placed Dulcie in his desk chair, and said, 'Now be a good girl, darling, and once I have made the telephone call we will go back and have tea. You'd like a piece of jam roll, wouldn't you? And strawberries and cream?'

'Ooh, yes, Papa. I'll be a good girl,' Dulcie told him, smiling up at him brightly. She loved Papa and she was glad she was here with him. Now her sisters would know *she* was his favourite. She settled back against the leather chair, still smiling broadly, her little face radiant.

Picking up the telephone, Charles asked the exchange for the London number on the piece of paper. A moment or two later, an operator was announcing that this was Claridge's Hotel on the line. He asked for Mr Hugo Stanton.

A moment later a masculine voice said, 'Hello. Stanton speaking.'

'Your cousin Charles here, Hugo. I received your message of earlier, and called you back as soon as I could.'

'How wonderful to hear your voice after all these years!' Hugo exclaimed, sounding genuinely pleased. 'I telephoned you because I was hoping I might be able to change the date of my visit to Yorkshire.'

For a moment Charles was taken aback, but he said evenly, 'Yes, of course. When would you prefer to come?'

'I was wondering, and rather hoping, that you would agree to this coming Friday. For a few days, as we'd always planned.'

Charles, startled, hesitated before saying, 'I think it will be all right, Hugo. I must warn you, we have a supper dance that evening. But if that does not disturb you . . . I must check with Felicity, of course. However, I don't see why not, old chap,' he finished, wanting to be cordial.

'Thank you, Charles. And by the way, I do like to dance, so I'll dance for my supper, so to speak. I don't usually change arrangements at short notice, I assure you,' he added. 'However, I have just been told there's an important meeting in Zurich that I must attend, the very weekend I was due to come to Yorkshire. The dates clash, I'm afraid.'

'I do understand, I assure you. These things happen occasionally. No problem at all. It's white tie, of course. I will telephone you tomorrow morning to confirm everything with you.'

'Thank you so much, Charles, and I can't wait to come back to Cavendon. Good night.'

'Good night,' Charles answered and put the receiver down. He then picked up Dulcie and left the library.

She exclaimed, 'You didn't let me speak.'

'I know. I'm sorry, Dulcie, the man was in a hurry. So now we can go and have jam roll and strawberries and cream. *Scrumptious.*'

From the doorway of the yellow sitting room, holding Dulcie in his arms, Charles announced, 'Now listen to this bit of news, all of you.'

Everyone turned to stare at him.

'I just spoke to Hugo Stanton and he's arriving here next Friday afternoon instead of later in July.'

'How wonderful!' Aunt Gwendolyn exclaimed. 'I can't wait to see him again.'

'Someone new to dance with, Papa!' DeLacy cried.

Felicity asked, 'How did this come about, Charles?'

'Hugo telephoned earlier, when I was out walking. I just spoke to him. He's staying at Claridge's Hotel. And he has a conflict with dates. It is all right, isn't it? Next weekend?'

'Yes. It's not a problem. And DeLacy is right. It will be nice to have a new guest, and especially a cousin we haven't seen for so long. He can dance with all the young ladies, as Lacy suggested. And perhaps some of the older ones, too.'

TWENTY-TWO

'Want to go out for a stroll?' Gordon Lane asked, smiling at Peggy. 'I feel like a cig, and a breath of air.'

She smiled back. 'Why not? I'll just tell Cook.'

Gordon nodded. He took off his tie, waistcoat and jacket, hung them on a peg, and pushed the packet of cigarettes and matches into a trouser pocket.

'Cook says it's all right,' Peggy told him, coming back into the servants' hall. 'But she says not to stay out too long. She'll wait for us.' Peggy grinned. 'Mrs Jackson says she doesn't want Hanson locking us out.'

'And he would too, the silly old bugger.'

'Gordon, be careful,' Peggy hissed, taking off her cap and apron and hanging them on another peg. 'Come on, let's have that stroll before he arrives on the scene and stops us.'

The two of them went out of the back door, and Gordon, taking hold of Peggy's hand, said, 'Let's walk down to the woods. I'll have a cig, and then we'll walk back. Half an hour at the most. All right with you?'

She nodded. 'I don't want to go into the woods though, Gordon. It's scary in there in the dark.'

He looked down, grinning at her. 'You've got me to protect you, my lass – and anyway, it's not so dark tonight. Look at that full moon shining down on us. Romantic, eh?'

Peggy was silent for a moment, then she said quietly in a firm voice, 'I won't do it, Gordon. I hope you understand that. I don't mind a bit of a cuddle and a few kisses, but that's all.'

'I know. You're always telling me that. Just a kiss and a cuddle then. Anyway, we can't be outside for too long, we don't want to get locked out. Then we'd have to sleep in the stables.'

Peggy just smiled, said nothing.

They walked on in silence, lost in their own thoughts. They had no way of knowing it, but they were thinking about each other.

Peggy had grown more and more enamoured of Gordon Lane over the last few weeks. He was tall, strongly built, and a handsome young man, but what appealed to her also was his kindness. He had been on her side ever since she'd started at Cavendon Hall, always ready to defend her when necessary.

Malcolm Smith, the head footman, was also nice looking, but not as nice a person as Gordon. And she'd seen him flirting with both the other maids, Mary Ince and Elsie Roland. Gordon had told her that Malcolm was a skirt chaser, and it was true.

Even though he knew she and Gordon were becoming close, he'd tried to feel her breast in the pantry, and she'd slapped his face hard. He hadn't come near her again.

Peggy knew she was infatuated with Gordon, and that he was with her. However, there was a problem. He wanted her to go all the way, and she wanted this too. But because of her last bad experience she was afraid; she had vowed to herself that she would not get herself into trouble a second time.

And so she was on her guard tonight as they walked towards

the woods. She must not let her desire for him get the better of her. She must be chaste, but without hurting his feelings.

For his part, Gordon was completely captivated by Peggy Swift. He had fallen hard for her almost the moment she had starting working at Cavendon. She was a good-looking woman, with expressive eyes, lovely curves, and an extremely nice nature. She was also intelligent, and clever, in many different ways.

He wanted to seduce her, yet he had also begun to realize she was a woman he would be happy to marry. He would have to curb his raging emotions, his lust for her; otherwise things could go horribly wrong.

Although she didn't know it, he was well aware she had a child. There was always gossip downstairs. He also knew that the man had left her in the lurch, and run off to America. *Bastard*, he cursed under his breath, as he came to a stop and got out his cigarettes.

Once he had lit the cigarette, the two of them ambled on. 'I'll be a good boy,' he suddenly announced. 'I won't hurt you in any way, or get you into trouble. Just a few kisses though, eh? You don't mind that, do you?'

'No,' she said. 'I'd like that, too. Nothing else though.'

By the time they came to the woods, Gordon had finished his cigarette. He stubbed it out on a log, and led her towards the edge of the woods, where there was a grassy glade. They sat down and Gordon put his arm around her, began to kiss her neck, and then unexpectedly he pushed her down, bent over her and kissed her passionately. He let his tongue linger against hers, and then brought his hand to her dress, opened the top buttons, feeling for her breast.

Peggy struggled. 'No, Gordon, don't. Please don't. You'll get me far too agitated.'

He paid no attention to her words.

Bending his head, he sucked on her nipple, and at the same time he pulled her closer, crushing himself against her body.

He was hard against her thigh, obviously highly charged, and she was melting inside as he sucked on her breast. Then a red flag went up in her head, and she knew she must keep a grip on herself.

'Let's stop,' she whispered. And he did at once, knowing he had no choice. He did not want to scare her away.

Gordon brought his mouth to hers, and devoured it. At the same time, he lifted her skirt with one hand, and was working his fingers inside her knickers until he found the core of her womanhood.

Pushing himself up on one elbow, Gordon looked down into her face, and whispered lovingly, 'You look so beautiful in the moonlight, Peggy. I want to touch you. I want you, but I won't force you . . . just say I can touch you . . . here, like this.' He stroked her, his fingers lingering inside her.

Her mouth was dry and she could only nod. He kissed her face and then continued to stroke her slowly until she was moaning.

Against her face, he whispered, 'Let go, relax, come on, let me give you pleasure. I just want to please you, Peg.' She did as he asked and within seconds she was stiffening, and then she began to spasm, calling his name.

Gordon clutched her to him with both his arms, holding her tightly as if never to let her go. 'Did I please you? I did, I know that, because I saw your face. I saw how much you enjoyed my loving touches.'

'Yes,' she whispered, sounding suddenly shy. 'You did please me, but that wasn't really fair to you. And I . . .' Peggy did not finish her sentence. She broke off, and stiffened in his arms, alert all of a sudden.

'What's wrong?' he asked, frowning, knowing something unusual had suddenly caught her attention.

'Shssss,' she said softly. 'There's someone else here in the woods, Gordon.'

They both sat up, listening attentively. They heard twigs snapping again. There *was* someone out there, hurrying away into the trees.

Gordon jumped up, pulled Peggy to her feet, and together they fled out of the woods and rushed up hill to Cavendon. They ran all the way there, and were out of breath when they reached the back yard.

The two of them stood panting near the stone wall, staring at each other. After a moment, Peggy said, 'It was a man, that I'm sure of, Gordon. His step was heavy; that's why we heard the twigs snapping. Knowing someone was there, maybe watching us, frightened me. Do you think it was a Peeping Tom?'

'Who'd be out there at this hour?' Gordon wondered aloud.

'Well, we were,' Peggy replied, and smiled at him, her love shining on her face. 'Thank you for being . . . respectful, Gordon.'

Bending closer to her, he took her face in his hands and kissed her lightly on the lips. Then he finally made an important decision, and said, 'Will you marry me, Peggy Swift? Will you be mine forever? Will you be my wife?'

She was so taken by surprise, so startled by his proposal that she couldn't speak for a moment. Finally she said, 'I will, Gordon Lane. I will! I will! I will!' She flung her arms around him, hugged him. And they kissed, then drew apart.

Peggy stood looking up at him, fully understanding that she loved this man with all her heart, and she knew she had to tell him the truth about herself. It would be deceitful not to explain about Kevin.

She said quietly, 'There's something I must tell you, Gordon. I have—'

He cut her off when he said, 'A child. Yes, I know that. And it doesn't change my feelings. I love you, Peggy, and when we are able to arrange it, he'll come and live with us. I'll be his father as well as your husband.'

Peggy drew close to him again, tears filling her eyes. She blinked them away. 'Thank you for saying that, Gordon. And I promise I'll be the best wife.'

At this moment the back door opened, and Cook stood in the corridor of bright light shining out from inside the kitchen. She beckoned to them urgently.

Holding hands, they ran towards her. She ushered them into the kitchen, and said, 'Hanson's on the prowl. Light a cigarette, Gordon, real quick, me lad. Now listen . . . yer've been outside in the yard for a few minutes, for a smoke. I just called yer to come in. Which I did, didn't I?'

Gordon nodded, and quickly lit up.

Hanson appeared in the kitchen several seconds later, and nodded when he saw them. After going over to the back door and locking it, he turned and went towards the corridor. 'Good night. Good night to you all,' he called, and headed off.

'Good night, Mr Hanson,' Gordon and Peggy said in unison with Cook.

Much later that night, as she lay in her bed in the maids' quarters, thinking of Gordon and about marrying him, Peggy was filled with growing happiness. She knew they would be good together, and that they'd make a good team. After a while, her thoughts went back to the woods that evening. She was certain someone had been there, hidden in amongst the trees, and so was Gordon. She couldn't help wondering if whoever it was had seen Gordon fondling her.

A Peeping Tom? But who? Surely not one of their woodsmen? Or a villager? She wondered if she should tell Cook or Mrs Thwaites? Perhaps even Mr Hanson? But almost instantly, Peggy decided against this. That would be revealing too much about where she had been with Gordon. Besides, what good would it do? She must warn Gordon tomorrow morning, tell him not to mention the man in the woods. No one must know they had been down there when they were not supposed to go out of the house at night. The rules were strict at Cavendon. And Hanson made sure they were kept.

Peggy was the first maid in the kitchen the following morning. She was so happy she felt like singing. But she couldn't do that. She had a smile firmly in place as she said good morning to Cook.

'Yer looking bright and cheerful, lass,' Nell Jackson said, returning her smile. 'He's a nice lad, that there Gordon Lane. Sincere, for one thing, and kind-hearted. Which is more than I can say about Malcolm Smith. He fancies himself, that one does. Vain as a peacock.'

'That's true, Cook,' Peggy agreed. Walking over to join her near the stove she whispered, 'It's a secret, but we're serious about each other.'

'That's nice for yer, Peggy. Couldn't wish for a finer young man for yer, lass.' Still smiling, the cook turned back to her stove and picked up a wooden spoon.

A moment later, Mrs Thwaites appeared, 'Good morning, Cook, morning Swift. Since you're down first today, I think you had better pop upstairs and light the fire in the library for the Earl. As soon as Ince arrives, I'll send her up to help you set the breakfast table. Come on, lass, hurry yourself along. We don't have all the day.'

Peggy did as she was told, and seconds later she was kneeling in front of the fireplace in the library, sweeping up yesterday's ashes into a dustpan.

After laying the grate with kindling, extra chips of wood, and the round newspaper circles made by the footmen, she struck a match and brought it to the paper. She soon had a roaring fire in the grate. She added several small logs, then stood up.

Peggy realized that her hands were dirty, and she ran downstairs to wash them.

Mary Ince and Elsie Roland, the two other maids, were standing near the china cupboard in the corridor, whispering together. They stopped speaking abruptly when they saw her.

'Good morning,' Peggy said, smiling at them.

They mumbled good morning in return, but both looked sullen, even unfriendly. Peggy couldn't help thinking they'd been talking about her and Gordon. They often made funny remarks these days.

There was a rush of footsteps, and Malcolm Smith came flying down the stairs, exclaiming, 'Mr Hanson wants another silver chafing dish. Hurry up, one of you, find one. Quick.'

Peggy was close to the small silver cupboard, and she opened the door, reached inside. Suddenly she felt Malcolm standing right behind her, breathing down her neck. 'Got you in the family way yet? I bet he has, you little trollop.' Before she could respond he squeezed her bottom, and stepped away from her quickly as the back door opened and Gordon walked in.

In a flash, Peggy turned around and said in an icy tone, 'Don't ever do that to me again, Malcolm Smith. If you do, I'll report you to Mr Hanson for being overly familiar.'

Malcolm burst out laughing. 'Every man around here's familiar with you, Peggy Swift, and the way you open your legs.'

There was a gasp, a sudden disturbance, a rush of air as Gordon flung himself across the kitchen and into the corridor in a giant leap. He fell on Malcolm and began to pummel him on the chest.

The head footman fought Gordon as best he could, but he

was not as strong as his junior. When he threw a punch at Gordon, he missed, slipped and fell down on his back, his arms flailing. Gordon was about to jump on him, when Peggy grabbed one arm and Cook the other. Together they pulled Gordon away from the fray.

A moment later, an irate Hanson was standing staring at them. 'What's all this about? Fighting like common street lads! And both footmen in the employment of one of the premier earls of England. The Earl of Mowbray would be appalled. This is the most reprehensible behaviour I've ever seen. You should know better. Aren't you ashamed of yourselves?' He looked down at Malcolm, and added in a scathing tone, 'Get up at once! And straighten your livery, Smith. As for you, Lane, explain yourself.'

Before Gordon could respond, Cook interrupted in a strong, determined voice, 'I was witness to this scene, Mr Hanson, and it was Malcolm's fault. He provoked Gordon no end. Take my word for it.'

'How?' Hanson demanded coldly, eyeing Cook. 'I need more details.'

'He insulted Peggy, who will one day be Gordon's wife. And Gordon was defending her good name.'

Hanson frowned and glanced across at Gordon. 'What did he say that created this ghastly uproar? Come along, speak up, Lane. Let's have it.'

Gordon remained silent, still angry with the other footman, and now growing nervous under Hanson's stern scrutiny. He shook his head. 'I'd rather not repeat it, Mr Hanson.'

'Please take my word for it,' Nell Jackson interjected. 'I heard every word. Oh my goodness!' She began to smile at a small, neatly dressed woman with bright red hair under a green hat, who had just entered the kitchen from outside, and was carrying a suitcase.

Nell rushed over to her, exclaiming, 'Miss Wilson! What a lovely surprise. Welcome back. Aren't yer a sight for sore eyes. I thought yer wasn't coming back to us till next week.'

'I managed to get everything straightened out sooner than I expected,' Olive Wilson responded. Smiling warmly, she took hold of Cook's outstretched hand and shook it, then squeezed it affectionately. They were old friends, good friends; both had worked at Cavendon for years.

With a glare at the two footmen, Hanson went over to greet Olive Wilson himself. She was lady's maid to the Countess, and he was well aware how much she had been missed. 'Welcome back. I trust all is well, Miss Wilson?' the butler said, shaking her hand.

'It was, Mr Hanson, until I walked into Bedlam here.'

Hanson grimaced. 'Bedlam indeed . . . or any other madhouse. Excuse me for a moment.' He swung around, looked at the footmen. 'I'll deal with the two of you later,' he announced. 'Now get a move on, both of you.' He stared at the kitchen clock. 'Get upstairs at once, and set the table for breakfast, prepare the sideboard. Ince, Roland, you'd better go with them and help to get the dining room up to snuff.'

The two footmen and the maids rushed out, and Hanson looked across at Peggy and said, 'You'd better stay down here. I think that's more appropriate today. You can help Polly . . .' He looked around for the girl, saw her cowering in a corner, and went on, 'You and she can get the food into the chafing dishes as soon as it's ready, help Cook in general.'

'Yes, Mr Hanson. And thank you very much, sir.'

He nodded. 'Stay out of Smith's way.'

'I will, sir. It *was* his fault, you know.'

Hanson sighed heavily. 'Speak to you later, Miss Wilson.' He walked out of the kitchen; he was angry and humiliated that the Countess's personal maid had seen this ridiculous display.

Olive Wilson came into the middle of the kitchen, and looked at Peggy. She smiled. 'Were they fighting over you?' she asked. There was a hint of laughter in her voice, and her green eyes were full of merriment.

'No. Gordon's my boyfriend, you see, and Malcolm made a nasty crack. Gordon took offence. So did I, to be honest.'

'Typical. He's a lout and a bottom-pincher, that one. Watch out for him. I'm Lady Mowbray's lady's maid, by the way.'

'I realize that. I've heard a lot about you.'

'Only nice things, I hope?'

'That's right – they only said nice things, sang your praises.'

Nell Jackson, always a bit nosey, said, 'So yer got it all sorted, and here yer are.' Suddenly puzzled, she remarked, 'It's very early. How did yer get here from the railway station in Harrogate?'

Olive Wilson began to laugh and explained, 'I arrived from London last night, and Her Ladyship had arranged ahead of time for Mrs Sedgewick's chauffeur to meet me at Harrogate Station. He drove me over here, and I spent the night at Miss Charlotte's. We knew it would be after ten when I got to the hall, and that was prearranged too. I didn't want to disturb the whole household.'

'Well, I'm glad yer back, Miss Wilson. It's seemed much longer than three months, though. More like three years.'

'I know what you mean, Mrs Jackson. I've missed all of you, too.'

Twenty-Three

He had been sixteen when he'd left, a slightly callow Eton schoolboy preparing to go to Oxford, and looking forward to it. He had returned to Yorkshire for the first time in sixteen years, a man in his prime at the age of thirty-two. Hugo Ingham Stanton was good looking, ambitious, highly motivated in whatever he did, and extremely successful.

He was a real-estate tycoon of no small measure, a go-getter, a dealmaker, and a supremely talented businessman. Fast moving and decisive, he was blessed with a charming manner as well. People easily fell under his spell, men as well as women, and children were instantly captivated by his marvellous ability to treat them as equals.

Now, as the Rolls-Royce moved smoothly along through the centre of Harrogate, Hugo sat looking out of the window. He couldn't help noticing that the town had changed. He was seeing new buildings and far more hotels. Harrogate had been a spa town for centuries, after the discovery in 1571 of underground wells filled with healing water. And apparently it was currently booming. From what he had read in *The Times* the other day, the first week of July had been spectacular, with all kinds of concerts and other entertainments, and a flock of royal guests visiting to sample the water and take the baths. It seemed that Harrogate was at its convivial best this summer.

It pleased Hugo that Charles had sent his Rolls-Royce and the chauffeur, Gregg, to pick him up at the railway station. The gesture was an indication that a warm welcome awaited him, although he had never really doubted that.

Charles Ingham had always been a first-class guy. Hugo smiled to himself, wondering if the family would find him too Americanized. He didn't believe he was, but others might think so.

He settled back against the leather seat, at ease with himself, and looking forward to visiting Charles, Felicity and the rest of the family.

Hugo had no qualms about returning to Cavendon, where he had grown up. He had not done anything wrong; nevertheless, he had been abruptly sent away by his mother, because she needed someone to blame for the loss of her favourite son. She hadn't been able to accept that his sibling was his own worst enemy: a daredevil, and spoilt.

Lady Evelyne Ingham Stanton, his mother and sister of the 5th Earl, had behaved unfairly and irrationally. Everyone thought that. His father, Ian, had backed him up, and together they had decided it would be better for Hugo if he went to New York, to work with his father's good friend, Benjamin Silver. 'If you stay, she'll only punish you in some way or other, and pick on you constantly,' his father had said. Hugo had agreed, and plans were made for his trip to New York City.

To Hugo's relief, his father had never cut off contact. He had written every week, and visited him in New York every year until his death eight years ago. They had remained close, the best of friends.

His parents had lived separate lives long before his brother's terrible accident, but they had never divorced. Sixteen years ago, his mother's treatment of him had so enraged his father, it had driven yet another wedge between them. They were very different people, and had lived in their own worlds. His mother had been wrapped up in Cavendon, where she had been born, and had become something of a recluse, her music and garden her only real interests.

His father had lived in the world of racehorses and horseracing, and the highly successful stud he owned in Middleham, not far from Ripon. The Stanton yard at Endersby House had been run for years by Major Gaunt, a breeder and trainer employed by his father. Since his father's death, the yard had belonged to him, but it continued to be under the control of Major Gaunt, which suited Hugo.

He loved horses, but not quite as much as his father had, and he did not want to be involved with the yard on a daily – or even weekly – basis. He left it to Gaunt.

Gaunt lived at Endersby House, and Hugo planned to go over to visit him during this visit. He wished to congratulate him on his continuing success, and reassure him about the future. Hugo had no plans to close the yard. It was a money-maker.

Endersby House was one of several properties Hugo owned in Yorkshire, but he would never sell the house and the stud as long as the Major was alive. It was his home, it meant everything to him, and it was there that he had bred so many racehorses for them. Then there was Little Skell Manor, which his mother had left to him, as well as his father's house in East Witton.

Oh, I'll deal with all that later, Hugo decided, pushing these thoughts to one side. As he settled back against the soft leather of the Rolls, Hugo thought of the last time he had driven through these great iron gates looming ahead; the gates of Cavendon Hall, which opened onto the long, tree-lined drive.

He had been with his father, and they had been on their way to Liverpool. It had been from there that he had set sail for New York.

As it turned out, Manhattan had been the perfect place for him. Benjamin Silver had taken to him at once, and it was not long before he had begun to treat him like the son he'd never had. And what a training Hugo had been given in the real-estate business, and in banking, and wheeling and dealing on Wall Street. Hugo had been an avid pupil, Benjamin an inspired teacher. They became inseparable.

And then one day he had become Benjamin's son-in-law, after marrying Loretta Silver, Benjamin's only child. It was through his own intelligence and talent that Hugo had become a million-aire many times over. Then, after her untimely death, Loretta had made him even richer. Hugo had inherited her entire estate, which Benjamin had bequeathed to his daughter on his death.

Benjamin and Loretta had been his best friends; he had loved them both dearly, and he knew how much he owed to them. And it was because of his loss, his loneliness, that he had decided he needed to come back to Yorkshire, where he had grown up and had family ties. He had been filled with optimism when Charles had been so warm and welcoming, first by letter and then on the telephone.

He had ended his youth here. In New York he had found himself, and started afresh, to become the man he was today. And now, perhaps, he would find a new beginning here, where he had once belonged, and where he wanted to belong again.

TWENTY-FOUR

A sense of excitement gripped Hugo as the Rolls-Royce finally pulled up at the huge, double-fronted door of Cavendon Hall. As he alighted from the motorcar, and stood looking up at one of the greatest stately homes in England, countless memories flooded through him and, momentarily, he was carried back into the past.

The front door opened and Charles and Felicity appeared in the doorway. Together they came hurrying down the few steps to meet him, followed by Hanson, who in turn was accompanied by two footmen to carry the luggage.

Charles embraced him, shook his hand, and exclaimed, 'Welcome, Hugo, welcome home!'

'It's wonderful to be here, Charles,' Hugo answered, and turned around to embrace Felicity, who, it seemed to him, had not changed one iota. She was still the beautiful strawberry blonde he remembered from his teen years: warm, friendly, and as elegantly dressed as always. As they drew apart, Hugo said, 'You haven't changed, haven't aged at all, Felicity. You're as lovely as ever, and not a line, not a wrinkle. I don't know how you do it.'

She laughed. 'It's the Yorkshire climate, Hugo darling. But I must admit, *you* have changed. You were a schoolboy when you left here, and look at you now. A grown man, and a successful man of the world, I sense.'

He nodded, and winked at her, then turned to greet Hanson, who had a huge smile on his face. 'How good it is to see you, Hanson,' he said, shaking Hanson's hand.

'And you too, Mr Hugo.' Leaning closer, the butler said in a lower tone, 'You've been missed by many. Your father usually filled me in when he got back from New York. You see, he knew I wanted to know how you were. All of the staff did.'

'He told me, Hanson,' Hugo responded, and nodded, as Felicity and Charles led him up the steps and into Cavendon.

In the front hall Hugo glanced around, his throat tightening with emotion. It was as he had remembered it over the years, but somehow it was just better in reality, more golden and embellished, if that were possible.

The hall had a gleam to it, and its beauty gave him great satisfaction . . . the grand staircase flowing down, with his ancestors' portraits on the walls, the crystal chandeliers, the mellow antiques, and the urns filled with flowers. He had yearned to be back here over the years, and now here he was, welcomed as family, and with enormous affection. He was filled with relief, and glad he had finally had the courage to take this step, to come back to his roots.

'Would you like anything?' Charles asked. 'A refreshment? Are you hungry, do you want something to eat? Or do you prefer to wait for tea?'

'Oh yes, I'll wait. There's nothing like afternoon tea at Cavendon, not anywhere in the world.'

'Let me take you up to your room, Hugo,' Felicity smiled, slipping her arm through his. 'The Blue Room. I know you always liked it.'

'It's my favourite.'

Charles said, 'Come down whenever you like, Hugo. I'll be in the library. There're a couple of things I would like to discuss with you, before you get surrounded by women at tea time.' Charles chuckled.

'I'd enjoy that. See you shortly, Charles.'

The moment Hugo stepped into the Blue Room, his face broke out in smiles. It was exactly the same as it had been the day he'd left for America. White walls, blue and white fabrics; every-thing so fresh and appealing to him. And, of course, the big bowls of flowers everywhere, including his favourite pink peonies. Felicity's trademark. He looked at her. 'I can't tell you how happy I am to be back at Cavendon.'

'And we're happy too, Hugo.' She smiled at him and walked to the door, adding, 'Hanson has assigned Gordon Lane to be your valet. He is most suitable, you'll find.'

'Thank you, Felicity.'

She simply nodded, and slipped out, leaving him alone, as usual aware of other people's need to have their privacy for a while.

He strolled around the room, looking out of the windows at the rolling lawns and the stand of trees near the rose garden. And then went into the bathroom to freshen up.

He was just about to go downstairs when there was a tapping on the bedroom door. He strode across the room and opened it, and gaped in surprise. Standing before him was the most beautiful child he had ever seen. A Botticelli angel. She was gazing up at him with great curiosity.

Crouching down to her level, he found himself staring into saucer-like blue eyes that were very serious indeed.

'Hello,' he said gently.

'I didn't speak on the teffalone because Papa said you were in a hurry,' she explained earnestly. 'I'm sorry.'

For a moment he was baffled, but said, 'Well, now we can speak in person. I am Hugo.' He held out his hand.

She took it, and answered, 'And I am Lady Dulcie Agatha Ingham. Pleased to meet you.' She did a small curtsy, and went on in a solemn tone, 'Am I the first of the sisters to meet you?'

Hugo swallowed a smile and, standing up, he opened the door and said, 'Please come in, Lady Dulcie, and yes indeed, you are the first one to meet me.'

Her face filled with radiance and then she giggled. 'I like to march a steal on them.'

'Steal a march,' he corrected, enjoying this unique little girl, who followed him into the room, looking him over, obviously assessing him.

'Oh dear I got that wrong. I sometimes do get things wrong. But DeLacy says it doesn't matter.'

'Of course it doesn't.'

'There you are!' a female voice cried, and a moment later a young woman who was obviously the nanny arrived in the room.

'Please do excuse Dulcie, Mr Stanton. I've been looking all over for her. I'd no idea she had found you so easily.'

Hugo began to laugh. 'That's all right,' he answered, still laughing, finding the situation amusing.

'She was longing to meet you first, before her sisters,' the nanny explained. 'And she did, I do believe.'

'That's right. And she wasn't a nuisance. On the contrary she was rather . . . charming.'

Dulcie flashed him a big smile. 'I shall have to go, Hugo.' She bobbed another curtsy and left with the nanny.

He stood there, shaking his head for a moment, and then he chuckled to himself. The child was beautiful and obviously competitive with her sisters, and a go-getter. I'd better keep an eye on her, he thought to himself, still chuckling as he went out into the corridor. That child's going places.

Twenty-Five

A s Hugo strode into the library a moment later, Charles immediately stood up and walked around his desk. 'There you are, Hugo. Come on, let us sit near the fire, and chat for a while. We've a lot of catching up to do.'

Hugo nodded, and stepped over to the fire, suddenly remembering how this room was always cold, even when there was a heatwave outside, and that there was always a fire blazing, whatever the time of year.

Turning to Charles, he asked, 'Did you ever discover what makes the library so cold all year round?'

Charles shook his head. 'Never managed that, old chap, although there are all sorts of old wives' tales: that Cavendon is built on an ancient druid cemetery; that far below Cavendon, in the bowels of the earth, there are hidden wells of water left over from the Ice Age . . . You name it, we've got it. But nobody really has an answer.'

Once the two men had settled down in the armchairs, Charles said, 'You mentioned your property in Yorkshire, in your letter to me from Zurich. Which particular house were you talking about, Hugo?'

'All of them. Well, not exactly. I mustn't include Endersby House, where Major Gaunt lives. That's his home for as long as he's running the yard. But my father left me Beldon Grange in East Witton, which I believe I'm going to sell, and then there's Little Skell Manor, here on the estate. I was—'

'You do know that Aunt Gwendolyn still lives there, Hugo,' Charles cut in. 'And she has for as long as I can remember.'

'Oh yes, I do know. And I must set her mind at rest as soon as I see her this afternoon.' He looked across at Charles and raised a brow. 'She is all right, isn't she? She is coming to tea?'

'Oh yes, wild horses couldn't keep her away. She can't wait to see you, and she hasn't stopped talking about your visit since I informed her you were coming to see us.'

'And perhaps to make my home here,' Hugo said. 'But getting back to Little Skell Manor, I want to reassure her that she can live there for as long as she wants. Until the day she dies, in fact. After that, I'll give it back to you. I know it has to stay in the family, and that it usually passes to a girl. And you have *four* daughters . . . one of them might need a roof over her head sometime, Charles, and it's really your call.'

'But your mother left Little Skell Manor to you in her will, Hugo. And now you're telling me you don't want it?' Charles was surprised, but pleasantly so.

'Not for myself, to live in, no I don't. It's not really large enough or grand enough. I aim to find a potential stately home, if there's one available around here, Charles, and I'm going to need your help to find it.'

'I'll do the best I can,' Charles replied, so filled with relief he would do anything to help Hugo acquire a grand property. How thrilled Aunt Gwendolyn would be, and Charlotte as well, that Little Skell Manor was safe. He was pleased an old lady wasn't going to be turfed out of her home, and also genuinely happy that the South Wing would remain unoccupied, so that they could use it themselves from time to time.

Charles said, 'I've opened up the South Wing, by the way, Hugo, and you're going to get a thrill seeing it again. It's perfectly beautiful, and we're holding the supper dance there tonight. The first of the season.'

'That's great to hear. I always thought it was one of the best parts of Cavendon. And I'm delighted I'm here for this event. I'm so pleased you were able to accommodate me; that you agreed to the change in dates.'

'No problem, Hugo, none at all. Getting back to homes, are you planning to keep your villa in Zurich?'

'Oh yes, for the moment. I might give it up if there's a war, but even then it should be safe, since Switzerland is a neutral country.'

Charles was frowning, his eyes tight on Hugo's face. 'Why do you mention war? Everything has been peaceful for a long time now. England is safe; we are the greatest empire the world has ever known, and the richest. London is the centre of the world, of the universe really. Prosperity reigns, don't you think?' His eyes remained riveted on his cousin.

Hugo said carefully, somewhat slowly for him, 'Yes, there is a lot of truth in what you say, Charles. The Empire with a capital E is the greatest there has ever been, no question about that. But I think this is the last summer . . . the last summer we're going to enjoy for a long time. There is trouble in the world. Trouble afoot.'

Noting the seriousness of Hugo's voice, the solemnity of his face, Charles felt a shiver run down his spine. 'Tell me more, Hugo. No one I know in London has spoken to me like this.'

'Nor would they. They don't want to face reality, or perhaps they don't know what I do. Remember, I live in Zurich and New York. I hear things, I'm told things.'

Hugo let out a long sigh and settled back in the chair. He made a steeple out of his hands and brought the point to his mouth. After a moment or two he said quietly, 'Germany is rearming. They want to rule the world. Kaiser Bill is on the march, or about to be. And quite soon. There's a heaviness in the air in Europe, and it spells trouble . . . war. Russia is in danger. Nicholas hasn't ruled well – too much influence from his queen. Alexandra is not the best advisor. The country is divided . . . the aristocracy and the serfs. Too many inequities. And then there are the Bolsheviks . . . watch out for a revolution in Russia. It's almost unavoidable, inevitable.'

'And it will affect us, won't it?'

'It will. That's one of the reasons I must go to Zurich for that meeting I mentioned. I can't miss it . . . the bankers of Zurich more often than not call the tune. I never miss a meeting, but I always listen without saying too much. Remember what my father used to say?'

'I do indeed. A still tongue and a wise head,' Charles was quick to answer.

'Exactly.'

There was a knock on the door, and it opened immediately. A young woman came in, exclaiming, 'Papa, about tonight, I've—' She stopped when she saw that Charles was not alone, and paused, waiting in the middle of the floor.

Hugo stood up and turned around. All speech left him. He felt as if he had been punched in the belly. The young woman he was staring at was the most beautiful creature he had ever seen. Breathtaking. She appeared to shimmer, from the top of her golden head filled with sunlight, to the hem of her satin dress. It was an unusual colour, not yellow, not peach, more like apricot. And it made her cornflower blue eyes seem even bluer.

She came towards him, smiling, her hand outstretched. 'Hugo, I presume. I am Daphne, the second daughter.'

Hugo still could not speak, and his legs felt weak. He took her hand in his, and felt its silkiness, and he said, 'I'm pleased to meet you again, Daphne. When we first met you were only twelve months old.' To his total surprise, his voice sounded normal.

Daphne merely smiled, and managed to extricate her hand from his, and walked across the room to her father.

Hugo watched her, noticing her grace and fluidity, the swirl of the clinging satin dress against her long legs, the proud set of her shoulders, the elegant tilt of her head.

He wanted her. Not for a night, not for a week, not for a month. *Forever*. He wanted to possess her. Keep her next to him. He had to have her; had to make her his entire life. And he would.

Sapphires, he thought. I want to drape her in sapphires that match those wondrous eyes. Sapphires around her neck . . . on her ears . . . encircling her arms. Sapphires, and diamonds, and anything else she wants . . . I will give her the world.

Clearing his throat, Hugo managed to say, 'Will you excuse me for a moment, Daphne, Charles.' He inclined his head to them both, smiled and hurried out.

Once he was in the Blue Room, he took off his jacket and threw it on a chair, then went into the bathroom where he soaked a towel in cold water. This he held against his burning face for a good few minutes. He noticed, later, as he looked in the mirror, that his shirt was damp. He had broken out in a cold sweat.

After a moment, he went and lay down on the bed, and closed his eyes. Schoolboy, he chastised himself. You're behaving like a silly schoolboy. It was true, he was, but he couldn't help himself.

He had never seen a woman who was as beautiful as her. Nor had he ever wanted a woman as much as he wanted Daphne. What was he going to do?

Hugo was startled by his forceful reaction to her. He had only just met her but she had affected him deeply, even though he believed he was too old for her. She was seventeen; he was thirty-two, and a widower, a man of experience. A big age-gap. Also, they were first cousins once removed, although he knew that had no legal bearing on anything in England. Still, the fifteen-year age difference was definitely a stumbling block.

Then there were her feelings. He had fallen instantly for her . . . love at first sight. She seemed hardly aware of him – had been polite, pleasant, and that was all. There had not been a flicker of interest.

She was probably in love with some dashing young man. Probably not, come to think of it. For it was more than likely that Charles had plans for her. She was, after all, a great beauty, and was obviously set to make a brilliant marriage.

Her father would want nothing less than an earl's son. Perhaps Charles already had his sights set on a duke's son. That was the way the Inghams thought and acted. Onwards and upwards. Ambition was endemic.

Hugo sighed to himself. Lady Daphne Ingham was beyond his reach. It would be best if he put her out of his mind, concentrated on buying a fine house and estate in Yorkshire, and focused on his business interests. Yes, that would be the thing to do. And money eased the pain.

There was a lot of excitement in the yellow sitting room. When Cecily arrived it was already half full, and anticipation was high. Everyone wanted to meet Hugo, either for the first time, or to become reunited with their long-lost cousin.

Cecily was thrilled to have been invited by DeLacy, who had been given permission to ask her by the Countess, and Alice had been invited by the Earl.

She looked across at her mother, who was seated next to Daphne. The latter looked as lovely as always; this afternoon she was wearing a delphinium-blue silk afternoon dress, made by Alice, and it matched her eyes.

Automatically, Cecily glanced at Lady Gwendolyn, who was staring at *her*. Great-Aunt Gwendolyn winked, and looked at Daphne, then shook her head.

Cecily had to swallow the laughter rising in her. Lady Gwendolyn was forever chastising the Ingham women for wearing dresses to match their eyes. Cecily thought it was funny, and always had to suppress her laughter when Lady Gwendolyn was on the warpath.

Diedre was sitting with Lady Gwendolyn; DeLacy was standing with Guy and Miles, near the doorway, waiting for Hugo. They had all been anxious to meet him, but he had still not appeared yet.

A moment later, the Earl entered the yellow sitting room, holding Dulcie's hand, and the Countess followed, accompanied by Charlotte Swann. Everyone had arrived. Only Hugo, the guest of honour, was missing.

Suddenly Dulcie broke free of her father's hold, and ran across the room. She came to a standstill in front of Diedre. 'I met Hugo first!' she announced proudly. Although she was afraid of her eldest sister, Dulcie was brave, and could be defiant at times; she was oddly combative for a little girl. Also, she enjoyed making announcements that were challenging.

Diedre merely raised an eyebrow eloquently, muttering offhandedly, 'As if anybody cares.'

Dulcie was instantly offended, and flounced away on her plump little legs, making for Daphne, whom she adored. '*You* are the most beautiful of the big sisters,' she exclaimed in a very loud voice.

Daphne reached for Dulcie, her face soft with love for her

little sister, and she embraced her. 'And you're the most beautiful girl I've ever seen.' Against her hair, she whispered, 'I'm going to give you one of my jewelled tortoiseshell hair slides later, and a new lace hankie.'

'Ooooo, thank you, Daphne.' Lowering her voice, Dulcie confided, 'Diedre's angry because I met Hugo first.'

'Oh, don't worry about that, darling. Just because he chose to meet you first is not your fault.'

Dulcie frowned for a second, and then laughed. 'Oh! I must tell Mama that . . .'

The Earl reclaimed Dulcie, and said, 'You'd better come with me to say hello to Great-Aunt Gwendolyn. You know she enjoys talking to you.'

'Oh yes, let's do that. I have a present for her, Papa.'

The Earl glanced down at Dulcie, frowning. 'Where is it?'

'In my pocket.' She patted the side of her flounced organdie frock, and walked sedately across the room with her father.

'Ah, here you are, Dulcie, and in such a nice party frock – *blue*, of course,' Lady Gwendolyn said, smiling at her, thinking how lucky Charles and Felicity were . . . the four Dees were all lovely, and the two boys were handsome. 'I can understand why everyone says you're like a Botticelli angel,' she added.

'With a will of steel,' Diedre muttered, and got up to go and talk to her mother, who was standing with Charlotte and Cecily near the bay window overlooking the lawns.

The Earl, surprised by this comment, raised a brow and glanced at his aunt. He shrugged, shook his head. 'She just can't resist making that kind of nasty remark,' Charles murmured, sounding slightly put out.

'I know what you mean,' his aunt responded, and wondered if Diedre had inherited that trait from her.

Dulcie said, 'She doesn't like me. I'm a nuisance, the little madam, that's what she says.'

Both Charles and Lady Gwendolyn were taken aback by these comments from the child, and simply stared at each other.

Drawing closer to her great-aunt, Dulcie now gave her a huge smile, and announced, 'I have a present for you.'

'Oh how nice, you're such a darling child. I like presents, you know. I suppose everyone does.'

Reaching into her pocket, Dulcie took out a barley-sugar hard sweet, and handed it to her great-aunt.

Lady Gwendolyn took it gingerly, gazing at it curiously for a moment, detecting bits of fluff and lint stuck to it. It looked to her as if it had been around for days without its paper wrapper. And who knew where, since it was decidedly grubby. 'How kind of you, Dulcie,' Lady Gwendolyn said at last, and smiled at her. She put the sweet in her handbag. 'I'll save it for later,' she explained, 'I don't want it to spoil my afternoon tea.'

'But don't forget the sweetie, will you? I saved it specially for you, Great-Aunt Gwendolyn.'

'I won't. And thank you again. You're very generous.'

Amused, Charles grinned at his aunt, then escorted his youngest child over to her mother, now sitting on the sofa in the bay. He was wondering where Hugo was when he suddenly appeared in the doorway of the yellow sitting room.

'I'm so sorry I'm late!' Hugo exclaimed, glancing around the room, taking in everyone. Some he knew, others he didn't. He went on, 'Well, here I am at last! Hello, everyone!'

They answered 'Hello' in unison, and laughed, and a few clapped as he strolled forward, greeting those he knew with a kiss, or a shake of the hand, and introducing himself to those he didn't know with ease and charm.

He was pleased when he saw Alice Swann, and stopped to speak to her for a few moments. He smiled at Daphne, who was seated next to her, and murmured, 'You look exceptionally beautiful, Daphne.'

She smiled back, 'Thank you, Hugo.'

Hugo felt himself growing hot all over, and he quickly stepped away, heading across the floor to join his aunt. He took charge of himself at once, knowing he must not display any emotions in front of his family, especially if Daphne was present. He had to be calm and collected: the absolute gentleman. Nothing must appear to be improper.

Lady Gwendolyn had a loving smile on her face when he bent down to kiss her cheek, and she squeezed his arm. He sat down on the sofa next to her, and took her hand in his.

There was a tremor of emotion in her voice when she told him, 'Thank God you've come home at last. I've worried about you for years, Hugo.'

'Well, here I am, Aunt Gwen, and glad to be back. I've missed *you* . . . missed everybody, really. But *you* most of all, you know.'

She was unable to speak for a moment, and he noticed the glint of tears in her blue eyes.

He said quietly, 'Before we start catching up, I just want you to know I haven't come here to claim Little Skell Manor. I don't want it; you can live there as long as you want, for the rest of your life, Aunt Gwen.'

'I never thought you were going to turf me out, Hugo. You were the kindest of boys, and I didn't think you'd have changed. I loved you, and I still love you. You're rather like the son I never had. I was devastated when you were sent away. It was unconscionable of your mother. She really was mentally unhinged after Peter drowned. Still, there was no reason to blame you.'

She sighed as she continued. 'I grieved for you, but your father told me he often saw you . . . I knew Ian would never abandon you. He loved you.' She smiled and squeezed his hand. 'Here you are now, and thank you, by the way, for Little Skell Manor. But I never thought you'd want it.'

Hugo was silent for a moment, touched by her words. At last, he said, 'So, tell me everything that's happened since I've been gone.'

Lady Gwendolyn chuckled. 'Not much, darling. I just carry on, potter around, go up to town occasionally, to see friends, have quiet dinners and, of course, I can't do without the theatre. So I'm quite sure you have more to tell me. Oh, and Hugo, I must offer you my deepest condolences. Charles told me you were widowed a year ago. I am so very, very sorry, my dear.'

'Thank you Aunt Gwen. I must admit, it has been hard. Unfortunately, Loretta was ill with consumption, which is why we moved to Zurich, for the mountain air, and the good sanatoriums.' He let out a sigh. 'She was too far gone, too ill to get better.'

He shifted slightly on the sofa, and looked off into the distance. 'I realized how lonely I was in Zurich, and one day I just knew I had to live in England again. It was such a strong desire that I finally made up my mind to come home . . . you see, I yearned for my own people, for all of you, and for this Yorkshire land I know so well.'

Later, once afternoon tea was over, Charlotte, Alice and Cecily walked back to Little Skell village together, taking the path through the park.

At one moment, Alice said, 'Hugo wants to buy a property here, as close to Cavendon as possible. But there isn't anything around, at least not for sale.'

'He told me the same thing,' Charlotte remarked. 'I mentioned a couple of estates near Middleham, but he wasn't interested.'

'I know he wants to settle in Yorkshire, he told me so. Now that he's widowed, he's lonely. He wishes to be with his own people,' Alice said. 'In the last year he's yearned for Yorkshire, so he said.'

Charlotte nodded. 'Maybe he wants to get married again. After all, he's only thirty-two. He's good looking, very eligible, and extremely successful in business.' She suddenly began to laugh. 'He's not only looking for a house, but a wife most probably.'

Cecily pricked up her ears, and looking at her mother, she said, 'I think he's found her already.'

Alice was taken aback. She came to a halt, staring at her daughter. 'What do you mean?'

'I think Hugo has found someone to be his wife.'

'Don't be so silly! He's only been here for a day!' Alice exclaimed.

'Yes, I know that, Mam, but I watched him, and he couldn't take his eyes off her. You were all talking to each other, eating, and mingling. I was sitting alone on the seat in the other bay window. I just sat and watched everyone, all of you. But it was Hugo I watched most because, whenever he thought no one would notice, he was staring at her . . . sort of . . . longingly.'

'But *who* was he staring at?' Charlotte asked, sounding a little impatient.

'Daphne . . .'

Charlotte was flabbergasted, and she exchanged a glance with Alice, who was also shocked.

There was a small silence.

Cecily broke the silence, when she cried, 'Don't you believe me, Mam? I'm not inventing it. I'm not. I'm not!'

'Yes, yes, I do believe you,' Alice was quick to answer, giving Charlotte a sideways glance, raising a brow. 'I just don't know how I could have missed his interest in her, that's all.'

'I do. He was very . . . clever about it, throwing her a glance, staring, eyeing her, sort of . . . *secretly*,' Cecily explained.

'Do you mean surreptitiously?' Charlotte asked.

'Yes, that's the word, Aunt Charlotte.'

'Did Daphne notice, do you think?' Alice wondered out loud.

Cecily shrugged. 'I'm not sure . . . maybe. No, I don't think so. She's used to people staring at her, because she's so beautiful. She probably didn't think anything about it, even if she did notice – just took it for granted, that's all.'

'And why did *you* notice so particularly, Cecily? What made you say Hugo might have found a wife already?' Charlotte asked softly.

Cecily stared at her great-aunt, whom she knew was very clever. After all, she'd worked for the 5th Earl for twenty years, and was considered very intelligent.

Better be careful, Cecily warned herself, and thought very hard. She cast her mind back to the tea; in her mind's eye, she pictured the yellow sitting room, Daphne in the blue dress, sitting with Alice. And Hugo. Handsome. Charming. Moving around the room. She focused on him intently, and closed her eyes, and when she opened them, she said, 'It was written all over his face.'

'What was?' Charlotte asked. Although she thought she knew what Cecily meant, she needed to probe deeper, to be sure.

'What he *felt*,' Cecily murmured. 'It was . . . like a *longing* . . .' She shook her head. 'I don't know how to describe it, not really.'

'I do,' Charlotte said softly, turning her gaze on Alice. 'I believe it's called love at first sight.'

Alice nodded. 'Perhaps,' she said noncommittally, but her mind was racing.

Charlotte was silent. She began walking again, and Alice and Cecily kept up with her until they arrived in the village. Once her house came into view, Charlotte said, 'I'd like you to come inside for a moment, Alice, and you too, Cecily.'

They did as she asked.

Charlotte led them into her sitting room overlooking the garden, and after turning on a couple of table lamps, she said, 'Please sit down for a moment. I won't keep you very long.'

Alice said, 'It's all right, Charlotte, we have plenty of time.'

Once Alice and Cecily were settled on the sofa, Charlotte took the chair opposite. Leaning forward intently, she looked from Alice to Cecily, and said quietly, 'I believe you, Cecily, because I know you are extremely observant. What you saw on Hugo's face was emotion . . . he probably is unusually attracted to Daphne.'

Cecily nodded. 'I know he is,' she asserted confidently.

'You cannot tell anyone what you've just told me and your mother. This must remain a secret. It must be our secret.'

'Oh,' Cecily said, sounding puzzled, then asked, 'Why?'

'At this moment, Daphne Ingham has to be protected. By the Swanns. Don't ask me why, because I cannot tell you. Eventually you will know, because your mother and I may well need your help. Do you understand?'

'You mean I can't tell Miles or DeLacy that I saw Hugo ogling Daphne all the time?'

'That is correct.'

'But they're Inghams.'

'That does not come into play here,' Charlotte responded adamantly. 'And if they noticed anything, and mention it to you, dismiss the idea as silly. What you told us about Hugo is our secret. No one else must know. Tell no one. Trust no one. Trust only the Swanns. You do understand this, don't you, Cecily?'

Cecily realized that her aunt was in deadly earnest, and extremely serious. She said, 'I understand that I cannot tell anyone anything. And I know what I saw must be a secret.'

'Correct. You know the motto? The oath?'

'Yes.'

'You will take it now, for the first time. And you will honour it all your life.'

'Yes, I will.' Cecily stretched out her arm and made a fist. 'Loyalty binds me,' she said.

Charlotte stiffened her arm, clenched her fist and put her hand on top of Cecily's. 'Loyalty binds me,' she repeated. Alice followed suit, and did exactly the same thing.

'It is done,' Charlotte said. 'You are sworn to protect the Inghams. You must never fail. No Swann ever has.'

It was twilight when Charlotte walked across the street to speak to Alice. She was opening the white garden gate when Alice appeared on the doorstep of her house, and walked down the path to meet her.

Charlotte said, 'I've been thinking . . . I believe it would be better for the Swanns to stay on the sidelines for the moment.'

'I'm not sure I understand,' Alice said, leaning against the gate.

'Ceci said that Hugo was ogling Daphne – that was the word she used. It doesn't really mean anything, does it? Men ogle women all the time.'

'That's true . . . you said you thought it was love at first sight, though,' Alice remarked, giving her a very direct look.

'Yes, because Ceci said Hugo had a look of *longing* on his face. Maybe I shouldn't have jumped to conclusions.'

Alice bit her lip. 'I understand, but you know she can't get involved with him on any level, Charlotte, not in her condition. My God, what if he somehow found out . . . discovered our secret? That would be disastrous!'

'You're up at the house all the time, handling the clothes, and I shall be there more often. Charlie asked me to do some secretarial work for him. We'll just have to keep our eyes wide open, Alice, and mostly focused on Daphne.'

'Yes, you're right. It's the only thing we can do really.'

A reflective look crossed Charlotte's face, and she said quietly,

'When I had a problem, or David had a problem, and we couldn't solve it, he'd just shrug and say, 'Life usually takes care of itself.' And in this instance, I suppose we must have that same attitude. Let's just leave it alone, and let life take care of itself.'

Alice reached out, touched her arm affectionately. 'That's right, we just have to wait and see what happens. You could be right: maybe it *was* love at first sight. Then we'll be in a pickle, won't we?'

Charlotte shook her head. 'Not necessarily,' she murmured, and gave Alice a knowing look.

TWENTY-SIX

F elicity knew within the first few minutes that the supper dance was going to be a great success. First her three eldest daughters, and then her two sons, had exclaimed about the beauty of the rooms in the South Wing as they arrived in the pale green drawing room. And now Hugo was doing exactly the same.

'I don't know how you managed to do it, but you've turned this into a fantastic garden, Felicity,' Hugo said, glancing around. 'It's quite magical, Charles, isn't it? And so are the other two rooms.'

Her husband smiled, nodded and looked pleased, but made no comment, because he knew as well as she did that she had not had anything to do with it.

Swiftly, Felicity explained, 'I can't take any bows, Hugo, and neither can Charles, for that matter. Hanson and Mrs Thwaites had the foresight to clear the three main public rooms. They moved some pieces of furniture into various bedrooms, and then the gardeners took over. They brought in the plants and flowers decorating this room, and the pink dining room and the blue drawing room as well.'

'And that room looks fantastic, too, Mama,' Guy interjected. 'It never occurred to me that it could be turned into a ballroom. But it works perfectly. It's just the right size. Now we'll know for the next time.'

Felicity smiled. 'Thank you but, as I said, I can't take any accolades this time.'

Diedre had been glancing around for a moment or two, and now she said, 'I love the way this room looks, Mama. It's like a . . . painting, yes, that's it. All the colours work together. The pink peonies, the white roses, the blue delphiniums and foxgloves all blend well together. It's very artistically done. I didn't think Bill Swann had that kind of talent. I know he's the head landscape gardener, but this is . . .' Her voice trailed off when she saw her father staring at her curiously, and frowning.

Charles said, 'Bill is certainly a good head gardener, but this room was created by a real artist. Charlotte Swann designed this. I suddenly remembered the other day that she often used to put together gorgeous indoor gardens for my father when he was alive, and when I asked her to do the same for me, Charlotte got to work immediately. And you're right, Diedre, it is like a painting.'

'Oh my goodness!' Daphne exclaimed, and they all followed her gaze, saw Dulcie standing in the doorway in her nightgown, her face covered in chocolate, and her hands as well.

'I've come to the party,' she said, and smiled at them.

Felicity took a step forward and stopped, looking down at the lavender chiffon gown she was wearing, thinking of the chocolate on her child. Then she shook her head as she saw DeLacy make a move to hurry to Dulcie. 'Don't go to her,' she said.

'We've either got the greatest escape artist in the world, or we need a new nanny,' Charles exclaimed, glancing at Miles. 'Go and find Miss Carlton, please, and ask her to come for Dulcie.'

'Why don't I just take her to Nanny?' Miles suggested.

'Because somehow she'll manage to get chocolate all over your white shirt and tie,' Charles explained, and shook his head, wondering how Dulcie had found her way to the South Wing.

At this moment, much to everyone's relief, Maureen Carlton, the nanny, appeared, looking flustered and upset. 'I'm so sorry, Your Ladyship,' she said, addressing Felicity. 'I turned my back for a moment and she managed, somehow, to vanish. I'm so very sorry. Really so sorry.'

'It's all right, Nanny,' Felicity answered in a low voice. 'But I think it would be a good idea to scoop her up right now and take her back to the nursery. Guests are about to arrive at any moment.'

'Yes, m'lady,' the young woman answered, and swept Dulcie up into her arms; she disappeared as fast as she could.

It was Hugo who broke the silence when he started to chuckle, and soon they were all laughing.

'Thank goodness you didn't go and pick her up, DeLacy,' Miles said. 'Your rose chiffon frock would have been ruined.'

The thought of another ruined frock made DeLacy wince, and she remained silent. The ink-stained white dress would haunt her forever.

Hugo said, 'One must admit, she is rather adorable, though.'

Charles laughed. 'True. And I must admit, I dread to think what she will be like when she's fifteen, and not five.'

'Still a little madam, I've no doubt,' Diedre muttered.

Great-Aunt Gwendolyn, who was standing next to her, whispered, 'Sshhhh, sshhhhh,' and drew her across the room towards a bank of lilies.

Hugo heard Diedre, and he quickly jumped into the conversation when he said, 'I must compliment you, Aunt Gwen, you do look wonderful in your royal purple tonight. So do all of you, ladies. Very beautiful indeed.'

His eyes lingered a moment too long on Daphne, who was wearing the extraordinary evening gown she'd tried on in May: a shimmering sliver of sea colours, made up entirely of blue, green and turquoise beads. Her beauty was incomparable.

Suddenly feeling self-conscious, he walked swiftly across the room to Felicity, and took hold of her hand, kissing it. 'You're as lovely as you were sixteen years ago; Charles is an awfully lucky man, Felicity, awfully lucky indeed. How I envy him.'

She smiled and touched his arm in an affectionate manner, answered in her low, soft voice, 'Thank you, Hugo. You always were very gallant. Hopefully you'll meet a fine woman one day who will become a lovely companion – and your wife, perhaps.'

'I hope so, yes.'

At this moment Hanson came in, accompanied by two footmen.

Charles looked across at him questioningly. 'Are the guests arriving?'

'Yes, my lord, they are. And all at once, it seems.'

Felicity sat with Lady Gwendolyn on a sofa at one end of the blue sitting room, which had been transformed into a ballroom.

Furniture had been moved around so that it encircled the room. It was set against the walls, and the large Persian rug had been removed to reveal a wood floor. An array of potted palms, flowering shrubs and urns of flowers gave the room a garden feeling, as in the pale green drawing room and the rose-pink dining room.

'The supper was particularly delicious,' Aunt Gwendolyn said, turning to Felicity, giving her a warm smile. 'I must say Cook outdid herself tonight. The salmon mousse was perfect, and I loved the tiny lamb chops. As for the desserts, they were mouth-watering.'

'Everything *was* delicious,' Felicity agreed. 'And Cook did have the foresight and experience to get in extra help from the village. So it all went smoothly. Altogether, we were sixty-two people at supper, you know. Quite a lot to cook for.'

'And most of them now appear to be dancing and having a grand time. Where did you find this rather good little orchestra?'

'Hanson discovered them in Harrogate – they are good, I agree with you.'

'Daphne has outshone herself tonight, Felicity,' Gwendolyn said admiringly. 'She looks wonderful, and her dress has caused quite a sensation. She only has to breathe and it shimmers. And this is certainly one time I'm not going to complain that it's blue.'

Felicity shot back, 'You can't, because it's also got green and turquoise beads in it. It was mine, you know. I had it made in Paris. I always thought it was a rather special piece of *haute couture*, and I kept it for that reason. Luckily, it fitted Daphne perfectly.'

Both women gazed at Daphne dancing with her father. Charles enjoyed dancing, and it showed. He moved around the ballroom gracefully, and Daphne was in perfect step with him. Because they were tall, they looked wonderful together, and seemed to be enjoying themselves.

A silence fell between the two women, and Felicity fell down into her thoughts. Her eyes were focused on Daphne, and for a few moments she was totally mesmerized by the girl's incredible beauty. Unexpectedly, her heart clenched when she thought of the rape, and her daughter's terrible dilemma. *Their dilemma.* They were in this together, the three of them. She was also thankful the Swanns were in the background, to help in any way they could. Daphne needed as much support as possible, and they would all give it to her, get her through. Hopefully her reputation would not be damaged in any way, and that she would be able to pick up her life in the early part of 1914.

A rush of overwhelming guilt about many things made Felicity slide further down into herself. This awful guilt invaded her frequently, because she knew she had been overly preoccupied with her sister's illness, and another dire and disturbing problem. She had neglected her family. And yet deep inside she knew she couldn't have prevented the rape; she hadn't been outside in the bluebell woods when Daphne had been so brutally attacked.

She and Charles had seized on the suggestion that Julian Torbett was to blame, and Daphne had done nothing to dissuade them. And yet Felicity had her doubts, and so did Charles. She had always thought Julian was a bit wishy-washy, and slightly feminine in certain ways.

She stifled a sigh. And what did it matter now? Julian was dead. And if it was some other man who had assaulted her, he was long gone. Far away.

In her opinion, her daughter might easily have been spotted by a poacher, a stranger on the estate . . .

Aunt Gwendolyn was saying something to her, and Felicity let the thought go.

'I'm sorry, my dear, I didn't quite catch that,' she said, turning to Gwendolyn.

'I was asking you if you thought Diedre might be unhappy in some way?'

Frowning, Felicity asked, 'Why do you say that?'

'It's just that she has a way of saying odd things.' Lady Gwendolyn lowered her voice. 'Rather mean things. And often people do that when they are discontented.'

'She's always been a little acerbic, you know: that's just her way.'

Lady Gwendolyn gave Felicity a long, pointed look and said,

'I hope it isn't a trait she has inherited from me. I've always been rather acerbic myself, and often had my knuckles rapped for it, I might add.'

Before Felicity could answer, Hugo appeared in front of them, looking impossibly handsome in his white tie and tails. 'Can I steal my aunt away, Felicity?'

'Of course,' she answered, and smiled as he led Gwendolyn onto the dance floor. She couldn't help thinking how graceful and elegant Gwendolyn looked in her purple evening gown and her amazing array of diamonds. Her back was straight and she stepped out with confidence, held in the arms of her nephew.

I hope I'm like her when I'm seventy-two, Felicity thought, and slipped back into her distressing ruminations. One of her concerns was keeping her own secret, as well as the secret about Daphne's pregnancy. She realized much of that would have to do with Daphne's clothes. They would conceal a lot. Tonight had been the best time for her to wear the slender column of beads, whilst she was still as thin as a reed.

'Mama, may I have this dance, please?' Guy said, stepping closer to her, offering her his hand.

'But of course, I'd love it,' she replied, and stood up, letting him lead her onto the floor and whirl her into a waltz.

Hugo found he could not sleep. He had tossed and turned in his bed for two hours, and finally, in frustration, he got up, put on his dressing gown and slippers, and went downstairs to the library. After switching on the light, he went over to the drinks table, and poured himself a large cognac.

After returning to his bedroom, he sat down near a window and sipped the brandy, thinking about Daphne. He was a sophisticated man of the world, and he had certainly behaved as one tonight. He had been the epitome of polished charm and good manners, attentive to all the women, and not only to Daphne. He had danced with them and with her. She had been pleasant and warm. And he had been totally in control of himself. No more schoolboy reactions. However, he did react to her, although he did not let it show. He *had* fallen in love with her, and he wanted her for the rest of his life.

Hugo was smart enough to know the situation had to be handled properly and with discretion. He would speak to Charles within the next few days, to ascertain what the situation was with his daughter. He needed to know if she was spoken for.

After another few swallows of the brandy, Hugo stood up to take off his dressing gown. As he did so, he happened to glance out of the window, and then stepped closer. He couldn't believe what he was seeing. There were flames in the stable block. *A fire.* My God, the horses, he thought, and rushed out of his room to raise the alarm.

TWENTY-SEVEN

H ugo was horrified when he reached the stable block. The first stall, with Diedre's brass nameplate on it, was empty except for bales of hay. It was the hay that was burning furiously, the flames shooting up into the night sky, turning it red.

In the stall next to it, Daphne's horse, Greensleeves, was panicked, rearing up on her hind legs, thrashing at the stall door with her front hooves. The animal was terrified, and Hugo knew he must release it at once. The horse's nostrils were flaring, and there was froth round her mouth.

In the process of trying to lift the latch, Hugo burnt his fingers on the hot metal, but hardly noticed. Someone had wedged a piece of wood behind the latch to keep it in place. Unable to move the wood, Hugo pulled off a shoe, and began striking at the latch with the heel, until it flew up and the door sprang open. Swiftly, Hugo stepped to one side as Greensleeves galloped out furiously and headed down the yard towards the meadows.

Immediately, Hugo ran to the next stall where DeLacy's horse,

Dreamer, was also panicked and rearing up on its back legs. He released the latch, opened the door and another horse sped away, heading after Greensleeves.

As he moved on to the third stall, he heard Charles shouting, 'Miles, get the fire extinguishers! Guy, pull out the pump and hose. We've got to stop the fire spreading! Walter, help him.'

Charles ran up to Hugo. 'Thanks for that warning. If you hadn't seen the blaze, all of this would have soon burnt to the ground.'

'I couldn't sleep, and got up. Lucky, wasn't it? When I saw the flames, everything I knew from my childhood rushed back to me. I knew I had to get here as fast as possible to save the horses.'

Charles nodded, and then, when he saw Hanson running into the yard, followed by two footmen, he cried, 'Please rescue Dulcie's little Shetland pony in the stall here, Hugo. I'll get Hanson and the footmen to free the horses on the other side of the yard. We must move them into the meadows for their safety.'

'Shall I take the pony into the fields?' Hugo asked.

'Good idea,' Charles shouted over his shoulder, already on his way to give Hanson and the footmen their instructions.

Within three hours, all of the flames had died down, most of the stalls had been hosed and cleaned out, and burnt and wet hay removed. Most importantly, none of the horses had been injured in any way.

The stable boys, who lived in the annexe near the estate offices at the far end of the stable block, had arrived soon after the fire started. Awakened by the furore, they had quickly come tumbling and running onto the scene. And they had done their fair share of work. Eventually, the horses had been led back to the yard, carefully examined, and then put in their stalls where they were watered and fed.

As the stable lads sat drinking their mugs of hot sweet tea and eating bacon sandwiches, they talked among themselves, wondering aloud how the fire had started. It had been huge. Hanson, Walter and the two footmen were doing the same thing in the servants' hall. The fire was a mystery to them all; and therefore it stayed in their minds.

Once they had cleaned themselves, and changed their clothes, Charles, Guy and Miles went down to the dining room for breakfast, where they found Hugo nursing a burnt hand. He had wrapped a towel around his fingers, but he kept anxiously looking at the burns, a frown on his face.

'Come on, old chap, let me take a look at that hand,' Charles said, striding over to his cousin at the other side of the dining table.

'It's nothing serious, Charles, but it does sting a bit, I must admit.' He lifted the towel.

Charles nodded. 'Wilson, Felicity's lady's maid, is very good at first-aid. Miles, do me a favour and go down to the kitchen. Ask Wilson to please come up and look at Hugo's hand. I think she will have the right salve and a bandage.'

'Right away, Papa.'

'You'll be fine in a couple of days,' Charles murmured. 'They're only surface burns. However, you were lucky.'

Hugo merely nodded. After a moment, he said, 'I can't fathom how that fire started . . . that hay wasn't merely smouldering, it was really burning . . . like a great bonfire. You don't think it was arson, do you?'

For a moment Charles was startled, and then he sat up

straighter, staring at Hugo. 'It hadn't crossed my mind. Why do you bring it up?'

'I thought of it when I was changing in my room. You see, Charles, I burnt my fingers on the metal latch, which was hot from the fire. The latch on the stall door wouldn't open, and when I looked closer I saw a piece of wood was wedged behind the latch. I had to take off my shoe and use it as a hammer to get the wood out. Only then could I open the stall door.'

Charles gazed at him. A worried expression had now settled on his face. His brows drew together in a frown, and he shook his head. 'Now why would anybody do that? A latch doesn't have to be so tightly shut. The horse isn't going to leave the stall. And you of all people know that; you spent most of your early years in the yard of your father's stud in Middleham.'

'That's why I wondered about the wedge. Which then led me to the thought of arson. Do you think you ought to call the police?'

'Perhaps I'd better, if only because of the insurance. Anyway, a fire must be reported.'

TWENTY-EIGHT

Inspector Michael Armitage of the West Riding Police and his sidekick, Sergeant Tim Pollard, were standing in the stable yard with the Earl of Mowbray, surveying the stall where the fire had started.

'I wasn't the first on the scene, Inspector,' Charles explained. 'It was my cousin, Hugo Stanton. He was the one who saw the flames from his bedroom window, and he literally banged on my door, shouted *fire*, and ran straight out here. Ah, here he is now.'

When Hugo reached them, Charles introduced the three men to each other, and said to Hugo, 'I was just explaining that you were the first on the scene.'

'That's right,' Hugo agreed. 'This particular stall was on fire – or rather, I should say, a large bale of hay was burning furiously. Fortunately, the stall was empty. But there was a horse in the adjoining stall.'

'And so you released the horse before doing anything else, am I right about that Mr Stanton?'

'You are, Inspector. Greensleeves, the horse in this stall . . .' He moved towards the second stall, indicated it, and continued,

'The horse had been spooked; she was up on her hind legs, frightened out of her wits.'

He told the inspector how he had discovered a piece of wood wedged behind the latch, and had knocked it out with his shoe. 'I didn't quite understand why it was there, since a horse isn't going to move out of a stall, even if the door is open. I grew up in a professional yard, my father's, and naturally I was puzzled. I suddenly wondered if the fire had been caused by arson. Perhaps someone with a grudge against the family? A person who had purposely trapped that horse.'

'I see what you mean. Tell me, Mr Stanton, did you smell anything when you arrived. Petrol, perhaps? Anything like that?'

'No, nothing. Just the stench of burning hay. Do you agree with me that it might have been arson, Inspector?'

'In one sense I do, because I can't quite fathom how hay would burst into flames of its own accord. Someone might have been out here in the stables, of course, having a smoke, and thrown the match away. Carelessly. But then I don't think a smouldering match would start that kind of huge fire.' He turned to the Earl, and said, 'From what you told me earlier, it was a big blaze before you got here, Lord Mowbray.'

'Almost out of hand, and the second stall had already caught fire when I arrived with Walter Swann, my valet, and my sons. They tackled the fire with extinguishers and the water pumps, and when the butler and the footmen came we were able to control it.'

'No strangers seen on the property, Lord Mowbray?'

Charles shook his head. 'Not the kind you mean, Inspector. However, we gave a supper dance last night, and we did have a number of guests. Approximately fifty friends. Naturally they came here in chauffeur-driven cars.'

'So, in a way, there *were* strangers on the estate. The chauffeurs,' Inspector Armitage asserted.

'That's right,' Charles replied. 'But I seriously doubt that one of them came into the stable block and started a fire.'

'Where were the motorcars parked, m'lord?' Sergeant Pollard asked politely.

'Mostly at the front of the house, and down the front drive. However, there were fewer cars than you might think. You see, our fifty guests were mostly made up of married couples, and some brought their daughters. So most of the motorcars contained a number of people.'

'I understand, m'lord,' Pollard answered.

Charles and Hugo walked around the yard with the two policemen, answering any questions they asked. But it was soon obvious that the professionals were at a dead end, just as Charles and Hugo had been earlier that morning. Quite simply, there were no real clues that could point to arson. How the fire had started *was* a mystery, as it had been right from the beginning.

Hugo was sitting on the terrace, reading *The Times*, when suddenly Daphne was standing there next to him, as if she had walked up to him in silken slippers, so quietly had she arrived.

'I hope I'm not interrupting you, Hugo,' she said in her soft, light voice.

'No, no, not at all,' he answered, putting the paper down, pushing himself to his feet.

'I just wanted to thank you again for saving Greensleeves. Father gave her to me, and I love her,' Daphne explained, and then glanced at his bandaged left hand. 'Does it hurt very much?'

He shook his head. 'No, just a few burned fingers, nothing too bad. They'll be healed in a couple of days, according to Doctor Shawcross. Please, sit down for a moment, won't you?'

Smiling at him, she did so, settling back in the chair next to his. 'I am in your debt. If ever you need anything, you must let me know.'

I need you. Marry me. Be my wife . . . those were the sudden thoughts running through his head, but he did not turn them into words. Instead he said, 'There is one thing I would like you to help me with, Daphne.'

She leaned forward slightly, and said swiftly, 'Please, tell me what it is. Of course I'll help you, Hugo.'

The scent of her freshly washed golden hair, the hint of roses emanating from her skin, the very closeness of her, made him feel weak. If he had had to stand up at this moment, he knew he wouldn't have been able to. He was also unable to speak. He simply stared into her deep blue eyes, smiling at her, and feeling dizzy, almost lightheaded.

'What is it?' she asked. 'Are you all right?'

He nodded and, before he could stop himself, blurted out, 'It's you, Daphne. You're the most beautiful woman I've ever set eyes on.' A small smile flickered on his mouth; lifting his hands in a helpless gesture, he said in a jocular manner, 'I am your devoted slave and always will be.'

His joking tone and his exaggerated words made her laugh out loud, and she exclaimed, 'Oh don't be silly, Hugo! I'm just another girl, and there are several of us in this house.'

Leaning towards her, wanting to breathe in the intoxicating scent of her yet again, he said, 'I'll tell you a secret . . . it's Dulcie who's really enslaved me.'

This comment made her laugh even more, and then she murmured, 'You haven't told me what you want me to help you with.'

'Ah yes, that's perfectly true.' Adopting a more serious tone, he explained, 'Last night Aunt Gwendolyn told me there is a house I should see nearby, that I should go there this afternoon. And I was wondering if you would accompany me? I think a second pair of eyes are always most helpful, especially when looking at bricks and mortar. Don't you agree?'

'I do indeed, and I will certainly come with you. What is it called?'

'Whernside House. It was the home of Lady Muschamp, widow of a local politician and Member of Parliament. She died, a few months ago. Her daughter told Aunt Gwendolyn she would sell to me, if I wanted it.'

Daphne had a beatific expression on her face when she said, 'I have only been there twice, but it is one of the most beautiful houses in Yorkshire. Not too far away from Cavendon, about twenty minutes in the motorcar. Have you checked that Gregg can take you there this afternoon?'

'I have indeed. I also mentioned it to your father, and he told me he will be here all day. Because of the fire, and other matters he has to attend to. What time shall we plan to go there, Daphne?'

'Immediately after lunch, I think. I know you're going to fall in love with it, Hugo.'

I'm already in love. With you. Forever, he thought, but did not utter a word. He was filled with longing for her, wanted to hold her to him, keep her close, keep her safe. Make her his. Stop it, he told himself sternly. Get a hold of yourself. And he did.

They sat on the terrace chatting casually, totally at ease with each other. And at one moment, Daphne couldn't help thinking what a truly lovely man he was. Most engaging.

TWENTY-NINE

Downstairs in the kitchen, there was an edginess in the air. Cook was well aware of this, and understood. The fire had upset everyone, and most of the staff had been up half the night, as she had herself. What an end to the gorgeous supper dance.

The mystery of how the fire had started was worrying, and she had already heard whispers and bits of gossipy talk about arson.

Now who would want to purposely set fire to the stable block and put those beautiful animals at risk? Only a maniac. Or somebody who harboured hatred for the family.

The latter did not seem possible to her. The Earl was a fine man, a good employer, loyal to his workers. And he was honest, straightforward and compassionate, felt responsible for everyone who worked on the estate, and those who lived in the villages of Little Skell, Mowbray and High Clough. There wasn't a better man alive, in her opinion, and Hanson and Mrs Thwaites agreed with her, as did Olive Wilson, the Countess's maid.

They were the long-time employees, who understood that

Cavendon was a superior place to be in service. The family behaved impeccably, and never gave the staff problems. Tempers and tantrums were unheard of, unless little Dulcie was carrying on.

It was Mrs Thwaites who squashed the idea that arson was involved, because she said there was no one alive who could possibly hold a grudge against Lord Mowbray.

They had gone along with her, put the matter to one side. But there were mutterings amongst the maids and the footmen; although Nell Jackson had noticed that Peggy Swift and Gordon Lane were quiet on the subject, attending to their duties efficiently and in silence.

Cook knew Malcolm Smith was a troublemaker, a bit of a rabble-rouser, and that he had influence over Mary Incé and Elsie Roland, who seemed to think he was a matinée idol who had stepped off the London stage and into their midst, just to entertain them.

Hearing a small mewling sound, Cook now turned away from the stove, where she was boiling pots of leeks and potatoes for a vichyssoise soup, and spotted Polly standing near the pantry door, weeping.

Hurrying over to the little kitchen maid, she looked down at her and said in a kindly tone, 'Whatever is it, Polly? What's upset yer?'

'It's Malcolm. He says t'house is goin' ter burn ter cinders next. When we be asleep. Is it?'

'No, it's not. Malcolm's daft. Wait till I see him – he'll soon know wot's wot around here. Come on, sit down, and I'll get yer a glass of lemonade.'

Several moments later the footman came into the kitchen carrying several silver trays, which he placed at the end of the long kitchen table. He was turning to leave, when Cook said, 'A word, Malcolm, if yer don't mind.'

He swung to face her, grumbling in a surly voice, 'I do mind.

Hanson's on me back. He needs me upstairs. I don't have time to mess around here.'

Nell Jackson moved across the kitchen floor at great speed and stood looking up at the footman, her face set in grim lines. 'Listen ter me, my lad. And that's all yer are, just a lad. So drop the airs and graces. If yer don't stop scaring Polly, I'll have yer guts for garters. Worse, I'll tell Hanson, then he'll *really* be on yer back. Then you'll know what trouble is. Leave the little one alone, or yer'll be sorry, my lad.'

'Who the hell do yer think yer are?' Malcolm growled in an angry voice, his face suddenly flushing. 'Yer just a cook. I'll do what I want, when I want to do it.'

'You certainly will not. Not here. This bit of Cavendon Hall is *my* domain, and I run it. I make the rules. Don't ever think otherwise. Go on, do what yer have ter do, but leave the little lass alone in future. *Understand*?'

Still bright red in the face, the footman left, ignoring Elsie and Mary who were coming down the stairs. They were giggling when they walked into the kitchen, but immediately sobered when they saw the stern look on Cook's face.

Cook paid no attention to them. Instead, she went over to her small desk, picked up the menu the Countess had made yesterday for today's lunch. First course, vichyssoise cold soup. Second course, cold poached salmon with mayonnaise and potato salad, and for dessert, a summer pudding made of red fruits with clotted cream. She nodded to herself. It was a lovely lunch for a warm day. Good choices.

Upstairs in the dining room, Gordon Lane glanced up and down. When he saw that he and Peggy were alone, he hurried over to her. 'What sort of questions did Inspector Armitage ask you, Peg?'

'He was mostly interested in trespassers on the property, any strangers loitering. I told him I hadn't seen anybody.'

'You didn't mention the woods then? The night we heard someone rattling around. You know – the Peeping Tom, you called him.'

'I didn't. We'd decided to keep quiet about that. You remember, don't you? We'd have been in trouble with Hanson if he'd known we'd been out that night, and we'd still be in trouble if word got about.'

Gordon nodded. 'I know, it's against the rules of the house. Anyway, the inspector asked me the same thing. *Arson*. That's what they've been thinking. The bobbies, I mean.'

'The bobbies might be right, Gordon. I grew up on a farm, and I've never seen a bale of hay catch fire unless a match has been put to it.'

Peggy stopped abruptly when she saw Hanson hurrying into the butler's pantry, just outside the dining room. Immediately she picked up some service plates and started to place them around the table.

Gordon took his soft, white glass cloth and began to polish a crystal wine glass.

After Hanson had uncorked a bottle of good white wine, a Pouilly Fuissé, to let it breathe, he walked into the dining room. 'Thank you, Lane, and you too, Swift. You've both carried out your duties in a most appropriate manner. Anyway, no trespassers have been seen, according to the inspector, so we must assume the fire was an accident.'

Peggy was silent, wondering if he was correct.

Gordon said in a quiet voice, 'You know something, Mr Hanson, one of the chauffeurs might have gone to the stable yard for a smoke. It was a long night. Maybe a smoker was gagging for a cig, had one, then threw the tab end away when it was still alight.' Gordon shrugged. 'You never know what people can do. Careless, that they are.'

Hanson ignored these words. He went over to the table, surveyed it with an eagle eye, then nodded in approval. 'Nine for lunch, Lane, so you and Smith will have to be on your toes.'

'Yes, sir,' Gordon answered, glad that he was in the butler's good books at the moment.

Walter Swann was restoring order in one of the Earl's wardrobes in the dressing room when Olive Wilson poked her head around the door.

Walter smiled the moment he saw her laughing green eyes, bright auburn hair and cheeky grin.

'Can I come in?' she asked.

Walter nodded. He liked Olive. They had always worked well together and she was reliable and diligent. Furthermore, she didn't have one bad bone in her body.

'I need to be filled in,' Olive explained, slipping into the room.

'What do you mean?' Walter asked, a brow lifting.

'I'm curious . . . what's been happening while I've been in London?'

'As you know, Mr Hugo finally came back, and he's had a very warm welcome. The most tragic thing is that the Countess's sister is very ill. I'm sure you know that, Olive. The Countess must have told you already.'

'Yes, she has, and it's very sad indeed. Her ladyship indicated to me that her sister doesn't have much time left on this earth.'

'So I've heard.' Walter carried a blue suit to the window, where the light was better, to inspect it. He said carefully, 'No other news, though, all has been normal. How was London?'

'I didn't get to see much of the city, I'm afraid. I was stuck in Croydon. After burying Mum, I had a lot to deal with – selling her house, all that sort of stuff. But her affairs weren't too complicated, after all. And to be honest I was pleasantly surprised by the legacy she left me.'

'A windfall?' Walter said, smiling at her.

'Yes, and a good one.'

'Dare I ask how your chap is, Olive? Mr Dayton?'

There was a moment of silence, and then Olive said in a low, sad voice, 'You'll never believe this, Walter. Ted left me. He ran away. With a married woman. They went to Canada . . . emigrated.'

Walter was flabbergasted, and couldn't speak for a moment. Then he said, 'What a rotten thing to do. I'm sorry, Olive, very sorry. You must be really upset.'

'No, I'm not, to tell you the truth, Walter. I'm relieved, actually. Can you imagine if we'd been married? Since we're not, I can say good riddance to bad rubbish. And mean it.'

Thirty

The house was Georgian. It had been built over two hundred and fifty years ago, and it was beautiful. It was designed in the style of Andrea Palladio, the great Italian architect, and was the perfect Palladian villa, standing on top of a small hill. Immediately below the house there was a man-made ornamental lake, in which was reflected an image of the house.

'How clever they were, those architects of the seventeenth and eighteenth centuries,' Hugo said as he and Daphne walked around the lake. 'They usually put a great house on top of a hill, if the topography was correct, and then made a lake to create a reflection, a mirror image. A bit of clever trickery. Two houses for the price of one. Well, let's say a house and the perfect image of it.' He laughed and added, 'So imaginative.'

Daphne looked closely at Hugo, thinking how intelligent he was. She had never heard anyone say this before about Whernside House. People only ever talked about the beauty of the interiors. She told him this, and went on, 'The rooms are lovely, perfectly proportioned, spacious and airy, but the outside is important too, isn't it?'

'Absolutely, and especially for me,' Hugo confided. 'I love an English park like Cavendon, and this park is very similar, although not as large. Let's go inside, shall we? I can't wait to see what's behind those walls. Maybe this place will be my new home.'

Together they walked the short distance up the hill, and were met on the terrace by the caretaker, Mrs Dodie Grant. 'The park's gorgeous, isn't it, Mr Stanton?' she said as Hugo and Daphne walked with her down the terrace to the French doors.

'It is indeed,' Hugo replied. 'And I'm impressed with all the ancient trees. They're just magnificent, especially the oaks.'

'Yes, they are, and the only other trees I've seen like them are in the park at Cavendon,' the caretaker remarked.

'That's so,' Daphne agreed, walking after the caretaker, going into the library, which opened off the terrace.

'I shall leave you alone to explore,' Mrs Grant now said. 'Lady Daphne has been here before, and I think she knows her way around the house. I'll be in my little office, off the kitchen, if you need me.'

'Thank you, Mrs Grant,' Hugo answered, offering her a pleasant smile. 'I plan to take my time, though. I hope that's all right?'

'It is. Take as long as you wish.'

Once the caretaker had hurried off, Hugo stood in the middle of the library and slowly turned around, taking everything in. 'I understand what you meant about perfect proportions, Daphne: this is a wonderful room. The windows and the French doors let in such an amazing amount of daylight.'

'The panelling helps too, Hugo. Mahogany is always too dark, in my opinion. I prefer pale wood.'

'I agree.'

After strolling around the library, discussing various aspects of it, they moved on, went to the drawing room, then the dining room, and toured every room on the ground floor. It seemed to Hugo that they became better and better.

The bedroom floor also had many lovely rooms, as spacious and airy as those downstairs. At one moment, he couldn't help thinking that the house was rather big . . . perhaps too big for one man. But then he wasn't going to be alone forever, was he? He would have a wife.

Only Daphne, he thought. *She is the only one I want. The house suits her. She looks perfect in it . . . but then she would be perfect anywhere. She's so beautiful. A truly luscious woman.*

He watched her intently as she walked down the master bedroom to the other end and looked out through one of the windows.

She said, 'There's a lovely view of the lake from here, Hugo. You could have swans, like we do at Cavendon. Yes, what this lake needs are two white swans. They mate for life, you know.'

'I did know that, yes,' he murmured, thinking: *we* should mate for life. Totally preoccupied with his thoughts about her, he fully understood he couldn't get her out of his mind. Would he ever?

This afternoon she was wearing a peach silk dress, similar in tone to the one she had worn when he first met her . . . yesterday. *Was it only yesterday?* It was. He had arrived here on Friday and today was Saturday. How was that possible? He felt as if he had known her for years. They had spent an evening together at the supper dance; they had breakfasted with the family this morning. There had been the chat on the terrace before lunch, then lunch, and later the drive over to Whernside House in the close proximity of the motorcar. And the long wander around these beautiful rooms for the past hour.

In a truly short space of time they had been in each other's company rather a lot . . . and he wanted to be with her constantly. She was not only the most beautiful of women, but intelligent, caring and charming. He felt completely at ease with her, but had no idea how she felt about him. However, she *was* comfortable with him, he was certain of that. Because he noticed she was relaxed.

He glanced around the bedroom. It was large, but then all of the rooms were. This was a house meant for a man and his wife and their family. Not for a lonely man, a widower, all alone and mooning over a woman far too young for him. A woman he was not likely ever to possess.

She turned around, came walking back, smiling. Sunlight gilded her golden hair, gave it a shimmer, cast a bright radiance across her face. The peach silk rippled around her long legs, was draped across her shapely bosom.

The dizziness returned, his mouth went dry. There had been women before he married; after all, he was a virile man. But he had not felt like this about any of them, not even his lovely Loretta, whom he had loved and been faithful to throughout their marriage.

Hugo, fully aware he was besotted with Daphne Ingham, did not know what to do about it. He, a sophisticated experienced man of the world, was flummoxed.

'Let's go up to the nursery floor,' Daphne suggested, breaking into his thoughts about her.

Pulling himself together, Hugo said, 'Why not?'

They climbed the stairs quickly. Once they entered the nursery, Daphne exclaimed, 'Oh! A rocking horse! Just like the one we have at Cavendon.'

She rushed across the room and started pushing the horse. It moved back and forth, and Hugo suddenly remembered the one in the nursery at Cavendon, which he'd ridden on as a child.

'Your rocking horse was a friend of mine, too,' he said in a hoarse voice. 'It's called Dobbin.'

Daphne nodded and laughed. She stopped the horse moving, and unexpectedly she flung one leg over its back and sat down on it. She started to rock back and forth. Her dress was caught on the horse's back and had ridden up to expose her leg.

He thought he would go mad with desire for her as she rocked to and fro. The movement had become highly suggestive to him, and he had to turn away. His desire was growing unbearable.

A moment later, Daphne left the horse and joined him near the window. Putting her hand on his arm, she said, 'Thank you again, Hugo, for saving Greensleeves.'

'It was a good thing I remembered to put on my shoes when I was running out of my bedroom.'

'What do you mean?' she asked, puzzled.

'I was in my slippers when I saw the flames out of the window. I started to run, but stopped to put on my shoes. So when I couldn't get the stall latch open, I used one of my shoes as a hammer,' Hugo explained.

Daphne was staring at him, frowning. 'Why couldn't you get the latch open? I don't understand.'

'Oh, I didn't tell you, did I? There was a piece of wood wedged behind the latch. That's how I burned my fingers, attempting to remove it. The shoe did it, of course, and I was able to get the stall door open and release Greensleeves.'

Daphne stood gaping at him. As his words sank in, she understood everything. She felt a shiver of fear run through her, and her legs were suddenly weak. She sat down on a chair, shaking her head.

'What's wrong? What is it, Daphne?' Hugo asked, noticing at once the change in her demeanour.

'The latch was a bit loose, but no one ever put a piece of wood there to wedge it, Hugo. I was at the stable on Friday morning to see Greensleeves, and everything was normal.' She felt chilled to the bone when she thought about Richard Torbett. He had threatened to kill her mother and Dulcie. And he had tried last night to kill her horse. *It was him.* She knew it without a question of a doubt. But why? She had not told a soul about his attack on her, nor mentioned his name.

'Don't you feel well?' Hugo pressed worriedly, wondering what was wrong with her. She was pale, appeared to be upset.

Daphne took control of her swimming senses. I must be careful what I say, she cautioned herself. *Tell no one. Trust no one. Only the Swanns. Only your parents.*

After a moment, she said slowly, '*It was arson*. I agree with the police. The bale of hay was torched. Whoever it was, they wanted to kill our horses and burn down the stables. Why they targeted Greensleeves, I don't know. But they had trapped her in her stall . . . obviously the other stalls were bound to ignite swiftly. There is somebody out there who has a grudge against our family.'

'I hate to think that, Daphne,' Hugo responded, concern written on his face. 'I'm afraid I just assumed the bit of wood had been wedged there as a safety measure, by one of the stable boys.'

'No!' she exclaimed. 'You know as well as I do that a horse rarely walks out of its stall, even when the door is wide open.'

He nodded, offered her his hand. 'Perhaps we'd better go, the fresh air will do you good. Also, you must tell your father of your suspicions.'

Taking his hand, Daphne stood staring into his face for a moment, and unexpectedly her eyes filled with tears. She said softly, 'Thank you for being so understanding, Hugo. I was a little shocked a moment ago, when I realized someone bears us ill will. They do, don't they?'

'Perhaps.'

THIRTY-ONE

Charlotte Swann walked slowly towards the lake at Cavendon. She had set off too early, but it was such a lovely day that she had not been able to resist leaving her house in the village.

She lifted her head and looked up at the sky. It was amazing this afternoon. A clear bright blue, without a cloud, and brimming with sunlight. They had been lucky so far this summer. Rain had been infrequent, the weather glorious. Unusual for Yorkshire.

She wondered, as she walked along, why Charles wanted to talk to her, and why he had chosen the gazebo at the edge of the lake as a meeting place. She could only imagine that what he had to discuss was extremely private; certainly nobody could hear them talking, unless they were in close vicinity, like under the gazebo floor. This thought brought a smile to her face.

She pushed her hands in the pockets of her pale green silk dress, and continued on at a steady pace, thinking about the clothes Cecily had been designing for Daphne to wear once her pregnancy began to show. Cecily had been taken into her confidence recently.

She was astounded at Cecily's talent. The suits and dresses

were brilliantly clever, and she had soon realized that this was all to do with their construction.

Because Cecily had explained this to her, and had shown her various drawings, each of which applied to a single garment, Charlotte had quickly understood how Cecily literally engineered the clothes.

Charlotte had telephoned her cousin Dorothy, who lived in London, and worked in the fashion department of Fortnum and Mason, on Piccadilly.

Without revealing anything about designing clothes for a pregnant woman, Charlotte had told Dorothy about Cecily, and how amazingly creative and talented the girl was.

'I want to send her to live with you one day,' Charlotte had explained. 'This one's a winner, Dottie; she will go places. I can guarantee that Cecily Swann will be a designer of great fame one day. World famous, in fact.'

Dorothy had listened carefully to every word, and had agreed that once Cecily was old enough to leave Cavendon, she could live with her and her husband, Howard Pinkerton, in London. And she guaranteed a job for Cecily at Fortnum's. She trusted Charlotte's judgement implicitly.

I want her out of here, Charlotte now thought. This place is too beautiful, too comfortable, too easy; too perfect, in so many ways. And dangerous. It was the Ingham men, of course. They were irresistible. And fatal.

Miles was only fourteen, but Charlotte had noticed more than ever before just how he looked at Cecily, especially over the past few weeks, since he had been home from Eton. They were rarely apart, and even though DeLacy was usually with them, Miles appeared joined at the hip to Ceci.

I've got to nip that in the bud. She can't be like me. I won't permit that, Charlotte reminded herself, then came to an abrupt stop.

Much to her amazement, Genevra, the gypsy girl, was suddenly in the middle of the path, gazing at her. Where had she sprung from so unexpectedly?

'Genevra! Goodness me! What are you doing here?'

The girl shrugged, smiled. 'Hello, Mrs Charlotte.'

'You know very well you're not supposed to come on this part of the estate,' Charlotte said in a soft but slightly reprimanding tone.

The Romany remained silent, but stretched out her hand, offered something to Charlotte. She said, 'A present.'

Fully aware that she could not offend the gypsy, Charlotte took the offered gift and examined it carefully. It appeared to be a piece of bone or ivory. Slender and smooth, it was carved with small crosses on either side of a tiny carved heart. There were small pieces of ribbon tied to it. One was scarlet, the other sky blue.

Charlotte frowned, looked at Genevra intently, and realized, suddenly, how important this offering was to the girl. She said, warmly, 'Thank you so much, Genevra, I shall treasure it always. Did you make it?'

Genevra nodded. 'It's lucky. A charm. Don't lose.'

Charlotte put it in her pocket. 'I shall keep it safe. I must hurry now, I am late.'

'Bluebell woods no good.' Genevra shook her head. 'Trespassers prosecuted,' she muttered, lifting one hand, moving it, as if writing those words in the air. And then she whirled around and ran off, racing across to the meadows, heading for the Romany wagons far away on the hill.

Staring after her, Charlotte couldn't help wondering about those words. They sounded familiar, and then she remembered. Years ago, the 5th Earl had had posters made warning exactly that, and they had been attached to trees in the bluebell woods and around the estate. Did Genevra mean they should be put back on the trees?

And why had she said the bluebell woods were bad? Oh my God! Had Genevra seen the attack on Daphne in May? Charlotte shuddered at this awful thought, and walked faster, hurrying to the gazebo, not even stopping to see the swans, as she usually did.

She was the first to arrive. Once inside, she sat down on one of the chairs, catching her breath, and attempting to put thoughts of trespassers out of her head.

Within a few minutes, Charles Ingham stepped into the gazebo, touched her lightly on the shoulder, and sat down opposite her. 'Hello. I hope I haven't kept you waiting, Charlotte.'

'No, you haven't, Charlie. I just got here.' She sat back in the chair. 'I suspect you wish to speak to me about something really important, very private, something that no one else must hear. Hence the choice of this famous beauty spot.'

'You know, you can sound quite pompous at times,' he said, obviously amused.

'And so can you,' she answered. 'I think we picked that up from each other when we were little. Anyway, here we are, so very private in the gazebo, with only the swans to eavesdrop. So, what is all this about?'

Leaning forward across the small bamboo table, Charles said in a serious tone, 'Before Hugo left, he came to see me. He told me that he had fallen in love with Daphne. To say that I was flabbergasted is the understatement of the year. In fact, I was speechless for a moment. Then he shocked me further, by saying he wanted my permission to court her, if she was not spoken for already. He explained he had serious intentions. He wants to marry her . . . if I didn't have any objections to his courtship of her, that is.'

'And what did you say?'

'When I'd stopped reeling, I sort of fudged it,' he said. 'I told him I must think about it, because he is, after all, fifteen years older than her. I also pointed out that I must ascertain how

Daphne herself felt about him, if anything. And whether or not she would consider him as a suitor for her hand in marriage.'

'I understand. It's all you could do. And when does he want an answer?' Charlotte asked, looking across at him, biting her lip.

'As you know, he went to Zurich for a meeting. He returns to Yorkshire on the thirtieth of July. He's coming back for the big summer ball on the second of August. I told him I would give him an answer then.'

'I see. What does Felicity think?'

'Actually, I haven't discussed it with her yet. She's been rather under the weather since the supper dance, unusually nervous and irritable. I didn't have the heart to bring it up now. I thought I'd wait until later this week.'

Charlotte nodded, but remained silent, her expression reflective.

After a moment, the Earl glanced at her, his eyes narrowing. 'Why do I have the strangest feeling that you're not surprised?' he said.

'Because I'm not.'

He was obviously perplexed. 'Why aren't you?'

'Because a twelve-year-old girl – Cecily Swann, to be precise – spotted Hugo's infatuation with Daphne when it was actually happening. That was at tea on the very day he arrived. She told Alice that he only had eyes for Daphne, and I was present when she said this. So he did speak the truth, Charles, it *was* love at first sight. He's serious all right.'

Charles sat staring at Charlotte, unable to say a word, wondering if she actually approved of Hugo courting Daphne. Finding his voice finally, he said, 'You sound as if you think I should consider his proposition.'

'Why not? If Daphne has no objection. Hugo is a charming man, interesting, worldly, good looking and, I have discovered, rather a kind soul, very caring. And I understand he's successful in business.'

'How can I possibly entertain such a preposterous idea? She's pregnant by another man, for God's sake!' Charles exclaimed, sounding indignant. 'And if that little situation isn't an impediment to a marriage between the two of them, then I don't know what is.'

'Charles, please, calm down. Don't become angry with me. I'm only trying to help. Let's go and walk around the lake, exchange a few thoughts . . . like I used to with your father. A bit of fresh air and the tranquillity outside does wonders.' Charlotte stood up. 'Come on, let's go and see the swans.'

THIRTY-TWO

They walked around the rim of the lake, not speaking, lost in their own thoughts, but compatible in their silence.

Charlotte knew that Charles was troubled, at a loss, and so she remained quiet for the moment, wanting to give him time to think. In her heart of hearts she believed that Hugo's arrival was a godsend, and that his falling in love with Daphne had been a miracle of sorts.

However, she wasn't sure Charles would see it that way. She could only hope he would understand the sense that a liaison between Hugo and Daphne would make. Marriage would protect his daughter.

As two swans floated by, Charles said, 'The Inghams have swans because of the First Earl, Humphrey.'

'Yes, and I know why,' she answered. 'Do you?'

'Because my ancestor wanted to honour your ancestor for his loyalty and devotion, and he promised James the Inghams would always have swans on this lake, to commemorate their name "Swann".'

'And ever since, the Inghams and the Swanns have been intertwined, involved with each other in a variety of ways, because of the friendship of our founding fathers,' she remarked. 'It's a bond no one can break, you know . . . it's lasted far too long now, over one hundred and sixty years.'

Charles nodded, paused, and looked at her. 'Ask anyone around here, "What do the Swanns know about the Inghams?" And they'll all answer, "What don't they know?"'

'Yes, we do know everything, I've been led to believe,' she said.

'You have the Swann record books, Charlotte, haven't you?'

'I do. Because I am the senior member of the family.' She peered at him quizzically. 'But why are you suddenly bringing this up? You don't want to see them, do you? Because you can't, you know – it's never been allowed.'

'I'd never ask that of you, Charlotte. No Ingham has the right. But I was just thinking how much the Inghams have relied on the Swanns over the generations. And how I always depend on you. I usually come to you when I have a problem, I always have done. Naturally, I discuss things with Felicity, seek her advice, as she does mine. But it's your judgement I really depend on, and I think that's because my father did.'

Charlotte did not reply to this comment, although Charles was right.

He glanced at her. 'Well, he did, didn't he?'

'Quite often, but not always.' She gave him a small smile. 'Sometimes he thought he knew better. And, of course, that was true: he was a very smart man. And wise. But let's talk about Hugo and Daphne, shall we? That's why we met this afternoon.'

'You're absolutely right. So tell me, what do you think about the situation? Should it be considered? Would it work?'

'I think it *could* work . . . providing Daphne is willing. We know exactly where Hugo stands, his intentions, but what about her? It has to be her decision. She has to be happy with it,' Charlotte responded.

Charles exclaimed, 'I wouldn't have it any other way! I don't think she could possibly be in love with him. However, if she likes him, trusts him, and if they get along well, then maybe a marriage between them would have a chance. But it must be her choice. I would never force her.'

Charlotte looked pleased, and said swiftly, 'I'm so glad you're saying this, Charles, because if they were together it would solve so many problems for Daphne, and for the entire family. It would be a relief for everyone.'

'I can see that now . . . and sometimes a marriage that is based on overwhelming passion dies out quickly, loses its fire – at least so I've been given to understand by some chaps I know.'

'And sometimes a passionate man can make a marriage work beautifully . . . if his partner is willing to go along. And just think, Charles, Daphne might genuinely welcome Hugo with open arms. The programme for her, for the next six months, is going to be tough, really hard. She has to go on living as she is living today, whilst hiding her pregnancy from the world. And hoping she gets away with it. Hoping she can start her life again, after the baby's born. And then there's the child to consider. Has it occurred to you that she might not want to give it up for adoption?'

'It hadn't crossed my mind,' he replied. 'Felicity and I just pushed that idea to one side. But the baby will have to be adopted. By a good family. Arranged by a solicitor. A family given financial support.'

'I understand. What do you think Felicity will say about Hugo and Daphne getting married? Would she go along with it?'

'She's practical by nature, so I'm sure she would, providing Daphne was happy,' he answered in a firm voice. 'She wanted Daphne to come out, be presented at court, and she was planning a grand debutante's ball for her next year . . .'

He broke off, shook his head. 'Every time we discuss this ghastly situation, the way Daphne was so brutally raped, we thank God she's alive. The most important thing is that we still have our daughter. He could have killed her.'

Charlotte said, 'Shall we go up to the house and talk to Daphne? I know Felicity has gone to see her sister . . . she told me yesterday that Anne was in hospital again.'

He nodded and grimaced. 'I'm afraid she is, poor woman. DeLacy and Miles went with their mother to keep her company. Diedre and Guy have gone up to London. I rather think you knew that, too, didn't you?'

'Yes. Diedre told me she and Guy had been invited to Maxine Lowe's twenty-first birthday party, and that they were going to be in London for a few days.'

'Aunt Gwendolyn went along with them yesterday.' He laughed. 'She wasn't invited to Maxine's birthday party, but since she had planned to go to London for 'a bit of Mayfair and the theatre,' as she called it, Diedre suggested they all travel on the train together.'

Just look at her, Charlotte thought, as she and Charles walked into the yellow sitting room a short while later. There she sat, Lady Daphne Ingham, looking beautiful in a pale blue silk tea gown, with a long strand of pearls and pearl earrings. She was one of the most extraordinary-looking young women imaginable. No wonder Hugo had fallen in love with her instantly. She was like a golden goddess.

Daphne's hair was a shining halo around her face, her skin was peaches-and-cream perfect, and her blue eyes were sparkling. She's sublime, Charlotte thought. No man would be able to resist her. She was breathtaking this afternoon.

The moment she saw Charlotte and her father, Daphne stood up, came to greet them, then took Charlotte's hand in hers. 'Come and sit with me on the sofa,' she murmured.

Hanson, forever on the hover, motioned to Gordon and Malcolm to push in the tea trolleys, and led the way forward. 'Good afternoon, m'lord, Miss Charlotte. Shall we serve now, Lord Mowbray?'

'Please do so, Hanson. And I'm sure you already knew that it would be just the three of us.'

'I did know, m'lord. However, I've had it on good authority that you will be joined for tea by Lady Dulcie. You will be four.'

'Oh really,' Charles said, and a moment later, as if on cue, his youngest daughter walked sedately into the room. 'Hello, Papa,' she said. 'Hello, Miss Charlotte. Daphne, can I sit with you on the sofa?'

'Of course,' Daphne answered, and made room for the child between herself and Charlotte.

A glass of milk was produced for Dulcie, while Gordon and Malcolm poured the tea and handed around the tea sandwiches. Hanson supervised, watching the footmen with eagle eyes, as was his way.

'When is my horse arriving, Papa?' Dulcie suddenly asked, staring at her father, her large blue eyes focused on him intently.

'A horse!' Daphne exclaimed, looking surprised. 'Goodness me!'

'Yes,' Dulcie said. 'A horse.'

'No,' Charles interjected. 'You are going to have a Shetland pony again. However, the new one will be a bit bigger than the one you now have.'

'A horse is for when you're more grown up,' Daphne explained.

The child nodded, concentrating on Charles. 'So when will the new pony arrive, Papa?'

'In about a week,' he replied, finding her irresistible. 'I had to

231

wait until I found exactly the right one for you. A special pony, Dulcie.'

A wide smile spread across her face, and she said, 'Thank you, Papa. I'm going to call him Hugo.'

There was a moment of quietness, and Charlotte glanced away, unable to look at Charles. Charles cleared his throat, and did the same.

It was Daphne who spoke first. 'And why have you chosen that particular name, Dulcie?' she asked curiously.

'Because I have a friend called Hugo. I was the first sister to meet him, and I can't help it that he chose me to meet him *first* . . . *you* told me that, Daphne. You said it wasn't my fault.'

'I did, yes. So the pony is to be given Hugo's name?'

'Yes. Because Hugo is nice, and the pony will be nice.'

'Hugo *is* nice, Papa. Dulcie's right about that. He's one of the nicest people I've ever met,' Daphne said to the room at large.

An hour later, Dulcie had gone back to the nursery, and Daphne sat in the library with her father and Charlotte. Charles told her everything, holding nothing back, repeating, almost verbatim, all of the things Hugo had said before returning to Zurich.

Daphne listened attentively, and then asked quietly, 'And so what happens next, Papa?'

'When Hugo comes back to Yorkshire, to attend the ball, he would like to know what your thoughts are.'

'Do you mean he wants some sort of an answer?' Daphne asked, giving her father a hard stare.

'He does indeed.' Charles leaned back on the Chesterfield sofa, and crossed his legs.

'But an answer to *what* exactly?' Daphne asked. 'Will I marry him? Or can he court me, with a view to marriage?'

'The latter, Daphne,' Charles answered. 'He indicated he wishes *you* to get to know *him* better. He is absolutely sure of his own feelings for you. He kept repeating that to me. He wants you to have enough time to make up *your* mind. In other words, he doesn't want you to dismiss him out of hand, and he doesn't want to push.'

Daphne did not answer immediately.

Charles looked at Charlotte and raised a brow, and Charlotte nodded.

She said softly, 'Hugo doesn't want to rush you, but he did want you to know how he truly feels, from what your father's said to me. I'll tell you something interesting.'

Charlotte now leaned forward, her eyes searching Daphne's face; the girl seemed very puzzled. 'You know, Daphne, Cecily spotted the way Hugo was reacting to you, the first day you met him, at tea that Friday afternoon. She told me he couldn't take his eyes off you. She added that he'd found a wife. What she meant was a potential wife.'

'I trust Cecily. She never misses anything, and she's very grown up and intelligent for her age,' Daphne responded. 'So what you're saying is that Hugo would court me, and if I like him enough to marry him, then that would be the ultimate result. Marriage. Eventually. But if I didn't grow to like him, more than I do already, then the courtship would die a natural death.' Daphne sat back in her chair, and looked at her father pointedly. 'Am I right? Have I summed it up?'

'You have, darling,' Charles said.

Daphne was thoughtful for a moment, before saying, 'I do like Hugo; he's a lovely man. Maybe it *would* work. We seem to get on well, we like the same things. But there's a huge problem, Papa. I'm pregnant. He would have to be told I'm having a baby. It would be wrong to hide that from him. Unethical, actually. Dishonourable, on my part. But there's a risk in telling him. He might walk away from me, lose interest in me, and yet he would know my secret. And he could talk. I would be ruined.'

'Don't think I haven't thought about all that,' Charles exclaimed. 'And so has Charlotte. I suppose we just have to take that chance.'

Charlotte cleared her throat, and said, 'Hugo is an Ingham, a member of the family, your father's first cousin, Daphne. I believe he is an honest and honourable man and, like all the Ingham men, completely loyal – true blue. I don't think for one moment that he would talk. Also, remember he will be told you were attacked and raped, and why would he reveal that? I doubt he would.'

'He would probably walk away and never come back,' Charles interjected, 'If he lost interest in you, or if you spurn his court-ship. He indicated that to me. He thought it would be intolerable to live here at Whernside House and not have you as his wife. "Untenable", that was the word he used.'

Daphne nodded. Her mind was racing with innumerable thoughts. An image of Peggy Swift leaning over her baby, Kevin, came rushing back, and she said, 'What about my pregnancy? Can I give this baby up? I don't know, Papa. It's an Ingham. I know I'm going to love it, the moment I hold it in my arms. Let us say we got together, and married, Hugo might not wish me to keep the baby.'

Charles was shocked by her words. It had not occurred to him that she would not give the baby up. He was astounded, but kept his voice level when he said, 'There are many things to consider, as well as the baby. If you marry Hugo, you won't be a duchess one day, as you've always dreamed of being. But he will treat you like a queen, and you will never want for anything. Hugo's exceedingly wealthy.'

'I know he's successful, a clever man in business, I realized that from our conversations.'

'He adores you, in my opinion. He'll spoil you, give you the world. He's a millionaire many times over,' Charles told her, and added, 'He was very candid and open, and explained a great deal about his wealth to me.'

'I can't let that influence me, Papa.' She turned to Charlotte. 'I can't, can I?'

'No, Daphne. However, I know you will think everything through before coming to a decision. That's the way you are made. You're very prudent.'

Daphne mused, almost to herself. 'He's kind and caring, and he makes me laugh. I like his energy . . . and he has a warm personality.' There was a pause, and then she said slowly, 'For the moment I think he can court me . . . but let me think it over for a few days. Then I will give you my final answer.'

'I wouldn't want it any other way,' Charles answered. 'It is up to you, darling.'

'What does Mama think about Hugo's serious interest in me?' Daphne asked, standing up.

'I haven't told her yet. She has been feeling rather poorly, and I haven't wanted to burden her in any way,' he explained.

Daphne said, 'Perhaps I'll speak to her later, when she gets back from Harrogate. Anyway, Mama is practical like me – or rather, I should say, I am like her.'

Upstairs in her room, Daphne locked the door, took off her dress, and all her other clothes, and went and stood in front of the cheval mirror in the corner.

She studied herself carefully, and from all angles. She wasn't showing yet. However, her breasts were bigger, and they were also sore on occasion. Once she started to show, and her bump began to grow, she would have to leave Cavendon. There was no alternative. She couldn't even go to their house in Mayfair. Because of the servants. They would notice her condition immediately.

Looking at herself in the mirror once again, she shook her head and turned away, went to her closet, picked out a silk robe. As she slipped it on, she wondered if she could carry it off: pretending not to be pregnant for the many months ahead of her; going to live in Paris when she was showing. Being taught like a student to speak French, to learn about art and French history. And being shown how to become elegant and chic in the French manner. Could she follow the programme Charlotte Swann had mapped out for her?

She could, she was positive about that. After all, she had a strong will, and once she made her mind up to do something, she did it.

But now, for the first time, she wondered if she wanted to go through that. It was play-acting and being dishonest, and she would certainly have to learn the art of dissimulation . . . she was open and honest by nature, not given to telling lies.

Walking over to her dressing table, she sat down, stared at her face, leaning closer to the mirror. For once in her life she saw herself objectively, and she understood how beautiful she was. Hugo had fallen in love with her because of that beauty.

Leaning back in the chair, she closed her eyes, and thought of Hugo. He was nice looking, and charming. She imagined he was a gentle soul, from what she had observed in those few days he had been here at Cavendon. And people who had never met him took to him immediately. Family and staff, who had known him as a young man, welcomed him with open arms. That said a lot, didn't it?

Marriage to a powerful and wealthy man would protect her, wouldn't it?

One thing was certain, it would ease the terrible burden on her parents. She had heard her mother say recently to her father that the situation was like living under the sword of Damocles.

Could she marry Hugo? Did she want to? Would he let her keep the baby? Or would she have to give it up for adoption? And could she do that? Give her baby away?

Then there was the question of intimacy. Eventually, she would have to be his wife, not only in name, but in every way. Sexual union would be part of that marriage. Was she ready for that? Could she share an intimate life with Hugo?

She shuddered, thinking of Richard Torbett and the way he had been rough and cruel with her when he had forced himself on her, raped her. She was still fearful of sex because of that fiend.

Thinking about Torbett now, she realized that being a married woman would, in fact, protect her from that vile man. He wouldn't dare do anything to her, or her family, if she had a husband like Hugo Stanton.

Then again, if she married Hugo, she would never experience that wonderful feeling of falling in love and adoring the man she loved, of wanting to be his in every way. She would never know true love . . .

What to do?

Daphne lay down on the bed, found her pillow and buried her face in it. She was on the horns of a dilemma . . . she did not know which way to turn.

There *was* one thing she was totally aware of, and that was the need to be strong, to be in control of her own destiny. She was determined to be her own woman, make her own decisions.

THIRTY-THREE

Felicity knew only too well that Charles loved the end of the evening, when dinner was over and everyone had retired for the night. It was then that he could be alone with her in her cosy upstairs sitting room, which adjoined her bedroom.

Comfortable in his nightclothes, he would sit in front of the fire chatting. Sometimes he brought a small glass of cognac with him, or a scotch. Her choice was always a glass of cold water flavoured with lemon.

Tonight, after the long afternoon in Harrogate, she was glad she could now relax in front of the fire in a comfortable chair, sipping her lemon water. And waiting for Charles. She wasn't looking forward to spending time alone with him, but she had no alternative.

She could hear his voice on the other side of the door. He was in his dressing room with Walter Swann, and the two of them were talking about Winston Churchill, the politician. From what she was hearing, they both seemed to favour him; they were talking about his brilliance and his aptitude for public speaking.

A moment later, the door opened and Charles walked in, wearing pyjamas, a dark blue silk dressing gown, and carrying a small balloon of brandy.

'You were being very laudatory about Winston Churchill,' Felicity said, looking up. 'There are some who don't like him, you know.'

Charles nodded, then gave her a knowing smile as he sat down in the chair opposite her. 'They're just envious of his brilliance, and his amazing ability to get things done, that's what all *that* is about.'

'I'm sure you're right,' she responded, and settled back in the chair.

'You didn't say much about Anne when you returned from Harrogate. How is she, actually?' Charles asked sympathetically.

'In her spirit she's more or less the same, Charles. Undefeated. Positive. Won't surrender to self-pity. She's extremely English in that sense . . . very stoical. Puts up a brave front. But I know she's in pain, and she is having morphine more frequently.' Felicity let out a long sigh. 'She is one of the bravest people I've ever known.'

'She is indeed, and I'm so sorry, darling, I do realize how much her cancer worries you. And I just want to say that I'm here whenever you need me. I'll always do what I can.'

She put out her hand, squeezed his arm, gave him a small smile. 'Thank you.'

After taking a sip of the Napoleon brandy, he said, 'I have something to tell you. I haven't had a chance before. Well, actually, I have, but I didn't want to burden you, I know you've been feeling a bit under the weather.'

Felicity looked across at him, and said in a firm voice, 'I'm much better today, and you sound serious. Is there something the matter?'

'Well, no, I couldn't say that . . .' He paused, took another swallow, and put his glass on a small table next to his chair. Leaning closer to her, he said, 'The day Hugo left for London, he came to see me. He told me he had fallen in love with Daphne and did he have my permission to court her? If she was not already spoken for, of course. He said it was love at first sight, and he had serious intentions.'

'I hope you said yes!' Felicity exclaimed, staring at him intently, her eyes bright, alive, her pale face filled with sudden animation.

'I did not,' Charles answered. 'I told him I would have to ask Daphne if she would like that. I explained it was her decision.'

'No! No! No!' Felicity cried, sounding unusually vehement. 'It's not for her to decide. We have to make the decision for her. Obviously Hugo is a solution to all her problems. And ours. What a coincidence that Hugo arrived at Cavendon when he did. Or perhaps it wasn't a coincidence at all. I think it was meant to be. No, it was God's will.'

For a moment Charles was stunned by her vehemence and the way she spoke so easily of God's will. Felicity didn't often invoke God's name. He frowned, then explained quietly, 'I cannot force Daphne to accept the overtures of a man she's not interested in. Nor would I ever push her into a marriage where there was no love involved on her part. That would be unthinkable. Monstrous, in my opinion. Living with someone you don't love would be impossible.'

Staring at him aghast, Felicity said, 'But you were going to marry her off to a duke's son, and she probably wouldn't have loved him either.'

'That was never my intention, Felicity, and you know that full well. I wanted to find the right young man, bring them together, and I hoped they would fall in love. I am far too modern a man to tolerate an arranged marriage for a daughter of mine.'

'Sometimes they work very well,' Felicity pointed out a little sharply. 'Arranged unions have been known to last a lifetime.'

Charles was angry, but he controlled himself and quietly said, 'But mostly they *don't* work. And both people are unhappy, *miserable*, and eventually get divorced. I don't want that for Daphne.'

'So Hugo is going to be turned away, is he?' she asked sarcastically.

'Far from it,' Charles responded swiftly. 'I have explained the situation to her, and Daphne confided that she likes Hugo. She thinks he's good looking, charming and rather nice. She will give me an answer in a day or two. In my opinion, she will agree to the courtship.'

'Well, let's hope it works, because to me it's the best solution there is. She would be married, protected, and there would be no gossip.' Felicity sat back in the chair, looking adamant.

'If she doesn't want to marry him, we will have to go back to the original plan of concealing it, sending her abroad,' Charles pointed out.

'I suppose we will, but that will be a strain on us all. You must persuade her, Charles, make her see the wisdom of marrying Hugo.'

Charles nodded, and picked up the brandy balloon, swirled the cognac around, staring into the amber depths. His wife had startled him with her immediate acceptance of the idea of Hugo and Daphne marrying, and without giving a thought to their daughter's desires, or her ultimate happiness. It was out of character, so unlike her. But then she had been under strain lately; she hadn't been herself at all.

Felicity picked up on his mood, even though he was silent, and ventured, 'I want the best for her, and this is the best solution. I think it's fantastic, and it's been handed to us on a plate. What did Charlotte say?'

He lifted his head and stared at her in surprise, struck by her knowledge of him. She had immediately assumed he had discussed the matter with Charlotte, without his having to tell her.

He sipped the brandy, put the glass down, and said in a low voice, 'She agrees with you that it would be the perfect solution to a ghastly problem – much easier for Daphne to handle, and us as well. However, she thinks it should be Daphne's decision.'

'I see.'

'Hugo would have to be told the truth, Felicity, and we would have to hope he would not turn away from her because of her pregnancy. It's a risk to take, confiding in him, but I tend to agree with Charlotte, who doesn't think he would talk . . . that he would keep our secret, protect the family. She thinks he's true blue, like all the Ingham men.'

'She would say that,' Felicity exclaimed tersely, her expression disdainful.

Charles frowned, studied her intently for a moment. 'What are you suggesting? That we Ingham men don't have honour and integrity?'

'No, I'm not. However, Charlotte was truly influenced in every way by your father, and she's also a Swann. It's ingrained in her to take the Ingham side, die for an Ingham if necessary. That's their role in life, and has been for generations.'

'I know all about the Swanns.'

'Not as much as they know about the Inghams,' Felicity countered. 'Anyway, she loved your father, doted on David.'

'Everyone loved my father: that was the kind of man he was.'

'Oh, you know what I mean, Charles!' she shot back, sounding exasperated. 'Don't pretend otherwise.'

'There was never one iota of gossip about my father and Charlotte, and you are fully aware of that.'

Felicity stood up. 'I must go to bed now.'

He also rose. 'Can I sleep in your bed tonight, or do you want to be alone?'

She offered him a small smile. 'You know you are always welcome in my bed,' she lied, trying not to show her dismay.

Not quite true, he thought, as he took her hand in his. Not lately anyway. He had been constantly spurned in the last six months, and had genuinely tried to understand. He couldn't entirely blame it on her worry about her sister. He sensed that she was no longer interested in the intimate side of their marriage. Why this was so, he had no idea. It puzzled him.

Felicity got into bed and turned out the bedside lamp. Charles also turned off a lamp, and as usual he strode to the window and drew back the draperies. There was a full moon tonight and it flooded the room with its silvery light.

Climbing into bed next to her, Charles put his arms around his wife and held her close. After a moment he bent over her and kissed her cheek, then found her mouth. She responded to his kisses, and this pleased him, and he began to touch her breasts lightly, murmuring how much he loved her.

Felicity was silent, held herself still, waiting for him to take her to him, to make love to her. And then it would all be over and she would be in peace.

He did not do that, and she was filled with relief. She did not desire him any more, but fought desperately to conceal this lack of interest in him. For her own preservation, at this moment.

As he continued to kiss and caress her, Charles recognized that he was unable to make love to Felicity. He was impotent. For a moment, he panicked, and then pushed that ridiculous feeling aside. He was, very simply, worn out, plagued by all the events of late. That was what this failure was all about.

After a few moments, he said softly, against her hair, 'I'm so sorry, darling. Like you, I'm totally exhausted.'

'It's perfectly all right,' she whispered. 'Good night, Charles.'

'Good night, darling,' he answered.

Charles was unable to sleep.

He lay awake for several hours. Finally, he slipped out of bed and went through his dressing room into his bathroom. Turning on the light, he stared at himself in the mirror, shaking his head in bafflement.

He could not understand why he had not been able to get an erection tonight. It had never happened to him before. Was he suddenly impotent? On a permanent basis? How could that be? He was only forty-four years old.

He closed his eyes for a moment, as an awful thought occurred to him. Had her rejection of him over all these months had a disastrous effect on him? He had no answer for himself.

Still troubled, he left the bathroom and went into his own bedroom. He would sleep alone tonight, as he mostly had lately. He had a busy day on the estate tomorrow.

THIRTY-FOUR

C harlotte sat at the Georgian desk near the window in her living room, making notes for her meeting tomorrow with Charles. They were to go over some of the old estate books; he had also explained that he wished to hire more men from the villages, and encourage tenanted farmers to work the land.

This had pleased her. She cared as much about their people as he did, and employment was important in Little Skell, Mowbray and High Clough.

That was the true reason for the existence of a landed estate and a great house owned by a titled aristocrat: employment for the local people, not only on the land but in the house. Housekeepers, maids, cooks and butlers, footmen and lady's maids; and, on the outside, gamekeepers, beaters and gardeners, and tenant farmers who worked the land around their villages. It was a whole world unto itself, something like a fiefdom.

Putting the notes aside, Charlotte took a sip of cognac and savoured it. She preferred brandy to the scotch Alice and Walter occasionally liked, which is why she served it to them when they visited her, if they asked for it.

She glanced at the photograph of David in its silver frame. She took it out of the desk drawer every night and placed it here on the desk, where she could constantly look at it. She missed him, and at times wept for him. He had died too young.

When she had seen his coffin being lowered into his grave, she had wanted to throw herself onto it, wrap her arms around it and be buried with him. She had even contemplated suicide, because she had nothing to live for without him.

She had not killed herself, because she saw that as an act of weakness, and she prided herself on being strong. Also, she had promised David she would look after Charles and help him whenever he needed it. And she had promised to remain at Cavendon.

'I need my devoted Swanns on the estate, where they belong, and you in particular,' he had said to her before he died. 'Then I will be able to rest in peace.'

And so she had stayed here . . . but where would she have gone? This was the only place on earth for her, where she had been so happy. And he was buried here.

Charlotte jumped up in surprise when there was a quick knock on the door, and Alice came straight in. She was earlier than Charlotte had expected her, and in her haste she forgot to return the photograph to the drawer. She never had it on display. It was only on the desk when she was alone.

'You look tired, Alice,' Charlotte said, walking over to the sideboard. 'Would you like a scotch?'

'Thank you,' Alice said, and sat down in one of the two armchairs. As Charlotte poured the drink, Alice looked across at the desk, and immediately saw the photograph of David Ingham, the 5th Earl. She was surprised it was not in the drawer.

Miraculously, there had never been any gossip about the two of them, yet Alice had known everything about their relationship. All that messing around between the Inghams and the Swanns had gone on for one hundred and sixty years.

They were intertwined and involved in every possible way. So why would it be different in this day and age? It would always happen. They couldn't help themselves, couldn't resist each other. In fact, they didn't even try. The Ingham men were fatal to the Swann women, and vice versa.

That was why she must get Ceci away from here, when she was old enough. Miles Ingham and Cecily Swann were too bound up in each other, far too close, joined at the hip. At the moment they were too young to become intimate, but they would eventually if they weren't separated. Walter agreed with her, and so did Charlotte. It had to be done.

Handing Alice the tumbler of scotch, Charlotte sat down next to her. 'Cheers,' she said.

'Cheers,' Alice echoed, as they clinked glasses. 'I think I might need a second one of these.' She shook her head and groaned. 'I've been sewing all day. Those clothes Ceci designs for Daphne are beautiful, they take a lot of work.'

'I realize that. They're engineered, effectively. I can't believe her talent, Alice; she's only twelve and yet she has an amazing ability as a designer. She's like . . . a child prodigy.'

'That's right,' Alice answered, and then glanced across at the silver-framed photograph again, but made no reference to it. She went on, 'I'm glad you telephoned Dottie. In a couple of years, Ceci will be old enough to go to London.'

'Yes,' Charlotte agreed, thinking not for the first time that the telephone the 5th Earl had had installed in her cottage was a godsend. She followed Alice's gaze, caught sight of the photograph and realized her mistake. 'I know what you're thinking. Ceci will leave here, I promise.'

'Thank you. Now, I'll have another scotch, if you don't mind.' Alice went over to pour it for herself.

Once Alice was settled in the chair again, Charlotte announced, 'I had a meeting with the Earl this morning, and he gave me some interesting news. That's why I wanted to see you this evening.'

Alice looked at her alertly. 'Go on then! Tell me! Don't keep me in suspense.'

'Before Hugo left for Zurich, he went to see Charles. He told him he had fallen in love with Daphne, that he wanted permission to court her – if she was not already spoken for. He confessed to Charles that it was love at first sight.'

'So Ceci was right.' Alice beamed at Charlotte. 'And did the Earl give his permission?'

'No. He said it was up to Daphne. Her decision.'

'I hope to God she says yes. It's a gift from heaven, isn't it? Hugo coming here when he did, I mean.'

'It is. And I believe Daphne is sensible enough to go along with it. She did tell me she thinks Hugo is nice, that she likes him.'

'But that's not love, is it? It's just not the same thing. You've got to want that particular man so much, you can't see straight. You *must* have him, be with him all the time. You must feel you can't live without him. That's being in love.' Alice stared at Charlotte, waiting for a response.

But Charlotte was silent, merely stared back at Alice, her expression enigmatic.

Finally Alice said, 'Certainly you know what I'm talking about. You wanted David so much you were crazed. And you devoted most of your life to him in the end. And from the age of seventeen.'

'True. I can't deny it.' There was a pause, a hesitation, then she added, 'But only the Swanns knew.'

'That's right. Because we protected you, always. Not only you, but the Earl as well. That's the reason there was never any gossip about you.' Alice took a small swig of the scotch, and added, 'Listen to me, Charlotte, we've got to try and influence Daphne. Don't you think that's right? Drop hints, say nice things about Hugo.'

'Daphne's smart, much brighter than most people realize. She'll see through that at once. So we must be subtle, Alice.'

'Oh, I know that. There's another thing, Charlotte. Daphne might just fall in love with Hugo, without any prompting from us. After all, he's an extremely attractive man, and there's something about him that's appealing, engaging. Let's not forget he's an Ingham. And you know better than anybody what the Ingham men are like, the effect they have on women. There's just something about them.'

Charlotte smiled. 'It's called fatal charm, Alice.'

Not far from Charlotte's house in Little Skell village, down near the lake in the park at Cavendon, Peggy Swift and Gordon Lane were taking a stroll.

It was a beautiful July night, with a bright full moon floating high in the sky. It silvered the surface of the lake, spreading a sheen across it.

The fact that they were in the park troubled Peggy; they were not supposed to be there. This was the private domain of the Ingham family, not like the woods and the meadows where anyone could roam.

'We're trespassing, Gordon,' she whispered at one moment. 'Hurry up and finish your cig, and then we can go back to the house.'

'What about a kiss and a canoodle, then? Am I not getting that tonight, Peg?'

'Yes, you are, but we must be quick, and I'm not going to do *it*, you know. Not *that*. Until we're married.'

'I know! I know! I'll be respectful, Miss Swift. Right up until the day you're Mrs Lane.' He dropped his tab end and ground it into the gravel path with his foot. 'Come on, Peg, let's go into that there boathouse for a couple of minutes.'

'We'd be trespassing more than ever,' Peggy protested, always afraid of authority.

'Aw, come on, love, just for a bit,' Gordon pleaded.

Reluctantly, and against her better judgement, Peggy allowed Gordon to lead her over to the boathouse. When he turned the knob, the door opened, and they went inside. There was no light switch, but the room was not too dark, because of the moonlight streaming in. Gordon spotted a candle stub in a saucer on the window ledge, pulled out a box of Swan Vestas, and struck a match. The candle flickered as he brought the flame to it.

'Not too bad, Peg. At least we can see a little bit. Oh, look, over there, a pile of ropes. A perfect spot to sit.'

'A bit grim,' Peggy spluttered, slightly indignant, but nonetheless she sat down on the ropes with him.

Immediately, and as usual, Gordon was kissing her, pulling her closer, smoothing his hand over her breasts, then opening her blouse, touching her skin. He was exciting her, arousing her, as he always did, and she was floundering.

He whispered against her neck, 'I promise you, I won't force you. But can I just touch you, Peg? Please.'

'I want you to, Gordon, but I think we should leave. We're servants, we're not supposed to be in the park, never mind in the boathouse. If we're not careful, we'll get the sack.'

'It's late. Everybody's gone to bed, believe me they have. Come on, just for a few minutes.' As he spoke he gently moved her back against the pile of ropes, and lifted her skirt, began to caress the top of her leg, her thigh, and beyond.

Gordon kissed her face, found her mouth. He knew he couldn't get enough of her. But he had promised not to force her into anything against her will, and he kept his word. She was too important to him; he didn't want to lose her.

Eventually they both sat up, and Peggy whispered, 'Gordon Lane, aren't you the naughty boy! A proper little devil.'

He grinned at her. 'The devil you love, though.'

'That's the truth, my lad.' Peggy straightened her skirt, fastened her blouse, and patted her hair. At that moment, the candle sputtered and died on them.

'The room's gone dark,' Peggy said in a low voice. 'I don't like the dark, Gordon.'

'I know that, love. But I can't help it. The candle went out, and the moon's gone behind a cloud. Wait a minute, I'll strike another match, and then we can find our way out of here.'

'That's a relief,' Peggy said, looking over at the window. 'It's really black outside without the light of the moon.'

Gordon struck the match, held it up. Peggy screamed. There was a man's face at the window.

'What the hell's the matter with you?' Gordon asked.

'There's a man outside, staring through the window at us.'

Gordon swung around to face the window, only to discover there was no one there. 'I think you must be seeing things,' he said, frowning at her.

Peggy scrambled to her feet, and so did Gordon. She said, 'Somebody's seen us in here. I saw his face. *I did.*'

'Oh my God. Then we're in trouble.' Grabbing hold of her hand, he led her towards the door. 'We'd better go and face the music.'

When they went outside, cautiously, they discovered they were entirely alone.

'Are you sure . . . ?' Gordon began, and stopped. Just ahead of them he saw a tall man running off, making for the far side of the lake.

'Course I'm sure,' Peggy exclaimed indignantly. 'I know what I saw and I'm not daft in the head. Look! He's running down there.'

'I know. I just saw him,' Gordon said in a low voice.

'It was a tramp,' Peggy announced.

Gordon peered at her. 'Why do you say that? You only caught sight of him for a second.'

'His face was dirty, and he had something strange wrapped around his head. It was like some old rags.'

Gordon made a face. 'I don't like the idea of somebody odd roaming around this park, it's too close to the house. And the family. We'd best get back there, Peg, before bloody old Hanson goes on his nightly prowl.'

As they ran together through the park, holding hands, Peggy couldn't help but think about the last time they had been to the woods, where there had been a Peeping Tom. Now they had just seen another one at the boathouse window. Someone was watching them, and it frightened her.

THIRTY-FIVE

The water gardens at Cavendon had been created in the eighteenth century and were truly beautiful. They were located on lower ground at the back of the West Wing of the house, and now, as she walked down the hill towards them, Daphne thought how tranquil this part of the parkland was.

Halfway down the small hill, she came to the platform that had been built by an earlier countess long ago. A large chunk of the hill had been dug out like a cave, granite slabs laid, and a resting spot created. There was a stone bench on the flagstones, and Daphne sat down for a moment, staring at the lovely scene below.

Manicured lawns stretched across the valley floor. In the centre, straight ahead, there was a large ornamental pond, and from this pond four canals branched out like spokes in a wheel. The wheel effect was emphasized by a circular canal that surrounded the long canals and the central pond. And further down were flowering bushes and another ornamental pond with a fountain, shooting water into the sky this afternoon.

Even as a child she had loved to come here, relishing the notion of a giant wheel set in the middle of green lawns. Water lilies floated on the ornamental pond, and there were statues placed on various parts of the lawns; at one end stood the Temple of the Moon. The lawn behind the Temple of the Moon was edged with beech trees, and the effect was spectacular. Eternal Serenity was the name that had been given to the water gardens when they were finished a century ago, and she thought it was indeed serene.

Earlier that morning, Daphne had written a short note to Hugo, asking him to meet her here at three o'clock, and requesting that he tell no one at all about the meeting.

She had sealed the note in an envelope, and left it on the chest of drawers in the Blue Bedroom. He had been due to arrive at two o'clock today, and he had been on time. Through the window she had seen her father and Dulcie greeting him on the front steps of Cavendon.

Rising, Daphne went on down the slope to the gravel path, and then followed the narrow flagstones that led directly to the Temple of the Moon.

There were two white-painted, carved wooden chairs inside, and she sat down on one, then glanced at the fob watch pinned to her pale green chiffon blouse. It was fifteen minutes to three, so she settled back, her thoughts concentrated on Hugo, and what she would say to him.

She had not told anyone about this meeting, because she had decided she must take her destiny into her own hands. She would do it alone, make her own life.

Suddenly he appeared at the top of the hill; he was early, so obviously he was anxious to see her. As he came down the slope her heart clenched, and she wondered if she had the nerve to go through with this. Yes, she told herself, I must do it. There is no other choice.

She noticed he was glancing around as he approached the bottom of the hill, and she stood up, went to the front of the temple, and waved to him.

He saw her at once, and waved back, a smile flashing on his face. He almost ran down the flagstone path to the temple, and came up the three steps and through the Doric columns.

Daphne thought he was going to embrace her, but somehow he held himself back, and took her hand, held it tightly in his, and kissed her cheek somewhat tentatively.

'Thank you for coming,' she said and, still holding his hand, she led him to the two chairs set against the back wall of the little building. She sat on one of them.

'I wondered where you were for a moment,' Hugo said, also sitting down. 'But now I realize these chairs are not visible from a distance.'

She merely nodded.

Getting straight to the point, he said, 'Your father told me that you would consider the idea of a courtship, and the prospect of marriage to me. That you would make up your mind before I left again. Thank you for that.'

'Papa said it was love at first sight when you met me a few weeks ago; that you knew there and then that you wished to marry me. It wasn't love at first sight for me, Hugo, I must confess. I like you enormously, I feel comfortable with you, and at ease. We get on well, we're compatible.' She suddenly laughed, 'And you are a handsome man, and very engaging. So . . .' She let her voice trail off, and then added softly, 'Although you are staying here for two weeks, I will give you an answer in one week. Because I'll be sure by then.'

He was pleased, and it showed on his face. He said swiftly, 'An answer to what, Daphne? A courtship or—'

'No, no,' she cut in swiftly. 'I will tell you whether or not I will marry you.'

This answer made him even happier, and he relaxed in the chair, feeling as if a great load had been lifted from his shoulders. A loving smile settled on his face. 'Thank you.'

Before he could start a conversation, Daphne said, 'There are several things I must discuss with you, Hugo. *Now.* Immediately. Before we talk about anything else.'

Looking at her intently, he frowned and exclaimed, 'You sound very serious.'

'These are serious matters.'

'I understand. I am listening, please tell me.'

'I believe there is an impediment to our marrying,' she announced.

Looking at her askance, extremely baffled, he exclaimed, 'But how could that be? I am a widower with no entanglements of any kind, and you are a single woman, totally free.'

She ignored these comments, and swiftly said, 'I would like to tell you a story. If that's all right?'

'Yes, of course it is.'

'A few months ago, on the third of May to be exact, I was attacked in the bluebell woods, and—'

'Oh my God!' he interjected, sounding aghast. 'You must have been hurt. My poor girl. Are you feeling all right now?'

Daphne held up her hand. 'Please, Hugo, I would like to tell you the rest of the story. Before I lose my nerve. We can talk about it once I've finished. Please, do listen. And I'd prefer it if you don't interrupt me.'

'I understand,' he answered quietly, wanting to know more. 'I shall absolutely keep quiet. You have the floor.'

'That afternoon something was thrown at me. It struck me between my shoulder blades. I fell forward, hitting my face and head on a log. Before I could get up, someone pounced on me.'

Slowly, carefully, she told Hugo about being raped, threatened, told that her mother and Dulcie would be killed if she talked, and how she was then left alone in the woods. She went on to explain how Genevra, the Romany girl, had found her much later and had helped her through the woods back to Cavendon Hall.

Pausing for breath, Daphne sat back in the chair, and looked deeply into his face. She saw that he was shocked and horrified, and she believed he was about to question her. But he didn't.

Instead, Hugo reached out, took hold of her hands, held them in his. 'My darling, my poor darling, what a horrendous thing to happen to you. Thank God you are alive. Men like that frequently have murderous intent. I'm so sorry this happened to *you*, of all women. Why you're just an innocent girl.'

He drew away, gazed into her eyes. 'I will look after you, keep you safe. And this is certainly not an impediment to our marriage. You are innocent, you are the victim.'

He rose, pulled her to her feet and, without saying another word, he brought her into his arms and held her close to him, murmuring soothing words. He couldn't bear to think what she had gone through, and his heart went out to her. At this moment he loved her more than ever. He was impressed by her immense courage, her integrity in wanting him to know about the horrific attack she had suffered. He cringed inside when he thought of this pure and inexperienced seventeen-year-old girl being brutally raped. It was unconscionable.

Moving away from him, looking into his worried face, Daphne said softly, 'Thank you, Hugo, thank you for saying that.'

'Who did this to you, Daphne?' he asked, his eyes narrowing. 'And what about your father? What did Charles say? Didn't he go after him? Have him apprehended by the police?'

'I didn't see the man's face at first, because he had a scarf wrapped around it. But after he'd, well . . . when he had finished with me, I reached up and pulled it off. I was stunned.' She took a deep breath and finished in a low voice. 'I was staring into the face of my childhood friend, Julian Torbett.'

'My God, how appalling of him! The wicked, evil man. He must be from the Torbett family of Havers Lodge?'

'Yes, he is.'

'What happened to him? What did your father *do*?' he asked in a harsh voice.

Daphne sat down again, and so did Hugo. Unable to resist, he took hold of her hand once more, as if never to let it go.

'Remember, he'd threatened me, frightened me, because of Dulcie and Mama. I didn't dare say a word to Papa. And then Julian actually had the nerve to come around with his fiancée, Madge Courtney, to go riding a week later. I had no choice but to agree, under the circumstances. My father and DeLacy rode with us, and I was safe, of course. But something strange happened, Hugo. Rifle shots went off in the fields, his horse was spooked, and bolted. Julian was thrown. He was unconscious when he was taken to Harrogate Hospital and he never regained consciousness. He died that night.'

Hugo drew closer, reached up and gently turned her face to his. He looked deeply into those marvellous blue eyes, and said in a sympathetic voice, 'You didn't tell Charles, did you? You kept the rape from your parents. That's true, isn't it?'

'What was the point of telling them? Especially when Julian Torbett had been killed in a freak riding accident.'

Hugo simply nodded, leaned back in the chair, and kept her hand in his. He was afraid to let go of her, and his love for her surged through him.

There was silence for a few moments; they were both lost in their own thoughts. Finally, it was Daphne who spoke.

She said, 'Mrs Alice knew. You see, she saw me come into the bedroom corridor, and grabbed me at once. She hurried me into my bedroom, before DeLacy and Ceci could question me. They were there and I was in a bedraggled state, my jacket torn and dirty. Mrs Alice helped me to get through the ordeal.'

'She would do that. She was my childhood friend, you know, and thoughtful, caring. I'm glad she knew, and that she helped you. That makes me feel a bit better, Daphne.'

'She told me something important. Mrs Alice said I should trust no one in this house, meaning Cavendon. Only my parents and the Swanns. Tell no one, trust no one, she said. And I haven't told anyone, and I don't trust anyone, except Mama and Papa. And the Swanns . . . and you, Hugo. I trust you with my life.'

He was touched by her words, and her faith in him. This gave him hope for a future with her. Before he could say anything, Daphne leaned into him, and kissed him on the cheek. 'Thank you,' she said. 'Thank you for being you, and what you are.'

'Daphne, I'm at a loss for words. I think you are enormously brave, and grown up beyond your years. You amaze me.'

'There is something else I must tell you, Hugo, and then I'm finished with my sad tales.'

'My darling Daphne, I'll listen to everything you have to say, sad or otherwise, and be happy to do so for the rest of my life.'

'There *is* an impediment to a marriage between us,' she insisted.

Puzzlement flickered in his blue eyes, and he gave her a curious look. 'Still talking about impediments, are we?'

'Yes.' Straightening in the chair, she gave him a pointed look. 'I'm pregnant, Hugo. I was raped and made pregnant.'

That he was stunned by this revelation was apparent; he gaped at her, stupefied, speechless for a moment, reeling from her words. It was a million-to-one chance she was raped on her father's land, and a million-to-one chance that the bastard had made her pregnant. He wished Torbett was alive. He would kill him.

After a moment, Hugo asked, 'How on earth have you been able to stand all this? To bear it, Daphne? You must have gone through hell, been worried to death. What a burden for you to carry.'

'It was, it is. But Mrs Alice and Miss Charlotte have been most supportive, and they take care of me.'

'Charles and Felicity do know about this, don't they? You have told your parents you're pregnant, haven't you?'

'I had to, and Miss Charlotte was helpful – she spoke to them first. Naturally, they have been loving and caring. Mama and Papa know it was not my fault.'

'Why do you say it's an impediment to our marriage?'

'Because I'm pregnant with another man's child.'

'A man who brutally raped you, ruined your life, in a sense, just like that!' He snapped his thumb and second finger together. 'I'm not going to let this situation ruin your life. Or mine. I'm going to give you a wonderful life, if you'll let me.'

She did not answer him, but sat there looking extremely worried.

Hugo said, 'Do you think I can stop loving you just like that? In an instant? Because you've told me something terrible, told me about a brutal attack on you? How can I possibly fall out of love? Actually, Daphne, your honesty, truthfulness and sense of honour have made me love you all the more. From the moment I met you I was in love with you, and I've never stopped thinking about you since. If you marry me, you will make my life complete. It will give me such happiness to be your husband. And believe me, I'll keep you safe from harm. Always. For the rest of your life.'

'But what about the baby? Would you want me to give it up? Give it away? Because I'm not certain I could do that.'

Hugo sat back in the chair, and closed his eyes, a familiar sadness flowing through him. A great sigh escaped. After a long moment, he opened his eyes and looked across at her. He half smiled.

'Do you see this man sitting here? He was a child once, a

child who was given away, banished from the father he loved, from the family he loved, from the home he had been born into, and loved. He was sent away from the country he loved. He was carelessly dismissed, sent to a place he didn't know, to people he had never met. Thrown away like a piece of rubbish. Do you think that this man, who was once that child, would let the woman he loves more than anyone else in the world, give her baby away? Never, not in a million years. Daphne, the baby you are carrying is an Ingham, and I'm an Ingham, as well as a Stanton. And I'll be damned if I'll allow anyone else but *us* to bring up your child.'

Later, as they walked up the hill back to the house, Hugo suddenly asked, 'What will you do, Daphne, if you don't marry me?'

Daphne answered at once. 'Charlotte came up with a plan to get me through the coming months.'

'What kind of plan?' He stopped walking and turned to look at her, obviously puzzled.

Daphne immediately told him all about Charlotte's idea, giving him all the details.

He listened attentively, and when she had finished, he remarked, 'It's a good plan, but it will be hard. You know that, don't you?'

'Yes, I do, but if I set my mind to it, I can do anything.'

Hugo smiled at her, and said lightly, almost offhandedly, 'But you'd have much more fun if you were married to me.'

THIRTY-SIX

When Cecily saw Genevra sitting on the wall just ahead of her, she groaned to herself. She was in a hurry this afternoon, and did not wish to waste time with the Romany girl.

But the moment Genevra spotted her, she jumped off the wall and stood in the middle of the path waiting, a huge smile on her face. She was blocking the path, as usual.

Cecily stopped, smiled back. 'Hello, Genevra.'

The gypsy didn't reply, just went on smiling, then handed a small package to Cecily.

Putting her satchel down on the ground, Cecily took the parcel and opened the grubby piece of pink paper. 'What is it?' she asked, frowning as she stared at the piece of bone tied with bits of narrow pale blue and scarlet ribbon.

'A charm for yer. I made it, carved it. Tek a look then.'

Cecily did so, and instantly saw the small carvings on the bone. She could just make out the shape of a swan, and what looked like the outline of a bell. She stared at Genevra and asked, 'What does it mean?'

'It's a charm. Lucky. Keep it. Don't lose.'

'I'll keep it, but what do the carvings mean?'

'Nowt,' Genevra said, and laughed loudly, as she always did, and went back to the wall. She cartwheeled over it, turned to face Cecily. 'Be safe, liddle Ceci,' she said, and ran off across the meadow without looking back as she sometimes did.

Cecily stared after her, as usual baffled by the strange girl, then put the piece of bone in her pocket, picked up her satchel and went on her way to Cavendon.

Once she arrived, she avoided the kitchen, which she knew would be full of hustle and bustle, since Cook would be preparing afternoon tea. Instead she went into the house through the conservatory, crossed the front entrance hall, and entered the library. All was still and quiet. There was no one around.

She had been given permission by Aunt Charlotte to copy the white rose of York and the white swan of Cavendon, which were on the big framed parchment bearing the Ingham family crest. She took out her sketching pad and sat down on the stool that Aunt Charlotte had left there for her.

Within twenty minutes Cecily had made several sketches of the swan, and the white rose. She nodded to herself as she stared down at them. Her copies were perfect in every detail.

'Hello, Ceci dear,' Charlotte said.

Startled, Cecily sat up with a jerk. 'Oh! You made me jump!' she cried, swinging around to face her great-aunt.

'I'm so sorry,' Charlotte apologized. 'I didn't mean to creep up on you and startle you like that.'

'It's all right. Look. I think my sketches are good, don't you?'

Charlotte stepped closer and stared at the drawing book and the images the girl had drawn. 'They are indeed.' She smiled at her and asked, 'But what are the images for, Ceci?'

Smiling back at her great-aunt, Cecily jumped up and explained, 'This swan will be on all the clothes I design. When I have my own shop. And I shall copy the white rose of York, in fabric. Cotton and silk, maybe even satin, and it will be like a brooch. To wear on the lapel of a suit or dress or even a coat. And it will always be white. It's like . . . well, a sort of trademark.'

Charlotte could not hide her astonishment. 'But how clever of you! What better trademark than the white rose of York? And, of course, the white swan will look wonderful on a label.'

Cecily beamed at her. 'I'm trying to think of everything.'

Nodding, still smiling, Charlotte said, 'Well, it's a good beginning, and if I have any ideas I shall pass them on to you. Are you going upstairs to the sewing room now?'

'Yes, to say hello to Mam, and to look at the white ball gown. Lady Daphne is going to wear it at the summer ball tomorrow night.'

'I think I'll come with you, I'd like to see it too.'

Cecily bent down to pick up her satchel and the piece of bone fell out of her pocket. As she picked it up, Charlotte exclaimed, 'Did Genevra give that to you?'

'Yes, she did. How did you know?'

'She gave me something similar the other day. May I look at it, Ceci?'

'Yes.' She handed it to her great-aunt, and said, 'There's a carving like a swan, and one like a bell.'

Examining it carefully, Charlotte saw that Cecily was right, although the carving was rough, amateurish, as were the symbols on her piece of bone. 'There was a heart and crosses on mine, and I've no idea what they mean.'

'Neither do I. I mean, I don't know why there's a bell. But I suppose the swan is for my name.'

'Well, she means no harm. She just wants to be friendly,' Charlotte remarked, walking with Cecily to the back staircase. 'Her family has been here for years. Actually, I think Genevra was born here on the estate.'

'Oh, I didn't know that,' Cecily said as they went upstairs together, heading to the sewing room, surprised by this comment.

Charlotte and Cecily had only been in the room for a few minutes, admiring the white ball gown hanging on the rack, when DeLacy came hurtling through the door.

Automatically, Alice and Cecily stood in front of the white gown protectively. And then they all laughed when DeLacy said, 'The white gown! I'd better stay in the doorway, hadn't I?'

'I think so,' Charlotte answered, but she was smiling.

'I came to thank you, Mrs Alice,' DeLacy said. 'My chiffon frock is lovely, and I'm glad we picked the pink and scarlet floral. It's so summery and pretty.'

'Lady Gwendolyn will be overjoyed,' Charlotte interjected pithily. 'She'll be thrilled that it's not blue.'

The two girls giggled, and DeLacy said, 'Can Cecily come down to have afternoon tea with us, Mrs Alice? Please say yes. Mama said I could invite her, and she's even letting me bring Dulcie.'

'Of course Cecily can go.' Alice smiled at the girl.

The two of them disappeared immediately, and Charlotte went and sat down in the small armchair in the corner. 'Join me for a minute,' she said to Alice. 'I've something important to tell you.'

Pulling up the other chair, Alice sat down, and looked at Charlotte quizzically. 'What is it? You have a funny look on your face.'

Charlotte whispered, 'She's told him everything . . . even that she's pregnant.'

'Oh my God!' Alice exclaimed, and then clapped a hand over her mouth, and her eyes widened in surprise.

'But it's all right,' Charlotte said, leaning even closer. 'He doesn't care and he still wants to marry her. So we've got to do everything we can to bring that about.'

Alice could only nod. But her heart lifted with genuine happiness for Daphne. Hugo was the perfect solution to her dilemma.

THIRTY-SEVEN

The ball was in full swing, and Lady Daphne Ingham was the belle of the ball. In her silver shoes, and the white lace gown, which swirled around her as she moved, she was a vision of beauty and grace.

Hugo had danced with her at the beginning of the evening, but then other men had clamoured around her and claimed their turn to whirl her across the dance floor. Now, at last, he had her in his arms once more and they were waltzing to the strains of Strauss's *Blue Danube*.

'You're as light as a feather,' Hugo murmured against her hair, breathing in the fragrance of her skin that smelled faintly of flowers, roses mingled with hyacinths.

'Soon I won't be,' she said, leaning back slightly, looking up at him, laughter in her eyes. 'I'll be as fat as a tub of butter.'

He gave her a huge smile. 'That's one of the things I love about you, Daphne, your sense of humour.'

'And what else do you love about me?' she asked, still gazing up into his face.

Hugo looked down at her, his eyes narrowing slightly. 'You're flirting with me,' he smiled in surprise, pleased and amused by this sudden turn of events.

'I know. And every other woman in the ballroom is jealous, because you're dancing with me instead of with them.'

'I hope not all the women are jealous. Some of them are quite old.'

Daphne laughed, and drew closer to him. 'I've noticed something about you, Hugo, something I find very intriguing.'

'And what's that?' he asked as he swirled her around, guiding her towards the terrace doors, which stood open on this balmy night.

'Women seem to swarm all over you, like bees around a pot of honey. They just won't leave you alone. At one moment, I couldn't get near you. Actually, what I—'

She stopped abruptly, merely offered him an enigmatic smile, and remained silent as they went on dancing towards the doors.

'And *what?* Finish your sentence, please,' he said.

'I felt something peculiar. Inside, I mean.'

'You were jealous. Admit it, Lady Daphne Ingham. You were jealous, weren't you?' His eyes were fixed on her intently.

'Yes,' she murmured. 'I suppose that was it.'

He held her tighter. 'It's *you* I love and adore. You I want to marry. You I want to spend the rest of my life with. I wouldn't know what to do with any of those women eyeing us now.'

'Would you know what to do with me?'

For a moment Hugo was startled by this question, which he thought was bold for her, and certainly a little provocative. He decided to respond accordingly. 'Oh yes indeed, I would know exactly what to do with you, my darling.'

'So tell me,' she answered, and then exclaimed in a low voice, 'Oh do look Hugo! Every woman is ogling you.'

'*Us,*' he replied. 'They're ogling *us,*' he repeated as he waltzed her through the French doors, out onto the terrace, and down to the far end. When he released her, he backed her into the corner, and stared into her eyes. 'The first thing I would do with you is kiss you. May I?'

She nodded.

Hugo took her in his arms and kissed her on the mouth. She responded ardently, and this emboldened him. His kisses grew more passionate, yet she did not pull away. She suddenly put her arms around him, moved much closer. And they went on kissing until he knew he must bring it to an end. He was dangerously close to exploding.

He gently pulled away, stepped back, and took several breaths.

Daphne leaned against the low terrace wall, also breathless.

After a moment or two, Hugo said, 'Has your mother explained anything about marriage to you, Daphne?'

She shook her head, grimaced. 'Mama would never bring up things like that, and I wouldn't dare ask her. Also, lately she's been worried about my aunt, as you know.'

'Yes, I do know,' Hugo responded, wondering why Felicity was so neglectful of Daphne at this moment, when there was so much at stake for her daughter. It beggared belief that all of Felicity's attention was focused on her sister. He knew how close they were, and that Anne had brought Felicity up after their mother's sudden death. But, nonetheless, he still believed her daughter deserved and needed her love and wisdom at this difficult time in her life.

Daphne broke the silence when she said softly, 'I spoke to Mrs Alice and Miss Charlotte the other day. They invited me to Miss Charlotte's for tea, and asked if I needed help . . . about those matters . . . to do with marriage. I told them I did, and I asked them some questions.'

'I'm sure they helped you, didn't they?' He raised a brow quizzically.

'Yes they did. They were kind, and explained a few important things they thought I should know. And I'm much less afraid now, actually.'

Hugo nodded, and then he laughed lightly, shaking his head. 'Thank God for the Swanns! Whatever would the Inghams have done without them over the years?'

Daphne laughed with him. 'I agree with you. Don't forget, it was a Swann who completely remade this dress I'm wearing. Which you so much admire.'

Hugo drew closer, put his arms around her, held her next to him as they both gazed out across the gardens and Cavendon Park beyond.

Daphne nestled against him, feeling comfortable and safe. Suddenly she said, 'I do feel much better about things now, Hugo. Honestly, I do.'

'About men and the marriage bed? That is what you mean, isn't it?'

Daphne nodded.

'I must admit, I've worried about those things myself. As any intelligent man would. Being violently attacked, the way you were, would make any woman fearful of men and marriage, and all that it entails.'

'I was afraid in the beginning, when it first happened. But I calmed down, and began to think more clearly. And then, when you first came here, I reminded myself there were nice men in this world. Men like you, like Papa and my two brothers. I thought you were so caring and charming. That was before Papa told me how you felt about me.'

'And how do *you* feel about *me*, my lady? And when will *I* know?'

A smile flickered on her mouth. 'Sooner than I thought. Miss Charlotte said I should make up my mind as quickly as possible, that it wasn't fair to you. And it's true.'

He was silent a moment, thinking of the right words to say,

words to reassure her. They came to him at once. 'I promise you that if you do marry me, I will expunge all of your bad memories, give you nothing but happiness, pleasure and love for the rest of my life.'

'I think I know that, Hugo . . .'

They continued to stand with their arms around each other, staring into the distance, now lost for a moment in their private thoughts.

It was a lovely evening. Bright stars littered the midnight sky; there was a full moon hanging so low it looked as if it was resting on the surface of the lake. The air was fragrant with the scent of flowers, and especially night-blooming jasmine.

This little corner on the terrace was tranquil and private, and no one could see them. It was entirely theirs for a moment.

I am home, I'm where I belong, Hugo thought. With the woman I belong to, and who I know belongs to me, even if she does not realize it yet. A sudden rush of happiness flowed through him. Vaguely, in the background, he could hear the music, the laughter, the chatter of people enjoying themselves. And here he was, in a cocoon of love. With Daphne. Nothing else mattered in this world. She was all he would ever need for as long as he lived.

'We'd better go inside, Hugo,' Daphne said gently, stirring in his arms.

'Yes.' He released her, took her hand in his and led her down the terrace. 'Tell me soon, my lady. Waiting for an answer is unbearable.'

'I will, I promise,' she said.

When they went back into the ballroom, Hugo was immediately conscious of everyone's eyes on them. And so he swept her into his arms and danced down the room with her, holding her apart from him, most properly and with total decorum. Once the music stopped, they went to join Charles, who was standing with Diedre and DeLacy near the entrance to the ballroom.

'There you are,' Charles said, smiling at them. 'I was beginning to wonder where you were.'

'Taking a breath of air,' Hugo answered.

'I'd like to have a chat with you later, Hugo,' the Earl continued. 'If you'd care to have a nightcap after the guests leave?'

'I'd enjoy that, Charles. Thank you.'

'We haven't had a chance to catch up since you arrived, and I must admit I'm anxious to hear what transpired in Zurich. Not your private business, of course, but things in general. What the mood is like over there, that sort of thing . . .' The Earl let his sentence drift off.

'I understand exactly, and I'll be happy to fill you in,' Hugo answered. Turning to Diedre, he said, 'Would you care to dance?'

'Thank you,' she replied, smiling at him, and immediately stepped towards him. He led her on to the dance floor, thinking how lovely she looked tonight. In fact, all of the Ingham women did, and their guests were equally elegantly gowned and bejewelled. The men too looked handsome and well dressed in white tie and tails.

It was one thirty in the morning when Charles and Hugo settled down with a brandy in front of the dying fire in the library. All the guests had departed. The family had gone to bed. And Charles had just told Hanson to lock up for the night.

'I've got guards on duty,' Charles confided quietly, once they were alone. 'After that damnable fire, Percy Swann deemed it vital that we have plenty of woodsmen out and about on the estate. Most especially when we're having guests, people from the outside. So he went ahead and hired extra men from our villages. They're all over the estate, and especially around the stable block. We've got to protect all our horses, you know.'

'I do indeed, and Percy's right: once bitten twice shy, that's my motto.'

'Percy has been a fine head gamekeeper – the best.'

'As all the Swanns who've gone before have been,' Hugo agreed, meaning what he said. But he couldn't help a small smile surfacing. There were Swanns here, there and everywhere, but then there had always been a bevy of Swanns at Cavendon. They were part of the scenery, virtually part of the family.

Settling back, Charles said, 'Our talk, when you were last here, alerted me. Now, when I read the newspapers, I notice things I might never have paid attention to before, Hugo. So thank you for that.'

'You're reading between the lines, as I do a lot,' Hugo said. 'Everything I talked to you about before is bound to happen, of that I am sure. I just don't know when. There is constant talk of the Kaiser's lust for power, his desire to rule the whole of Europe, and basically that's where all of the trouble is . . . between Germany and the Austro-Hungarian Empire. I'm just afraid we might get drawn into the conflict. If they go to war, that is.'

'But how?' Charles stared at Hugo, frowning. 'We're not part of their quarrels, surely, and anyway, the Kaiser would avoid involving England. After all, he and the King are first cousins, through Queen Victoria, their grandmother.'

Hugo let out a loud chuckle, and shook his head vehemently. 'You don't think a man like the Kaiser, a power-hungry tyrant, would consider *family*, do you, Charles? He couldn't care less about the King, or the English. Actually, I have a feeling he's jealous of our great Empire, the success we enjoy in the world.'

'That's why we shouldn't let ourselves get drawn into anything that could prove dangerous to the Empire and especially our country.'

'I agree.' Hugo swallowed some of the cognac, and put the glass down on a side table. He leaned forward. 'If you have any foreign investments – and by that, I mean in Europe – I suggest you sell. On Monday. Certainly as soon as you can. I have divested myself of all my foreign holdings, except for those in Switzerland. The Swiss banks are rock solid. I know my money is safe there.'

'I'll certainly take your advice,' Charles answered.

Thirty-Eight

H ugo sat back, nursing his brandy balloon in both hands, listening attentively. Charles had started to speak about Cavendon a short while ago, and Hugo was fascinated.

'So, after I had gone through the old estate record books, guided by Charlotte, I decided to financially back more tenanted farming, and I've put a great emphasis on this, and also on livestock. In my great-grandfather's day, Cavendon truly was a farming estate. What I want is to get back to that level of agriculture,' Charles explained.

'I think it's a very wise move,' Hugo replied. 'I don't wish to frighten you, but I still believe there will be a war in Europe. That we'll get dragged into it . . . rightly or wrongly. Local produce is going to play a big part in the feeding of this country, because if there's a war, then we won't be importing any goods.'

'I must admit, I hadn't thought of that when I decided to increase the farming here, but after you left for Zurich, it did strike me that I'd made a good decision.'

'What've you got? It's about three thousand acres here, isn't it?' Hugo frowned. 'If I'm remembering correctly.'

'Yes. Without the grouse moor, of course, but—' Charles broke off, and looked at the door.

There had been a light knocking, and now it flew open to reveal Daphne hovering there.

Charles stood up, and so did Hugo, as she glided into the room. It was obvious from the expressions on their faces that they were genuinely surprised to see her.

Before her father could say a word, she exclaimed, 'Sorry, Papa, to disturb you in this way, but I have something important to say. May I come in?'

The Earl laughed. 'You're already *in*, so you might as well stay and tell us what's on your mind. And why you're up at this late hour and still dressed in your evening gown?'

Walking forward, Daphne did not answer. Instead she focused her eyes on Hugo. When she was a foot away from him, she said, 'I will marry you, Hugo, I *want* to marry you, actually. I just came to this decision, and I wanted to tell you *immediately*. I went to your room. But you weren't there. I realized you were probably down here with Papa. Anyway, here I am. With my decision.'

Completely taken aback, Hugo was speechless. He just stood there gaping at her, and then slowly a huge smile spread across his face.

Daphne exclaimed, 'Oh, I forgot! Does Hugo have to ask your permission, Papa?'

'Don't be a silly girl. He already has it!' Charles said.

Hugo rushed forward, took hold of Daphne, and stared into her face. 'Are you sure?'

'I am.'

'Are you *sure* you're sure?'

She nodded. 'I am, I really am. So you can kiss me, if you like.'

Pulling her into his arms, he kissed her on the mouth, and then they stood back, smiling at each other.

It was this ease and affection he saw between them that convinced the Earl his daughter had made the right decision for herself; that, in her own way, she loved Hugo. And he was filled with relief, plus the kind of happiness a father feels when he knows his daughter is in the right hands – the safest hands in the world.

Daphne walked over to him. He hugged her, kissed her cheek. 'I'm glad, Daphne, truly happy you made this decision. And on your own,' the Earl told her in a loving voice.

With the help of two Swanns, Hugo thought, but remained silent. Whatever they had said to her, he would be eternally grateful to those extraordinary women.

Daphne said, 'Let's sit down, shall we? You see, I have a few . . . conditions. I'd like to discuss them with you, Hugo. And you too, Papa.'

'Conditions,' Charles repeated slowly, a frown crossing his face.

'I'll agree to anything,' Hugo cried, laughter shining in his eyes. Earlier, he had thought he would explode with desire for her. Now he believed he might just explode with sheer joy. He didn't care what her conditions were; he'd agree to anything. More or less.

'Papa, the first condition is that you and Mama make the announcement of our engagement immediately. I would like to read it in *The Times* by the middle of next week. No later.' She looked at Hugo. 'Do you agree?'

'Absolutely.'

'I would prefer to get married quickly. As soon as possible, actually. And for a number of reasons, the main one being that Aunt Anne could die at any moment. I don't want my wedding postponed because of a bereavement in the family.'

'But how *soon* is soon? What do you have in mind, darling?' her father asked. 'Look here, Daphne, I don't want your marriage to Hugo to appear to be a shotgun affair.'

'September. At the latest early October,' Daphne answered. 'Naturally, I would like to marry Hugo next week, or certainly later in August. However, I know the Glorious Twelfth is imminent. And that Mama and you would not agree to August because of the grouse shooting. So September it is. Is that all right with you, Hugo? Does it suit?'

'Anything you say, anything you want, I'm totally on your side,' was his immediate response. He still couldn't quite believe all this was happening, and at two thirty in the morning, no less.

'I would be happy with a small wedding, Papa. Just our immediate family, and that includes Aunt Lavinia and Aunt Vanessa. Will they come? They're not here much these days, are they?'

'No, because they have busy lives in London,' Charles replied. 'I'm quite certain they will want to be here. I know your uncle Jack wouldn't miss it for the world.'

'If Aunt Lavinia allows him to come . . . you know they're a bit off track with each other these days.'

'Daphne, really! That's silly gossip Diedre has planted in your head.'

Daphne shrugged and sat back. She went on, 'I hope you don't mind, but I don't really think I want to have any bridesmaids, Papa. Just a flower girl. In other words, Dulcie.'

Charles was startled by this statement, and he said in a perplexed tone, 'But DeLacy and Diedre will be hurt, Daphne. You really must have them as bridesmaids, they're your sisters.'

'DeLacy will be happy to walk behind me with Dulcie, but I don't think Diedre will take to that role quite as easily. After all, she's older than I am, and she'll be angry with me because she isn't getting married first.'

'Oh I don't know about that, my dear. Diedre loves you. Perhaps you have to speak with your mother about this. However, I genuinely believe Diedre will be cut to the quick if she isn't a bridesmaid with DeLacy.'

'I really only want a flower girl . . . Dulcie,' Daphne said again.

'She's a bit of a handful. We need a bridesmaid to take control of her, you know,' Charles pointed out.

Daphne looked across at Hugo. 'What are your feelings about bridesmaids?'

'I understand you wish to keep the wedding small, Daphne, darling. Still, I think your father is right. Dulcie might well need someone to mind her during the service. He certainly has a good point there. One you must consider.'

'All right. Two bridesmaids and a flower girl. Now, Hugo, Papa will be giving me away. And you need a best man. I was wondering how you felt about Guy taking on that role.'

'I'd be honoured,' Hugo answered swiftly, wondering when she had thought all this out.

'Regarding the church, Papa, I was thinking we ought to use the church here on the estate. I know it's not huge, but it will hold the entire Ingham family and all of the Swanns. They must be at the ceremony, don't you agree?'

'I most certainly do. They've been at every Ingham marriage for years. They were at mine, and they should be at yours. Just a thought about the church here on the estate, Daphne. It's not big enough to hold the villagers. So perhaps we should have your marriage ceremony in the village church – then everyone can come. How does that strike you?'

Before she could answer, Hugo said, 'I agree with you, Charles, and there's something else. If I'm not mistaken, the villagers usually have a tea party in the village hall afterwards, don't they? To celebrate the wedding of an Ingham.'

'You're absolutely right, Hugo. It had slipped my mind. I must arrange for that to be given, and at my expense.'

'Holding the ceremony in the village church is a lovely idea,' Daphne interjected. 'As for our wedding reception . . .' She broke off, looked at Hugo, and continued, 'Shall we have it in the South Wing? What do you think, Hugo? Papa?'

'There's no place better, in my opinion. What about you, Charles?'

'Of course, it's the ideal spot,' the Earl agreed.

Daphne smiled at them both, and said to Hugo, 'Now you must decide about the honeymoon . . . where we should go. I'll go anywhere with you.'

'I'm so happy to hear that,' Hugo answered. 'How about Paris? One of my favourite cities, and then we could travel to Zurich. My villa is on the lake, and it is very beautiful.'

'I would like that, Hugo.'

Charles said, 'The baby must be born at Cavendon. It is an Ingham, after all.'

'We'll come back for Christmas, Papa. The baby is due in January.'

THIRTY-NINE

'Something *old*, something *new*, something *borrowed*, something *blue*,' Cecily said to DeLacy, and then took a small package out of her satchel and placed it on the long table.

The two girls were in the sewing room at Cavendon, Alice Swann's domain on the floor above the family bedroom corridor. It was two days before Daphne's marriage to Hugo, and Cecily was waiting for Daphne to arrive, to have the final fitting of her wedding gown.

'So what is it you got for her, Ceci?' DeLacy asked, eyeing the package. 'Come on, show me, before Daphne gets here.'

'No, I can't, Lacy, I don't want to open it. Mam wrapped it up so nicely with ribbon. But I can describe it.'

'Oh, all right, that will have to do for now.'

'It's a blue silk garter for her leg. My mother told me a blue garter is popular with brides . . . it provides the *blue* without being seen.'

DeLacy laughed. 'How clever. I bought her a lace wedding handkerchief, which is new. Mama is lending Daphne her diamond bow brooch, and that means *new*, *blue* and *borrowed* are taken care of nicely. I don't know who's giving her something old.'

'I do,' Ceci said, throwing the large white sheet over the wedding gown hanging on a clothes rack.

'You do! Who is it? Who's giving her something old?'

'My great-aunt Charlotte. It's a bracelet, I think.'

'Oh, that's kind of her,' DeLacy responded. 'So that part is settled. Hugo has given Daphne diamond earrings as a wedding present. I think Diedre's green with envy.'

Cecily simply nodded, not wanting to become involved in a discussion about Lady Diedre, who was not one of her favourites.

Walking over to the large closet, she took out DeLacy's bridesmaid's dress and carried it to the rack. 'Do you want to try it one more time?' Ceci asked. 'Just to be sure.'

'No, it fits perfectly,' DeLacy replied, and went to join Cecily, began touching the dress. 'It's so pretty. I love the rose pink taffeta and tulle, the way you've combined them.' DeLacy smiled at her. 'You are clever.' She turned around. There was a loud knock on the door, and it swung open to admit her brother, Miles.

'I've done it!' he exclaimed, striding into the sewing room, closing the door behind him. 'Hello, Ceci, DeLacy.'

'Hello, Miles,' Cecily responded.

'Done what?' DeLacy asked.

'Managed to get my ushers together. Finally. I have Mark Stanton, Hugo's only living relative on his father's side, plus the three sons of Major Gaunt, who runs the Stanton yard. Hugo's cousin Mark, and the Gaunts, are his only guests, as you know. So with me and Uncle Jack, we're six. That's fine, because it's not a huge fancy society wedding.'

'Oh don't say that!' DeLacy cried. 'It will be fancy. We're all going to be dressed beautifully, and wear jewels, and you and the other men will be in morning suits. And Miss Charlotte is making the South Wing look beautiful, with lots of plants and flowers.'

'So Guy told me. He also said there's going to be a small orchestra, or quartet – something like that. Apparently Cook's got in extra help and we're going to have a delicious high tea. All of my favourite things, like sausage rolls and pork pies. I'm glad it's an afternoon wedding, aren't you?'

'Yes.' DeLacy touched the pink bridesmaid's dress and said, 'Look, Miles, isn't it lovely? Ceci made it for me.'

Miles nodded. He looked across at Ceci, gave her a huge smile. 'You've outdone yourself, Ceci. I hear from Daphne that her wedding gown is fantastically gorgeous.'

Cecily nodded, her eyes sparkling. 'That might be a bit of an exaggeration, but it is rather lovely, even if I do say so myself.'

'Did Daphne show you her diamonds, Miles?'

'She did, and the sapphires as well. She's going to wear those tonight, she told me.' He grinned at his sister. 'I can't wait to see Diedre's face when Daphne comes down to dinner. She's always been jealous of her.'

'I know. And Papa never helped, always claiming Daphne would marry the son of a duke. That really made Diedre crazy.'

'I asked Papa why Hugo and Daphne are getting married so quickly. The engagement was just announced in *The Times* in August, and today is only the eighteenth of September. She'll be a married woman on September twentieth. Gosh, just imagine that. Daphne a married woman.' Miles walked over to the window and opened it. 'It's stuffy in here,' he said.

'What did Papa say?' DeLacy asked, curious herself.

'He said Daphne was worried that Aunt Anne might die suddenly, which she will, most probably. Daphne didn't want the marriage postponed for a year because we were all in mourning.'

'Oh gosh, yes, that's true.' DeLacy went and sat down on a chair. 'Who's arrived so far, Miles? Do you know?'

'Uncle Jack and Aunt Lavinia. I ran into them, and bagged him for an usher immediately. He was his usual genial self, but I thought Aunt Lavinia looked put out. Sort of sulky.'

DeLacy said in a low voice, 'She's got another man.'

'Who told you that bit of nasty gossip?' Miles asked sharply.

'Diedre. She said Papa was furious because Lavinia might bring a big scandal down on the family. This new boyfriend is a married man. He's a Member of Parliament. Papa's quite upset about it all.'

'Good heavens! That's some nasty charge against Lavinia. And how does Diedre know?'

'I think she overheard Papa telling Mama.'

'Eavesdropping again, I bet you anything,' Miles shot back, making a face.

Cecily, going about her work of hanging up the bridesmaids' dresses, and checking the shoes and gloves, was laughing inside. Miles always complained to her that DeLacy loved to gossip about the family, but he did too. She was well aware he thought Diedre was mean about everyone, and certainly it was common knowledge that she was jealous of Daphne, especially of her great beauty.

Daphne was the sweetest of the four Dees, and Cecily was relieved and glad she was marrying Hugo. She had made the right decision, according to her mother and Great-Aunt Charlotte. Cecily knew everything about the situation, but was under oath not to reveal anything. *Loyalty binds me*, she said to herself under her breath. That was the oath. She would never break it.

Cecily hadn't been listening to DeLacy and Miles chattering about the family for the last few minutes, preoccupied as she was with the clothes for the wedding. But when DeLacy began to laugh uproariously, she glanced across at her and then looked at Miles, who was still standing at the window. Cecily raised a brow, and asked, 'What did I miss?'

Miles, grinning, answered, 'DeLacy mentioned the famous sapphires from Hugo, and I said that no doubt Great-Aunt Gwendolyn would not like them because they match Daphne's eyes. Like all the frocks you make for her.'

Cecily grinned.

And so did DeLacy, who then said, 'I bet you a sixpence Great-Aunt Gwendolyn asks if they're real. She can be very odd.'

They all laughed.

A few minutes later, Daphne arrived in the sewing room, looking elegant, dressed entirely in cream with touches of black. Cecily nodded approvingly.

DeLacy said, 'Oh how chic you are, Daphers. Just elegance personified.'

'Thank you, Lacy. It's a new outfit Mrs Alice made for me. It was designed by Cecily, of course. I love all the black touches, the black patent belt, the shiny black buttons, the black piping.'

Looking across at Miles, she went on, 'I hear you now have six ushers, with yourself. I'm happy, Miles. You were so worried.'

Miles strolled across the room and squeezed her shoulder. 'I'll never let you down, old thing. I suppose I had better scoot . . . you're going to try on your gown. Nobody's supposed to see it, right?'

Daphne nodded and took hold of his arm, leading him to the door. 'Thanks for everything, Miles, you're really a very nice brother.'

Miles stood in the doorway, smiling, his eyes resting on Cecily, as he said, 'Farewell, my beauties, see you anon.'

Once they were alone, Cecily took the sheet off the wedding dress, and said, 'I'll help you to try this on now, Lady Daphne. I don't think there's anything for me to do, but I had better check.'

They walked over to the screened-off corner, with Cecily carrying the wedding gown on its hanger.

A few moments later, when Daphne came from behind the screen and stood in the middle of the floor, DeLacy began to clap. 'Oh Daphne, you are just gorgeous! The dress is . . . unbelievably beautiful. Congratulations, Cecily.'

The wedding gown was made entirely of pure white Chantilly lace, laid over a white taffeta bodice and skirt. The latter was narrow, very slender, and the lace fell into a long train at the back. The waist was cut very high, in the French Empire style, so favoured by Napoleon's Empress, Josephine. The sleeves were long, made only of the white lace, while the neckline was scooped out, just covering the shoulders.

Daphne looked down at the bodice. 'Mama's diamond brooch will be pinned here, just below the scoop and in the middle. Am I right, Cecily?'

'You are, m'lady.' Cecily brought her a headdress composed of white silk-and-lace flowers made into a coronet, and put it on top of Daphne's head, pressing it down.

She said, 'This will hold your veil in place, Lady Daphne. Don't worry, it won't fall off. I'll make sure of that.'

Cecily stood away, looked at her, and smiled, thrilled at the effect. 'The veil will complete the picture, but I don't want to try it on you again. It's so delicate.'

Daphne smiled at her. 'I know it works, Ceci; certainly it did the other day. And I've no doubt it will on Saturday. Thank you. Thank you so much for all your hard work.'

Daphne had just returned to her bedroom when there was a light knock on the door. She went to open it and saw Charlotte Swann standing there.

'I have something for you, Lady Daphne. May I come in for a moment?'

'Yes, please do, Miss Charlotte.' As she spoke, Daphne opened the door wider and stepped to one side.

As was her way, Charlotte Swann went straight to the heart of the matter. 'I want to give you this, Lady Daphne. It's very old, and you must have something old as well as new, blue and borrowed.' She handed Daphne the gift. It was wrapped in silver paper and tied with grey silk ribbon.

'Thank you, Miss Charlotte,' Daphne said, staring down at the package. 'I have something borrowed from Mama, her bow brooch. Cecily gave me something blue, a garter.' She laughed as she said this, shaking her head. 'And DeLacy gave me a lace wedding handkerchief that is brand new. Yours is the last gift to fulfil the ancient saying. Can I open it now?'

Charlotte smiled. 'Why not?'

Once the paper was removed, Daphne found she was holding a blue velvet box. When she lifted the lid she gasped. She was staring at a narrow strand of diamonds. 'Why it's beautiful!' she exclaimed. She held the diamond bracelet in her hands, marvelling at it. 'But this is too valuable. You can't possibly give me this, Miss Charlotte. And I certainly can't accept it.'

'Yes, you can. And you must.' Charlotte waved her hand in front of Daphne, as the young woman attempted to give the bracelet back to her. She said, 'Listen to me, Lady Daphne, this is meant for you. It is an Ingham family heirloom, and therefore rightfully yours. I want you to wear it, knowing that your grandfather, David, the Fifth Earl, gave it to me for my twenty-first birthday. I've treasured it all these years, and now it's yours to enjoy.'

Daphne stood holding the bracelet, knowing that to insist Charlotte take it back would be to insult her. That was the last thing she wanted to do to this woman, who had been such a comfort and wise counsellor.

Daphne took a deep breath. 'If it is an Ingham family heirloom, then who did it belong to originally? Do you know, Miss Charlotte?'

'Yes, it belonged to the Fifth Earl's mother, the Fourth Countess . . . your great-grandmother.' Charlotte reached out for the bracelet. Daphne gave it to her, and Charlotte fastened it on Daphne's wrist. '*There*. You see, it looks beautiful, and it's very simple, not at all ostentatious.'

'Thank you, Miss Charlotte. I shall treasure it always.'

Charles was ensconced in the library with his sister Lavinia, and he was having a hard time controlling himself. To say he was angry was an understatement.

The Earl of Mowbray was fuming inside, yet he did not dare let go of his self-control. There were already guests at Cavendon, who had arrived for Daphne's wedding. Hugo's cousin, Mark Stanton, was here, having come up from London earlier, and so was his other sister Vanessa, who had her own suite of rooms in the house.

Lavinia suddenly said, 'I know you're furious, Charles, but I'm not entirely to blame. Jack and I have problems.'

'Yes, you have been saying that for a while now. But that doesn't mean you can go off and find another man, and get hopelessly involved with him, as you obviously are.'

'I didn't go off and look for another man. It just happened. That's the way of the world, Charles. Things just happen in life.'

'If you have to take a lover, why in God's name did you choose a famous politician, someone who's very much in the public eye? And married, to boot.' Charles glared at her.

Lavinia let out a long sigh, and fell back against the cushions on the sofa. 'I didn't. What I mean is, it was Alex who pursued me, not the other way around.'

Charles compressed his lips. 'I'd heard he was a bit of a bounder, and now you've just confirmed it.'

'Charles, please get down off your high horse, and tell me what you want me to do.'

'You must break off this relationship at once, Lavinia. Before you involve this family – your family as well as mine – in a scandal of no mean proportions. There's gossip about you floating around already. The next thing you know, it'll be in the bloody newspapers.'

Lavinia sat up straighter, pushed back her blonde hair, her bright blue eyes flashing angrily. Watching her closely, Charles couldn't help thinking that when Daphne was forty she would have a look of his sister at this moment. They had always had a strong resemblance to each other, physically at any rate. As for their characters, they were very different. Lavinia was imprudent and impulsive, whilst Daphne was cautious and thought things through.

Lavinia said, 'I don't know how there could be gossip. I haven't told anyone about Alex.'

Charles threw her a pointed look. 'Yet several people have told me. Friends I trust, and who seem to know all about your affair. Perhaps your lover has spoken out of turn. It wouldn't surprise me. He doesn't have an ounce of class.'

Lavinia looked stricken, and she exclaimed, 'I can't believe he would talk about me, reveal we're involved. That's so dishonourable – it's very dismaying.' There was a pause and she said, 'Are you sure?'

'I am. Absolutely. How would anyone know otherwise? If you haven't told anyone, then he obviously did. You're quite a catch, you know. An Earl's daughter from one of the leading families in England, with a title in your own right, married to a notable business tycoon. Good God, Lavinia, don't you understand? He's boasted about you being his mistress.'

'Were you serious when you said it might get into the newspapers?' She leaned forward. Her face was very pale.

'I was indeed. I don't want a scandal surrounding us, Lavinia. Especially not at this moment, when Daphne is marrying.'

'Neither do I. What shall I do?'

'I'd break it off immediately, and don't put a bloody thing in writing. Just be unavailable, and if you have to speak to him, do it on the telephone. I wouldn't see him ever again if I were you.'

'I won't, I promise, and I'll do as you say.'

'Look, I'm not making a moral judgement about you, Lavinia. I'm just being protective. Many women take lovers because of problems in their marriage. But usually both parties are discreet, and so protect each other from gossip. And trouble. You just picked the wrong chap, that's all.'

'He picked me.'

'And there you have your answer, don't you think?'

'I do.' She sighed. 'By the way, I meant to ask you before, why is there this rush to wed on Daphne's part?'

'Several reasons,' he answered in a confident voice. 'Firstly, Daphne is worried that she and Hugo might have to postpone their marriage if Anne suddenly dies, which is very probable. That's why it's *this* Saturday, and not planned for a Saturday six months from now. And Felicity and I agreed with her about that. Secondly, Hugo has a great deal of travelling to do. He has to be in Zurich and then New York. They didn't want to be separated for long stretches of time.'

'I understand. They fell in love very quickly. Was it a *coup de foudre*, as the French say?'

'It was indeed. They took one look at each other, and that was it.'

'How lovely,' Lavinia said. 'She's a lucky girl. Hugo is a real charmer.'

'And very solid; he'll make a good husband. Now I think we'd better go to the yellow sitting room for tea. I'm sure everyone is waiting for us.'

FORTY

As she walked towards Cavendon, Charlotte couldn't help wondering why Olive Wilson wanted to speak to her, and why she had suggested the late afternoon today. The kitchen was very busy: Cook and the maids were bustling around with plates of sandwiches, scones, cakes and pots of tea, and Hanson was commanding the footmen, hustling them upstairs. Then it struck her. Olive, as lady's maid, would not be busy at that hour. The Countess would be presiding over afternoon tea with her guests in the yellow sitting room.

Olive must have something serious on her mind. Obviously she wanted to speak to Charlotte in private, probably in the servants' hall, which would be empty, with only Cook in the kitchen.

'Cooee! Cooee!' a voice suddenly called, attracting her attention.

Charlotte paused, swung her head, and saw Lady Vanessa, the younger sister of Charles and Lavinia, running down the terrace steps. She was waving and her face was full of smiles.

Waving in return, she waited for Vanessa, who reached her a moment later and threw her arms around Charlotte.

The two women hugged, and Vanessa exclaimed, 'Char, you look beautiful! And that lavender frock does suit you.'

Charlotte said, 'You look marvellous yourself, Vans.' As usual, these two women reverted to their childhood nicknames for each other whenever they met after an absence. Vanessa lived mostly in London now, and only came to Cavendon for holidays and special occasions.

'I'm feeling good. On top form, actually,' Vanessa answered.

'I suppose you're still banging the drum for the suffragettes, aren't you?'

'Yes, but I'm not so militant these days. We are making good progress. Emmeline Pankhurst is a charming, brilliant and powerful woman, and she's getting people to listen to her, to pay attention. You'll see, Char, one day women will have equal rights.' She paused and asked, 'Where are you heading now?'

'To the South Wing, I'm doing the floral decorations for the rooms being used for the wedding on Saturday.'

'Then you're in your element: gardens and gardening are your vocation. I'll keep you company for a few minutes.'

The two women started walking, Vanessa falling into step with Charlotte. They had been close since they were children, had grown up together, were completely at ease with each other. Vanessa Ingham was a modern woman, something of a visionary, tolerant, liberal minded and without any side to her.

After a moment, Vanessa casually remarked, 'I must admit, I was awfully surprised when I received the wedding invitation. They'd only just got engaged. Is there a reason for this headlong rush to the altar?' She gave Charlotte a penetrating stare.

'Anne Sedgewick's illness is one of the reasons. Sadly, she's at death's door, and could pass away at any moment. Daphne asked her parents to let her get married as soon as possible, while Anne is still alive. She knew that if she made the date for later in the year, she and Hugo might have to postpone the wedding for the mandatory mourning period.'

'Oh gosh yes, I hadn't thought of that. What are the other reasons?' Vanessa probed.

'Hugo's business interests. He's very successful. I'm sure Charlie told you. He has to be in Zurich and also New York very soon, and he wishes Daphne to travel with him. I can't say I blame him.'

'Neither can I. They're lucky they found each other, aren't they? It's not so easy to fall in love these days. There aren't that many eligible men around. Charles told me it was love at first sight for those two.'

'Yes. And you'll see how happy they are together. They're well suited. Hugo's a rather special man.'

'I'm glad. Has Charlie said anything to you about Lavinia?'

Charlotte stopped in her tracks, gave Vanessa a direct look, and nodded. 'He's been a little worried about her and a new male friend. But he didn't really say much more than that.'

'He's truly angry with her, Char, and he thinks she's making a fool of herself with that awful Alex Mellor. A seasoned womanizer, if ever there was one, and I tend to agree with Charles. He's terrified of scandal touching the family.'

'I know that. Don't you remember how upset he was when we were young, when the Hateful Harriette was falling about drunk, making scenes in Mayfair nightclubs, and getting herself in the newspapers? Charlie was mortified his father had to go through that ghastly episode.'

Vanessa made a face and said, 'It was tremendously embarrassing for him, and he doesn't want to have scandal blight the family name ever again.' She squeezed Charlotte's arm. 'I'd better dash. I'm going to be the last one in for tea, as usual. See you later.'

'I'll be around if you need me, Vans. In the South Wing all day tomorrow.'

Charlotte watched Vanessa flying off, racing across the lawn. She had always been thin, fast and elegant, like a pedigree filly. A thoroughbred. Charlotte loved her and appreciated what a true and loyal friend she was. They were devoted.

A few seconds later she went into the kitchen, and was greeted by the sound of Cook singing, 'Here comes the bride! Here comes the bride!'

Mrs Jackson was alone, standing in front of her long oak table, waving a wooden spoon in the air like the conductor of an orchestra.

She stopped singing abruptly when she spotted Charlotte. 'Luvely ter see yer, Miss Charlotte. Miss Wilson said ter tell yer she won't be a minute.'

'I'm not in a hurry, Cook, and I must say, you're certainly in the right mood for the wedding.'

'I am that, right thrilled. It's a treat ter see Lady Daphne so happy. Mr Hugo's luvely, that he is.'

Charlotte agreed, and continued, 'Are you sure you don't need extra help on Saturday? I can get a few more of the village girls to come in if you need them, Mrs Jackson.'

'I don't, but thank yer, Miss Charlotte. We're well prepared. As yer knows, Hanson is the master of organization.'

Before Charlotte could make any comment, Olive Wilson, lady's maid to the Countess, walked into the kitchen. 'Sorry to keep you waiting, Charlotte. I had to check on something for Her Ladyship.'

'That's all right, Olive.'

'I'll make yer a pot of tea,' Cook announced.

Charlotte glanced at Olive, who nodded and said, 'That would be nice, Cook, thanks ever so much.'

Within seconds, Olive was carrying a tray holding two cups of tea into the servants' hall down the corridor. It was quiet and cool after the warm kitchen.

Olive poured the tea and said, 'Thank you for coming. Alice said you'd be here in the South Wing, but I didn't want to miss you. That's why I sent a message.'

'I gather you wish to speak about something private,' Charlotte said, giving Olive a questioning look.

'I do, and I realize that this might not be a good time, just before the wedding. But I'm very worried about Her Ladyship. Sick with worry, really.'

'Why? What's the matter with her?'

'She's . . . well, she's just not *right*. Not the way she was before I went to London to deal with my mother's affairs. I really do believe she's ill.'

'What leads you to think that?' Charlotte pressed, leaning forward, wanting to know more. Had Olive seen something in Felicity that she had missed?

'She's not behaving like the woman I know – and obviously I've known her for quite a few years. She's remote, preoccupied, absent minded. I know she's not sleeping well, because she told me so, and certainly she has no appetite. Actually, Charlotte, Her Ladyship seems to be living in her own world. I feel, somehow, that she's isolated.'

Charlotte was thoughtful for a moment before she said slowly, carefully, 'I've noticed a remoteness in her, a distance, and I do know she has been preoccupied, Olive. I'm sure the latter has something to do with her sister's illness. The Countess has been, and no doubt still is, very worried about Anne Sedgewick.'

'She goes to the hospital a lot, to visit her sister, but I have a feeling she's also seeing a doctor there, getting advice,' Olive confided quietly.

Startled by this comment, Charlotte exclaimed, 'How could you know that?'

'I don't, not for sure. It's intuition on my part. I think that she might have an illness, and is trying to keep it a secret. From all of us, including the Earl.'

'I hope not, Olive. Look, why don't you just come out and ask her if she's feeling unwell?'

'I have thought of doing that.' Olive compressed her mouth, looking more worried than ever. 'But I don't like to intrude.'

'You *must* ask her. She'll confide in *you*; after all, you're with her all the time. She depends on you for so many personal things. You help her to dress and undress, and you do her hair. You look after her clothes and jewels, all of those things. You're on a truly personal footing with Her Ladyship. Ask her, and let me know what she says. Maybe *we* can help her, you and I. Maybe she needs some loving care, and someone to unburden herself to . . . like *you*.'

Olive nodded and smiled for the first time in days. 'Thank you for listening. I do appreciate that you came to see me at once. I trust your judgement and I will have a word with the Countess. But after the wedding. I don't want to venture down that road and upset her, just before her daughter gets married.'

'That's a good thought. Don't bring anything up until after Lady Daphne and Mr Hugo have left for their honeymoon.' Charlotte finished her cup of tea and stood up. 'I'm sorry, but I do have to leave now, Olive. I've such a lot to do in the South Wing.'

'I understand, and thanks for coming.'

Charlotte smiled at her. 'Try not to worry, we'll solve this. Keep me informed, won't you?'

'I will.'

Leaving the servants' hall, Charlotte went up the back stairs, and made her way through the house to the South Wing. She swiftly processed everything Olive had said, impressed with her acuity. Olive had picked up on Felicity's strange behaviour very quickly since returning to Cavendon. And now she thought about it, she agreed that there *was* something wrong with the Countess, although Charlotte had no inkling what this was. Certainly it did not have anything to do with Anne Sedgewick, of that Charlotte was certain. Rather, it must be something to do with Felicity herself. She just wasn't sure what that could be. It was a puzzle. After Daphne's safely married I'll tackle it, Charlotte decided. One step at a time.

FORTY-ONE

When the bride and groom came through the church porch and out onto the steps, the rain had stopped, the sun was shining and the sky was blue. Daphne lifted her eyes and looked up, breaking into smiles when she saw the arc of the rainbow in the sky.

'Hugo, look! There's a rainbow! And aren't we lucky the rain has stopped?'

'We're lucky to have each other, that's what I think, Lady Daphne Ingham Stanton.' He grinned at her. 'We're married, Daphne, well and truly married by the good vicar of Little Skell, and that's what matters most to me.'

The clapping and the cheering started as the villagers, standing on both sides of the path, edged closer to see their own beautiful bride, the daughter of their Earl and Countess. And beautiful she truly was, in her white lace wedding gown and flowing veil that surrounded her like a cloud.

'Congratulations, Lady Daphne! Congratulations, Mr Hugo!' some of the villagers were already shouting, while others took up the chant, 'Hip, hip, hooray, hip, hip, hooray, for the bride and groom today!'

Stepping forward, Daphne and Hugo went along the path to greet their well-wishers, laughing when they were showered with rose petals. Some of the women were singing 'Here Comes the Bride', and they had lovely voices, Daphne thought.

Daphne was surprised there were so many of their people in the grounds, but then the church could only hold a certain number.

On their way to the church earlier, her father had said that everyone from the three villages would be turning out to enjoy the wedding and give her a good send-off. Afterward, they would attend the tea party in Little Skell village hall, a treat paid for by the Earl.

It was when she was lifting her hand to wave at the crowd outside the church gates that Daphne saw him. *Richard Torbett.* She was stunned. He was standing there, as bold as brass, glaring at her.

Taken by surprise, she stiffened and drew closer to Hugo, who sensed something was wrong and glanced at her. 'What is it? Are you all right?' he asked worriedly.

'I'm fine. I almost slipped on the wet stones, that's all,' she quickly improvised.

Daphne couldn't resist glancing towards the road again and was shocked to see he was no longer there. He had been, hadn't he? Or had she imagined it?

Thoughts of Torbett fled as soon as she and Hugo were surrounded by their family. Her parents, Aunt Gwendolyn in her usual royal purple, her aunts Lavinia and Vanessa, Uncle Jack, her brothers, Guy and Miles, so smart in their morning suits, and the three Dees in their pink taffeta bridesmaids' dresses. How adorable Dulcie was in her long dress, carrying her posy of pink roses.

Then came Major Gaunt and his three sons, thrilled to be with Hugo and attending his marriage, and incredibly excited that he was returning to live in Yorkshire.

Finally they were able to extricate themselves. They went down the path and through the gate to the waiting car, which was trimmed with white satin ribbons.

'Lady Daphne! Lady Daphne!'

She turned around and saw Genevra running across the road, waving something in the air. The Romany girl came to a stop, stood a few feet away from her and offered her something. 'Lucky charm,' the gypsy said, coming closer. 'Don't lose.'

'Thank you, Genevra,' she said, taking the bit of bone from her, wondering what on earth it meant.

'You be happy,' Genevra muttered, and in her usual fashion she ran off without saying another word.

'Who was that?' Hugo asked, looking puzzled.

Before she could answer him, Daphne was surrounded by DeLacy, Cecily, Mrs Alice and Miss Charlotte. They began to help her into the car, lifting up her voluminous veil and long train, and DeLacy was taking her bouquet of white roses from her. A moment later she and Hugo were being driven away from Little Skell village and back to Cavendon Hall.

The house was virtually deserted since the entire staff had gone to the wedding. Hugo took hold of her arm and led her into the library. Once inside the room, Daphne put down her bouquet and looked at the piece of bone. On it were tied little bits of silver and white ribbon, and there were carvings down one side. 'They're little hearts,' Daphne said after a moment, showing it to Hugo. 'Genevra's strange, but she's harmless.'

Hugo studied the bone. 'Seven hearts altogether. What do they mean?'

'Lots of love perhaps,' Daphne said, turning to him.

'Then keep it safe.' Putting his arms around her, Hugo brought her close to him. 'I love you, Daphne, with all my heart, now and forever, as long as we both shall live. I meant those vows I just made in church, I truly did.'

'And so did I,' Daphne answered, standing on tiptoe, kissing his cheek. 'And it will be all right. Don't worry.'

'Oh Daphne, I know that, my darling.'

'I meant tonight. You and I together, starting our honeymoon here at Cavendon. It must begin tonight . . . our married life, I mean. I want it to be that way.'

Hugo's face was full of love for her as he handed her the bouquet of white roses and led her out of the library.

'We must go to the pink drawing room,' Daphne explained. 'For the family photographs. And then after that we can relax and dance the night away.'

'Not the whole night, I hope,' Hugo grinned, his smile suddenly flirtatious.

'Don't be a silly boy, I've better plans than that,' Daphne answered. And the look in her deep blue eyes told him everything he needed to know.

PART THREE

Frost on Glass
January 1914–January
1915

I'll break and forge the stars anew,
Shatter the heavens with a song;
Immortal in my love for you,
Because I love you, very strong.

                              Rupert Brooke

We are dancing on a volcano.

                         Comte de Salvandy

FORTY-TWO

Daphne gave birth to a baby girl in the South Wing of Cavendon Hall on Thursday 29 January 1914 at three o'clock in the afternoon.

The baby had a small pouf of blonde hair on top of her shapely little head, and she was healthy and perfect in every way, very much to the relief of the mother.

Daphne had been in labour for ten hours, and her silent but constant prayer had been for the safe delivery of a baby without any deformities or the slightest blemish. And her prayers had been answered.

Now, two days later, on Saturday afternoon, Daphne was seated on the sofa in the pale green sitting room of the South Wing, holding the baby in her arms.

She couldn't stop looking at the little girl, constantly moving the lacy cashmere shawl slightly in order to study her small, delicate face, her tiny hands with those perfect minuscule nails. What a miracle the child was. Daphne overflowed with enormous love for this tiny creature who was hers.

As she had recognized months ago, she would never have been

able to give her away for adoption. This precious little bundle, all silky and pink, was part of her and always would be. There was an unbreakable bond between them that would last forever.

Daphne was relieved she was a married woman with a wonderful husband who had claimed the baby as his own. Because of Hugo, the baby would be forever safe as his child, under his protection and bearing his name.

The story given out was that the baby was premature, and everyone accepted this, whatever they actually believed. And Daphne and Hugo kept a cool front, turned a blind eye to any hint of gossip, and just kept on smiling serenely. As they were doing this afternoon.

Hugo was sitting next to Daphne on the sofa, being charming to everyone, but occasionally giving his total attention to his child. He kept peering at her sweet face, love reflected in his eyes, and in his demeanour in general.

Felicity was sitting in a chair next to Daphne, accompanied by Olive Wilson. The Countess had been suffering from exhaustion, and was only now more like her old self. The arrival of the baby had brought smiles to her pale face, and a new lightness of spirit was evident in her.

The Earl of Mowbray, the baby's grandfather, was as happy as his wife, genial and outgoing today. Like Hugo, he kept glancing at the child in his daughter's arms. He was fascinated by the new arrival, his first grandchild, who was the start of a new generation of Inghams.

'You look positively radiant, Daphne,' Charles remarked at one moment. 'You did have a bit of a rough time, I realize that. But you came through so well. I'm proud of you.'

'And so am I,' Hugo interjected. 'You've been marvellous, darling.' Glancing at his watch, he added, 'I wonder what's happened to everyone? They were invited to come at three o'clock to see the baby, before afternoon tea is served.'

The words had hardly left his mouth when Hanson appeared in the doorway and announced, 'Lady Gwendolyn has just arrived, m'lord, and so has Miss Charlotte.'

'Thank you, Hanson. Do show them in, would you please?'

'I will, Lord Mowbray. The footmen are helping them with their outerwear. I'm afraid it's started to snow again, m'lord.'

Charles nodded and glanced out of the window, and saw that the snow was indeed falling rather heavily.

Charles and Hugo immediately stood up when Lady Gwendolyn came sweeping in, looking her usual elegant self. This afternoon she wore a grey wool suit and a blue silk blouse.

After greeting her, Daphne couldn't help chuckling. 'I love the blue blouse, Great-Aunt Gwendolyn.'

Lady Gwendolyn, acerbic and outspoken, also had a great sense of humour, and had the good grace to laugh when she said, 'I chose it in order to reflect the baby's eyes, don't you know? And I do want her to feel at home, since you all wear blue most of the time.'

'Oh she does feel that, Aunt Gwen,' Hugo exclaimed. 'In fact, she really is at home here in the South Wing. The other day Charles offered us the South Wing as a place to live, and we've happily accepted. We shall reside here permanently. I'll not be buying Whernside House.'

'You've made a wise decision, Hugo, and I like the idea of the three of you being here under one roof at Cavendon. And walking distance from me.'

As she spoke, Lady Gwendolyn had glided across the room and was already peeping at the baby in Daphne's arms. 'An Ingham through and through,' she announced. 'I can tell from her thin wrists and delicate hands. They're aristocratic.'

'And so are her ankles,' Felicity interjected. 'Slender and neat.'

Charlotte came into the room, greeting everyone, then adding, 'The weather is bad. I think we might be in for a snowstorm.'

'Perhaps,' Charles said. 'But don't worry, Charlotte. Gregg can drive Aunt Gwendolyn and you back to the village later.'

'Thank you, that's very kind,' Charlotte replied, and went to join Daphne on the sofa.

'Isn't she sweet,' Daphne said, smiling at Charlotte, and moving the shawl. 'Look, her mouth is like a little rosebud.'

Charlotte could only nod, suddenly choked with emotion. The baby was beautiful, and she was safe, as was Daphne herself. How different things might have been if not for Hugo. Thank God he had decided to come to Cavendon at exactly the right time. What is meant to be is meant to be, she added to herself, believing this.

Charles helped his aunt to sit down in a chair next to him. He swung around as Hanson appeared once again, announcing the arrival of Mrs Alice, Cecily, and the Earl's three daughters, Diedre, DeLacy and Dulcie.

Of course it was Dulcie who came bouncing into the room, as usual in a hurry to be the first, although she was obviously trying to be a bit more restrained than she normally was.

When she came to a stop in front of Daphne, she said, 'I want this baby, Daphers. Will you give her to me? *Please.*' She offered her favourite sister her biggest smile.

'I'm afraid I can't, Dulcie dear. However, you can be her best friend. Yes, that's a good idea, I appoint you her best friend. That's a very special honour, and it means you can spend a lot of time with her.'

'Ooooh, thank you, Daphs. YOU'RE THE SWEETEST OF THE SISTERS.' She shouted these last few words in a loud voice then, reverting to her normal speech, she added, 'I'll look after her careful.'

'Carefully,' Daphne corrected, and smoothed her hand over Dulcie's blonde curls lovingly. 'And when you're grown up and married, you will be able to have a baby of your own, just like mine.'

'I'll marry Hugo.' Dulcie looked across at him and smiled. He winked at her.

'That's not possible, darling, but I will find you a second Hugo, just for yourself,' Daphne promised.

'Oh thank you,' Dulcie responded, and leaning forward she looked at the child and asked, 'Why is her face all crumpled up like an old apple?'

'Because she's just two days old. Tomorrow she will be . . . uncrumpled, you'll see,' Daphne smiled.

Dulcie said, 'I'll come and check.' She ran across to her father, and climbed up onto his knee, settling against his broad chest.

Daphne said, 'Come along, Mrs Alice, and you too, Cecily. Come and see the little one.'

They did as she asked, and admired the child, and exclaimed what a beautiful baby she was, and then DeLacy joined them. Immediately she cried, 'She's got a rosebud mouth. You should call her Rosebud, Daphers. Or Rose. Or Rosalie. Or Rosamund or Rosemarie.' DeLacy continued to laugh, as she added, 'There are so many *rose* names. But what are you going to call her?'

'I'm about to tell you,' Daphne replied.

Diedre crossed the room in a sedate fashion, stopped in front of Daphne, and looked down at the baby. Quite suddenly, unexpectedly, she moved the shawl away, revealing the baby in her long nightgown. 'Lovely child, Daphne,' she said. 'And quite a good size for a premature baby, wouldn't you say?'

'Quite the *normal* size for a premature baby,' Hugo cut in swiftly, his voice controlled. Being protective of Daphne, he was annoyed. He had discovered Diedre was a sour puss with a mean streak, and it was obvious she was envious of all her sisters, and not just his wife.

He fully understood why Dulcie didn't like her and was afraid of her. Since they had been living in the South Wing, Hugo had befriended Dulcie, who was neglected by her mother, in his opinion. But then Felicity was recovering from a bout of exhaustion. He thought she looked on edge today, and there was a faded air about her. Sometimes she seemed distracted, he thought, and acted very strangely. She had changed a lot lately.

Once everyone was seated, Daphne handed the baby to Charlotte and stood up. She walked across to the fireplace and beckoned for Hugo to join her.

Together they faced the room and their guests, and Daphne said, 'We've been calling our daughter Baby, as everyone else has, but we have been considering names for her. And now that we've settled on them we thought this afternoon was as good a time as any to reveal them to you.'

'She has four names,' Hugo told them. 'And lovely names they are too, as far as we're concerned. And very meaningful to *us*.'

Daphne looked across at Alice Swann. 'Baby's first name is Alicia, and she will be called that. She is named in honour of you, Mrs Alice. Because you have been so wonderful to me all my life, and especially lately.'

Alice was so startled and touched she couldn't respond, and her eyes filled with tears. After a moment, she said, in a trembling voice, 'Thank you, Lady Daphne. You too, Mr Hugo.' She paused, unable to continue; then, after taking a deep breath, she finished, 'I am very honoured.'

'Her second name is Felicity, for you Mama, and for all the reasons you know. Hugo and I hope this pleases you.'

'It does indeed, Daphne and Hugo, and I thank you with all my heart.'

Hugo now spoke. 'We come to Baby's third name. It is Gwendolyn, and she's called after you, Aunt Gwen, because of what you have meant to me, especially as a child. And also to the entire family.'

Lady Gwendolyn's eyes were moist when she answered in the most surprised voice, 'Thank you, Hugo, and you too, Daphne.

I'm afraid I can't say anything else. You see, you've knocked the breath out of an old lady, who for once in her life has been rendered speechless.'

Everyone laughed.

When the room was silent again, Daphne spoke. 'Finally, we come to the last name, but by no means the least. It is Charlotte, and she's named for you, Miss Charlotte. For your devotion and wisdom. And the help you've always given me . . . and for being a fine example of true Swann loyalty to the Inghams.'

Charlotte was genuinely moved; she choked up for a second and was unable to respond. Finally, she said, 'Thank you, Lady Daphne, for those kind words, and how lovely of you both to give your first child my name. I'm so very touched.'

Charlotte looked down at the sleeping child in her arms. 'As a Swann I will always be there for her, whenever she needs me. I will protect her always.'

FORTY-THREE

Hugo stood at the French doors in the library, looking out at the terrace. Except that he couldn't see a thing. Frost on glass had made an intricate pattern and was blurring his view. It was already March but snow had been falling for several days now, and it didn't look like stopping.

Outside everything was covered in a blanket of pure white, and the surrounding countryside was beautiful, but it was hard to get around the estate and the weather was icy cold. Fortunately Hanson had fires burning brightly throughout the house and there was a cheerful atmosphere.

How glad he was that he had not bought Whernside House. They would have been isolated out there in weather like this. Daphne had suddenly understood that, and she had also pointed out that the house was far too large for them anyway. Shortly after this conversation, the surveyors he had hired presented him with a bad report about the roof and the underpinnings of the house. All needed extensive work. That was that, as far as he was concerned. He agreed with Daphne they should pass on the house.

Charles had invited them to live in the South Wing, and they had accepted with alacrity. He and Daphne had enjoyed being there so much that Daphne had eventually told her father they would prefer to live at Cavendon permanently, rather than seek a home of their own. Nobody had been happier than the Earl.

They had soon discovered that the unusually beautiful South Wing was also comfortable and easy to manage; it was also private, whilst still allowing them to be in the midst of the family, and with the downstairs staff readily available.

Hugo was genuinely happy about the arrangement, and one of the reasons was that he would have to travel soon. He must be in Zurich for several meetings, and also in London. He had been putting the trip off, but now he would be leaving tomorrow. It was imperative.

Knowing that Daphne and the baby were with her family made him feel more at ease about them. He loved them both very much, and he was filled with the kind of happiness he had not thought possible. He knew he was a lucky man.

Charles came into the library, breaking into his thoughts. 'I had Gregg drive to Harrogate and back,' the Earl announced. 'And I'm happy to tell you the roads are clear. He'll have no problems driving you to the station tomorrow, and the trains are running on time.'

'Thanks for doing that, Charles. It's good to know,' Hugo answered.

'Are you sure you don't want to stay at the Mayfair house?' Charles now stood in front of the fireplace, warming his back, and he threw Hugo a questioning look.

Walking over to join him, Hugo shook his head. 'Thank you, Charles, it's awfully good of you to offer. But I'll be in London for only two nights. It's not worth opening up the house for such a short stay.'

Charles nodded. 'Whatever suits you best, old chap.'

'The reason I'm going to Switzerland via London is to see my former personal assistant, Jill Handelsman. She worked alongside Ben Silver first, and then became my PA after his death. She and her husband came to live in London about five years ago, and I've stayed in contact with her. I'm hoping she'll agree to find and open a London office for me, and run it.'

'She's that good, is she?' Charles raised a brow.

'One of the smartest women in business I've ever met,' Hugo replied.

Charles sat down on the Chesterfield and leaned back, his expression thoughtful. He said, after a moment, 'I don't mean to pry, but I'm curious. Why do you need a London office?'

'I need a proper organization to handle my private money, and my personal investments around the world. In other words, what I made myself, as opposed to what I inherited from the Silvers. Which is the whole real-estate company, by the way. That is run in New York by Leonard Peters, who has been president of the corporation for years, even when Ben was alive. I've no worries about him; he's doing a superlative job. He likes me to visit New York from time to time, but basically he's in charge, reporting to me every week.'

'And when do you plan to go to New York?' Charles asked. 'And do you plan to take Daphne with you every time you go? You did tell me you wanted to travel back and forth.'

'I did want to do that, but not any more. I don't believe it will be possible, or, quite frankly, very safe. The high seas are going to be very dangerous, in my opinion.'

'War? You're thinking of war again, aren't you?' Charles stared at his son-in-law intently.

Hugo nodded.

'So the Kaiser is ready to march?'

'I believe he is. He's building up the German Navy, for one thing. And, thankfully, Churchill's doing the same with ours.

He's been doing that since he became First Lord of the Admiralty in 1911. He's very aware of the Kaiser's aims. As the Germans build one new dreadnought battleship, Churchill builds two for the Royal Navy. When Germany builds two, Churchill builds three.'

'An arms race, obviously.'

'Correct. That's why Winston is always trying to squeeze more and more money out of Parliament for his naval budget. I guess he drives them mad with his demands, but by God he's right as far as I'm concerned.'

'Asquith likes Winston, I'm told by my friends in the know,' Charles said. 'And that's good enough for me.'

'I'd go as far as to say that the Prime Minister admires Winston Churchill and likes Lloyd George. There are some good men in Asquith's government and they'll cope with a war. It's a bloody awful thing to think about, though.'

'I trust Churchill's judgement. He has enormous potential,' Charles remarked.

'I wish we could avoid a conflict, but unfortunately England promised France that we would come to their aid if they were invaded,' Hugo pointed out.

'I know. If push comes to shove, that's what we'll have to do, I suppose.'

'And God help us all.' Hugo shook his head, and looked off into the distance, as if contemplating something only visible to himself. After a long moment, he said in a low voice, 'Bad times are coming, and the world will never be the same again.'

FORTY-FOUR

'Thank you so much, Hanson. The room looks elegant yet suitably masculine,' Daphne said, smiling at the butler.

'It was a pleasure to help you, Lady Daphne, but I can't really take credit for this. It's all your doing.'

Daphne and Hanson were standing in the doorway of a small sitting room in the South Wing, which together they had redecorated as a library.

In the three days Hugo had been away, most of the furniture had been removed to the attics, and other pieces brought down. The room now boasted a mahogany bookcase, a small Georgian desk and desk chair, plus the sofa and an armchair that had stayed in place.

'It'll be very comfortable for Mr Hugo,' Hanson said, his eyes sweeping around the room. 'And I'm glad we found those hunting prints; they look well in here, m'lady.'

'They do indeed, Hanson. Now, I just have to go and borrow a few books from the library to fill the bookcase.'

Hanson pondered for a moment, and said, 'I do believe there

are some boxes of leather-bound books in the attics above the East Wing, Lady Daphne. Mrs Thwaites always stores things very well, and I'm certain they will be in perfect condition. Shall I have them brought down for you to look at?'

'Certainly, Hanson, thank you very much. And now, if you'll excuse me, I must pop into the nursery to see the baby.'

'Yes, my lady, of course, and the books will be here and unpacked in a jiffy.'

She smiled, thanked him again, and the two of them went their separate ways: Hanson to the East Wing, Daphne to the nursery further down the corridor.

Miss Jane Willis was the baby nurse, and she had arrived at Cavendon a few days before the baby had been born. She was in her mid-twenties, young, energetic and very caring of Alicia, and Daphne was pleased with her.

Miss Willis had trained at Norland College, where baby nurses and nannies were schooled in the best tradition. Daphne was glad she had listened to her mother. It was Felicity who had suggested she hire a baby nurse for the first six weeks, to help get on her feet and also to create a proper routine for the child. Daphne thought of Miss Willis as a godsend.

Miss Willis held her fingers to her lips when Daphne appeared in the doorway of the nursery, and then smiled, beckoning her into the room. Alicia was fast asleep in her cradle, and Daphne looked down at her child, marvelling at her yet again. 'I'll come back later,' she mouthed silently, and slipped out, making her way to the lavender room she shared with Hugo. He had a dressing room next door, which had a French daybed in it. 'But that's just for show, I hope,' Hugo had said when he had seen it. 'I've no intention of sleeping alone. I want you next to me in bed always.' And that was the way it was, and always would be.

Daphne smiled to herself when she thought of Hugo's comments, not only about their sleeping arrangements, but also about many other things as well. He was very modern in his way of thinking, and forthright, and spoke to her openly about a variety of subjects.

Opening the wardrobe door, Daphne glanced at the dresses hanging there, wondering what to wear that evening for dinner. Something simple, she thought, since she and her mother would be the only two people dining. Unless Great-Aunt Gwendolyn had been invited to join them. She would ask Hanson about that later.

It seemed to Daphne that the house was deserted and quieter than usual today. Guy was at Oxford, Miles at Eton; Diedre had gone to Gloucestershire yesterday, to stay with Maxine Lowe at her house near Cirencester, and her father had driven to Northallerton this morning. He was to be a pallbearer at the funeral of one of his oldest friends. He had insisted Felicity stay at Cavendon, pointing out that there was no need for her to go. And Hugo was off on his business trip and would be arriving in Zurich tonight. In particular, she missed his cheerful and loving presence; she felt lost without him, and couldn't wait for him to get back.

There was a knock on the door, and it opened at once. Peggy Swift looked into the bedroom and said, 'Could I speak to you for a minute, Lady Daphne?'

'Of course, Swift, come in,' Daphne answered with a warm smile. Peggy Swift had become her lady's maid after her marriage, and Daphne liked her, favoured her. She was a good worker, took wonderful care of Daphne's clothes and was efficient. And she had a nice disposition.

The young woman stepped into the room and closed the door behind her. Daphne looked across at her and frowned. 'What is it, Peggy? You look upset.'

'No, I'm not really, m'lady, but something had been preying on my mind a bit, and I wanted to . . . well, get it off my chest. But first I must ask you not to repeat what I tell you.'

Daphne sat down in a chair and said, 'I promise I won't break your confidence.'

Peggy Swift liked and admired Lady Daphne, and genuinely trusted her, knowing her to be a good person – caring and compassionate. There was a sweetness about her that touched Peggy. Yet she now found she couldn't speak out.

Daphne said, 'It's very private here, Peggy, as you well know. You can speak freely.' When still Peggy hesitated, Daphne said, 'You're not ill, are you?'

'No, no, it's nothing like that, Lady Daphne. It's just that I don't know how to begin.'

'Just blurt it out. I've found that's the only way,' Daphne advised, smiling encouragingly.

'It's about Gordon, and me too, and I don't want to get him into trouble. Will you keep my secret, m'lady?'

'I said I would, Peggy, and I mean it. So come along, tell me.' As she spoke, Daphne couldn't help wondering if Peggy was pregnant, but then dismissed this thought. Peggy wouldn't fall into that trap again. Leaning back in the chair, she waited patiently.

'Well, you see, it's like this. Sometimes Gordon and I sneak out at night. After our supper, and the cleaning up is finished. Gordon likes to go for a little stroll and have a cigarette. When the weather's nice. And well, last summer we went out for a bit . . .' Peggy paused, took a deep breath, and said in a low voice, 'Several times I think we were being watched.'

'What on earth do you mean?' Daphne sat up straighter in the chair, concerned by this comment.

'When we were in the bluebell woods, having a little kiss, a cuddle, I heard noises. Like someone was there in the bushes, watching us. Rustling noises, twigs snapping. So we ran back to the house. And then another time, we'd gone to have a walk round the lake.'

Peggy shook her head, rested her hand on a chest of drawers.

'I know we shouldn't have been there—' She broke off, looking worried.

Daphne said, 'Go on, Peggy. I'm not going to tell Hanson you were outside when you should have been indoors.'

'We went into the old boathouse, Lady Daphne. It was filled with moonlight and Gordon saw a stub of a candle and lit it. So we could see. I don't like the dark. We were just having a cuddle . . . you know we're going to get married when we can.' Peggy bit her lip, and after a moment she continued. 'A bit later the candle died, then the moon went behind the clouds, and Gordon lit a match. So we could see our way out. And I was facing the window and there was a man staring in, watching us.'

'Oh my goodness! That must have been upsetting!' Daphne exclaimed.

'It was, my lady. Gordon and I, well, we rushed outside. And we saw the man, he was running away.'

'Who was it?' Daphne asked, more concerned than ever.

'I don't know, Lady Daphne. But it was a funny feeling, knowing somebody was watching us. Like a Peeping Tom. We came back to the house. And we didn't go for strolls again.'

'And you're sure it wasn't anyone you know?' Daphne probed.

'Well, it was always dark, but who'd do that? Not anybody who works here, I don't think.'

'That's true.'

Peggy said, 'Don't give us away, Lady Daphne. Gordon doesn't want to get sacked. I don't either. I'm telling you this because it's sort of . . . well, it's worried me that someone is lurking around Cavendon.'

'I promise I won't involve you and Gordon, Peggy, but I can't just leave it like this. I've got to say something to someone.'

'But not Hanson or Mrs Thwaites. Please, Lady Daphne.'

'I suppose I could speak to Miss Charlotte, and she in turn

could have a word with Percy Swann. As the head gamekeeper he's basically in charge of the estate. At least it would alert him.'

Peggy nodded, and after a moment's hesitation, she said slowly, 'There's just one other thing, m'lady. Now that she's left to go to another job, I can tell you that Mary Ince was once surprised by a man. He jumped out of the bushes and tried to grab her. But she was quick, and ran. He ran after her, but the minute she left the woods he stopped chasing her.'

Daphne was now truly alarmed by these stories, but she kept her expression neutral when she said, 'I shall definitely confide in Miss Charlotte. She will know the best thing to do.'

'Will you keep us out of it, m'lady?' Peggy asked nervously.

'I will have to tell her about you and Gordon, Peggy. There's no other way. But she won't bring you into it, I promise you. On my word of honour.'

'I'm glad I told you, Lady Daphne, it's really been bothering me. We can't have trespassers lurking around Cavendon, now can we?'

'We certainly can't . . . Leave it to me, Peggy, and in the meantime, let us decide what I might wear for dinner.'

FORTY-FIVE

'You look so well, Mama,' Daphne said sounding surprised, staring at her mother's reflection in the mirror on the dressing table. 'Better than I've seen you for a long time.'

'I feel better, Daphne,' Felicity answered, and smiled back at her daughter's reflection.

Daphne moved away to sit in a chair so that Olive Wilson could finish doing Felicity's hair, and within minutes the maid had put in the last hairpins and, as a finishing touch, a diamond and tortoiseshell comb.

'There, that's it, Your Ladyship,' Wilson said, stepping back, checking the Countess's hairdo from various angles, nodding to herself.

'Honestly, Wilson, you're quite brilliant with hair!' Daphne exclaimed. 'I love these fancy curls, and the way you've then swept one side back with the comb. Just lovely.'

'Thank you, Lady Daphne,' Wilson answered, and helped Felicity up out of the small chair.

'For the first time in months, I feel like going downstairs

and having a lovely dinner with you, Daphne. It's been ages since I've even felt like getting dressed for dinner, never mind eating it.'

'You look so elegant, Mama, I must say. The burgundy dress is very flattering.'

Felicity laughed. 'It's one of my old Paris frocks, revamped by Cecily. I don't know how she does it, but that clever girl can make anything look brand new. And chic.'

'I know. Charlotte says her designs are complex – she calls them *engineered*. I do know Mrs Alice has a devil of a time sewing them. But there's no question Ceci's got a huge talent.'

'A little genius, I'd say.' Felicity turned to Olive Wilson. 'Thank you, Olive. You've outdone yourself tonight with my hair.'

'It's my pleasure, my lady.' She hesitated, then asked, 'Do you need help down the stairs, Lady Mowbray?'

'I don't think I do, thank you. I believe I can navigate the corridors of Cavendon without any assistance tonight.'

As they went downstairs, Daphne made sure her mother's right hand was on the balustrade, and she kept her watchful eyes on her as they descended. Once they were in the grand entrance foyer, Felicity turned to her daughter, and half smiled, 'You see, I did well, didn't I?'

Daphne nodded and took hold of her mother's arm, walking with her into the sitting room next door to the dining room, where they always assembled.

'Just the two of us tonight, but I think that's rather nice. We haven't had a chance to talk alone together for a long time.'

'I know, and it's silly when you think about it, Mama, since we do live in the same house.'

'The same *big* house,' Felicity corrected. 'Your grandfather always said you need a bicycle to get around it, and I think he was right.'

'I hadn't realized Papa wasn't coming back tonight, until

Hanson told me. Or that Great-Aunt Gwendolyn wasn't going to be with us for dinner either.'

'It's very slushy outside apparently, with all that melting snow, and of course Gregg and the motorcar are with your father in Northallerton, so there's no way to send him to get her. Your father had to stay because a dinner was arranged for the family and closest friends.'

'I understand. Anyway, it's cosy, just the two of us, and I'm especially glad that you're doing so well.' Daphne threw her mother a pointed look, and said, with a hint of laughter in her voice, 'It's all because of Baby. She's given you a new lease of life, Mama.'

'You're laughing, and I'm happy to laugh with you, Daphne. But it just so happens it's true. I've felt so much better since Baby's arrival – but we've got to stop calling her that or it will stick, and she'll hate us when she grows up.'

'I agree. We must call her Alicia from this moment on.'

'I'm sorry, Daphne, sorry I've been so absent in your life for such a long time. I'm afraid I've neglected you, and all of my daughters. However, it was you who needed me the most, and I let you down most dreadfully.'

'Oh, Mama, please don't say that,' Daphne cried, and rising she went and sat next to her mother on the sofa. 'I know how worried you were about Aunt Anne, and frustrated that you couldn't change the course her life had taken.'

Felicity reached out and took hold of Daphne's hand, and held it tightly in hers. 'Well as you know, she brought me up from the age of three; she was ten years older than me. It was like losing a mother as well as a sister when she died. A double loss in a sense.' Felicity grimaced, and gave her daughter a knowing look. 'I was frustrated, you're right about that, and especially annoyed with Grace and Adrian. After all, Grace was her only child, and she should have returned when Anne became so seriously ill. I'll never know why they lingered in Cairo.'

'I agree but, as Papa would say, that's water under the bridge.'

'I'm happy you married Hugo when you did, and that you insisted on an early marriage. And I'm glad I wouldn't let you spoil the honeymoon and come back for the funeral. There would have been no point, and Anne had made me promise I wouldn't allow that. She understood, and she knew you loved her, and that was good enough for her.'

Daphne found it hard to sleep that night. She had far too much on her mind. Her foremost worry was the news Peggy Swift had given her about a trespasser in the private grounds of Cavendon and in the woods and park.

When Peggy had mentioned the woods she had felt the goose-flesh rising on her neck and arms, and instantly she had thought of Richard Torbett. But surely he wasn't lurking around the woods, being a Peeping Tom, or attacking young women, was he? But he had attacked her, hadn't he?

She pushed the thought of him away. She had vowed to do that on her wedding day, when she had seen him standing on the other side of the road, across from the church. She had looked again, and discovered he wasn't there. Had he ever been there at all? Perhaps she had imagined it.

Until today he had been gone from her thoughts. Not even when she had given birth to her daughter had she thought of him. Because by then she had been loved by Hugo in the most passionate and tender way, and she had loved him in return. And it was Hugo who was the father of her child, as far as she was concerned.

Turning in the bed, holding onto the pillow, Daphne remembered her wedding night. Here, with Hugo. Slowly, tenderly, and with infinite patience, he had aroused her, and in the most sensual way. She had discovered desire and passion, and had become his.

Later he had said to her, 'If you weren't pregnant already, I'd have made you pregnant tonight, my darling. I've never made love to any woman like this . . . with such fervour, love, intensity and passion.'

And she knew that he spoke the truth. Their nights of love-making continued, and as always when he took her to him, she experienced ecstasy and joy.

She let these thoughts of desire and passion slide away. They were too tantalizing. Instead she turned her thoughts to Charlotte.

She would meet her tomorrow and tell her Peggy's stories, and perhaps something could be done about the Peeping Tom. If there was one, that is. Maybe it was not a Peeping Tom at all, but another man intent on doing damage to a young couple. Or a girl.

This thought sent a shiver through her, but she calmed herself, and finally she fell asleep. It was not a dreamless sleep. Nightmares hounded her all through the night, and she was relieved when daylight broke.

The following morning, Daphne went to see Charlotte, who was now working for the Earl in the office annexe next to the stable block.

Bundled up in a warm coat and rain boots, Daphne glanced around as she made her way to the building. It had rained during the night, and the slush and melting snow had been washed away. The sun was shining and, even though it was cold, it was a nice day. The sky was blue, and the sun brightened the day.

More like March at last than the dead of winter, Daphne

thought, as she made her way along the path. Soon the daffodils will be blooming, as they should be.

'Lady Daphne!' Charlotte exclaimed, sounding surprised when Daphne walked into her office. 'How lovely to see you. Good morning.' She stood up, smiling.

'Morning, Miss Charlotte. I wonder if you can spare me a few minutes? There's something I need to talk to you about.'

'Of course, please do sit down,' Charlotte answered.

Glancing around, Daphne said, 'I know that the estate staff are in the offices across the hall, and perhaps we ought to go out for a few minutes. Do you mind?'

'No, I don't, let me put my coat on.' Charlotte was struggling into a heavy wool overcoat a moment later, and the two women went outside.

'Let's walk down to the stables,' Daphne suggested. 'I'd like to see Greensleeves.'

Charlotte nodded and said, as they moved from the building, 'You want to talk about something . . . *sensitive*, shall we say?'

'I do, yes.' Daphne launched into the story of Peggy Swift and Gordon Lane, and repeated everything Peggy had told her yesterday.

She finished, 'They're afraid of being sacked, because they broke the rule and went strolling around at night. They don't want Hanson's wrath coming down on them for being outside when they should have been asleep. Peggy begged me not to tell anyone, and I did promise. Although I warned her I must talk to you.'

'It's a strange story, Lady Daphne. You know there are a lot of estate workers in the grounds these days, but obviously they're not out late at night. Do you think we should have some of them patrolling after dark? Is that what you're saying?'

Daphne shook her head, answered vehemently, 'No, not at all! I think that would really alarm everyone. It's not necessary, actually, because – as far as I know – most of the staff are inside at that time.' Daphne was silent, before adding, 'I trust Peggy. She's down to earth, not at all fanciful. I'm certain she was telling me the truth.'

'I agree. And why would she invent something like that?' Charlotte gave Daphne a pointed look, and asked, 'I assume this was happening last summer, wasn't it? After you had been . . . assaulted in the bluebell woods.'

'Yes, but I knew my attacker,' Daphne was quick to respond. 'And he's dead. So what shall we do?'

'*Nothing*,' Charlotte answered in a firm tone. 'I can't ask Percy Swann to put men out at night. He'll tell the Earl, and how would I explain it without breaking Peggy's confidence?'

'I understand.' Daphne was thoughtful as they went down to the stable yard, heading towards the stalls. 'Perhaps you could just ask him to make sure the men are patrolling during the day.'

'They're doing that already, Lady Daphne, and have been for months.' Charlotte fell silent, wondering who could be loitering on the estate, watching people. It didn't make sense.

Daphne went up to the stall, and Greensleeves moved towards her, whinnying. She stroked her head. She had loved this horse since the first moment she had seen her, and suddenly her thoughts rushed back to the fire. 'What a lucky escape Greensleeves had,' Daphne remarked, looking at Charlotte. 'I mean, in the fire.'

'Yes, indeed she did. Listen to me, Lady Daphne, I think what we ought to do is to say nothing. We should simply keep quiet. Apparently these incidents happened last summer, some time ago now. Just warn Peggy Swift not to go strolling with Gordon Lane late at night. Say that if she does, you'll have to tell Hanson everything.'

'You're right, Miss Charlotte. I don't really have any other choice, do I?'

'I'm afraid not. But do rest assured that there are plenty of estate workers out and about during the day.'

'I know. I see them all the time.'

Together the two women walked back to the office annexe. On the way there, Daphne shared the news about the Countess's improved health and then, with a laugh, she added, 'It's all because of Baby. I'm sure of that, and Mama agreed. We also agreed to stop calling the baby Baby, because Mama thinks it will stick.'

'And then she'll hate us all when she grows up,' Charlotte murmured, also laughing. 'So Alicia it is from now on.'

FORTY-SIX

Alicia Felicity Gwendolyn Charlotte Ingham Stanton, a little baby with a very long name, was the star attraction at Cavendon Hall these days. Everyone wanted to see her, touch her, even hold her, although they weren't actually able to do so.

Family and friends were only ever allowed to view her, and Nurse Willis made sure they did not break her rules. Daphne had been so taken with Jane Willis she had asked her to stay on permanently at Cavendon.

The Norland-trained baby nurse usually gave her 'new baby' only six weeks, and then moved on to a new family. But she broke her rule for Alicia. Like everyone else, she had been captivated by this gorgeous infant with bright blue eyes, blonde tufts of silky hair and a peaches-and-cream complexion. All inherited from her mother.

Like Daphne, she had a sweet disposition, was a baby who rarely cried, forever smiled, chortled and laughed.

Her parents and grandparents doted on her, as did her aunts. Except for Diedre, of course, who was always mumbling to herself that too much fuss was being made over 'just a baby'. For the last few months, Diedre had been absent from Cavendon. She was travelling in Europe with her friend Maxine Lowe, an heiress of great wealth. Dulcie, in particular, was pleased she was away.

Dulcie adored Alicia and was forever making her small gifts: lavender sachets, cut-out paper tulips coloured red and yellow, and ribbon bows for her tufts of blonde hair. And DeLacy was truly proud when Daphne allowed her and Cecily to push the Silver Cross pram up and down the terrace.

DeLacy was doing that on this Sunday afternoon in May. The weather was lovely, and the rain clouds of earlier had blown away. DeLacy pushed the pram carefully, leaning forward, cooing to the baby, smiling and talking to her. The child simply laughed and kicked her chubby little legs in the air, as contented as always.

Daphne was seated at the round table with Jill Handelsman, who, with her husband Marty, had been guests at Cavendon for the weekend. The two women were finishing their coffee before the Handelsmans took their leave. They were being driven to Harrogate by Gregg, and would take a late afternoon train to London.

Daphne liked them, and she was impressed with Jill's business acumen, appreciative of the way she had swiftly found a nice office for Hugo, and had it up and running within a couple of weeks. He went to London twice a month for a couple of days and always returned singing Jill's praises. Hugo felt he had everything under control because of her help.

After a few moments of silence, Jill said, 'I want to thank you again for arranging for me to see Cavendon's collection of antique silver. Your father was most gracious and informative.'

'Hugo told me you collected Regency and Georgian silver, Jill, and I knew you would enjoy seeing the Paul Storr pieces.'

'I did, especially those gorgeous candlesticks dated 1815. I've always admired his work – he was one of the great master silversmiths.'

'He was. I reminded Papa to show you the impressive silver bowl, too, that Queen Anne montieth by William Denny. He was another of the great English silversmiths, though much earlier than Storr.'

'I know. I made a note of that. Your father told me that the montieth was crafted in 1702. The Earl is very knowledgeable about silver – probably more so than anyone I've ever met.'

Daphne smiled, 'And about almost everything else at Cavendon, too. My father considers himself the custodian of all this . . .' Daphne paused, swept out an arm, added, 'The house, its contents, the land, the grouse moor. Everything as far as the eye can see. He always says he's keeping it intact, and in perfect condition, for the next generation, and generations after that. As for his knowledge, this was passed down from his father, the Fifth Earl, and Papa will pass it on to Guy . . . that's how it works. Father to son, the next heir, and so on—'

'Here we are!' Hugo exclaimed, interrupting Daphne, walking onto the terrace with Marty. 'I'm afraid I've got to break this up, ladies. Gregg is waiting at the front with the Rolls-Royce to whisk you off to the railway station.'

Later that afternoon, as they were walking from the South Wing to the yellow sitting room in the East Wing, for afternoon tea, Daphne suddenly stopped and took hold of Hugo's arm.

He turned and looked at her. 'What is it?'

'Something's been bothering me for a few weeks, since the christening . . . Do you think I offended Diedre when I didn't ask her to be a godmother to Alicia?'

Hugo exclaimed, 'No, of course not! None of your sisters was asked, so how could she take offence?'

Daphne couldn't help laughing. 'Dulcie's only five years old, so she could hardly be a godmother.'

Laughing with her, he replied, after a moment. 'I think you made the right choices. Lavinia and Vanessa will do their duty as far as Alicia's concerned, and let's face it, they are grown-ups.'

'Not Lavinia, according to Papa. He's forever announcing she's childish.'

'I know, but he doesn't really mean it . . . not *actually*. You're worrying about Diedre because she's been away for weeks, but it was that kind of trip, you know. Paris, Rome, Berlin, Vienna. The whole works. The Grand Tour. Anyway, if it still bothers you, when you have your next baby you can ask her then.'

Daphne nodded. 'Yes, how right you are. You always manage to make me feel better, Hugo.' She stood on tiptoe and kissed his cheek. 'And you were right to ask Guy and your cousin Mark to be her godfathers.'

Hanson was decanting a bottle of Pomerol in the little pantry next to the dining room when Gordon Lane suddenly appeared at his side.

'Excuse me, Hanson, but could I have a quick word with you, please?'

'Can't we speak later, Lane? As you can see, I am busy.'

'I know, and I'm sorry, but there's never a chance to ask a question. You're so busy, Mr Hanson. It won't take but a second. It's important.'

Hanson, conscious of the serious tone in the footman's voice, turned around. 'Very well then. What is it?'

'As you know, Peggy Swift and I are engaged, and we'd like

to get married soon, Mr Hanson. In August, if that's all right with you?'

Hanson nodded. 'You're asking for a day off, I presume?'

'Yes, for the two of us, Mr Hanson. Do I have to go to Mrs Thwaites to ask about Peggy's day off?'

'No, no, that won't be necessary, Lane. Why don't you take the first Saturday in August, and I'll have a word with Mrs Thwaites later. You and Swift worked very well this weekend, and I was particularly pleased with the way you looked after Mr and Mrs Handelsman. Will you be marrying in the village church?'

'I expect so, Mr Hanson, and thank you very much. It'll make Peggy happy, knowing we can now set a date.'

'Congratulations,' Hanson said, and turned back to his work.

Dulcie hummed to herself as she went through the conservatory and down the little hill, heading for the woods. The bluebells were in full flower, and she had been longing to pick a bunch for Alicia all day, but had not found the opportunity until now. Now Nanny was preparing the bath for her and putting out her nightclothes; as usual she was preoccupied, and Dulcie seized the moment.

It was only six thirty and still light. The child strode into the woods determinedly, her eyes darting from side to side, until she saw a patch of the flowers, and ran towards them, a happy smile on her face. She bent down and began to pick the bluebells, and then suddenly stopped. Next to her hand was a big black shoe.

Glancing up, Dulcie saw a man standing there, staring down at her. She had never seen him before. As she straightened up, he said, 'Why if it isn't little Dulcie.'

'Lady Dulcie,' she said. 'And who are you?'

'I'm the Bluebell Man,' he answered, and grinned at her.

Dulcie frowned. 'I've never heard of you. And this is my father's land.'

'I know. And he's the one who appointed me the Bluebell Man, *Lady* Dulcie.' He stared at the flowers in her hand. 'That's not a nice enough bunch. Come with me. I can take you to the best patch in the wood.'

Dulcie hesitated. She was not afraid of the man, but she was wary all of a sudden. Before she could step back, he snatched her hand in his, and said, 'Let's hurry. We must get the best before it gets too dark to see.'

'I think I have enough,' Dulcie exclaimed, and tried to break free of him, but he held her hand tightly in his. She tugged; he wouldn't let go.

The man was about to walk off with her when he heard the sound of a gun being cocked. He let go of Dulcie's hand and ran. He rushed forward, crashing through the bushes, disappearing into the woods.

A moment later Dulcie was looking up at Percy Swann, the head gamekeeper, who was standing there with a rifle in his hands.

She smiled at him. 'Hello, Mr Percy. I didn't like that man. He wanted to take me to another bluebell patch. But I wouldn't go.'

'You did the right thing, Lady Dulcie. Come along, I'll take you home.' He bent down, picked her up in his arms, and carried her back to the house, holding the rifle in one hand.

It didn't take him long to get to the conservatory. The hue and cry had already started, and he saw the enormous relief flooding the Earl's worried face as he put Dulcie down on the ground.

She ran towards her father, exclaiming, 'I went to pick bluebells for Alicia, Papa, and Mr Percy came and sent the funny man away. And then he carried me home.' She smiled at Percy and said, 'Thank you.'

Felicity was as white as chalk, also worried. She came forward and took hold of Dulcie's hand. Looking at Percy, her red-rimmed eyes full of gratitude, she said, 'My thanks, Mr Swann. It's a good thing you were down there.' She hurried away with Dulcie, who was still clutching the bluebells. The weeping nanny trailed after them, unable to quell her tears.

Pulling himself together, Lord Mowbray said, 'What exactly happened, Percy?'

'I always patrol the area near the bluebell woods while it's still light. I've been doing so since last year, when there were rumours of poachers. I was walking up from the lake when I spotted Lady Dulcie going into the woods by herself. I ran hell for leather, m'lord. As I went into the bluebell woods I saw a man holding Lady Dulcie's hand, about to lead her away. I surprised him. I cocked the trigger, and he heard it, as I knew he would. He took off, ran into the woods. I lifted her up and brought her home.'

'Did you recognize the man?'

'I didn't, Your Lordship. He had muttonchop whiskers and was wearing a flat cap; it was impossible to see much of his face. He was badly dressed. Tallish though, a man with long legs and long arms.'

'Disguised perhaps?' Charles asked.

'Maybe, m'lord. I think it would've been hard for anyone to identify him. Muttonchop whiskers cover most of the face.' Percy Swann shook his head. 'I suppose I could have run after him, but I wouldn't have caught him, and I thought it was better to get Lady Dulcie home.'

'You did the right thing. Miss Charlotte insists the bluebell woods in particular are watched by your outdoors team. Why do you think that is, Swann?'

'Because they are quite dense in parts and also they're at the end of our property on that side of Cavendon land. Once the woods end, there's that dirt road that separates our land from the Havers' land, and the land belonging to Lord Judson.'

Charles said, 'We need a barbed-wire fence, don't we?'

'I think we should build a very high wall, if you don't mind me saying so, Lord Mowbray. With barbed wire along the top.'

'That would block entry to the woods from the road. What about the rest of the property?'

'We should build more walls where there are gaps.'

'Parts of Cavendon on the perimeters have always been open, but times have changed. I think we'd better make our lands safer than they are. I'll talk to the estate manager tomorrow. He can make the plans and carry them forward. And thank you, Swann, I dread to think what might have happened to Lady Dulcie if you hadn't been around.'

'It's a good thing I was on my rounds, m'lord. Well, I'll say goodnight.'

'Goodnight, Swann, I'm extremely grateful to you,' Charles replied. He left the conservatory and went upstairs to the nursery floor, fuming inside. He found Felicity in the nursery, talking to the nanny, Maureen Carlton, who was still in tears.

Instructing her to come outside into the corridor, he informed her she had been in dereliction of her duties, and that he could no longer employ her. He added that she had until tomorrow at noon to leave Cavendon.

Felicity came out and joined him, and together they went downstairs to the bedroom floor. Once alone in her bedroom, Charles said, 'She had to go. She has no brains. I can't have any child of ours put at risk because of another person's stupidity.'

'I agree, Charles,' she answered, and added, 'I was about to give her notice myself when you arrived.' Felicity sat down in a chair, feeling nauseous. 'Thank goodness Dulcie doesn't understand, and she's sitting happily in the bathtub.' She shook her head. 'I can't bear to think what might have happened if Percy Swann hadn't been out there in the grounds.'

'She would have been abducted,' Charles replied in a terse voice. And he shuddered when he considered the harm that could have been done to little Dulcie, his Botticelli angel. It didn't bear thinking about. Later, he couldn't help wondering who the trespasser was. He also knew he had no way of ever finding out, much to his frustration.

Charles excused himself, went into his dressing room, and removed his jacket. He put on his silk dressing gown and returned to Felicity's bedroom.

To his surprise, she was still sitting in the chair, and had not changed from her dinner dress. And now she had her head in her hands.

When she looked up he was taken aback. There was a bleak expression on her face. She had obviously had one of those sudden mood swings that had been occurring frequently lately.

'What is it?' he asked from the doorway, reluctant to intrude on her when she was like this.

'This is your fault, Charles. You have been lax in securing this estate,' she said in a low, flat voice. 'It needs proper armed guards, not woodsmen. Dulcie might have been taken, raped and murdered tonight.'

He was flabbergasted, and exclaimed, 'It was one of my *armed* men who found her, and very quickly. She's safe because of Percy Swann, and you said so yourself. You praised him, Felicity. His armed teams are all over the estate, and have been for a long time. And we're doing repairs to the walls tomorrow.'

Taking a step forward, he said quietly, 'This has been terribly upsetting for both of us – for everyone here, in fact. And frightening, I know that. I know how distressed you were, but the estate is safe now, and it will be even safer.'

When she made no response, he added, 'I don't want you to become upset again. Dulcie is safe, and always will be safe from now on.'

'I've never worried about Dulcie because you've got all your devoted Swann women here. I know full well they keep an eye on her just to stay in your good graces.'

Annoyed though he was by this comment, he did not want to bicker with his wife. She seemed like a stranger to him these days. There was an unbelievable change in her that puzzled him, and he could not help wondering at times what had caused it. She was certainly not the woman he had married.

Turning, walking back to the door of his dressing room, he said in a level voice, 'I'll be back in a moment. And then perhaps we can draw a line under this . . . be more relaxed with each other. Like we used to be. Perhaps I can share your bed tonight, darling.'

'I don't think so,' she said in that same lifeless, flat tone of voice.

Charles frowned. 'Why not? What's wrong?' he asked.

She told him.

FORTY-SEVEN

T he story of Dulcie wandering off into the bluebell woods, and her near abduction by a stranger on the property, sent a shock wave through Cavendon. By eight o'clock that Sunday evening, the news had even travelled to the village of Little Skell.

Before he went home, Percy Swann went to see his Aunt Charlotte, who as matriarch of the Swann family was always informed first about everything that happened at Cavendon. And then she wrote it up in the record book. At least that was the assumption everyone made.

Charlotte's face broke into a smile when she answered the knock on her front door, opened it and saw Percy standing there. Like his older brother Walter, Percy was a good-looking young man; tall, athletic and strong. Although he was thirty-three, he appeared younger, as did Walter and Charlotte as well. It seemed to be a Swann trait, and one they were all happy to have inherited. Percy, despite his age, was the head gamekeeper, and ran the grouse moor and grounds with enormous skill and much love. He had been born on the estate and he knew every inch of it. He was a great marksman and had never missed a target yet; he was known affectionately as 'The Perfect Shot' by his fellow workers.

Within a second Charlotte knew that something wasn't quite right on the estate, simply because Percy would not have disturbed her on a Sunday evening, unless there was some sort of issue.

As was her way, she did not question him, but simply ushered him into the parlour, went over to the sideboard and asked if he would like a drink.

'Thanks, Aunt Charlotte, I wouldn't say no to a scotch, providing you're going to join me.'

'I will indeed,' she answered, and poured the liquor into two glasses.

Once she had handed him the drink, and they had touched glasses, they sat down opposite each other. There were a few moments of silence as they both took sips of the scotch, and then Charlotte said, 'Is there something wrong, Percy? Or is this a social visit?'

He told her everything in great detail, described the stranger on the estate, and confided the Earl's plan to build a high wall at the end of the bluebell woods, and wherever there were gaps.

Charlotte had turned paler than ever as she listened to him, and her stomach had lurched when she realized that if Percy hadn't shown up at exactly the moment he had, Dulcie would have been taken. When she picked up her glass she noticed that her hand was shaking.

After steadying herself, she said, 'I am breaking a confidence now, Percy, but I know it will remain between us. Peggy Swift and Gordon Lane, who are engaged, as you know, occasionally used to go for a stroll late at night. Mostly in the woods. Peggy told Lady Daphne that she, in particular, felt they were being watched by a Peeping Tom. The reason she confided in Her

Ladyship was because she was troubled someone was wandering around Cavendon. Peggy gave her permission to tell me.'

Percy had listened to her attentively and now said, 'It has to be a stranger to these parts, someone who has moved to a town nearby, because I know every Tom, Dick and Harry in all of the Earl's three villages.' Percy sat back in the chair, sipping his drink, and then said swiftly, 'I know one thing, it's not any of the gypsy lads. They keep to themselves, and always have. It's only their sister Genevra that roams around, but she's harmless enough.'

'Oh yes, I know that. The Romany family is happy to live on this land with the Earl's permission.'

'This is not a poacher roaming about, Aunt Charlotte. This is someone with criminal intent, someone out to hurt people,' he told her, his voice grim.

Charlotte closed her eyes and a shiver ran through her. 'Oh please don't say that, Percy. It worries me so much when I think that there's danger lurking out there in the park or in the woods . . . it's always been so safe here.'

'It is safe, Aunt Charlotte, please don't worry. I've always got my lads out till it gets dark.' Percy paused, his eyes narrowing slightly, and then he said, 'Please tell Lord Mowbray that he has to have a curfew, something like that anyway. He has to tell the family they can't go wandering about in the grounds at night. Hanson should be instructed to tell the staff the same thing.'

'I will explain, of course, but it's an awful thing to have to do. To have a curfew, I mean. This is Cavendon Hall, for good-ness' sake.'

'I know, but it's a necessity. When I was walking back to the village, it occurred to me that I could get a band of the lads together, and we could lay in wait in the woods every night. But I do believe I frightened the chap off when I cocked the rifle. He realized I had a gun.'

'And thank God you did!' Charlotte exclaimed.

'So you will talk to the Earl, won't you?'

'I will, I promise. I'm sure he'll want to discuss it anyway. I will actually be working with him tomorrow morning, so he will no doubt bring the matter up.'

Percy nodded. 'I did think about putting traps down, but what if a small animal was caught and not the trespasser?'

'No, don't do that, Percy. It will only hurt the wildlife. I doubt he'll come back knowing there's a man with a rifle waiting for him.'

Much later, after Percy had gone home to his wife Edna and his waiting supper, Charlotte went upstairs and opened the safe in the cupboard. She took out the record book for 1914, and wrote in details of her meeting with Percy. As she put the record book away, she noticed the dark blue one at the bottom of the pile, and pulled it out as she often had before.

Taking it over to a chair, she sat down and opened it to the page she had read countless times, intrigued by the one entry. It had been written thirty-seven years ago.

In mine own hand. July 1876
I loveth my ladie. Beyond all.
The swann fits the ingham glove tight.
I have lain with her. She is mine.
She gives me all. I got her with child.
Oh our joy. The child dead in her belly. Destroyed us. She
   left me. She came
back to me. My nights are hers
again. Til the day I die. M. Swann.

For years Charlotte had tried to fathom out which of the Ingham women had been the lover of M. Swann. She was quite certain this particular Swann was Percy's father, Mark; he had been the patriarch of the Swanns in those years.

Sighing, she closed the book, went and put it away, locked the safe. Secrets, she thought. So many secrets between the Swanns and the Inghams . . . intertwined for all time. And once she had also been part of it, hadn't she? Living a secret life.

Charlotte found she was unable to sleep. Finally, she got up, put on a dressing gown and went downstairs. She boiled a cupful of milk, made herself some soothing Ovaltine, and took it into the parlour. She went and sat by the window, her favourite spot. There was a full moon tonight, and the garden beyond the French doors was glossed over with a silver sheen.

Her garden looked beautiful in the moonlight and everything was peaceful out there, the tall sycamores and oaks a towering wall of green darkness at the end of the lawn.

But it wasn't peaceful out there, was it? Not any more. There was a stranger lurking around the parkland and the woods. It was unthinkable that this was happening at Cavendon, and she couldn't quite fathom it out. No one else could, she was sure. The only reason she could come up with was that there was some sort of vendetta going on, someone with a hatred for the family, a grudge against them; someone out to do them no good. If it was not that, it was a sexual pervert doing this, one who preyed on women and little girls.

Shuddering at the thought of Dulcie being taken away and sexually assaulted, Charlotte took a few swallows of the hot Ovaltine and hunched into the chair. Eventually she calmed down, and tried to sort out the myriad thoughts rushing through her mind.

Begin at the beginning, she told herself, and she did.

The first incident was a year ago last May. Daphne was raped in the bluebell woods. Was she raped by the stranger? Or by Julian Torbett, as she claimed? Why would she lie?

To protect her parents? They had seized on the idea of it being Julian, because she had gone to see him that day. But what if that wasn't the truth? Wasn't it far better to let her mother and father *believe* it was Julian, a well-born young man, rather than a dubious stranger from God knows where? On the other hand, Daphne was so honest and honourable, Charlotte couldn't imagine her lying.

Yes, I can, she suddenly decided. To protect Charles. Daphne was extremely close to her father, adored him, and had gone along with all his elaborate plans for her . . . their shared dreams.

If the stranger had raped her, he had done so to hurt her and the family. To bring the Inghams down, perhaps, if she got pregnant from the rape? Then there had been the fire in the stables. Daphne's horse Greensleeves had been targeted. It had obviously been arson.

Charles and Hugo believed that, and so did she. Not to mention the West Riding police. They had even interviewed every chauffeur who had been at the supper dance that night. Their aim was to ascertain if any of the men had gone up to the stables to smoke and left a smouldering tab end around. But none of the drivers had, so they said.

According to Peggy Swift, she and Gordon Lane had been watched when they were canoodling in the woods and the boathouse. Mary Ince, the maid who had recently left, confided in Peggy that she had been surprised by a man in the woods. A man who had attempted to grab her without success.

And now, earlier this evening, a strange-looking man had tried to take Dulcie. It had to be the same man. There couldn't be a bunch of trespassers moving around the estate, of that she was certain.

But what to do about it? *Make Cavendon safer than it was.* But according to Percy, that was going to be set in motion tomorrow. High walls and barbed wire. She sighed, loathing the idea, and thinking how much the 5th Earl would have loathed it too.

On the other hand, the Ingham family had to be protected. And perhaps now the Swanns needed help to do that, in the world they lived in today. Nothing was the same any more.

FORTY-EIGHT

Charles Ingham, 6th Earl of Mowbray, was upset, angry and exhausted.

He was exhausted because he hadn't slept a wink all night, but had lain awake in his bed, restlessly tossing and turning. He was upset because he knew his marriage was at an end, and had been for a very long time. And he was angry with himself for not taking charge of his household over a year ago.

Rising early, he had shaved, taken a bath, and dressed rapidly. Now, at eight thirty, he was on his way downstairs for breakfast, knowing full well he was in a foul mood.

Waiting for a moment when he arrived at the bottom of the staircase, he took a deep breath, straightened his shoulders, and walked across the grand entrance foyer towards the dining room, calming himself, taking full control of his emotions. A smile slipped easily onto his face.

Hanson was waiting for him when he walked into the room. As always the butler's manner was pleasant, his quiet authority intact.

'Good morning, Lord Mowbray,' Hanson said, immediately pulling out the chair at the head of the table for the Earl.

'Morning, Hanson, and thank you. I suppose I'm the first this morning.'

'Not exactly, m'lord. Lady Daphne popped in about forty-five minutes ago, to tell me that she and Mr Hugo would join you for breakfast around nine. Then she went upstairs with Nurse Willis. Shortly after they took Lady Dulcie to the South Wing, where Nurse Willis was going to give her breakfast and look after her until Lady Daphne is free.'

'I'm pleased to hear that, Hanson. I must say Lady Daphne thinks of everything. I'm happy the child is safely away from the nanny. I want *her* out of here by noon, Hanson, make sure of that. Miss Carlton is incompetent, to say the least.'

'Yes, she is and I'll deal with it, m'lord. What can I serve you this morning?'

'I'd like a cup of tea first, and then perhaps some of Cook's scrambled eggs and bacon. I must admit I'm feeling hungry this morning, Hanson. I didn't really eat dinner last night.'

'I'm not surprised, m'lord. Not with all the goings-on yesterday. Frightening really, and upsetting.'

'That's right. Oh, and Hanson, I believe Her Ladyship will take breakfast in bed this morning. Wilson told me she's still asleep.'

'Yes, my lord.' Hanson poured tea for the Earl, and stepped over to the sideboard where the silver chafing dishes were lined up. A moment later he placed the plate of food in front of Charles.

'Thank you, Hanson.'

The butler nodded and retreated into his pantry behind the dining room.

Charles ate slowly, and soon began to feel better with the warm food inside him. Dinner had been somewhat chaotic last night, after the near-abduction of Dulcie.

He had been beside himself, and slowly, over the evening, he had begun to realize how stupidly he had behaved with Felicity in the past. She had been an absentee mother for most of last year, devoting herself totally to her sister, and he had done nothing about it. He had understood her concern for Anne, and had offered her his full support. But it had been to the detriment of his children. Well, his daughters, anyway. His sons, thankfully, were away, being educated at Eton and Oxford.

It still rankled that his wife had not been there for Daphne, when she had needed her the most after the rape. Felicity had jumped at the idea of Daphne marrying Hugo, without giving a single thought to Daphne's own desires, her happiness. She had just wanted to get rid of the problem as fast as she could.

Dulcie had been neglected, left to her own devices, and had been in the hands of a nanny who was stupid, had been unsupervised, and was extremely careless.

Diedre, who was the eldest, and capable of looking after herself, had spent more time with their mother than the others.

DeLacy, forever with Cecily, had at least had Alice to deal with her clothes for the summer season, and probably other matters as well, if the truth be known. Certainly it was Alice who had helped and supported Daphne after the rape. And there was always Charlotte in the background – reliable, devoted, involved with the family, and ready to look after his girls, if need be. Once again, thank God for the Swanns, he thought.

Charles chastised himself now. He should have put his foot down long ago; not been quite so sympathetic and understanding of Felicity's almost abnormal devotion to her sister. In point of fact, she had put Anne before their children, and he had allowed that to happen.

As for his marriage, it was over. Felicity had informed him of that last night, taking him by surprise.

Distressed, exhausted and anxious after the terrible incident involving Dulcie, he had needed to share his thoughts and feelings with his wife. He had made the assumption she would want that too, under the circumstances, and because of the child's close call. And so he had asked her to let him share her bed. He hadn't even been thinking of making love, only of comfort and affection, and sharing their thoughts.

She had rejected him in the coldest manner and he had been shocked, thrown off balance by her words, her tone of voice.

He could hear her voice reverberating in his head. 'Our marriage is over, Charles,' she had said. 'I cannot share my bed with you. Or be intimate with you ever again.'

He had been unable to respond, but had just stood there, staring at her, feeling as if he'd been hit in the stomach with a sledgehammer.

'Why?' he had eventually asked. 'What's suddenly gone wrong?'

'It's not sudden,' she had answered. 'It's been a long time since I actually cared about you sexually. It has been pretence on my part, and I can't pretend any more, or fake pleasure. So I would like you to sleep in your own bedroom in future.'

'If that's what you want, then I shall.' As he now remembered saying this to her, he couldn't help wondering why he had gone on standing there, looking helpless, when he was angry and hurt. He had been dismissed, as if his feelings didn't matter, as though he were of no account.

Felicity had then added, 'If you want a divorce, you can have it.'

Growing even more incredulous, he had been unable to think straight; he was shocked and bewildered by this unexpected turn of events.

She had asked again, 'Well, *do* you want a divorce?'

'I'll let you know,' he had snapped in a tense voice, finally pulling himself together. Then he had turned and walked towards his dressing room. In the doorway, he had swung around to look at her. 'I'm forty-five years old. I'm not an old man. What am I supposed to do?' His eyes had not left her face.

'Anything you wish. You're as free as a bird,' she had replied.

Sitting there, drinking his cup of morning tea, it struck Charles that when she had so icily spurned him last night it had been wounding, and emasculating. However, she had done something else. She had given him his freedom to do whatever he wanted. But at this moment he had no idea what that might be.

He was still appalled by the chilliness of her manner, her total lack of emotion and feelings for him. And her blunt words. After all, they had been married for over twenty years, had six children, and he had genuinely believed his marriage was as solid as a rock. Apparently not. He had been wrong, hadn't he?

For a moment, he wondered if her bout of exhaustion had affected her more than he'd thought, bringing about this odd change in her. But then her behaviour had been strange for some years – even before Anne became sick, in fact.

He remembered that she had become an unwilling and passionless lover a year after Dulcie's birth; five years ago, actually. He had endeavoured to ignore her coldness, to turn a blind eye. And in doing so he had become impotent. She had done that to him, hadn't she? He couldn't get an erection because she didn't desire him, had no interest in him, and he knew it. He just couldn't accept it; perhaps that was it.

'Good morning, Papa,' Daphne said, floating into the dining room in a lovely, lilac-coloured dress. 'I have Dulcie safe and sound with Nurse Willis, so you don't have to worry.'

Standing up, Charles said, 'She's all right?'

'Oh yes, she didn't really understand any of it,' Daphne reassured him.

After embracing Daphne, Charles said, 'Thanks for taking care of her, you're the best, and very well organized. You can come and help me run the estate if you wish.'

She laughed. 'Thank you for the kind words. And any time you need me, I'll be there. I'm like you, Papa, very efficient.' She stepped away, gazed up at him, and said, 'You look tired.'

'I am a little, but there's nothing wrong that a good night's sleep won't cure.'

Hugo hove into view, and Charles called, 'Good morning, Hugo.'

'Morning, Charles,' Hugo answered. He pulled out a chair for Daphne and sat down in another.

A moment later Hanson was by their side, with a footman standing in the wings.

While they were discussing breakfast choices with Hanson, Charles pushed thoughts of Felicity away. He focused instead on Olive Wilson. He had run into Felicity's personal maid in the bedroom corridor a little earlier, and she had said something about having a lot of packing to do. He had not lingered to ask her questions because he had a splitting headache.

It occurred to him that Felicity might be going up to London today. She had muttered several times last week about missing the summer season yet again, and being disappointed by this.

Perhaps she was being smart and going away for a few weeks. It would certainly make life easier for them both if they were in different homes.

Charles had a busy morning ahead of him, working with Percy Swann and Jim Waters, the estate manager. There were no two ways about it, new walls had to be built to make Cavendon safe and private.

Daphne broke into his thoughts when she said, 'I think Nurse Willis will be able to get a nanny for us, Papa. She has a friend, also a Norland-trained nurse, who is looking for work as a nanny. I asked her to get in touch with this friend. I hope that's all right?'

'Naturally it is, and let's hope this person wants to come here.'

Now, turning to Hanson, Charles said, 'By the way, where's DeLacy this morning? Do you know?'

'Lady DeLacy is out on the terrace with Cecily. They are sitting with Miss Payne, chatting to her. She will be leaving shortly. The governess starts her summer holidays today, m'lord.'

'Oh, of course. I'd forgotten.'

'They wanted to say goodbye to her,' Hanson added.

'I understand.'

The ringing of the telephone in the butler's pantry interrupted their conversation. Hanson went to answer it. A moment later he came back. 'It's Lady Diedre, Your Lordship. She is telephoning from Berlin, she said.'

'My goodness!' Charles exclaimed. He excused himself to Hugo and Daphne, and went to speak on the telephone.

'Hello, Diedre. How nice of you to call. Hanson said you're in Berlin.'

After these comments, there was a silence as Charles listened to his eldest daughter. After a few seconds, he said, 'You've made the right decision. Let us know when you arrive in London. Safe travelling, my dear.'

'What did Diedre have to say? Is she on her way home already?' Daphne asked when he sat down again.

'Yes, but she was due back soon, you know. She detests Berlin, says it's militant, and that all they talk about is war and Wagner. Tomorrow she's taking a train to Paris, and from there she will go to London. So we can expect her in a few days.'

'I still think the trip's been cut short,' Daphne said, then decided to let the matter drop.

Charles said, 'Oh by the way, your mother is thinking of going to London today. She feels like a change, a few days in town. You can deal with the menus, can't you?'

'I can. But is she well enough to go by herself?' Daphne asked.

'Very much so. She's tons better, and anyway, Wilson will be with her, so you don't have to worry. And there is a full staff at the Mayfair house. With Eric Swann in charge, she'll not have to worry about a thing. Hanson trained him, remember. And Laura Swann is a housekeeper par excellence.'

Walking across to the stable block and the office annexe, Charles asked himself why Felicity had chosen last night to tell him their marriage was over. Especially since there had been such an upset about Dulcie's safety. Then it hit him between the eyes. He had mentioned he would like to share her bed. And she had not been able to tolerate that idea. Obviously she couldn't stand having him near her any more. So be it, he said under his breath. His marriage was over and he was a free man.

FORTY-NINE

'They've found the excuse they were looking for,' Adam
Fairley said, turning to Charles. 'We'll be in the middle
of a war before we can blink. No question about that.'
Everyone at the dinner table was silent, staring at Adam. They
took his words seriously. He was the new chairman of the board
of *The Yorkshire Morning Gazette*, and the majority stockholder
in the newspaper. He usually had the latest news before everyone
else, because he had access to so many news sources, including
Reuters.

'You're referring to the assassination of Archduke Franz
Ferdinand and his wife, aren't you, Adam?' Charles asserted.

'I am indeed. A Serbian nationalist killed them late in June,
in Sarajevo, as we all know. Suddenly Austria-Hungary are
bearing down on little Serbia, issuing fierce ultimatums,
demanding that their officials should be allowed to go into Serbia
to find and punish those responsible for the deaths of the
Archduke and his Duchess. From what I gather, the Serbians
have agreed to certain demands, but want to negotiate others,
and there's some kind of standoff between them.'

'Let's hope that someone over there has a bit of common sense,' Hugo exclaimed. 'Because if war breaks out, it will be a war of attrition, and it won't be over in a couple of months.'

'Why not?' Guy asked. 'Wars don't usually last long.'

'One did!' Charles cut in. 'It was called the Hundred Years' War.' He winked at his son and everyone laughed.

Olivia Fairley, Adam's second wife, spoke up in her lovely, lilting voice. 'My mother believed that if the world was run by women, there would be no more wars. I tend to agree with her.'

Guy gazed at Olivia with interest. She was one of the most beautiful women he had ever seen, and her words intrigued him. He asked, 'Why is that? I mean, how could women avoid wars, if men can't?'

'As my mother said, men don't bear children, women do,' Olivia explained, smiling at him warmly. 'And after carrying a child for nine months, a woman isn't going to put her son at risk when he's an adult. So no more wars, no more killing. The Woman's Rule, she called it.'

'Actually, I believe there's a lot of truth in that,' Daphne said. She was tired of all this talk of war. It frightened her. She was certain Hugo would want to go and fight, he was such a patriotic Englishman. His country meant a lot to him, which was why he had come back here.

Diedre cleared her throat and said to her father, 'I told you what it was like in Berlin when I was there in May, Papa. The Germans do nothing but discuss war. If they do get into the fray, it will be a *bloody* war, lots of casualties.'

Adam said, with a quick nod, 'You're absolutely right, Diedre. Thank God Churchill was aware of the Kaiser's efforts to create a stronger German Navy in 1911. That was when Churchill started to build the new Dreadnought battleships, and powerful ships they are indeed. Winston was determined to uphold our naval superiority on the high seas, and he has done that, thank

God. The Royal Navy is the greatest in the world; nothing compares to it. Can't say that about the Army, or the Air Force, though.'

'I understand from a friend of mine that the Army is a bit disorganized,' Hugo remarked. 'Although I hear Churchill is now trying to do something about that, and about the Air Force as well.'

Before anyone could respond or comment, Hanson appeared with the two footmen and dessert was served.

Daphne, wanting to lighten the atmosphere, started to talk about the start of the grouse season on the Glorious Twelfth of August. Adam Fairley joined in immediately, understanding what she was attempting to do. Talk of war ended, and was replaced with more social topics, gossip and discussions about the latest plays in London, the newest books.

Later, after dinner, the men retired to the library for cognac and cigars, and the subject of war instantly came up again. It was Adam who started it. He said to Charles, 'Look here, there are a few things you should know, old chap. If a war starts in Europe, we'll be in it because we signed an Entente with France . . . to come to their aid, if they're attacked.'

Charles nodded. 'And I think we have one with Russia as well, if I'm not mistaken. It's called the Triple Entente.'

'We do. As you know, we don't have a compulsory draft system here. Joining any of the armed services is voluntary. But you and I will not be expected to fight.'

'Why not?' Hugo asked, then answered the question himself when he said swiftly, 'Oh, that's because you're both over forty. That's right, isn't it?'

'Yes,' Adam replied. 'I've been informed privately that the War Office will ask young men from eighteen to thirty to join up. Anyway, I'm afraid I have bad eyesight, so I wouldn't be any use to them, even if they needed me.'

Charles grinned. 'So do I. I just had an eye test the other day, and apparently I need spectacles.'

Glancing at Charles, Hugo said in a low voice, 'My friend with the connection in the War Office told me that the aristocracy may be asked to make a truly big sacrifice. If there is a war. And that is opening up part of their stately homes, to help the country.'

Charles eyed Hugo quizzically. He then sat back in the chair when a terrible truth dawned on him. 'For the wounded soldiers! That's what you're getting at, isn't it? The government anticipates huge casualties, don't they? And they foresee most of our hospitals being overloaded, filled to capacity. The War Office will need our homes because they are so large. They're going to need wards for wounded soldiers.'

Hugo stared at him and nodded.

'I don't care,' Charles said fervently. 'I'm willing to open up two wings of this house if it helps our troops. What troubles me is hearing that the War Office expects such huge casualties before we're even at war. Why in God's name would we allow ourselves to be pulled into this quarrel? We're hard to invade. We're an island race. We can defend ourselves with our fantastic Navy, if we're attacked. So we should just stay out of it.' Charles sounded irate.

'It's the politicians,' Adam answered in a voice of disapproval. 'And the noisy, greedy, hungry, ambitious rulers. King George's cousin leads the way. Kaiser Bill is about to go on that rampage we've been expecting, mark my words. He wants an Empire like ours.'

'That he'll never have!' Guy exclaimed, his face flushed, his blue eyes flashing.

Charles looked across at his oldest son, and thought: Oh my God, he'll want to volunteer, to be a true patriot, to fight for King and Country. I've got to stop him if war does come. I can't let him put himself at risk. He's my heir. He's the future of the Inghams.

The following morning, Charles went to the library to read the newspapers. As usual he became even more alarmed when he saw the dire stories, blaring headlines predicting that war was imminent.

He had only been in the library for fifteen minutes when there was a knock on the door and Daphne looked in. 'Am I disturbing you, Papa?' she asked.

He shook his head, smiling at her. 'No, and you look lovely. I missed you at breakfast.'

She walked across to the Chesterfield sofa where he was sitting, surrounded by the newspapers. 'Well, now that I'm a married woman, I'm allowed to have breakfast in bed, you know. And it was a rather late night.'

'It was. But what a treat to have Adam Fairley for dinner. We're such old friends, and we don't get to see enough of each other. His wife is nice, isn't she?'

'Olivia is charming, and beautiful. I liked her tremendously,' Daphne said, and sat down opposite her father. 'I want to speak to you about something,' she went on. 'Something that's been troubling me.'

'You sound serious. What is it, darling?'

'It's about you and Mother, Papa. Is there something wrong? What's going on? I don't understand.'

'Please close the door,' he said.

She did as he asked, and then returned to the chair. She sat looking at him, waiting for his response to her question.

She couldn't help thinking how handsome he looked today. The July weather had been nice so far, and he had been outside a lot, checking on the walls going up. And he had acquired a light tan, which made his eyes look bluer, and his hair blonder, bleached by the sun. He was forty-five, but he appeared younger, his face relatively unlined. He was also a good man, kind and caring, not only towards his family and the Swanns, but everyone who lived in the three villages. They were his people, and he felt responsible for them and their wellbeing. Unlike many titled aristocrats, he treated everyone the same, with graciousness and dignity, and he was not at all snobbish. He was her moral compass and she respected him. She had always striven to be like him.

Daphne focused her deep blue eyes on her father intently, and said, 'Why are you so silent? Aren't you going to tell me why the two of you are more or less living apart?'

Charles sighed, and stretched out his long legs, and after a moment he said in a low voice, 'I was wondering where to begin, actually.'

'Just blurt it out, Papa, that's what I do when I've something difficult to say,' Daphne said solemnly.

Charles laughed for the first time in weeks. 'That's what I'll do too, then. Your mother left me the morning after Dulcie was almost abducted in the bluebell woods. If you recall, she went to London. In fact, the night before, she told me she didn't want to . . . live with me any more. She even told me I could have a divorce, if I wished.'

'I can't believe this!' Daphne cried, her eyes wide with shock. 'Why on earth did she pick that night, when we'd all been so upset and strained at dinner, because of Dulcie's narrow escape? I don't understand. Did *you*? Do you?'

'To be honest, no. Not really. Look, I've given you this in a nutshell, and it's between us. Nobody else has mentioned your mother, none of your sisters or brothers. At least, they haven't asked why she's away. What I'm telling you is confidential, Daphne. I know you realize that.'

'I do, and I would never discuss it with anyone, not even Hugo, if you don't want me to, Papa.'

'I think, at the moment, I would prefer to keep this between us, Daphne. Not that Hugo would talk, but, well, it's nicer to keep quiet for your mother's sake, don't you think?'

Daphne nodded, then exclaimed, 'Why would she leave *you*? You're the most wonderful man in the world, and you've always looked after her, been so caring and loving. You've been a good husband, and you're a good father . . .' Daphne stopped abruptly. Tears came into her eyes. 'I can't understand it.' She began to cry.

Charles got up and went over to his daughter, pulled her to her feet and put his arms around her, holding her close. 'I'm all right, you know. It was a bit of a shock, but I've accepted it. Come along, darling, stop weeping and sit down here with me on the sofa.'

She did as he asked. He took hold of her hand and said in a steady voice, 'We've had some good years together, your mother and I, but sometimes people change. And I think *she* has. At least in the way she feels about me. Putting it simply, she just doesn't want to be with me, not in any way. I didn't put up a fight, or try to dissuade her from leaving me, because she did change after Dulcie was born, and I've known that for a long time.'

'In what way?'

'Her feelings for me changed. She . . . cooled, I think is the best way of putting it,' Charles said very quietly.

'Maybe her exhaustion and dealing with Aunt Anne affected her in some way,' Daphne ventured. What a fool her mother was to leave in the way she had.

'I considered that, Daphne, but the change in Felicity happened long before your aunt became ill with cancer.'

Daphne looked at him intently. 'What you're saying is that this . . . separation might have been a long time coming.'

'Yes. A year after Dulcie was born there was a difference, but I ignored it, turned a blind eye. Which I now believe was foolish on my part.'

'Do you think, I mean, could there be . . . another man?'

Charles laughed again. 'I don't think so, but I don't know, to be honest.'

Daphne took a deep breath and plunged in. 'Well, I know one thing, you don't have another woman, Papa. Do you?'

He shook his head, and said in a serious tone, 'You're right there, Daphne. I've never been unfaithful to your mother, never strayed. And you mustn't worry about this situation, or be concerned about me. I'm feeling fine now. I must admit, I was rather shaken up at first. But I'm calm, and it's better for us to live apart than be at loggerheads.'

'I'm here to help you any way I can, Papa.' Daphne hesitated for a moment before asking, 'What are you going to do?'

'Nothing. I'm going to let sleeping dogs lie, as they say. I've no reason to get a divorce. Unless your mother wants one, that is. I've a lot to do on the estate, and if there is a war I will have my hands full. War changes everything.'

FIFTY

Two weeks later Charles remembered those words he had uttered to his daughter, and he repeated them to Charlotte Swann on 5 August 1914.

'War changes everything,' he said. 'And it changes everyone as well. The world becomes a different place.'

'We've expected it for such a long time, and now it's finally here,' she remarked in disbelief, shaking her head. 'I never really thought it would happen, though. I was positive it would go away.'

The two of them were in the library at Cavendon. Several newspapers were piled up on the floor near the Chesterfield; the night before, on Tuesday 4 August, Britain had declared war on Germany, after it had invaded neutral Belgium.

'The German attack was unprovoked,' Charles explained to her. 'And it tipped the balance in our government. Our Triple Entente with France and Russia was made in order to provide mutual defence of each other, if a war with Germany came. But Britain and the other great powers pledged to guarantee Belgian neutrality as well. So that's the reason we're involved now.'

'Do you think it will be a long war?' Charlotte asked.

'I'm afraid it may well be. Adam Fairley confirmed that to me last night, when he telephoned to tell me about the declaration of war. It was late when we spoke, past midnight, and the paper had just gone to press. He always keeps me posted these days. He thinks it is likely to be a prolonged affair.'

'So you knew before you read about it in the *Gazette* this morning?'

'I did, yes. In a funny way, it came as a relief to finally know. At least we are now able to look at our options now. Much better than being in limbo, in the dark, worrying. And I do believe our government had no option but to take us in, I see that very clearly now. We cannot afford to let the Germans capture Belgium's Channel ports. We will be at a strategic disadvantage if that happens.' Charles sat back. 'But I trust Churchill and Asquith,' he added, not wanting to appear too gloomy.

'Are we in for a long siege, Charles?' Charlotte sat, twisting her hands in her lap, aware that hordes of young men would be leaving to fight. It was always the young who rushed to the front, fired up by youthful enthusiasm, strength and fortitude. Unfortunately, war excited them.

Charles had been thoughtful for a few moments, and finally he answered her question. 'This is going to be a big war, Charlotte. Other countries are already in it, and yes, I can see it lasting a year at least.'

'So long?' She sounded surprised.

He nodded. 'Germany has amassed an enormous amount of armaments. They will be able to fight on for months and months.' He shook his head, and rose. 'Let's go and tour the West and North Wings, shall we? That's why you came up this morning. Those wings are the ones we will have to transform. We must be ready to start operating when the government asks us to take in wounded troops. And they will, there's no doubt of that in my mind.'

By Thursday 6 August, Austria-Hungary had declared war on Russia. On the twelfth of the month, France and Britain went to war with Austria-Hungary, since they were allied to Russia in the Triple Entente. As Charles had predicted, it was going to be a big war, a great war, and some people would describe it as the war to end all wars. But would it be? Charles had his doubts about that.

Across the country, in cities, towns and little villages, government posters went up, were pasted to lampposts, trees, walls, and doors. Anywhere there was enough space for one, in fact.

YOUR COUNTRY NEEDS YOU, they read, and men responded, just as they had responded to Lord Kitchener's request for volunteers. One hundred thousand men joined the Army after his first appeal.

Kitchener had been made Secretary of State for War, and there was much relief everywhere that he had taken on this arduous job. He was not only a great war hero, but a legend.

The posters appeared in the three Ingham villages in the Dales, and recruitment offices opened all over Yorkshire and the rest of the country.

Wherever Charles went, his people asked him questions and wanted to know about the war, what it would mean to them, and what they should do to help.

'I think I had better call a meeting at the church hall in Little Skell,' he said to Hugo and Daphne one afternoon in the middle of August.

'For this coming Friday. I must also include the villagers

from Mowbray and High Clough. And all of the outside workers on the estate. I do think it's important that I speak to them, answer their questions. The women must come, if they wish. They have as much right as their husbands to hear everything I have to say.'

Daphne and Hugo agreed with him, and Daphne said, 'Don't you think you should speak with the indoor staff at Cavendon also, Papa? Perhaps just before dinner tonight.'

'Good thought, Daphne,' her father answered. After a moment's reflection, he went on, 'I believe it is vital we go to meet our villagers as the Ingham family. So we must take the children, including Alicia, in the care of Nurse Willis, and Dulcie with Nanny Clarice. By the way, she's turned out well, hasn't she, Daphne?'

Daphne nodded, and then broke into laughter. 'She never takes her eyes off Dulcie. Fortunately, Dulcie fell in love with her at once. They get on like a house on fire because Nanny Clarice treats her as an adult. She asks her opinion about all kinds of things, including what she would like to wear. In that quarter, we're doing well, Papa.'

Hugo asked, 'Are you going to ask Felicity to come to Yorkshire to join us for this event?'

'No. I don't think she would be interested, Hugo,' Charles answered. 'I understand from Diedre the Countess has been feeling exhausted lately. As for Diedre, I think she prefers her life in Mayfair. She certainly wouldn't want to be *here*, I can assure you of that.'

When Lady Gwendolyn heard about the impending meeting at Little Skell church hall, she immediately told Charles she would love to come with them – would be offended if she were left out, in fact.

'After all, I am the *oldest* Ingham,' she reminded her nephew. Charles agreed it was most important that she was there, being the great Ingham matriarch that she was.

'Well, Papa, we're quite a group as a family,' Daphne said to him as they stood together on the terrace on Friday afternoon, as everyone assembled.

Alongside them were Hugo, and Guy, who had not yet returned to Oxford. Lady Gwendolyn was seated in a chair and Nanny Clarice was holding Dulcie's hand. DeLacy, and Miles, still at home from Eton, were standing on the garden path below the terrace with Nurse Willis and Alicia. The baby was sitting up in her Silver Cross perambulator and looked beautiful.

'*She* is going to be the hit of the show,' Miles said, grinning at Nurse Willis.

The Ingham family walked through the park, heading for the village of Little Skell. Nurse Willis, pushing Alicia in the pram, was the leader, along with Nanny Clarice and Dulcie, walking hand in hand. This amused Charles. As usual, Dulcie had to be the first, no matter what.

He followed behind them with Hugo, Lady Gwendolyn, Daphne, DeLacy, Guy and Miles. As he glanced at his family, he felt a little surge of pride. They were, each one of them, individuals in their own right, confident and secure and well behaved. Not to mention good looking.

When they reached the church hall, a bevy of Swanns was there to greet them: Charlotte, Alice, Cecily and Harry, with their father, Walter, who had been given permission to be present by Charles.

Percy was there with his wife Edna, and their thirteen-year-old son Joe, who was a junior woodsman, and Percy's nephew, Bill, head landscape gardener at Cavendon, aged twenty-eight.

There was a lot of cheering and clapping as the Inghams trooped into the church hall. Once things had calmed down,

Charles went and stood in front of his villagers and spoke to them in his usual well-modulated voice, his charisma holding them spellbound.

'I've come here with my family to speak to you about the war. Unfortunately, the Countess is in London and was unable to join us today, but she sends her best wishes, as does our daughter, Lady Diedre, who is also away.

'I believe all of us here today know what we must do, and that is to support our country in its hour of greatest need. That is what we of the three Ingham villages are going to do most wholeheartedly, as we have done in other times of strife and trouble in our land.

'I know Lord Kitchener has raised a force of one hundred thousand men, who will be shipping out soon to fight in the fields of Flanders. The Army is still requesting men from the ages of eighteen to thirty to volunteer. Single men at the moment. And those who feel they must go to the front must do so.

'I am not going to tell anyone what they can or cannot do, because this is a free country. We make our own choices as Englishmen. What I do ask is that married men consider their options. It might be wise to wait until married men are called to duty, because of their family responsibilities.

'I must explain something to you. I am converting two wings of Cavendon Hall into hospital wards. We have been alerted that the government might need beds for our wounded troops coming back from the front. I would like to ask any of you who have nursing or medical skills to volunteer now, to help with the wounded later. Miss Charlotte is starting a list today to hold in reserve.

'There might be rationing of food, since we won't be able to import. That is why I am relying on our tenant farmers to keep tilling the land.

'I will end by saying that we are in this great fight together.

We will stand together shoulder to shoulder, to bring victory to our country. And we shall prevail. Now Miss Mayhew will play the national anthem, and then refreshments will be served.'

There was clapping and cheering and then Miss Viola Mayhew, the church organist, began to thump the piano in one corner of the hall, and the voices of the villagers rang to the rafters as they began to sing:

'God save our gracious King, long live our noble King, God save the King. Send him victorious, happy and glorious, long to reign over us, God save the King.'

When the national anthem finally finished, many of the men came to speak with their Earl, asking crucial questions about the war, earnestly seeking his advice.

As usual, Charles Ingham, the 6th Earl of Mowbray, listened attentively, and answered them all with graciousness, respect and kindness, which was his way.

And the women of the three villages flocked around the women of Cavendon Hall, and especially the children, and, as Miles had predicted, baby Alicia, in her Silver Cross pram, was indeed the star of the show.

By 20 August the first four divisions of the British Expeditionary Force had crossed the English Channel, and by early September, the fifth and sixth divisions had followed.

Not a ship was sunk, not a life was lost. It was called a triumph for Winston Churchill, brilliant leader and militant trustee of the British Royal Navy.

Great Britain mobilized for war with ferocity and enormous speed. Every citizen was affected in some way or other as the grim days sped on, and on, and on. Endless days that seemed without hope.

The guns that had started to roar in August went on roaring through the following months and into the new year. Suddenly it was 1915 and success was nowhere in sight.

Hundreds of thousands of young men had died on the blood-soaked fields of Belgium and France. And as the dead piled up, the wounded were being shipped home to Britain, the country they loved and had fought for so bravely.

PART FOUR

River of Blood
May 1916–November 1918

We few, we happy few, we band of brothers;
For he today who sheds his blood with me
Shall be my brother.

William Shakespeare

If I should die, think only this of me:
That there's some corner of a foreign field
That is for ever England. There shall be
In that rich earth a richer dust concealed;
A dust whom England bore, shaped, made aware,
Gave, once, her flowers to love, her ways to roam;
A body of England's, breathing English air,
Washed by the rivers, blest by suns of home.

And think, this heart, all evil shed away,
A pulse in the eternal mind, no less
Gives somewhere back the thoughts by England given;
Her sights and sounds; dreams happy as her day;
And laughter, learnt of friends; and gentleness,
In hearts at peace, under an English heaven.

Rupert Brooke

FIFTY-ONE

D aphne sat at her desk in the conservatory, making the work sheet for the coming week. She glanced at her daily engagement book: today was Sunday 28 May 1916.

Nineteen sixteen, she said under her breath, wondering what had happened to time. It had passed so quickly, she was momentarily startled.

Her eye caught the photograph of Guy and Miles in the silver frame, the two of them looking so grown up and handsome. Hugo had taken it last summer on the terrace. Miles was still at Eton, but Guy was at the front, fighting in France with the Seaforth Highlanders, a regiment favoured by many Yorkshire men.

She sat back in her chair and closed her eyes, thinking of her brother, and saying a silent prayer for his safety. She did this every morning and every night, as she knew her father did. He had not wanted Guy to join up, but her eldest brother had explained to their father why he must go.

Like all of the Inghams, he was patriotic, loved his country, and was proud of his heritage. Their father had finally given in.

But Daphne realized her father had not had any alternative. Guy was of age and could do as he wished. They all worried about Guy. The news from the front line was horrific, and seemed to grow worse every day. Thousands upon thousands of young men had been slaughtered. And as the dead piled up on foreign fields, the wounded were brought home to be treated and healed.

The two wings at Cavendon were now filled. Once the war had started in 1914, her father had immediately converted the North and West Wings.

All of the antiques, paintings and other precious objects had been taken up to the attics to be stored, and extra beds moved in. Her father had, in the end, had to buy additional beds so that the largest number of wounded soldiers could be accommodated.

The entire staff at Cavendon had pitched in, in order to turn those beautiful eighteenth-century rooms into hospital wards.

Once the wounded had started to arrive, the women from the villages had come to help, as had all of the Swann women, and she herself. DeLacy had done her bit in different ways, and Cecily too before she left.

It was a joint effort, and it was working well. Dr Shawcross dropped by from time to time. Her father had hired several matrons to run the wards, as well as professional nursing staff and doctors. He had also purchased all of the equipment needed to make the wings as efficient as possible.

Her father was a wonder. He was managing the estate as best he could; this was a difficult task, since so many men had left the three villages to go and fight the enemy. But their wives had taken over, many with great skill, and the tenant farms continued to run.

Teenage boys, too young to go to war, helped out, and so did teenage girls and young women. Daphne was constantly amazed how everyone pulled together, to properly ensure that things continued as normally as possible.

Eventually Daphne finished her list, and read through it one more time. Today she was off, and would be able to have lunch with her father and Hugo. It would be just the three of them because DeLacy was on duty in the other wings, as was Cecily.

She smiled to herself as she thought of the two of them. They were fifteen now, and both lovely, and very determined to lend a hand in the war effort. They rolled bandages, took hot and cold drinks to the patients, handed out magazines and newspapers to those who wanted them, straightened bed sheets and plumped up pillows. And ran errands.

Alice would be running the North Wing kitchen this afternoon. It had been enlarged and was now used for the West Wing as well. Mrs Thwaites would be helping Alice, and so would Peggy Swift, who had been kept on after her marriage as she was needed. She still used her maiden name, so there was no confusion with two Lanes in service. Peggy had managed to keep Gordon by her side.

Malcolm Smith, the other footman, had gone long ago, glad to be out of domestic service and into the armed services. Hanson was not eligible to fight, nor was Percy Swann, who discovered he had a weak chest when he tried to enlist.

Walter Swann had also remained at Cavendon, because married men had not yet been called up, and he had promised Alice he wouldn't volunteer.

Daphne thanked God that Hugo had stayed with her, even though she knew he was itching to go and fight. She was happy he was here. Turning pages in her engagement book, Daphne saw her notations about her aunts, Lavinia and Vanessa.

Her father's sisters had turned out to be true Inghams, ready to help however they could. Vanessa would be returning from London on Tuesday of the coming week. She would stay for the whole of June, as would her older sister, Lavinia, both working in the wards.

Lavinia had proved herself to be a gifted nurse, caring, compassionate, efficient and skilled, much to Daphne's surprise. Her aunt was tireless, and her disposition was so warm and loving that the soldiers adored her. Lavinia always managed to bring a smile to their faces. Likewise Vanessa also helped to cheer them up, and made them laugh when she was on the wards. There wasn't anything the two women wouldn't do for their patients.

Daphne was proud of her family, and of the Swanns and the villagers, the way they had responded to war and the adverse conditions they faced. Although she had to exclude Diedre and Felicity.

Diedre was not around any more. She had a job at the War Office. Meanwhile Felicity had not come back to Cavendon very often since she had left in May 1914. She had remained in London and was hardly ever in contact, much to Daphne's surprise. But her mother hated the idea of Cavendon as a hospital and was squeamish about working on the wards.

To her astonishment, Daphne had discovered that her brothers and sisters didn't seem to care that their mother was absent. Before he had left for France, Guy had gone to say goodbye to her at the new London house she had bought, but that was only out of politeness. He had, after all, been brought up to be a gentleman.

Miles confessed to Daphne that he found their mother irritating, and thought she was flighty. This was a word Daphne had never thought would be used to describe their mother. DeLacy, deep down, was angry about Felicity's departure, and called it, 'the worst defection I've ever heard of.'

But Daphne knew that DeLacy was enveloped in the warm embrace of the Swann women, as she was herself. Dulcie, now eight, was as independent as always, but she loved Nanny Clarice, who had taught her manners, amongst other things. Since Felicity had been absent so much when Anne was ill, Dulcie didn't miss her mother at all.

Nor does Papa, Daphne thought. She knew how busy he was. He had so much to do with Jim Waters, the estate manager, and the outside workers; plus he visited the hospital wings as much as he could. Work and more work, she thought, pursing her lips. All work and no play make Jack a dull boy, she muttered under her breath. She also knew her father was lonely, and she worried about him.

After writing all of the names down, their days of work, and their duties next week, Daphne closed her book and got up. She would now join her father and Hugo for lunch. And this afternoon, when she and Hugo were alone, she would tell him a secret.

Fifteen minutes later, when Daphne walked into the dining room, she knew at once that something was wrong. Hugo and her father were standing talking as they waited for her. Their faces were grim.

'What's happened? What is it?' she cried, looking from one to the other, fearing the worst, that there was bad news about Guy.

'The government's just passed a new law. Every man, whether single or married, and who is well and able, will be called up,' Charles said. 'It went through the House of Commons last night. It's the new Military Service Act and it has received royal assent.'

Daphne looked from her father to Hugo, her eyes filling with tears, understanding exactly what it meant.

Hugo went over to her, and put his arm around her. He said quietly, 'Serving in the armed forces has now become compulsory. I will have to go, Daphne. I really will.'

Tears spilled, ran down her cheeks, and she clung to him, but after a moment she pulled herself together. He gave her a handkerchief and she wiped her eyes. She said, 'I understand. I know every man must do his duty.' Swallowing, she added, 'And Ingham women don't weep. They stand up to be counted. And get on with it, keep going.'

'That's the spirit!' her father said admiringly. 'Let's sit down, and try to eat lunch . . . since Cook has made such an effort.'

'Yes, we must eat. At least I must,' she said, looking at her father, then turning to Hugo. 'I have a secret,' she said to her husband. 'I was going to tell you later, and you too, Papa. After lunch. But I might as well tell you both now.' Taking a deep breath, pushing a big smile onto her face, she said, 'I'm pregnant, Hugo. I'm going to give you another baby.'

It was obvious that Hugo was overjoyed. He jumped up, pulled her to her feet, hugged her, kissed her cheek, and hugged her again. 'How wonderful, my darling. How very wonderful indeed. And this time I think it will be a boy.'

Her father was also smiling, and once Hugo released her from his grip, Charles went to her and held her close. 'Congratulations, Daphne. I'm so happy for you and Hugo, and glad to know I will soon have another grandchild.'

FIFTY-TWO

'Lord Mowbray!' Alice exclaimed, taken by surprise and quickly closing the oven door as Charles Ingham walked into the kitchen in the North Wing. 'Do you need me? How can I help you, m'lord?'

'Sorry to burst in like this, Mrs Alice, but I can't find Miss Charlotte. No one seems to know where she is. Not even Lady Daphne. I've been to the West Wing, and gone through the wards here. There's no sign of her. I thought you could enlighten me perhaps.'

'She did tell me on Friday that she was going to be working in the wards this weekend. I don't think she has the weekend off. Maybe she's gone home for some reason.'

'I did try telephoning her, Mrs Alice, but there is no answer,' Charles replied.

Alice looked thoughtful for a split second, and then said, 'She might have gone to rest for a while, m'lord. At home. She could be in her garden, and didn't hear the telephone. Do you want me to find Cecily and send her with a message, m'lord?'

'No, no,' he said, shaking his head. 'That won't be necessary.

I need to talk to her about something quite urgently. I'll walk down there myself. But thank you, Mrs Alice.' He smiled at her, and added, 'The chicken smells delicious. Those boys are going to enjoy their dinner tonight.'

'Thank you, m'lord. We always try to give them a good nourishing meal at night. They deserve it, after all they've been through.'

He nodded and left the kitchen, went out to the front entrance hall. He couldn't help smiling as he went down the terrace steps. Alice had looked positively astonished when he had burst into her domain unannounced, and no wonder. Whenever had anyone seen the 6th Earl of Mowbray in a kitchen at Cavendon?

Walking through the park to the village, Charles tried to control his anxiety. He had been worried about Charlotte all week. She had looked worn out and unwell, troubled even, and it had concerned him. They had both been so busy there hadn't been a chance to talk. Then, on Saturday, he had gone looking for her, and again this afternoon. The odd thing was, nobody seemed to think she had the weekend off. He decided he had just kept missing her. After lunch today, when he had come to the North Wing, his anxiety about her had spiralled. Usually she told him where she would be at the weekend, but she hadn't done so on Friday.

Perhaps she was really ill, and alone in her house in the village. And with no one to look after her.

He increased his pace, convinced she needed help. The good thing was that her house was at the edge of the village, close to the park. She didn't answer when he knocked on her door a few minutes later. He went inside the house.

'There you are!' he exclaimed when he saw her standing on a ladder in the living room, straightening a painting.

Charlotte had not heard him come in. She was so startled when she heard his voice, she swung around too quickly and lost her balance.

He saw it happening, her foot slipping, her body tumbling forward. He rushed towards her, managed to break her fall, caught her in his arms and held onto her tightly.

He staggered slightly, then regained his balance. She wasn't heavy but the impact of her body against his had almost brought them to the floor.

He held her in his arms, looking down at her.

She gazed up at him. He gazed back. Their eyes locked and held. Neither of them could look away, mesmerized by each other.

'I've been so terribly worried about you, Charlotte,' he said softly, and before he could stop himself, losing all restraint, he bent his head and kissed her on the mouth.

Charlotte kissed him back. Her arms were around him. She was clinging to him. Somehow they managed to right themselves, and he got her safely onto her feet. They were clutching each other again, kissing passionately, as if they were trying to slake some kind of thirst for each other.

Suddenly, Charles stopped, left her alone, standing in the middle of the floor looking startled. He strode over to the front door and locked it, came back to her swiftly, filled with a raging desire for her, wanting to make her his own right now, here in this room.

He took her in his arms at once, their mouths meeting with urgency. He heart was racing, his yearning for her so enormous he was startled at himself. He pulled her closer, pressing his body against hers, and he knew immediately that he was not impotent. No, not at all.

Charles reached up, pulled the pins out of her hair. It came tumbling down around her face, luxuriant and filled with auburn lights. He stood away from her, his eyes fixing on hers . . . those wondrous, translucent eyes, a funny greyish-blue tinted with lavender, so unique to the Swanns. And what he saw in them moved him, touched his heart. He recognized how much she wanted him, as he wanted her. Her desire for him was reflected in her unwavering gaze.

She reached out, touched his cheek, stroking it lovingly. His heart twisted in him and he pulled her even closer, pushing his body against hers. His control was slipping, he was growing harder, and his need for her was something he had never known with any other woman. It was overwhelming.

Charles began to open the buttons on her blouse, and he bent down, kissed her neck, and then he said softly, against her hair, 'Might we go and find a bed? We've wasted too much time already. Too many years.'

Taking hold of his hand, Charlotte led him upstairs, guiding him into her bedroom and towards the large four-poster bed.

Unexpectedly, Charles stood still in the centre of the room. He looked down into her face, his own intense and serious. There was a questioning look in his eyes when he said, 'Are you sure you want to continue? Because if you do there will be no going back. Not for me. I realize you long for us to be together, just as I do. I see that. But if we make love now, it will never end. It will be forever, Charlotte Swann.'

'I know it will, Charles Ingham. That's the way it is, and always has been . . . between yours and mine.'

She put her hands on either side of his face, and kissed him deeply, her tongue slipping into his mouth and entwining with his. And for the first time in his life, as she cleaved to him, he experienced the thrill of raging mutual desire.

A moment later, she stopped kissing him and began to undress. Charles threw his jacket onto a chair, and within seconds they found themselves stretched out naked on the bed.

He pushed himself up on one elbow, and looked into her beautiful face. Her hair fanned out behind her on the pillow, and its richness of colour made the pallor of her face seem all that more striking. Leaning over her he touched her face with tenderness as he marvelled at her lovely long body, so slender and shapely.

He stroked her breasts and moved his hands over her stomach, and down onto her thighs. Her skin was so soft it was like satin. He brought his mouth to hers, and let one hand slide down to the silky triangle between her legs. When he touched the core of her femininity, she stiffened and then relaxed. And she let him do whatever he wanted. Because he was hers at last, and she knew he loved her, just as she loved him, and that was all that mattered.

She was so quickly aroused under his hands, so responsive to him, Charles wrapped his arms around her, and pulled himself onto her body.

He said, 'I want to savour every part of you, prolong this, but I need to take you to me, to be inside you.' His voice was low, thick with desire and heightened emotion.

'I want that too, Charles,' she said. He heard the urgency in her voice, and she was breathing rapidly. She was as aroused as he was, and her ardour excited him even more. He began to kiss her, slipped his hands under her back, and slid into her quickly and with some force. As the moist warmth of her enveloped him, he thought he was being held in a velvet vice, and he groaned with pleasure. He lay still, savouring her, and then, as he moved with sudden swiftness, she moved with him. They were feverish in their need for each other, their bodies clamouring wildly.

Charlotte thought she was melting into Charles, becoming a part of him. It was as if they were consumed by their own heat. Her quivering body arched up to meet his, her arms and legs went around him, and he began to quiver with her. His heart was hammering next to hers. They soared together, and he clung to her as if to never let her go. And he knew he never would. She was part of him, and she always had been, without him ever realizing it.

Charles held Charlotte in his arms, filled with the kind of peacefulness he had never ever known before. It was a total absence of pain . . . contentment, and something else, something he could not quite define.

Charlotte spoke first when she said, 'You're very quiet, Charles.'

'I was thinking about you, and how peaceful and contented I feel,' he said, his voice full of love and tenderness.

'I'm glad.' She drew closer to him, resting her head on his shoulder. 'Why did you come looking for me this afternoon?'

'I looked for you yesterday as well. I wanted to see you, talk to you, just be with you, actually. And when I couldn't find you I became very anxious.'

'Why?'

'Because I've been awfully worried about you. You've been looking unwell for several weeks, and somehow troubled. I couldn't imagine where you were yesterday and today, when everyone kept telling me you were in the wards. And yet I couldn't find you. And I must confess, I became frantic, desperate, and filled with anxiety, if you want the truth.'

After a while, she said softly, 'I discovered I couldn't come to Cavendon this weekend. I didn't want to, so I stayed at home.'

Releasing her, sitting up, Charles turned to look at her. 'What's wrong, Charlotte? Are you ill?'

'No, I'm not,' she replied, propping herself up against the

pillows and returning his gaze. She touched his face with her fingertips and, quite unexpectedly, her eyes filled with tears.

He caught her hand in his, staring at her, looking more worried than ever. 'What on earth's the matter? What is it?' he asked.

'Nothing. I can deal with it.'

'I must take care of you better than I do. You're working too hard. So am I. We need a change. We must go to London for a few days, take a break from Cavendon . . .' He stopped abruptly, realizing what he was saying. Turning slightly, glancing at her, Charles grabbed hold of her shoulders. 'I need you. I want you with me. I love you, oh my darling Charlotte, I do love you so much.'

She smiled wanly. 'We've loved each other since we were children.'

'Let me rephrase that at once. What I mean is that *I am in love with you*. And you're in love with me, aren't you?'

'Yes. And I worry about you. I know how lonely you are, and so am I. And I keep wondering why we aren't together. And that's why I didn't come up this weekend. Because I knew I couldn't bear it any longer. It was torture, seeing you every day, loving you so much, wanting to touch you, hold you in my arms. To comfort you, to make you happy. And to make love with you.' The tears had welled again and she flicked them away with her fingers. 'And I couldn't do any of those things.'

'Oh darling, don't cry.' He reached for her, held her close to him. 'We're such fools. We've been such fools for a long time. We're in our forties, and we've been behaving like children. We must be together, take this chance of happiness, before it's too late. In any case, I told you earlier there was no going back if we made love today, and you agreed. So I'm afraid you're stuck with me.'

'Thank God,' she exclaimed, smiling at him.

'You've often said when certain things happen, that it was meant to be . . . and this was meant to be,' Charles murmured.

'I know . . . it's our destiny, I suppose.' She glanced at him through the corner of her eye, and bit back a smile. 'I found something in one of the old Swann record books, years ago, and then came across it again recently. It's something that has always stayed with me.'

'I do know about those Swann record books. They are forbidden to the Inghams. But what did you find? Are you allowed to tell me?'

She nodded. 'I can tell you a bit of it, yes. It was a notation by a Swann, an M. Swann, to be exact, and it was dated 1876. This M. Swann had a long affair with an Ingham woman, and he wrote this: *The Swann fits the Ingham like a glove.* Do you think it's true?'

He saw the flirtatious look in her eyes, and he began to laugh. 'I'd like to put it another way, my darling. In this instance, I think it's the Ingham that fits the Swann like a glove. What do you think of that?'

'I think it's true,' Charlotte replied, laughing with him. She got out of bed, and went across to the wardrobe. As she took out a silk robe and put it on, she said, 'Let's go downstairs and light a fire, have a drink together. Wouldn't you like that?'

'I would indeed. I wish I had a dressing gown here. Should I bring one tomorrow?'

He was still laughing when he said this, obviously happy; she was filled with happiness herself. She said, 'I've never stolen anything in my life, but after David died I took a dressing gown of his, from his dressing room at Cavendon—'

'Why?' he asked curiously, cutting in, looking across the room at her, his love for her reflected in his blue eyes.

'Because I wanted something personal that had belonged to him, something I could wear.'

'Did you love him?'

'Yes.'

'And he loved you, didn't he?'

'I think so.'

'Don't be so silly, darling. I know he did. How could any man *not* love you? I *sensed* he loved you, and I became convinced of it recently. You were with him all those years, how could he ever have resisted you? Surely you know you are a beautiful, intelligent woman. He was widowed twice, and lonely, and you worked with him, grew close to him.'

'There's something I must tell you, Charles.'

'What?'

'Although I worked with your father from the age of seventeen, it wasn't until I was over twenty-one that we became personally involved. He was always very proper, always the gentleman.'

'Yes, I know he was. And there's something I must say to you, Charlotte. Your relationship with my father has never troubled me, nor does it now. I just want you to be aware of that. I'm glad he could share a bit of happiness with you, truly I am.'

'In that case, you can wear his silk dressing gown. I know it will fit you.'

FIFTY-THREE

They went downstairs together. There were wood chips and newspaper rolls in the fireplace grate in the living room, and Charlotte struck a Swan Vesta, bringing the match to the rolls of paper. They flared immediately. After turning on a couple of table lamps, she went and sat on the sofa in front of the fire. Charles joined her, carrying two glasses of scotch and water.

After handing her one, he sat down in the armchair next to the fireplace. When Charlotte looked at him questioningly, he said, 'I want to sit and admire you. The cat can look at the queen, can't he?'

She nodded, and leaned forward, clinked her glass to his, and they said cheers in unison.

Charles leaned back in the chair, a reflective expression settling on his face, and eventually he said, 'I would like to tell you something, but it involves Felicity. You wouldn't mind if I spoke about her, would you, Charlie?'

'No, that's perfectly all right.'

'Firstly, I want to make something clear to you. I know there's been gossip here at Cavendon about Felicity's absence; in case you hadn't guessed, she is the one who left me.'

'I thought as much. Well, eventually. When she didn't come back, except on the odd brief visit, I realized you were probably separated. But why did she leave you? Will you tell me?'

'Of course. Felicity told me she had lost interest in me, and especially sexually. She said I could no longer share her bed, and that the marriage was over.'

'Did she actually use those words?'

'Absolutely. And she was rather blunt, and very, very icy. I realized she had no feelings for me whatsoever, except perhaps contempt. I was rather stupid, I think. I just stood there in shock, staring at her flabbergasted.'

Charlotte was appalled, and she stared at him, shaking her head. 'I don't understand her. Why would any woman want to leave *you*?'

He laughed. 'You're prejudiced, my darling. I think what hurt the most was that she made this announcement on the night that Dulcie had almost been abducted. All I wanted was to share her bed, talk about that terrible incident, exchange thoughts. When she started her little speech I was taken aback, and later I understood that she had come to the point in her life where she simply couldn't stand having me near her. She left the next morning and has barely been back, as you are aware.'

'I can't bear to hear this!' Charlotte exclaimed, looking across at him. How hurt he must have been, and humiliated. And emasculated. She found herself growing angry at Felicity, but kept tight control on herself. Certainly she would never say a word against his wife. That was a dangerous game to play, whatever the circumstances.

'When I reminded her that I was a young man, only forty-five, and asked her what I was supposed to do, meaning about my life, she told me I was as free as a bird.' Charles gave a small chuckle after he said this, looking across at Charlotte pointedly.

Through her laughter, she said, 'I'm so happy it's my nest you flew into, Charles Ingham. Very, very happy.'

'I suppose everyone at Cavendon knows it was my wife who left me? Am I right?' he asked, raising a brow.

'Naturally. She's the one who did the moonlight flit,' Charlotte answered, using a well-used Yorkshire expression. 'And anyway, you're the Sixth Earl of Mowbray, don't forget that.'

'I won't, but what are you actually saying?' he asked, obviously baffled.

'That you are genuinely loved here on this estate, admired and respected and looked up to. And you are everyone's moral compass. In other words, the villagers and staff will always side with you, Charles.'

He nodded. 'I just wanted *you* to know I wasn't cheating on my wife, because she was the one who left me.'

An amused glint flickered in Charlotte's translucent eyes, and she observed, 'You didn't really have to say that, you know, Charlie. Especially since a short while ago you said I was an intelligent woman.'

'I know that, but I've always had a certain moral code, and I never strayed, nor have I ever had a mistress. But you know that, since the Swanns know everything.'

Charlotte took a long swallow of the scotch, fully aware that Charles Ingham's pride had been savagely dented by the woman he had married and with whom he had fathered six children. Finally, she said, 'Perhaps her exhaustion played a part in it,' although she was fully aware it hadn't.

'No, it didn't. I toyed with that idea, and so did Daphne. Felicity became extremely strange about a year after the birth of Dulcie.'

Charlotte noticed that the light had changed outside. Twilight was descending. She rose, went to the French doors, drew the curtains, and then did the same at the other windows in the room. All the time her mind was racing, wondering what to do. She was sitting here with a man she had known since child-hood, who was, in fact, her dearest friend. She had lived all of her life close to him. She had fallen in love with him several years ago. And this afternoon they had become lovers. Didn't she owe him something? Didn't she owe him the truth? The only real reason she had hesitated about telling him before was the fear of hurting him. He had had enough hurt lately.

When she came back to the fireside, he said, 'What was all that about?'

'What do you mean?'

'All that busy fussing around with the draperies. What are you hiding from me, Charlie?'

She shook her head, unable to lie to him, and sipped her scotch.

'I know there's another man,' Charles told her. 'I know that Felicity has another man in her life, to be precise,' he announced in a steady voice.

'How do you know?'

'My sister Lavinia told me, about six months ago. I suspected it, though. There's usually another man when a woman leaves the way Felicity did, without giving a thought to her children, never mind her husband. Sex in itself is a powerful aphrodisiac, and especially with a man ten years younger. When he left his wife and the hospital in Harrogate, and opened a private practice in Harley Street, she followed him to London.'

'How did Lavinia find out?'

'She saw them together, and there had been a bit of gossip in London. As I just said, he's younger than her, and it's been going on for years, since Dulcie was a year old.' He leaned closer to Charlotte and put his hand on her knee, his clear blue eyes locked onto hers. 'You know all this, though, don't you, darling?'

'I didn't know that she announced it so bluntly or spoke to you so coldly or what exactly she said. All I know is that there is another man in the Countess's life, and that he's a surgeon.'

'Who else knows this?'

'Walter and Alice, that's all. It was Walter who told me.'

'Oh my God, my valet knows all about my wife's sex life!' he exclaimed, shaking his head. 'What next!'

She knew he wasn't angry, and she explained, 'It was Olive Wilson who told Walter, Charles. When she came up to get some of the Countess's clothes. About six months ago.'

'I wish he'd told me, I really do,' Charles murmured.

'There's a certain line even we can't cross, and we Swanns respect that.'

'We can fornicate, the Swanns and the Inghams, and have done so for generations, from what I gather. But we can't confide?'

Charlotte nodded. 'Yes, I suppose that is so, but I didn't make the rules.'

Rising, she went and knelt down in front of him and looked into his face.

He was a very handsome man, irresistible to her. There was also a certain gentleness in his face, and his features were finely drawn, classical and genteel. He was well bred, kind and caring, and she had never heard a bad word said about him. Not by anyone. And she told him that, and then she said, 'Walter didn't know what to do, to be honest, Charles. He explained that to me. On several occasions he was on the point of telling you, but lost his nerve. None of us wants to hurt you.'

Leaning forward, Charles kissed her lightly. 'I'm not angry with Walter. I hope you know that. In fact, I can't ever remember any Ingham being angry with a Swann. What else did Wilson have to impart? Will you tell me?'

'Yes, I will. She disapproves, and is not really very happy with working for Her Ladyship any more. But she needs the job, you know.' She left it at that, not wanting to repeat the gory details that Olive Wilson had imparted to Walter.

He simply nodded, then asked, 'Are you going to let me stay for supper? May I?'

'Yes, but whatever will Hanson think if you don't return home for dinner?'

'I don't know, nor do I care. But I will telephone and explain I'm having supper here with you. Just so he knows where I am, in case I'm needed.'

Charlotte realized, as she knelt there looking at him so adoringly, that he was trying very hard not to laugh, and then suddenly he did. He was convulsed, and she laughed with him, because his laughter was so infectious.

When they had calmed down, she asked, in all seriousness, 'Why did you start laughing like that?'

'Because I am now forty-seven years old. I'm the Sixth Earl of Mowbray, and you're asking me how I'm going to explain to my butler where I am. I'm not that ten-year-old schoolboy you used to boss around, you know.'

'I never bossed you around. And I was only thinking of discretion, of being careful. There'll be gossip otherwise.'

'Oh bugger gossip!' he exclaimed, and then leaned forward and grabbed her, said against her flowing hair, 'Sorry. I know you don't like me to swear.'

'As far as I'm concerned you can do anything you want,' Charlotte said and meant it.

'I will tell Hanson that if anyone asks where I am, he must simply say I'm out. But not where. He's my man, and he's totally loyal.'

'So is Walter, Charles. Don't be cross with him.'

'I'm not, don't be silly.' Charles let out a sigh. 'I've a bit of bad news for you, Charlie. All able-bodied men are going to be called up. Enlistment is now compulsory.' He told her about the new Act that had just been passed in Parliament the day before, and gave her the details.

'You won't have to go, will you?' she asked, suddenly sounding genuinely concerned.

He looked at her, and said quietly, 'I'm too old, and I have bad eyesight.'

'You're not too old in my book, and your eyes are beautiful. And I'm relieved you won't have to go to the front.'

'We'll have a lot of villagers and estate workers leaving,' he said, sounding grim. And they did go off to war in droves.

FIFTY-FOUR

The day that Daphne had been dreading finally arrived. Hugo was going to leave Cavendon and go for field training at Catterick, before embarking for France to fight in the trenches.

She had several important things to say to him, and she rose early so that she could speak with him privately before they had breakfast with her father.

Hugo found her waiting for him in the little library she had created two years ago. As he walked in, he thought she looked more stunning than he had ever seen her. She was always beautiful, his Daphne, but today there was something about her that stirred his heart.

She stood up quickly when he entered the room, and said, 'Will you come outside with me, Hugo? And go for a very short stroll? To the rose garden.'

'Why not? You said you needed to speak to me, and that's the perfect place. Very private, my darling.'

'That's right.' She stretched out her hand.

He took hold of it, and went out of the library with her, and walked towards the grand entrance hall. He knew she was going to tell him something very secret or inflammatory, otherwise she wouldn't have suggested they take a stroll. No one could overhear her in the gardens.

There was no one around. The park was deserted. Many men had gone already. Kitchener was desperate for soldiers; the troops were being mowed down by the thousands. And that was where he was going. To the killing grounds of France. And the Battle of the Somme.

He pushed these thoughts to one side as they walked down the steps and sat on one of the iron garden seats. She clung to his hand, and he looked at her and he thought his heart would break. He had to leave her to go and do his duty for King and Country, and he might not come back. And he could not bear that thought. If he lost his life he would never see her again. And what would she do without him?

She was wearing pink today, and she blended in with the roses all around them, and he had that perfect picture of her in his mind's eye, and he would keep it there, and remember, when he was on the front. It would sustain him, as would the thought of their child she was carrying.

'Hugo, listen, I want to tell you something very important,' Daphne announced, leaning into him, her cornflower blue eyes fastened on his face. She sounded and looked more serious than he had ever seen her.

'Yes, I'm listening, sweetheart,' he said quietly, holding himself still, also steeling himself for bad news.

'When you first met me, it was love at first sight,' Daphne said. 'That's how you described it. And when we went to Paris on our honeymoon, I felt a *coup de foudre* too. Not for Paris. But for you, Hugo. I want you to know I fell in love with you then. And I love you with all my heart, I always will. And you will come back to me, I am truly certain of that.'

Tears had filled his eyes, and he took her in his arms and held her close to him, breathing in her scent, as he always did, that mixture of roses and hyacinth so unique to her.

'You're right, I will come back, Daphne. Because we have a long life to live, and much joy to share. And it makes me happy that you fell in love with me on our honeymoon. I thought you had.'

'We're going to have five children,' she whispered.

Leaning away from her, he smiled, love for her spilling out of his eyes. 'Why not six?' he asked.

'Because Genevra says it will be five. I begged her to tell me what the seven hearts mean on that piece of bone, and she wouldn't. But then when I said you were going to war and I was afraid for you, she told me. She said you would be safe because we were going to have five children altogether. The other two hearts were for you and me. I trust her predictions, Hugo, I really do.'

'And so do I,' Hugo agreed quickly, wanting to please her, and wanting to believe he would come home.

'What I have to say now is a sort of confession. About something I never told anyone. You must promise me that you will keep this entirely confidential all your life, Hugo.'

She spoke so solemnly and she was so tense, he knew this was the serious matter she had not wanted anyone to overhear. 'I won't betray you,' he said. 'I'm ready. Tell me what you've been hiding from me.'

Daphne took a deep breath, and began. 'When my parents knew I had been raped and was pregnant, they jumped to a conclusion. They were fixated on Julian Torbett. Because we had been friends for so long, and also because I had been over to Havers Lodge that afternoon. He wasn't there. He was out. And when I walked back through the bluebell woods, I was attacked. The man who attacked me wore a scarf around his face. When

I managed to pull it off later, I was horrified. It was Richard, Julian's brother. He is the one who raped me. But I let my parents believe it was Julian because he was dead. And I lied to you when I said it was Julian. For the same reason.'

'Oh my God! Isn't Torbett still alive? Daphne, you might not be safe. He could come after you again. And what about Alicia? We say she's mine, but she's his, and you know that.' Hugo was full of sudden apprehension.

'No, she's not his. She is your child, and no one will ever say otherwise. Neither must you, because you are her father. The story is simple. I slept with you the first time you came to Cavendon in July, because we couldn't resist each other. The baby was premature.'

He nodded, understanding her reasoning. Hugo Stanton knew he must back her at all costs. But he needed to know more about Torbett and where he was at this moment. 'Is that horrific man still living here? Or is he in London?' he demanded.

'Neither, Hugo. Torbett joined the Army about a year ago. He volunteered and he was shipped to France.'

'How do you know this, Daphne? Have you been making enquiries about him? That would be dangerous!' Hugo exclaimed.

'No, no, I haven't. I wouldn't do that, Hugo. But by chance Cook ran into the Torbett's cook, Annie Thorpe. It was Annie who told Cook that there were no Torbett sons at home these days. One dead, killed in a riding accident on Ingham land, and the other two gone off to fight the Huns, as she called them.'

'Cook told you?' he asked, looking at her oddly. She was never in the kitchen.

'No, no, she told Hanson. Who told Miss Charlotte. Who told my father, who told me . . . just in passing, a bit of local gossip.' Daphne took hold of his hand. 'He can't harm us.'

'I hope he catches a German bullet, and if I run across the bastard, I'll shoot him myself.' Hugo sounded so angry, his voice shrill. Daphne wrapped her arms around him, to calm him, soothing him until he was himself again.

'Do you forgive me for lying to you, and keeping this awful truth a secret from you?' she asked a little later, looking at him, biting her lip nervously.

'Oh course, my darling Daphne, my beautiful wife. You did what you thought was for the best. And you are right, we must put this behind us. Look to the future and believe in Genevra's prediction.'

'There is just one other thing. I know you want to explain about your Last Will and Testament, and your business affairs, and Jill Handelsman. Plus all your financial affairs. Papa told me he has a full understanding of everything. He said he will do as you suggested, and telephone Mrs Handelsman every week, and look after all matters for me.'

'I'm relieved you know all about these arrangements,' Hugo said. 'But I was ready to explain, if you wanted me to do so.'

'I didn't and I don't. Especially your Will. Because you're coming home to me, my darling. I trust Genevra, she has the sight. Put your hand here, Hugo, please.'

She took his hand and put it on her stomach. 'That's my bump. It's the baby, our baby, your son, Hugo. Oh, let's pick a name now, so we can refer to him properly, waiting for him to be born.'

'What a lovely idea,' Hugo said, lightly moving his hand around her belly. 'How does Charles sound to you? For your most loving father and my very best friend.'

'I think it's a wonderful name, and we can tell him over breakfast.'

'And what if it happens to be a girl?' Hugo asked.

'I think she should be called Charlotte, because Miss Charlotte did so much for me.'

'But Alicia has that name,' he reminded her.

'I know, but we'll never use it. She is Alicia, and that's what we call her, isn't it?'

'It is.' He kept his hand on Daphne's belly for a short while longer as they sat together, dreaming a little about the future, when they would be reunited. Hugo held this memory in his head and his heart, and it would sustain him in the terrible times he was facing when he risked his life on the fields of France in the war to end all wars.

FIFTY-FIVE

Lieutenant Hugo Stanton, a platoon commander in the 2nd Battalion of the Yorkshire Regiment, sat down on the large box filled with cans of corned beef. It was their rations and the only thing that didn't sink deep into the mud in the trench.

Finding a packet of cigarettes in his pocket, he pulled one out, and brought a match to it, took a deep drag of the nicotine.

He was really weary today. He was only thirty-six, but he felt like a hundred and five. And he had been here far too long. Eleven months too long. He had arrived to fight on the Western Front in September of 1916. It was now July of 1917, and the British and their Allies were nowhere nearer to winning this war than they had been then.

Whilst he had been training at Catterick last year, he had received a telephone call from Charles. It was Charles in steely control of himself, yet nonetheless heartbroken. He had received a telegram from the War Office, informing him that his eldest son Guy was missing in action, presumed dead. Yet Charles was hopeful that Guy would be found in a hospital somewhere in

Verdun. Or perhaps he had been taken prisoner by the Germans, Charles had suggested.

Hugo had spoken to Daphne afterward and she, too, was hopeful, praying that her brother was alive. It had been wonderful to hear her voice, and have other news of the family. But when he had hung up he had been full of sorrow.

Hugo let out a deep sigh, knowing in his heart that Guy was more than likely dead. Everyone knew the story of Verdun, and how last year the Germans had been waiting for the large British force approaching the gates of that city.

During the preliminary shelling, the Germans had been in deep underground bunkers as the guns thundered above them. They had come out unharmed to meet the British troops, who were instantly mowed down by German machine guns.

General Haig had then ordered a second assault. On the first day there were 20,000 dead and 40,000 wounded or missing, yet the British went on fighting, their losses growing daily, and in the end it was a lost cause. By mid-November that battle was over, and at an enormous cost. The Allies reported 615,000 men killed, wounded, missing in action, or taken prisoner. And perhaps Guy Ingham had been there.

The Major in charge of their battalion had recounted all this to Hugo on his arrival at the front, and he had been shocked at the loss of lives, the wholesale slaughtering of men. It was barbaric. If Guy had been in that battle, there was little likelihood of him being alive.

Major Thompson had told him other hair-raising stories, and Hugo had seen enough for himself already to understand how horrific this war was. He was relieved he had not joined a cavalry regiment, as he had thought of doing, and was in the infantry instead. The horses were at risk every day from the gunfire, shelling, barbed-wire fences, diseases and the mud.

He had only been in the Somme sector for a few days last

year, when the Major had taken him out to shoot three horses, which were impaled on barbed wire, and to rescue several others drowning in the mud.

Having grown up with horses at his father's stud, and having been around them all of his life, it was heartbreaking for him to witness these horrendous scenes. But he had shot the horses willingly, knowing he was releasing them from agonizing pain. Their stomachs were torn open by the barbed wire and they were bleeding to death. A bullet in the head was quick and painless.

There had been British victories that had given Hugo hope. In April of this year, the Canadian Corps, the right wing of the British 1st Army, had captured Vimy Ridge near Arras, held until then by the Germans.

It had been a courageous assault by the Canadians, and at least there had been a reason to cheer for once. But Hugo had been genuinely troubled for the last few weeks. Major Thompson had told him that the French cabinet had called a halt to the fighting in the Somme region in May, because there had been outbreaks of mutiny in many of the French units. The Major had explained that a lot of French soldiers had reached a breaking point, and that their spirits were low.

'It's now up to us,' the Major had said to Hugo and his platoon last night. 'We seem to have been left to shoulder the burden of this war. We British will have to defend the Western Front by ourselves.'

And now here he was, sitting in a trench full of mud with his rifle on his knee on the outskirts of Ypres. In June, General Herbert Plumer, leading the 2nd Army, attacked Messines Ridge, a German stronghold. After exploding more than 500 tons of TNT beneath the ridge, Plumer's nine divisions took the ridge, much to Hugo's relief. But he couldn't help thinking that there would eventually be retaliation, and he wondered what would hit them next.

It seemed to him that he had been in so many battles in the last eight months he had lost track, and he was bone tired.

Even in his sleep he heard the sound of metal hitting metal with precision, as a strong voice yelled, 'Fix bayonets,' and instantly they went out to do hand-to-hand fighting with the Germans. Echoes of the thundering cannon reverberated in his brain, even when they were not being fired.

Hugo leaned back against the trench wall and closed his eyes, shutting out the war, focusing on his memories. He pictured Daphne sitting in the rose garden at Cavendon in her rose-pink frock. She had looked very beautiful that day, and he could almost feel the sleek satin of it under his hands, remembering when she had told him to feel the baby. And he had, and now their little bump had arrived, had been born in December. It was a boy who was now seven months old. He felt a rush of warmth as he saw Charles Hugo Ian Ingham Stanton in his mind's eye.

He chuckled to himself. Another little baby with a very long name. But that was the tradition, the way of their world, the world he and Daphne had been born into.

For as long as he was alive, Hugo knew that particular morning in June, a year ago, would live on in his mind and heart. She had been so loving and lovely, and he had been filled with enormous fury when she had told him about Richard Torbett, and how he had frightened her into silence after he had raped her. He had threatened her, and said he would have her mother and the little Dulcie killed if she revealed what he had done to her. Even now, as he thought of that bastard Torbett, he felt the anger rising inside him like bitter bile in his mouth.

Dropping the cigarette end in the mud beneath his boots, Hugo ground it down, then grimaced at the awful stench that immediately rose up, making him gag. The mud wasn't merely mud. It was mud mixed with the blood of men and horses, and some poor sod's guts, and horse manure and excrement, and the effluvium rising off this foul mixture was vile. He began to cough.

'It's the bleeding mud, Lieutenant,' Private Robby Layton said, as he hove into view in the trench. 'If a bullet don't kill us, the frigging mud will. Here, sir, I've brought yer a cuppa.'

'Thanks, Layton,' Hugo said, and gratefully accepted the tin mug of tea. He was in need of it. It was hot, strong and sweet, and very welcome.

'Have yer noticed summat, sir?'

Hugo looked at Layton and frowned. 'No, what do you mean?' He glanced around; it was late morning, cloudy and warm.

'The bleeding guns have stopped, Lieutenant. The Jerries are suddenly silent.'

'By Jove, Layton, you're right!' Hugo grinned at the Private. 'I was a bit preoccupied; I didn't even notice the silence.'

'Thinking of yer lady, was yer, sir?'

'I was indeed. By the way, where is Sergeant Crocker? I haven't seen him for an hour or so.'

'I don't know, sir, but I'll go have a look for him, if yer wants.'

Hugo shook his head. 'No, it's all right. I don't need him right now. Seen Major Thompson at all?'

'No, sir. I think he was at headquarters. There's been a lull, yer knows.'

'I hope to God it's not the lull before the storm,' Hugo muttered and stood up.

At that moment it started. A barrage of guns. Cannons going off. Bombs exploding. Bursts of machine-gun fire. Everywhere. And German soldiers were now running through No Man's Land, crossing the stretch of open land between them.

'Holy Christ!' the Private shouted as he and Hugo looked over the top of their trench. 'The frigging Huns are up our arses.'

'More like down our throats,' Hugo responded, and shouted

to his men running down the trench towards him, 'Fix bayonets!' Then he yelled, 'And over the top, lads. Stand fast to the end.'

Hugo was up and out of the trench, his platoon following him. Instantly, they were in the middle of the fighting, engulfed by German troops, also with fixed bayonets.

The fighting was deadly, hand-to-hand combat of the most frightening kind. Men were falling all around him, their blood splashing onto his uniform. British and German troops died together, their screams of agony strident on the warm summer air.

And the bombing and explosion continued, were unending. Hugo was well aware the enemy was almost undefeatable with the huge manpower and armaments they had. The Allies were weak against this powerful onslaught.

He fought on valiantly. His total focus was on defending himself and staying alive. Hugo prayed to God his men were doing the same, the way he had taught them. Think of nothing but surviving, he had drilled into them.

Then, just as he thought he could not sustain himself any longer, that he was going to fall down from fatigue, Hugo heard a strange sound, a noise he couldn't define because of the deafening guns. It became almost a roar, or so it seemed to him. Suddenly he was startled. The Germans were retreating, going back to their trenches. Then running to their trenches.

Hugo stood stock-still. He heard Sergeant Crocker's voice just behind him. 'It's the ladies from hell, Lieutenant.'

Glancing to his left, a grin spread across Hugo's face. He saw a large contingent of Seaforth Highlanders marching towards them, their kilts swinging in the breeze, the skirl of the bagpipes filling the air with a sound that was most joyous to him. Their saviours were here.

'From now on they're the *angels* from hell, as far as I'm concerned,' Hugo shouted back to Crocker.

FIFTY-SIX

After the arrival of the Seaforth Highlanders, there were two days of respite. Both sides tended to their wounded, buried their dead, and got themselves back into shape.

Always alert, and poised for the unexpected and ready to rush into action, Hugo sensed the Germans might be revving up again. He sent his Sergeant, Bill Crocker, and a four-man team out to do a recce.

Within an hour they were back, jumping into their trench. 'We'd better start gearing up, sir,' Crocker said quietly to Hugo. 'The buggers are slowly getting ready. They'll probably strike tomorrow or the day after.'

Hugo simply nodded. 'Do what you have to do, Sergeant.'

Later that afternoon, Crocker was back at headquarters, looking for his Lieutenant. When he found him, he said to Hugo, 'There's a few stragglers, sir, they've just come into our trench. Will you come and question them, Lieutenant?'

'I will,' Hugo answered, sighing under his breath. 'Do you think they might be deserters, Crocker? Is that it?'

'No, sir. Well, I don't know, Lieutenant, I'm just not sure. But they seem like three Tommies who got separated from their regiments.'

'Knowing you, you got their ranks and serial numbers, all of that?'

'I did. Written it down, sir.'

'Which regiments?'

'Two from the Lancashires, and one from the West Kents.'

'What are their names, Crocker?'

'Private Arthur Jones and Private Sam Tyler from the Lancashires. And a Lieutenant Richard Torbett from the West Kents.'

Hugo couldn't believe what he had just heard. 'Richard Torbett,' he repeated, and stood absolutely still, frozen to the spot. His heart was suddenly beating very rapidly; he felt the blood rushing to his face. My God, the rapist was here! And he had him in the palm of his hand. I'm going to kill him. I'm damn well going to shoot that vile bastard, Hugo vowed silently. Revenge for Daphne.

Vaguely, Hugo heard Crocker's voice saying, 'Are you all right, sir?'

'Never better, Crocker,' Hugo answered, recouping, pulling himself together. 'Any of them wounded?'

'The two lads from the Lancashires both look as if they're about to collapse.'

'Bring Layton and Macklin, and let's go. The Torbett chap? He's been wounded?'

'No, sir.'

Crocker turned around, strode out of the tent. Hugo picked up his revolver, put it in his pocket. He followed Crocker out to the trenches, heading to the one his platoon usually holed up in.

Hugo virtually ignored Lieutenant Richard Torbett of the West Kents. Instead he spoke to the two privates, asked them a few leading questions. Satisfied they were genuine stragglers and not deserters, he sent them off with Layton and Macklin.

He stood opposite Torbett, and looked him over swiftly. He saw a tall man, probably in his early thirties, with a swarthy skin. He was not very good looking, rather weak and ordinary in appearance. A nonentity.

After asking him the usual standard questions, about how he had become separated from his unit and regiment, and so forth, he then said, 'You don't happen to come from Yorkshire, do you, Lieutenant Torbett?'

For the first time Torbett relaxed, and a smile flashed. His dark eyes filled with curiosity when he said, 'I do indeed, Lieutenant. Why do you ask?'

'I know your name. Isn't your family home Havers Lodge on the Havers estate?'

'Why, yes it is,' Torbett replied, smiling again.

Hugo stepped forward, took hold of his arm firmly, and brought out his revolver. He stuck it against Torbett's forehead and said in a low, threatening voice, 'You bloody bastard! You son-of-a-bitch! You raped a young girl, you vile bugger. I'm going to shoot you for ruining a young innocent girl. You deserve to die. Shooting's too good for you, in point of fact.'

'Lieutenant! Lieutenant! Take it easy,' Crocker was shouting. 'Put your gun away. Please, sir. He's not worth it. You'll be court-martialled if you pull that trigger.'

'I don't bloody well care. He's going to die for what he did,' Hugo shouted back without turning around.

Torbett was shaking from head to foot. So terrified he wet his pants. And like all bullies he started to beg. 'Don't kill me. Don't kill me. Please, don't kill me.'

Hugo cocked the trigger, stared into Torbett's eyes. 'I am going to shoot you.'

'Please, Lieutenant, please,' Crocker pleaded. He loved and admired his company leader and wanted to prevent a ruinous action taking place. The head of their platoon was true blue. The best. He didn't want his life in ruins after the war.

Torbett shouted, 'She was always tempting me! It wasn't my fault. She was flirtatious. Leading me on.'

'You liar. What a vile creature you are,' Hugo replied in a dangerous voice. 'You went looking. For her. For other women. Even little girls. You were the trespasser always roaming the Ingham estate. I know that for a fact. You were recognized.'

Torbett was still shaking. He moaned, 'I didn't mean any harm.' He was on the verge of tears.

'But you *did* harm, you frigging bastard! What were you going to do with the child? Tell me the truth. And I won't kill you. Just for that information, Torbett, I'll let you live.'

'Nothing. I wasn't going to do anything to her. Just take her to the bluebells. I was going to let her go.'

'You fucking liar! You weren't. You were going to rape that child, just as you raped her sister. You deserve to die.'

'Please Lieutenant, put the gun down,' Crocker said in a quiet, steady voice. He did not dare go near the Lieutenant for fear of startling him. Just moving closer might make him pull the trigger, which was already cocked.

Hugo did not answer. Torbett was snivelling.

'He's not worth it, sir,' Crocker went on in a calm voice. 'Just put the gun away. Think of your lady, sir. Please, please, don't do this. Think of your children. Lieutenant, don't sink to his level. Rise above this coward. Please, sir.'

Hugo remained standing close to Torbett, staring intently into the other man's face. The revolver was pressed to Torbett's temple. And Hugo's face was set in determined lines. There was unremitting fury in his eyes.

Crocker spoke once again. 'For God's sake, please, don't do this, Lieutenant Stanton. They'll court-martial you if you kill him. Think, sir, please think. Remember you're an officer and a gentleman. And remember your lady, how much you love Lady Daphne?'

Hearing Daphne's name brought Hugo up sharp.

He had to go home to her. What would she do without him? She needed him. His children needed him. Charles needed him. Very slowly, Hugo Stanton lowered his arm, and held the gun pointing to the ground.

'Let go of his arm, sir,' Crocker instructed.

Hugo did so.

A look of relief surfaced on Torbett's face, but his eyes were still filled with fear.

'Run, Torbett!' Crocker shouted. 'Run for your life. Go on! Run down the trench. Find another unit.'

Torbett did as instructed. He turned, leapt away from the Sergeant and his Lieutenant. He ran for his life and into death.

Hugo turned around and peered at his Sergeant. 'Thank you, Crocker. You brought me to my senses.' Hugo's brows came together, and his eyes narrowed as he looked down the trench. 'But you've sent him the wrong way. You've sent him into the German lines. Our other units are back there, behind us. You sent him the wrong way.'

'No, I didn't, sir,' Crocker answered very calmly. 'I sent him the right way. I sent him into hell, Lieutenant, which is where he belongs.'

At that moment the German guns started to roar in a great crescendo. Hugo and Crocker swung to face the German lines. There was a huge deafening roar as bombs began to explode further down in their trench. And the machine-gun fire started its inevitable rat-a-tat.

'Well, he's a goner, sir. Torbett's just been blown to smithereens,' Crocker announced. He took hold of his Lieutenant's arm and led him back to headquarters.

The Yorkshire Regiment stayed on in Ypres. In August came the rains, turning the area into a sea of mud. Hugo's division moved closer to Passchendaele where it soon grew worse. The earlier bombings in the region had ruined the drainage system of the Flanders lowlands, and all of the British divisions were trapped in the mud. So were the Germans. It was a strange standoff.

One afternoon Crocker said, 'I just want to tell you this, sir. It's been an honour to serve under you. I've never met a man like you before. A true officer and a gentleman. And I just want to thank you for being so good to the lads. And for leading us so well.'

Hugo was touched by Crocker's words but rather puzzled. He asked, 'Are you leaving me, Sergeant? Joining another platoon?'

'No, sir.'

'Then why are you thanking me? You sound as if you're saying goodbye.'

'In a way, I am, sir. Because I don't think we're going to get out of this bleeding mud alive. We're going to drown in it.'

Hugo shook his head. 'No, we're not, Sergeant. Remember what you said about thinking of my lady. That's what I do every day. And I'm going home to her.'

In April of 1917 the United States had declared war on Germany, joining the Allies in their battle against the Axis

Powers. They had the manpower to build and train an Army, but it took them months to do this. Finally, they were well prepared. American troops and armaments were shipped off to the Western Front, to the relief of Churchill and the government.

This reinforcement for the British and their Allies turned the tide of war. The Americans had a massive and destructive impact on the Germany Army, and by the summer of 1918 they held the upper hand in the war. Success was in the air, boosting morale and re-energizing the fighting men.

By October 1918 the Germans knew they had lost the Great War. In November they surrendered to the Allies in a railway carriage in the Forest of Compiègne in France. It was at 11 a.m. on the eleventh day of the eleventh month that the war to end all wars was finally over.

There was rejoicing everywhere, and sorrow as well. Many soldiers went home relatively intact. Many others were wounded. Others were left behind, thousands and thousands of them mown down in the line of duty.

Hugo Stanton was lucky, and so was Sergeant Crocker. They were on the same British battleship that took them safely home to the country they loved and had fought so valiantly for. Hugo could hardly wait to see his beloved Daphne.

Walter Swann and his son Harry returned to Cavendon and the waiting arms of Alice, and Gordon Lane to Peggy Swift. And many of the men from all three Cavendon villages also returned safely, and were welcomed with relief and delight by their families.

The Honourable Guy Ingham did not return. He had died at Verdun and was buried in some far corner of a foreign field.

Charles was filled with grief for Guy, and mourned him. But he was comforted by Miles, who had not passed the physical because of poor eyesight and had not gone to war. Charles had his heir to the earldom. The Ingham line was safe.

PART FIVE

A Matter of Choice
September 1920

And so it began: the most relentless pursuit of success and fame ever embarked upon, the most grinding and merciless work schedule ever conceived and willingly undertaken by a young woman.

Emma Harte: *A Woman of Substance*

Remember me when I am gone away,
Gone far away into the silent land;
When you can no more hold me by the hand,
Nor I half turn to go, yet turning stay.
Remember me when no more day by day,
You tell me of our future that you plann'd;
Only remember me; you understand
It will be late to counsel then or pray.

Christina Rossetti

FIFTY-SEVEN

The evening gown was breathtaking. It was made of different shades of blue chiffon, from indigo to delphinium, cornflower to sky blue, and a final greyish-blue tone that emphasized the vivid blueness of the other shades. From a moulded bodice and a tight waist were layered petals of chiffon, which fell down to mid-calf length. And each petal had a hand-kerchief point.

Dorothy Pinkerton, née Swann, Cecily's aunt, kept nodding her head and beaming. Finally, she said, 'It's extraordinary, Ceci, a dream of a dress. You've outdone yourself.'

Cecily nodded, looking pleased, and said, 'Thank you.' She then turned to DeLacy. 'You look so beautiful, Lacy, you really do. And I'm glad I had the shoes dyed sky blue, because they look so . . . light, as light as air.'

'I can't thank you enough for making something so special for me, Ceci. You're a genius.'

'I don't know about that, but I know what suits women, and you in particular.'

At nineteen Lady DeLacy Ingham was a ravishing blonde,

effervescent and slightly scatterbrained. She was fun loving and forever rushing around Mayfair, caught up in the social whirl of London society, eyeing the young men and flirting with them.

Her best friend, Cecily Swann, who was also nineteen, was now a blossoming fashion designer with a tiny shop in South Audley Street. She was serious, hardworking to the point of obsession, driven by enormous ambition to succeed, and to fulfil her childhood dream. She was sincere and loyal; honesty and integrity were the keynotes of her character.

'Wherever it is you're going on Friday, m'lady, you'll be the belle of the ball,' Dorothy said.

'Thank you, Dorothy, but it's not a ball. I'm going to Miles's engagement party.'

Cecily stared at DeLacy, unable to believe what she was hearing. But DeLacy sounded serious and Cecily knew it must be true. An icy chill swept through her and unexpectedly she began to shake. She took a step closer to the chair and held onto it in order to steady herself; her legs had turned to jelly. It wasn't possible! How could Miles be engaged? He was hers, and she was his, and they belonged to each other. Vaguely, in the distance, she heard her aunt asking who the lucky young woman was.

'Clarissa Meldrew,' DeLacy answered, and grinned at Cecily. 'Don't you remember, we all used to call her Mildew?'

Cecily did not respond. She could not. Her mouth was dry and her throat was choked with sobs.

Dorothy noticed Cecily had gone as white as chalk and looked stricken, and for a moment she didn't know what to do, what to say. How stupid DeLacy had been, to blurt something out like that, and so bluntly, thoughtlessly!

Something suddenly dawned on DeLacy, and she cried, 'You didn't know! Miles didn't tell you! Oh my God, Cecily. I'm so sorry I was the one to break this news. I can see you're . . . a bit upset.'

'No, he didn't tell me,' Cecily managed to say in a low, tight voice. After a moment, she added, 'He asked *me* to marry him.'

DeLacy stared at her. 'You mean when you were younger. You were only twelve, weren't you?'

Cecily nodded. Then added in a whisper, 'And also not too long ago.'

DeLacy was shaking her head. 'Whatever made you think he could marry you, Ceci? He's the heir to the earldom. He has to marry an aristocrat, not an ordinary girl like you. He has to have aristocratic children to carry on the Ingham line.'

Cecily stood there without saying a word. Her heart had turned to ice, and she was frozen in the spot where she stood, unable to move.

Dorothy was in a fury, but she did not want to upset Cecily further. So she held her tongue, and gave Lady DeLacy her hand, helping her step down from the platform. 'I think you should change into your own clothes, m'lady. I will pack the gown and the shoes, and then you can be off. We're closing in about ten minutes. I don't mean to rush you, but we have an appointment on the outside, you see.'

'Oh yes, of course, Dorothy. And perhaps you'll be kind enough to send the dress by messenger.'

'Oh dear, Lady DeLacy, Tim has left our employment. We don't have a messenger boy at the moment. I'm afraid you will have to carry the box yourself.'

A few minutes later, Dorothy was ushering DeLacy out of the shop. On the doorstep, DeLacy swung around and waved. 'See you later, Ceci. And thanks again for the gorgeous frock.'

In the street, Dorothy flagged down a taxi, opened the door, helped DeLacy into it, and then shoved the box in after her. She gave her a cold smile and slammed the cab door very hard.

Once she was inside the shop again, Dorothy locked the door and went to Cecily, who still stood next to the chair, hanging onto it to steady herself, looking as if she was on the verge of fainting.

'Are you all right, lovey?' Dorothy asked, knowing full well that she wasn't. 'Sit down, and I'll make us a cup of tea.'

Cecily shook her head. 'I'll be all right in a few minutes, I really will. Don't bother with the tea.'

'I'm going to tidy up. I'll send Flossie home, and then we'll go to our appointment with Charlotte.'

'Yes,' Cecily said automatically, but she looked as if she wasn't listening. And she wasn't.

A little later there was a loud knocking on the door. Cecily managed to rouse herself from the chair. She went to open the front door, and found Miles standing there. 'Hello, Ceci,' he said, and walked inside before she could stop him.

Dorothy had heard the knocking and came out from the small sewing room behind the fitting area. When she saw Miles she nodded to him, turned around and fled.

Miles attempted to take hold of her arm, but Cecily shrugged him off and stood staring at him. 'When were you going to tell me?'

He knew what she meant. Immediately he said, 'Today. That's why I'm here. I was going to ask you to come out for tea. I needed to talk to you about my problems.' His eyes swept over her and he was not only aware she knew, but that she was hurt beyond belief.

'Who told you?' he asked, leaning against the chair.

'DeLacy. But that doesn't matter. What matters is that *you* didn't tell me, Miles.'

'Look, Ceci, this was forced on me. I know you might not

believe me, but it was. I can't help it. I suppose it comes with being who I am. But I didn't want this . . .' Quite unexpectedly his voice broke, and he began to blink rapidly.

She saw the tears in his eyes, and looked away, so that he wouldn't see that she was crying too.

'There has to be a way we can work something out—'

'Never!' she shouted, cutting him off. 'I will not become your mistress.'

'I wasn't going to suggest that. I wasn't, Ceci. I love you. I've always loved you, and I could never demean you. I was thinking that maybe, after a few years, once I've got an heir, I could leave. Get a divorce—'

'You know that's not going to happen. Don't be stupid, it won't. Miles, if you do love me, as you say, then you must leave now. Immediately. I just can't continue this conversation. Please do that for me. Walk out and let me keep my dignity.'

It was almost impossible for him to leave her. It was like tearing a limb off. But he did. He didn't say another word, nor did he try to touch her or embrace her. He walked out of the shop and closed the door behind him very quietly.

Although she did not know it, he half stumbled along South Audley Street, like a man deranged, tears streaming from his eyes as he made for his father's house in Grosvenor Square. He let himself inside with his key and got to his room without anyone seeing him.

Locking his bedroom door, Miles threw himself onto the bed. He howled into his pillow, trying to smother his sobs. He had just given up the only person in this world who truly mattered to him, other than his father. The only woman he had ever loved, and whom he would love for the rest of his life. He knew he was entering a loveless marriage and he dreaded it. But he had been brought up to do his duty to the family. There was no way out.

As he lay there on his bed, his face pushed into the pillow, he experienced genuine physical pain. The pain of losing Cecily Swann was actually something he could feel in his bones. And he knew it would never leave him, that aching yearning, that longing for her. It would remain with him for the rest of his life.

FIFTY-EIGHT

Cecily had managed to regain her equilibrium somewhat, and she and Dorothy agreed to walk to Burlington Arcade in Piccadilly. They were meeting Charlotte there at five o'clock, and it was Dorothy who had suggested they walk. She explained that fresh air would do them both good, and most especially Cecily.

'Where are we actually meeting Charlotte?' Cecily asked as they walked into the arcade from the Piccadilly entrance.

'Just a bit further along. Not far. She wants you to see some special windows. Windows she thought might interest you.'

'Oh all right, why not,' Cecily replied, trying to get the image of Miles out of her head, though without success.

'Here we are,' Dorothy suddenly exclaimed, sounding excited. She took hold of Cecily's arm and led her to the double-fronted large shop, which had two windows, one on either side of the door.

'Just look at this, isn't it chic?' Dorothy said. Drawing Cecily to the left window, she added, 'Less is more.' In the window was a simple French ballroom chair on which sat a hat . . . a bit of nothing, a frou-frou. Black lace and a black flower. In the second window on the right, a mannequin was draped with yards of scarlet silk that fell in a pool on the floor of the window. Next to this pool of fabric was a pair of scarlet shoes.

'There's nothing valuable in the windows, I realize that, but they're certainly striking,' Cecily said, studying both of them, intrigued.

'I agree,' Dorothy answered, and went on. 'Look up, lift your head.'

Cecily did so and gasped. 'Oh Dorothy! Oh my goodness!'

Written in white across the black board above the door and windows was a name. CECILY SWANN. Also in white paint, and at each end of her name, was a white swan. They faced each other.

The door of the shop opened and Charlotte was standing there, smiling hugely. 'Do you like it, Ceci?' she asked, taking hold of her hand, drawing her inside the shop.

'How could I not? And it's such a huge surprise, Aunt Charlotte. When ever did you do all this?'

'I did it over the past few months. I wanted it to be a surprise. That's why only Dorothy knew. She helped me tremendously and, as of tomorrow, she will be running the shop for you. And you'll be upstairs in your studio, designing.'

'Thank you, Aunt Charlotte, thank you so much, and you too Dorothy.' Cecily kept shaking her head in disbelief as they walked her around the shop. It was huge, much larger than her other tiny shop, which had been just a hole in the wall really. The new premises had two dressing rooms, a fitting area, plenty of storage space in the basement for fabrics, plus the studio upstairs and a small office.

When they came downstairs again, Dorothy said, 'I'd better be going, Charlotte, Cecily. I have to get home to make Howard's dinner. But we would like to invite you both to supper tomorrow, take you out to celebrate the launch of Cecily Swann Couture.'

'That would be lovely, thank you,' Charlotte said.

'Thank you,' Cecily added, offering a smile.

Dorothy hugged Cecily, and whispered, 'Chin up, there's a big wide world out there.'

As she left the new shop, Dorothy looked back and caught Charlotte's eye. Charlotte understood at once that Dorothy wanted to speak to her privately, and followed her to the door. Cecily noticed this unspoken communication between them, but made no comment. Dorothy was obviously about to tell her about Miles as they walked into the arcade together.

'Dorothy told me that you've been upset today. By the Inghams. Both DeLacy and Miles. Please tell me about it.' Charlotte sat back in the chair, in the sitting room of her suite at Brown's Hotel. She smiled at Cecily warmly, wanting to encourage her.

'DeLacy blurted out that the dress I'd designed for her was to wear at Miles's engagement party. And I was shocked, distressed.'

'You didn't know he'd become engaged?'

'No, I didn't. I haven't seen a lot of DeLacy. I work and she plays. We're still close friends, and as you know she insisted on lending me money for the hole in the wall. But right now we have slightly different interests. There'd been no occasion for her to tell me.'

'I understand. And Miles didn't tell you either?'

Cecily shook her head, suddenly unable to speak. She thought she was about to burst into tears and she struggled not to cry.

Charlotte stood up and walked over to the window, where she looked out at Green Park. The most terrible thought had just occurred to her and she was frightened . . . frightened for Cecily. Had she been seeing Miles all these years she'd been living in London with Dorothy and Howard? *Five years.* Since she was fourteen. Working at Fortnum's in Dorothy's fashion department at first, then in the little pokey place she had rented with DeLacy's help.

Miles had been at Eton, not so very far from London. And Oxford wasn't very far either. How easy it would have been for them to meet and become romantically entangled with each other. Oh God, I hope not, Charlotte thought, her heart sinking as she returned to the chair and sat down.

She looked at Cecily and saw the tears streaming down her face, and she was startled. The stricken look on her face and the tears told her everything she needed to know.

Rising, she went to sit next to Cecily on the sofa, and gave her a handkerchief.

Cecily wiped her tears, and eventually she stopped crying.

She forced a smile and said, 'I'm sorry, Aunt Charlotte, I didn't mean to break down like that.'

'That's all right. I understand. At least, I think I do.' Charlotte sat for a moment, and then she said in a soft voice, 'You're in love with Miles, aren't you?'

Cecily's mouth trembled, and the tiny 'Yes' she uttered was so filled with anguish that it tore at Charlotte's heart. She took hold of her hand, and held it tightly in hers. 'You've been seeing him, haven't you? All these years you've lived with Dorothy?'

'Yes,' she whispered.

'He's in love with you, isn't he?' Charlotte wondered why she'd asked. Obviously he was . . . he was an Ingham.

'Yes,' Cecily whispered in that same tiny, heartbroken voice.

Charlotte leaned back and closed her eyes. What was this terrible obsession that existed between the Inghams and the Swanns? Was it something in their blood? God knows what it is, she thought. But it pulls us together. We are irresistible to each other, and have been over many generations. Will it ever end? She knew it wouldn't, because they needed each other. Strange as that was, it was the truth.

'I want to ask you something, Cecily,' Charlotte began, and gave her a small smile. 'Have you and Miles . . .' She paused, and finally said, 'Been together? Had intercourse?'

'No!' Cecily cried. 'We haven't. He wouldn't do anything like that. He's a gentleman.'

Charlotte found it hard to believe they hadn't made love, but she made no comment for the moment. After a short while, she said, 'When you were twelve, you took the vow? Remember?'

'Yes, I do. *Loyalty binds me*, that's what I said. I will always be loyal to the Inghams, and even to Miles, because I took the oath.'

'That's what I'm thinking. Are you protecting him now? Are you saying you didn't sleep with him to protect him? From my anger? Or his father's anger?'

'No, I'm not,' Cecily answered with some vehemence. 'And if you don't believe me, Aunt Charlotte, you can take me to a doctor and have me examined. You'll soon know I speak the truth, that I'm a virgin.'

'I don't think I have to do that, Cecily. I believe you.'

'Thank you,' Cecily said, and gave her a wan little smile.

'You can't see him any more – privately, I mean. I'm sure you'll run into him at Cavendon, but you can't continue this . . . romantic liaison. You can't become his mistress after he's married.'

'I wouldn't want to! I really wouldn't!' Cecily said quietly.

Charlotte looked at her. 'I'm so sorry, darling, so very sorry this happened. I tried to protect you. I got you away. I saw it happening even when you were children.' She shook her head helplessly.

'I know,' Cecily nodded, and then she looked into Charlotte's eyes, so like her own, and asked, 'Whatever am I going to do without him? I love him so much. He's part of me. Part of my heart and soul.' She began to weep.

Charlotte put her arms around Cecily and held her close. Twice in her life she had been where Cecily was now. Two Ingham men she had loved, and one she still loved. She had no answer. She was crying herself.

Ten minutes later, after they had both composed themselves, Charlotte said, 'Let me change the subject for a moment. I'd like to discuss business. To be precise, your business. The shop in Burlington Arcade to begin with. All right?'

'Yes, of course.'

'It is yours. The lease is in your name, and you have a five-year lease. The first year's rent is paid, and it will be paid by me for the next five years. And—'

'But Aunt Charlotte, I can't let you do that,' Cecily interjected. 'Not unless you become my partner.'

'I was just going to suggest that. I will be your financial, but silent, partner. You can run the business the way you see fit. And it is yours.' She moved slightly on the sofa, and went on, 'How much did DeLacy lend you to open the little shop?'

'About a thousand pounds, and then she gave me some extra money for fabrics. Altogether I owe her about fifteen hundred pounds,' Cecily explained.

'Is she a partner? Did you make a contract with her?'

'No, I didn't. Why?'

'I'm happy she just loaned you the money as a friend. Tomorrow I'll work out the interest you owe her. I will give you the money to repay her everything. I really don't want you to have any financial obligations to anyone outside the Swann family.'

'I understand. And thank you, from the bottom of my heart.'

'I was leaving you this money in my Will; better you have it now.' Charlotte sat up straighter on the sofa, and took Cecily's hand in hers again. 'You are nineteen years old, and your life is ahead of you. You have two choices, Cecily. You can grab hold of that life and make something of it. You have beauty and charm, but most important of all, you have a God-given talent that borders on genius. Or, if you prefer, you can yearn after Miles, become his mistress, and let everything else fall by the wayside. Which is it going to be?'

'I told him I wouldn't become his mistress, even though he didn't ask me. And I won't,' Cecily said in that vehement tone.

'He'll still come after you, Cecily. I know the Ingham men. They just can't resist Swann women. You'll have to be very strong.'

Cecily was silent. She knew her aunt spoke the truth.

After a while Charlotte said, 'Come on, give me an answer, Cecily. What's it going to be?'

'My choice is to become a famous fashion designer. A success.' She paused, took a deep breath and said, 'I want to follow my dream. And I choose to walk alone.'

And she did.

FIFTY-NINE

Miles was the first Ingham to arrive at Lord and Lady Meldrew's Mayfair house, located in Charles Street, just off Berkeley Square. It was his engagement party after all, and he had to be there before everyone else, to greet the guests along with the Meldrews.

And so there he was, standing next to Lady Sara and Lord John, with Clarissa by his side. He had a confident smile on his face, but inside he was filled with dismay as he contemplated his future. No changing that, he thought, his smile growing wider.

He knew Clarissa was nervous about the imminent arrival of his family. He couldn't say he blamed her. The Inghams were something to behold. Many people were intimidated by them, because of their amazing looks, and their wealth and standing in society, although they themselves played everything down.

Turning to Clarissa, he said, 'You know my sisters, Clarissa, and they're easy to get along with, so don't worry. All right?' He raised a brow.

She nodded and replied, with a hint of humour, 'I do know

your sisters, and that DeLacy used to call me the Honourable Miss Mildew behind my back.'

Miles knew this was true, but he simply flashed her a bright smile, which was the only thing to do. There was nothing too terrible about Clarissa. She was a nice-looking, pleasant girl with an aristocratic background and wealthy parents. By nature she was shy, but once she relaxed she was easy to talk to, and get along with.

Most men would have been happy to marry her, would have leapfrogged over each other to get her to the altar. For him it was a duty. He loved someone else.

Just as he was wondering where his family was, they arrived all together, all of them blonde and smiling and full of bonhomie.

His father strode across the hall, looking impossibly handsome and impeccably dressed, his natural charm engaging the Meldrews at once. He was accompanied by DeLacy and Dulcie, who was now twelve and a beauty. As DeLacy floated towards him, shod in pale blue silk shoes and wearing an extraordinary frock of mingled blues, Miles caught his breath. She looked absolutely stunning. No doubt that frock was Cecily's creation. His heart clenched. Don't think of her, he warned himself sternly.

Once his father, DeLacy and Dulcie had spoken to the Meldrews and Clarissa, they moved on and entered the drawing room.

Hugo and Daphne were the next to walk in. His sister was as glorious as always, and extremely happy. She was four months pregnant with her third child, and Hugo looked as proud as Punch.

Following immediately behind came Great-Aunt Gwendolyn, wearing a flowing satin gown of her favourite royal purple, and enough diamonds to sink a battleship. But she carried them off with total aplomb, as only she – the matriarch of the Ingham family – could.

Lady Gwendolyn was leaning on the arm of Diedre, to whom she was close. Diedre was also stunning this evening, and smiling for once. Miles was rather proud of his oldest sister, who was still working at the War Office and committed to her position, even though the war had been over for two years.

Aunt Lavinia and Uncle Jack arrived with Aunt Vanessa in their wake, and now everyone he had invited was here. Except for his mother. This thought had just entered his mind when she too finally appeared. She was alone because Miles had not thought it proper to invite her lover, Lawrence Pierce, the now-famous neurological surgeon. He had only met the man once and had disliked him on sight. Pierce might be brilliant but he was arrogant. Diedre had told him all surgeons were arrogant because they thought they were God.

Miles took a step forward, not wishing his mother to walk in alone, but his father beat him to it. Charles, ever the true gentleman, hurried over to greet Felicity, and it was he who escorted her to the receiving line.

She knew the Meldrews, so there was no discomfort, and they all chatted pleasantly together. Miles thought his mother looked chic but thin, and her makeup was too vivid, but at least she appeared to be relaxed.

After a few moments, Clarissa touched his arm, and said, 'The Meldrews and the Fosters will be here any minute, Miles, and my friend Annabelle.'

Miles replied, 'My father told me he knows your uncle, Sir Malcolm Foster, and his wife, Phyllis.'

'That's my mother's sister, and their two sons are coming with them; also my other cousin, Johanna Meldrew, will be here.' She gave him an odd look. 'There are not as many of us as there are of you. And I must admit, I envy you your siblings.'

Miles began to laugh. 'I know. We're quite a clan, aren't we?' He scanned the room, realized it truly was full of Inghams, and this pleased him. He liked having that support they gave him.

The dinner was well done. The food and the wine were incomparable, and Miles was relieved when the conversation turned to important things, away from gossip and the social whirl of London. He loathed trivial conversation; it didn't seem appropriate these days.

The world had been irrevocably changed by the Great War. Things were very different now. The aristocracy was being heavily taxed. This was an entirely new innovation.

The villages across England, and theirs in particular, had been diminished. So many men had been killed in the war, and acres of land were sadly neglected. The men who had gone off with a deferential manner had returned from the war in a different frame of mind. They weren't quite the same. They had seen their brothers die in blood and mud on the fields of France. They had fought for their country, and they believed they were owed something. A better living, higher wages, more respect. He didn't blame them for expecting this. Surely it was their due.

He thought then of Guy. Lost to them forever. Killed at the Battle of Verdun. He and Guy had been close, despite the difference in their ages, and Miles had always looked up to his brother, the heir. He would miss Guy for the rest of his life. He would mourn him and love him until *he* died.

Violet Lansing had loved Guy. At the end of the war, she had sought Miles out, and asked for details of Guy's death, or whatever he knew about his passing. And she had wept in his arms, and confessed her love for his brother. Miles had understood then that Violet had been forbidden to Guy. Because she was not an aristocrat. He sighed under his breath. That had to change too, sooner or later, that class difference. But would it?

He did not know the answer. He didn't seem to have answers for many things at this moment in time. The world is in a strange kind of limbo, Miles thought. Suddenly he wished the dinner would end so that he could escape. Be on his own. Think of her. His lost love. Also forbidden to him, as Violet was to his brother.

Out on the pavement, several hours later, Miles refused his father's offer of a ride home to Grosvenor Square in the Rolls. Miles explained he would prefer to walk, get some fresh air, stretch his legs. His father merely nodded, touched his arm, and departed with Dulcie and DeLacy. Everyone else had their own cars.

Miles headed down to Berkeley Square, strolled slowly towards Mount Street, then he turned around and walked back. He headed to Charles Street, walking in the direction of Park Lane.

It was a lovely September evening, an Indian summer kind of evening, the air soft and balmy. He lifted his head and looked up. The sky was as black as ink, and hundreds of stars were tiny, bright pinpoints of light, surrounding a glorious full moon. And he thought of Cecily, wishing she were with him, that he had her in his arms on such a night as this, a night for love and lovers like them.

He realized that he had stopped at South Audley Street and he was unable to resist turning right, heading for her little hole in the wall. It was just one room with a small space for sewing. But no matter what it was, she loved it. He knew she wouldn't be there at this hour but he just wanted to feel her shadowy presence, the spirit of her.

When he got there Miles couldn't believe what he was reading on the white card attached to the door. SHOP FOR RENT. He read it again in total disbelief. She had been here on Monday, and today was only Friday. Three days and she had gone.

What had happened? Where was she? Was she all right? Had she left London? Or just found another shop? He was frantic, filled with panic and worry.

He held himself very still. Was it always going to be like this? Was he going to worry about her for the rest of his life? Fret about her? Care about her? Yes, it was. Nothing would ever change when it came to the woman he loved beyond reason, and more than anyone else in the world.

He could not have her. But Cecily would always own his heart and his soul. His life had been mapped out for him, and he could not change it. He would have to walk the path he had inherited because of Guy's death, but he would walk it alone. And he would marry Clarissa. He had no choice.

The die was cast.

Acknowledgements

I enjoyed writing *Cavendon Hall*, but once the manuscript was finished on my desk, my solitary life ended. As usual I was then joined by a lot of other people, whose job it is to see that the manuscript is properly edited, designed, and finally sent off to the printer. That's when I finally sighed with relief.

I must now mention all those people who are involved with my books. I owe special thanks to Lynne Drew, Publishing Director of HarperCollins, London, for being a superb editor and sounding board. Her ideas and suggestions are much appreciated, as is her enormous enthusiasm. Thanks are also due to Kate Elton, Publisher, Harper Fiction; editor Thalia Suzuma, who is always there to handle so many details, and does so cheerfully and with efficiency. My thanks to her assistant, Martha Ashby. I want to thank my editor Susan Opie, and my copy editor Penny Isaac.

Elizabeth Dawson, PR Director Harper Fiction deserves a huge thank you from me for all of her work in the promotion of my books. Roger Cazalet, Publishing Strategy Director, and Oliver Wright, UK Sales Director, also have my thanks, as well as the entire team at HarperCollins in London, who are involved in the publication of my books.

I have to thank Lonnie Ostrow of Bradford Enterprises, for his help with preparing the manuscript for publication. A computer whiz, he gets all of my numerous rewrites and edits onto the computer with good humor. Thanks to Linda Sullivan of WordSmart, the best typist I ever had.

It is usually my husband Robert Bradford who gets thanked last, but he really should come first. He is as much a part of my novels as I am myself, listening to plot lines endlessly and without complaint. His insights are invaluable. His is a true partner in every sense, taking care of a huge part of my career. He does so with the skill of a business man and the creativity of a movie producer. I am lucky that I have his support, love and devotion, and that he never gets upset when a book consumes me and seems to take over the entire household. And he always manages to make me laugh every day, even if it's at myself.

Barbara Taylor Bradford is proud to support the National Literacy Trust, a charity dedicated to improving literacy across the UK. Barbara is passionate about improving life chances, particularly among women, to ensure everyone reaches their full potential. To find out more about Barbara's involvement, please go to: www.literacytrust.org.uk/barbarataylorbradford